Also by Serena Burdick

The Girls with No Names
Girl in the Afternoon
Find Me in Havana

the STOLEN BOOK of EVELYN AUBREY

SERENA BURDICK

PARK ROW BOOKS

PARK
ROW
BOOKS™

Recycling programs
for this product may
not exist in your area.

ISBN-13: 978-0-7783-8686-5

The Stolen Book of Evelyn Aubrey

Park Row Books
22 Adelaide St. West, 41st Floor
Toronto, Ontario M5H 4E3, Canada
ParkRowBooks.com
BookClubbish.com

Printed in U.S.A.

To Stephen,
my love,
for everything

the
STOLEN
BOOK
of
EVELYN
AUBREY

PROLOGUE

This will go on forever, life and death, stretching out over the expansive body of water, chill and slick and seductive against my skin. It is so cold, and I do not like the cold. There is the acrid smell of fish, the weeds tangled around my ankles. The wind is strong and the water froths and roars around me. I feel trapped in my body. Exhaustion presses down. I am glad there is a moon, for it is like my dream and it comforts me as I struggle to stay afloat.

I want to go back, to take it all back, to start over, but it is too late. This is my ending. I have known it all along, the darkness, the solitude, the words in my head. It is not as I imagined, and exactly as I imagined. Where does fiction end, and truth begin? Is this my pen, or reality? I have lost track. I have lost myself in the sea, in the river, in the moon, in all the watery images of life that fold over my head like fabric.

When I finally let go and sink, I find, beneath the chaos, that the silence is astounding, it is a relief, and I wonder then, if I have been entirely wrong.

This, I realize, might actually be the beginning.

Part One

THE MEANING OF A NAME

I am writing to reach you,
Both of you,
Only my eyes and mouth are full of water.
Consider a voice as obvious as the beat of your own heart,
But, like the pounding in your chest
You can't hear it.
Imagine you hear it now,
Try,
Because there are things I remember
And so much I have to tell you.

CHAPTER 1

Godstow, England, 1898

April 5

I put pen to paper in a drafty room of the Yateley Inn early on a Tuesday morning.

Yesterday, William Aubrey and I were married at St. Paul's Cathedral, and this journal was a parting gift from my father. I have never kept a lady's journal as I do not care to write of the things I ate, or where I walked on a particular day, or what I read in a particular week. How tedious. I have only ever written stories, so if I am to honor my father's wish that I keep a journal, I will record my story as such.

The April chill has sneaked her way through the cracks between the floorboards, and the fire does nothing to fight off the cold. William is still asleep and it is all I can do to keep from climbing back into bed with him, to touch his parted lips, run my fingers over the inside of his wrists. I can hardly believe we are married. It happened so fast; I feel as if everything changed in an instant. I was prepared to marry Peter Emsley, happy in my sated comfortability, totally ignorant of the heat and desire that can devour a person.

When William and I arrived at the inn last night, I didn't care that the room smelled of mildew, or that it was cold and damp. We did not bother to light a lamp or the fire. I could not speak a single word as he pulled the curtains closed and drew me to him. He was not hurried about it, but slow and methodic, peeling each garment away before easing me backward onto the bed. I shook uncontrollably as he drew his hands along the inside of my thighs, thrilled and terrified, grateful for the darkness as inexplicable tears sprang from my eyes and rolled over my temples, wetting the tops of my ears. William kissed my tears, licked them with the tip of his tongue, as he pressed himself into me with a shock of pain and pleasure. I clawed his back as the rain thundered outside like a million horses were trampling down the earth.

When he stopped moving against me, a pungent odor rose from the sheets, and his breath came hot and quick against my shoulder. The room was utterly black. In my blindness, every sound was magnified: the thrash of rain against the window, our breath rising, the creak of the bed, the blood pounding in my ears.

William rolled away and lit the candle on the nightstand, his blue eyes flaring into view. "You are so lovely," he said. "I want to look at you."

Embarrassed, I pulled a pillow over my face as he yanked the quilt off of me and a chill hit my naked body. "William, don't!" I tossed the pillow aside and scrambled for the quilt but he held it out of reach, eyeing me devilishly. Completely undone, I flipped over on my stomach and buried my head into the mattress. "I'm cold," I said, my voice muffled.

The quilt came down with a burst of air that sent goose bumps up the back of my neck. William's warm body pressed against me, one leg wrapping over mine. I wanted to slide under him, to feel the weight of him again.

"I have never known you to be shy," he breathed in my ear.

I shifted onto my side, his face so close I could feel his breath on my lips. "Only in front of you."

I traced a finger along his jaw and he bit the tip of it. "Never in front of Peter Emsley?"

I yanked my hand away. "Why would you ask me that?"

"It is not an entirely unreasonable question. You were engaged for six months."

"Are you implying that I laid with him?" I sat up, drawing the blanket over my bare chest. I did not like to think of Peter. I had broken off our engagement abruptly, thoughtlessly, and without regret. My mother said it was the most heartless thing I had ever done. I told her I hadn't meant to be cruel. I was trying to be honest, something my father instilled in me. *"Tell the truth at all costs,"* he'd told me. Better that Peter have it straight, I thought. That's what I would have wanted.

William slid off the bed. "I didn't ask if you ever laid with the man. Simply if he ever made you feel shy." He strode naked across the room, picking his waistcoat up off the floor and pulling a small silver snuffbox from the inside pocket. I had never seen a naked man before, and despite the confidence with which he stood sniffing a pinch of tobacco completely exposed, his pale, taut, sinewy body looked vulnerable to me.

"If by that you mean, did I care for him," I replied, "I will answer truthfully and say that, yes, I did care for him, once."

William clicked the box shut, tossed it onto the night table and jumped back into bed, pulling the covers loose from my legs and crawling under them. "I am asking if you ever loved him."

William had the same look on his face that he had the night I met him when a guest at the dinner table challenged him on the truth of a certain fact he wrote in *The Beaumont Man*. He looked childlike, hurt and slightly bewildered, as if he didn't know what it was to defend himself.

I slid down and wrapped my arm around his hairless chest. Finding his hand, I wove my fingers in between his and laid my head on his breast. "I have never loved anyone but you." I considered asking him if he'd ever loved anyone else. There had been other women; of course there had. Better not to have him confirm it. He was mine now. That was all that mattered.

The light flickered and dimmed, the room melting into darkness and then brightening as the lamp flared up. I shivered.

"You're cold." William slid out from under me. "I will light a fire. No sense in ringing someone at this hour."

Resting my head on the inside of my arm, I watched him pull on his trousers and slide his arms into his white shirt, leaving it unbuttoned, the collar standing straight up as he squatted in front of the fire. My chest ached looking at him, and I wondered if it was possible to love someone too much.

I have always felt that things ought to be more exciting than they turn out to be. Mother says I expect too much from life and will be endlessly disappointed. Father says my restlessness is what makes me a good writer. My parents have little in common: Father is tall and stubborn and overbearing, Mother dark-haired and birdlike and submissive. She was twenty-five when they married, a huge relief to her family, who had decided that she was already an old maid. I came along three years later, another huge relief as the family had also decided she was barren. My father, at thirty, was considered a perfect catch, a gentleman of means to match the family inheritance. It was just a shame they didn't have a son, the family said.

I am like my father, tall and stubborn with a head of curly red hair that stands out in a crowd. I am proud to look like him, and secretly ashamed of my mother's meek civility. I was afraid of becoming meek with Peter, of becoming my mother, complacent and accommodating. Unimpassioned.

With William, life has become everything I imagined it to be.

We met at a dinner party thrown by my friend Gwyneth, newly married and already with child. I knew William by reputation only. We were not introduced during predinner cocktails, but ended up sitting across from each other at the dining table. I hardly noticed him until he looked up at me with a flash in his eyes that made me feel stripped naked. The room suddenly became too bright and noisy, everything overwhelming.

He said something over the glinting urns and sparkling glasses, but I don't remember what, only that I became giddy and ridiculous, spilling my wine and fumbling every word out of my mouth. At the end of the evening, I stood alone in the hallway while Peter retrieved our coats. William came up to me from behind. I was wearing a short-sleeved gown and he put his hand on my bare arm and leaned so close, for a shocking moment I thought he meant to kiss me.

"You are a delight," he'd whispered in my ear, sliding his hand down my arm with an intimacy that set my freckled cheeks on fire.

The next day he called on me and we sat in the drawing room with a tension between us that made every cell in my body pulse. He did not care that I was engaged. He said my company delighted him, and that sitting together was no sin.

After that, I thought of nothing but his next visit, waking each morning with a desperate, thrilling sensation rolling through me. I tried to name the desire I felt for William, to figure out exactly what it was about him that appealed to me in order to rid myself of the obsession and be content with Peter. William had a reputation for being eccentric, flirtatious, and given to moods. He will suddenly drop from society without explanation, everyone remarking on how dull it is without him. Many women, even married ones, have found themselves the object of his desire. His behavior is excused on account of his having written a brilliantly successful novel. He is an artist, they say. Artists are allowed flirtations. They are allowed their moods.

No matter how hard I tried, my feelings could not be restrained. William pursued me and I let him. People gossiped. Mother was shocked, and said as much. Father warned me to be careful, but he didn't dissuade me. It pleases him that William is a successful writer. My father always wanted to write, but never had the talent for it, or so he says. It's why he's encouraged me all these years. When I confided in him how much I cared for

William, he said it was only natural that we would be drawn to each other through our similar interests.

Peter Emsley, on the other hand, remained silent on the subject, honorably continuing to call on me, sitting speaking of trifles while I thought only of William.

Mother wept the day I broke off our engagement. She said I would regret it. Father said I could do as I pleased. Peter, frustratingly, said absolutely nothing. We were in the garden, standing behind a shrubbery, so close he could have done any number of things to express his love—grabbed my hands, pulled me into an embrace, kissed me—not that it would have made any difference. The stoic way he tucked his arms to his sides, saying that if I'd made up my mind he'd be happy for me, made me even more relieved I wasn't marrying him.

I have never felt desire like this before. It is all of William I long for, his laugh, his vivacious stream of dialogue, the excitement on his face when he speaks on any subject. He describes things to me in a way that makes me see differently. The mundane becomes brilliant. I have never felt so alive.

The fire crackled to a start and William propped the poker against the wall, brushed the soot from his hands and ran his fingers through his long hair. I like the way it falls in wavy clumps around his face and the back of his neck. It makes him look unruly. Pulling the curtain aside, he peered into the darkness. "I hope the roads aren't too washed out to make the rest of the trip to Burford tomorrow. Sorry about this, darling. A shabby way to spend our honeymoon."

The chimney was in need of a cleaning and the smoke curled into the room, but I said, "It is perfectly suitable."

"I doubt that. I have yet to see Abbington Hall, but, knowing your father, I imagine it is quite grand."

"I do remember it being lovely, but I haven't seen it since I was a child and childhood memories are not to be relied upon."

William crawled back in bed and settled his head on my shoulder.

"Did you spend much time there?" he asked.

"In the summers before Mother decided it was more fashionable to vacation in Bath."

"Has it stood empty?"

"No, Father let it."

"Did he put the tenants out for us?"

"I'm afraid so, but they knew Father was giving us the house, so it wasn't a surprise."

"Will you miss your father?" William looked up at me and I could see the underside of his jaw, the dark stubble of hair beginning.

"I will miss my studies with him. But I have my writing." I drew my finger along his cheek. "And, I have you."

"Your father taught you a lot. You are a lucky woman."

"Yes, I am. He gave me 'an Oxford education. A man's education.'" I mocked the sound of my father's voice. "Doesn't that intimidate you?"

"Absolutely, but I will bear it since you hold a better conversation than any woman I have ever met. It's why I married you." William circled the palm of his hand over my nipple, the sensation weakening me.

"You've held conversations with so many women. I doubt all of them were dull." I shouldn't have said it, but I am jealous of the women he has been with. I can't stand to think of him giving his attention to anyone else.

Instead of angering him, this made him smile. "Trust me, they were all duffers. I wouldn't have been able to live all the way out in the country with a single one of them."

"Am I to entertain you then?"

"I imagine we will entertain each other."

I closed my eyes as he brushed the hair from my shoulder and kissed the side of my neck.

"You won't have time to entertain me," I murmured. "Chapman & Hall will be expecting your next book."

"*The Beaumont Man* hasn't even finished its first serialized publication," he whispered. "Don't rush me."

I heard a log fall in the fire and behind my closed lids, I felt the room brighten.

You cannot see a thing coming.
You have no idea in the beginning.

CHAPTER 2

Berkeley, California, 2006

The photograph was tucked inside the pages of a book Abby found shoved behind nude briefs and organic cotton sports bras in her grandma's underwear drawer. She'd been looking for Grandma Maggie's sterling silver jewelry case, where her grandma kept every imaginable type of earring—Abby had in mind a thread-thin gold pair with tiny balls on the end. Her grandma had excellent taste. If Abby could fit into her clothes, she would have been ferreting around in her closet too.

It was August, two years since Abby and Josiah met at a Mazzy Star concert, drunk, swaying to the singer's boozy voice on the dance floor. Their first official date was a week later at the Green's restaurant where, tonight, Josiah had booked them reservations to mark the occasion, just as he had last year.

Abby didn't like marking occasions. She liked to forget dates, and times, when certain things happened. Moving blindly forward into an unknown future was what suited her. But it meant something to Josiah, so she'd decided to suppress the low-level hum of anxiety in her stomach and go to dinner, knowing she'd talk too much and drink too much. At least last year she'd managed a cute outfit. Tonight, she hadn't even found the motivation to change out of her jeans. Hence the rummaging in Grandma Maggie's drawer for her jewelry, hoping a pair of earrings would at least make it look like she'd tried.

When Abby's hand hit the book, she imagined a journal—why else hide a book in your underwear drawer? She'd once found *The Joy of Sex* as a kid on her grandparents' night table, guilt and embarrassment and curiosity running through her as she peeked inside. This was neither. It was an old book with a faded yellow cover and a rose embossed under gold lettering that read, *Poems of Solitude*, by Evelyn Aubrey.

Carelessly, Abby cracked it open, the skeletal insides of the binding poking out like tea-stained cheesecloth. On the inside cover, under a film of paper thin as tissue, was a photograph of a woman sitting sideways at a desk with her elbow propped next to a globe. Her fingers rested lightly against the side of her full, freckled face and her hair was piled thickly on top of her head, the round pouf failing to soften the woman's arresting expression. She leaned slightly forward, lips pressed together, eyes guarded and accusing, as if whoever stood on the other side of the camera had just insulted her. Stray curls escaped down her neck and scattered over her temples. Her blouse was askew, sliding unevenly over one shoulder, and she wore a double string of pearls that she had twisted tightly around her finger as if threatening to yank it from her neck. Under the picture was a signature in a looping, elegant hand, "Evelyn Madeline Aubrey, 1905."

An otherworldly sensation pulsed through Abby. She was looking at a version of herself she'd never met, in a time she couldn't comprehend, and it gave her the disorienting feeling of intimacy with the woman. What's more, the woman was mocking her for it, her expression taunting, almost mean. She was daring Abby to have walked into the room right before the camera flashed. *Then*, she seemed to be saying, *would I have explained this extraordinary, illogical, quite possibly illusory moment.* But Abby had missed it. *You missed everything*, this woman's wordless mouth said.

When Abby sat down on the foot of the bed, a loose photograph fell from somewhere between the pages of the book and skittered to the floor. She picked it up, holding the edge like she might a shard of glass, her whole body tensing as she stared into the bright, youthful eyes of her mother. It was a square Polaroid, the earthy, muted tones of the '70s washing her mother and a man Abby had never seen before in golden light. He was jaunty, thin and shirtless, wearing paint-splattered shorts with an arm wrapped tight around Eva's waist. He had Abby's green eyes, ginger hair and freckles. On the back was written:

August 1974.
To Eva, my love, these poems were written by my great-grandmother. Who knows, maybe our child will grow up to be a poet one day.

Hot tears stung Abby's eyes, her tender, pliable hope reshaping inside her. She brought the photograph close to her face as if every unanswerable question could be found in that tinted past. The photo smelled like her grandma, like the lavender-and-bergamot essential oil she spritzed over the laundry and bedspreads. Why would her grandma keep this from her? Seventeen years after her mother's death, seventeen years of aching desire to find the only parent she had left, and here he was, shoved behind a pile of underwear. Here was his smile, his narrow chest, his gangly teenage legs, his large, lovely hand resting on her mother's hip.

Overwhelmed, Abby dropped onto her back and held the book to her stomach. The room was Grandma Maggie's now, but it looked the same as it had when her mother was alive: the white iron bed frame, the tiny-flowered wallpaper, and lacquer dresser. There were even the black scribble marks on the closet door where Abby had taken a pen as a toddler. Her mother was eighteen when Abby was born, and they had never moved from her grandparents' home. Abby had practically grown up in this bedroom. A room that had been her mother's until the day in October when Eva flew off the side of a cliff.

Don't lose sight of her, Abby had told herself over and over, as if she knew it was going to happen. In a crowded street, her mother's lean legs too far ahead, the calf muscles flexed, her heels clicking. *Don't lose sight of her,* at a party, her mother blowing her a kiss from the center of her outstretched hand before disappearing behind a closed door. *Don't lose sight of her.*

Abby remembered sitting on the edge of the bathroom sink that day—a day that had no significant meaning yet—with the sick feeling she always got when her mother was about to leave. She was fourteen years old, and still, the feeling hadn't gone away.

"Why can't I go?" She hated being left behind more than she hated falling asleep on strange couches.

"Because it's a school night." Eva teased the ends of her hair with a comb, the light brown strands feathering out.

"So?" Abby yanked the top off the lipstick she held. Cherry Berry. It smelled like the head of her old Strawberry Patch doll.

Eva plucked the lipstick from Abby's hand. "Gram would have both our heads if I let you go out on a school night." Abby puckered her lips, offering them to her mother. Eva twisted the tube. "One, two, three," she said, applying the lipstick to Abby's mouth in three swift strokes—right, left and bottom. Abby looked in the mirror and ran her tongue over her top lip. It tasted like a red starburst. Eva did her own lips and they both leaned over and kissed the glass.

In this room, on this same bed, Abby had said, "Don't go," and laid her head in the curve below her mother's neck, breathing in her cucumber lotion. Her mother had taken a stick of gum from her purse, unwrapped it and broken it in two, putting half in her mouth and holding the other half out to Abby. Abby had bitten the inside of her cheek and shook her head. She always took half, but in that moment, she had wanted to deny her mother something. Eva had just shrugged and popped the other half in her mouth.

In the doorway, her mother turned to her, purse swinging at her side. "I love you, baby," she said. Mad, Abby said nothing. She listened to the click of her mother's heels on the wooden stairs, the sound of the front door opening and shutting, and then her mother was gone.

Abby sat up, her grandma's neatly arranged Turkish throw bunching beneath her. There was a burning sensation in the middle of her chest, right underneath her breastbone. She and Grandma Maggie never talked about that night, and yet the grief was there, clawing at them, keeping them tangled in a relationship that was full of holes. Here was evidence of it in the stashed-away photograph, Grandma Maggie keeping Eva's secrets for her. Honoring her relationship with the dead over the living.

"Gram?" Abby shouted, indignation propelling her out of the room, the book and photo clutched in her hand. She went down the stairs to the front hall, her toes rolling over the tatami mats. A few years ago, Grandma Maggie replaced their plush pillows and flowered wallpaper with slim-cushioned, pale wood furnishings, sheepskin rugs and white walls. Her mother's room was the only one in the house that hadn't been remodeled, but Grandpa Carl dismantled it anyway. He removed the altar of Eva's things: a stuffed bunny, a pink plastic ring, a wooden rattle, a china doll in a white dress, elementary school drawings, report cards from high school. Maggie argued while Carl quietly labeled boxes and packed everything neatly away.

"Gram?" Abby called again. The kitchen was empty, the shades in the living room drawn, the house silent.

Sliding the photo into her pocket, Abby set the book on the hall table and stepped outside into a light drizzle, walking barefoot down the slick stone path, past the split oak, the trunks like ancient legs coming up from the earth. The house was the smallest on the street, muddied stucco from a century ago, but beautiful, with purple asters and burnt daylilies lining the walk-way, and Grandma Maggie's herb garden, a jumble of weeds and wildflowers, taking up the whole front yard. Her grandma was nowhere to be found.

A car swished past. The rain came down harder. Abby went back inside and looked at the photograph of Evelyn Aubrey. Holding the book at arm's length, she inspected her own image in the hall mirror, her damp shirt clinging to her breasts, her red hair springing around her head, frizzing at the temples. She eyed the bridge of her nose, the height of bone under her cheeks, the storm of freckles over her skin. No matter what angle, her reflection was the same as the author photo. The face, but also the body.

In high school, Abby was teased for her large breasts. Grandma Maggie had sat her down and shown her a book of nude, Pre-Raphaelite women. "See how beautiful these women are? You're like a model," she'd told her. Abby did resemble those women, soft and round with seashell pale skin, but she'd slammed the book shut and said, "They're fat," stomping her sixteen-year-old attitude out of the room, because all anyone wanted in 1991 was to be skinny, tan and blond.

Her grandma had done her best, Abby knew this, and she still resented her. Before Eva's death, Grandma Maggie had been a predictable disciplinarian who liked dinner at six and checked to make sure homework assignments were done. Then Eva died and all order was lost. Boundaries swept away. At night, Grandma Maggie used to climb in bed with Abby, her body hard and bony where Eva's had been soft and squishy. Her grandma was trying to comfort her, but Abby didn't want to be comforted; she wanted to be alone. She had nowhere to grieve; Grandma Maggie took up all the space.

Just then the door burst open. "I can't believe this rain. It never rains in Berkeley in August!" Maggie propped her yoga mat against the wall and leaned down to remove her rubber boots, her gray bun flopping over. "Not that I'm complaining. We can always use rain."

Maggie straightened, brushed the hair from her eyes and gave her granddaughter an effortless smile. Maggie was tiny, with a figure she kept fit against age and a face that held an expression of genuineness that she did not always live up to.

With a silent, accusatory stare, Abby held the book out to her. The photograph was still in her pocket, forming to the shape of her thigh.

Maggie glanced at it and said, "Found a poet to admire?" before taking a small bag of groceries from her gym bag and walking to the kitchen. For the most part, Maggie was a good listener, but there were times, like right now, when she did not listen, which was intentional and deliberate.

"No, Gram. Look again." Abby trailed her, hating how child-like she sounded.

"Just let me get this salmon in the fridge."

Maggie knew exactly what that book of poetry held and she planned to ignore it for as long as possible. She put the salmon, goat milk and flaxseed in the fridge, a can of tomatoes in the cupboard and a bunch of garlic in the fruit basket before reaching for the book, her stomach tensing. "Oh," she said, recognition showing for the first time. "What are you doing with this?" Her voice was thin.

"What are *you* doing with it?"

"It's mine."

"No." Abby opened the book. "It's my mother's."

Written in light pencil on the title page it said, *"For Eva, Love B."*

"How could you keep this from me?" Abby was on the verge of tears.

Maggie couldn't bear those tears. She started folding up the empty grocery bag, pinching in the corners. "I forgot my cloth bags again. I got them just so I wouldn't waste paper and then I never remember to bring them with me." She always did this. If her house were on fire, Maggie would watch with casual annoyance and comment on the library book she'd left inside, ignoring the real crisis as it exploded in front of her.

Abby drew the photograph from her pocket. "Why have you never shown me this picture of my father?"

Maggie gave a perfunctory shrug and shoved the paper bag under the counter, fiddling with the edges as she angled it in.

Abby sank onto a stool at the kitchen island. "Gram, why did you keep him from me?" she insisted, knowing she would not get an honest answer—theirs had never been an honest relationship.

Maggie said nothing, going about her business with efficient evasiveness. She filled a glass of water and took a jar of vitamins from the shelf, removing the top a little too forcefully, sending vitamins pinging to the floor. "Damn it!" She got down on her knees to pick them up. From the ground, she said, "I don't think you should be making accusations when you're the one snooping in people's underwear drawers."

"It wasn't *people's underwear drawers*. It was *your* underwear drawer." Abby did not get up to help her grandma. She kept her eyes on the countertop, tracing the swirls in the marble with the tip of her finger.

Maggie stood with a fistful of vitamins clutched in her hand and started dropping them back into the jar. She recognized Abby's tone, and that look of anguish. It was the same look Abby wore for weeks as a child after that painter told her the meaning of her name. It was the same look Abby had when she came home from the library announcing that she had found her father; he was the man who checked out the books. He had her freckles, she insisted, begging Maggie to take a picture of Eva to the library and ask the man if he had ever slept with her. Maggie said she would do no such thing. Abby simply did it herself, which

Maggie suspected she would. When the man told her he had never seen the woman in his life, Abby had come home crying.

Her need was so desperate that she had always been irrational.

"I kept this from you for your own good." Maggie put the vitamins back on the shelf, forgetting she had intended to take one.

"I don't see how this is for my own good." Abby didn't want a fight, just an explanation.

"Abigail," Maggie said in her *come-on-already* tone. "Your mother was with a lot of men."

Flipping open the book of poems, Abby rapped her finger on the picture of Evelyn Aubrey. "Have you seen this? She looks just like me. Exactly like me."

Maggie looked at the photograph as if she hadn't already seen it a hundred times. If Abby only knew how much she'd agonized over this book. "It doesn't mean anything. Some woman in a photograph looks like you, so what?"

"Gram!" Abby pulled the photo from her pocket. "This is my father. The photo says *'Who knows, maybe our child will grow up to be a poet one day.'* It says *'August 1974.'* Do the math. I was born seven months later!"

"Fine, okay." Maggie pressed her hand into her forehead, smoothing her fingers over her eyebrows. "You were always so anxious about it, Abigail, I figured it would only make things worse, having a photo with no name or location or any way of finding him."

"You could have at least let me decide that."

Maggie threw up her hands. "Alright, I apologize." She walked to the refrigerator, the rain tapping on the terra-cotta roof tiles. Hoping food would ease the tension in her stomach, she took a cardboard container from the top shelf and said, "I am going to eat leftover Thai. Do you want any?"

"Oh no! Shit." Abby looked at the clock on the stove, remembering Josiah. Grabbing the old-fashioned landline her grandmother had kept during the remodeling, Abby dialed his number.

"Abby?" he answered on the first ring. "Is everything alright?"

"Yes, fine. I'm so sorry. I'm still at home. Something came up."

There was a pause. "Are you still coming?"

"At this point, with traffic, it would take me over an hour to get there."

Josiah was quiet. Abby could hear the din of the restaurant around him, clinking dishes and muffled voices. He would have booked them a window table months ago. Right now, she should be eating mesquite grilled brioches and Vietnamese yellow curry looking out at the fog surrounding the bay, the bridge and headlands hidden somewhere in the mist.

"I'm seriously sorry," Abby tried again. "We'll reschedule for another night."

Another night would not be their anniversary. From Josiah's strained voice Abby couldn't tell whether he was being sincere or sarcastic when he said, "Sure, yup. You just let me know," and hung up.

Maggie stirred the food in the pan. Her tiny back firmly erect. "You should have invited Josiah for dinner. We could have ordered more Thai."

Abby knew she should have. She should have explained, convinced him that missing their anniversary had nothing to do with him. She could see him sitting alone, his hands clasped, his dark hair falling into his eyes. He would probably still order, not wanting to offend the waiter. She loved that about him, how thoughtfully he went through the world.

Maggie scooped her food into a bowl.

"I couldn't find your jewelry box," Abby said. "I was looking for some earrings. That's why I was in your drawer."

Maggie nodded, staking her chopstick into her curried rice.

"Help yourself." She jutted her chin at the food on the stove. "I'm going to eat in the living room."

When Maggie sat down in her Scandinavian lounge chair, she had no appetite. She set her bowl on the coffee table, went to the window and opened the shade. Big glass beads of rain spilled down the palm leaves. She drew a breath and pressed her fingers into her abdomen, massaging away the tension.

She had thought Abigail's obsession with finding her father would pass, that her granddaughter would make a career for herself, fall in love, start a family. Then maybe Maggie might get a chance to be a real grandmother. Abigail was such a smart girl. They'd sent her to Brown with high hopes, but she'd done nothing with her degree. Maggie couldn't even remember what she'd majored in. Something to do with film. Now, Abigail just bounced from one underpaid job to the next. All the therapy Maggie paid for didn't seem to be doing any good. No waitressing gig or coffee shop job ever lasted very long, and then there were the boyfriends who came and went. Josiah wasn't going to last; Maggie could see that. She put her hand on the glass. She had failed Eva. She knew that, and had desperately tried not to fail Abigail.

The rain was falling harder, pushing the delicate heads of her flowers to the ground. Carl was in Chicago. He wouldn't be home until tomorrow. He would tell her it was a mistake to keep the photograph from Abigail.

Maggie cracked the window open and let a finger of mist curl in. She really had been trying to do the right thing.

CHAPTER 3

Burford, England, 1898

April 6

By the time William woke, the clouds had lifted and the day was bright and promising. We ate a hurried breakfast of boiled eggs, toast and tea, and William ordered our chaise ready as soon as possible. We were both anxious to leave the inn. Once we were seated, the horses picked up speed and it took only a few hours to make the rest of the journey to Burford.

It was one of those brilliant mornings that follow a good rain and the fields gleamed in the sunlight. Everything was delightful, even the smell of manure from the nearby farms that rose sharply in my nose. William kissed my gloved fingers, squeezed my hand and held it tight to his chest, looking at me as if he meant to pull me down in the carriage that moment. Flushed with embarrassment, I bit back a smile and looked away. I am not used to such open affection, and certainly not in the light of day. My parents are rarely affectionate. I grew up believing you touched your husband in a reserved and controlled manner, and that he rarely touched you.

Childhood memories rushed back at me as our chaise rounded the corner atop a hill, the town dropping below us. I insisted on getting out and walking the rest of the distance to Abbington Hall. William was anxious to see the house and rode on ahead, kissing me heartily before leaving me to make my way down the steep, cobblestone street that runs through the heart of Burford.

The view was magnificent, sloping meadows dropping away to thatched and shingled roofs that descended into the wooded valley at the edge of the River Windrush. From this height, the water looked like a silver ribbon winding through the fields.

Observing this, I stepped directly into a pile of sheep droppings, which made me grimace, but did not alter my mood entirely. Burford is known for its production of fine wool, and the sheep often wander the streets unattended. Scraping my boot over a cobblestone, I smiled remembering the stories I used to tell my friends back in London about how the sheep not only walked the streets, but roamed the houses in the middle of the night bleating pitifully. I always stated stories as fact, which drove my friends mad since I refused to be proved wrong. It was amusing getting them to believe whatever I wanted, telling tall tales with such conviction their eyes grew wide and fearful. I'd throw in a bit of terror, ghosts and what have you, which always got me into trouble. Mother told me lying was wicked, but Father said to leave me be, I was using my imagination, and hadn't Mary Shelley told the best ghost story in the world?

My boot mostly clean, I pulled the jaconet collar of my traveling dress tighter around my neck and hurried along, passing congeries of cottages huddled together in crooked rows, peaked roofs sloping away from tall chimneys, smoke billowing into the clear sky. I did not take a direct route, but turned down Lawrence Street and walked to the church green, an open space of well-tended grass before the gates of Saint John the Baptist Church. I used to spend hours reading on that green with Father, listening to the deep baritone of his voice reciting *The Faerie Queene* to me.

Inside the gate, I looked up at the Norman tower with its steeple ascending toward heaven and felt an astounding sense of peace. The sheep bleated in the distance; a bird twittered. I understood why William wanted to come here to write, how one's mind could be clear and open without all the demands the city imposes. How easily my stories came as a child.

Leaving the church, I crossed Packhorse Bridge and followed the footpath up a steep hill toward Abbington Hall, the gray stone exterior flexing across the horizon, the gables casting triangular shadows over the grass. Seeing it, I felt a clutch of nostalgia. The old oak tree is still here, growing so close to the house the branches practically reach through the windows. I used to climb out onto it from the upstairs hall window and scale down the drainpipes, battling the ivy with a butter knife, pretending the vines were thick-bodied serpents, a game that tormented my mother and resulted in endless pairs of ripped stockings. I had not realized how much this place would make me miss my parents. We were so happy at Abbington Hall. Why did we stop coming?

I heard a shout and saw William running across the field, his jacket flapping open. "It's enormous," he cried, reaching me with a small leap. "Splendid, and I have already found my study. There's a room off the library with two long windows overlooking the gardens. It's simply perfection." He wrapped his arms around me, and my parents were instantly forgotten. "All it needs is a desk, chair, stack of paper and a proper fountain pen." He let go of me, bounded ahead a few yards and then came running back.

"A simple thing to arrange." I laughed.

"Yes, a simple thing. I'm famished. Are you hungry? The servants are all waiting to meet you and be ordered about. I don't know how any of this works." He ran a hand through his windblown hair.

"I'm sure you've charmed them already."

"Hardly. I think I've startled them, bursting from one room to the next. You'll have to do the charming. Domestic life eludes me. I have always been alone with my work. I took meals in restaurants and roamed where I pleased. This is all new to me."

I wanted to tell him that I have spent my youth alone with my work as well, buried in books, much to my mother's chagrin.

She did her best to prepare me for domesticity, but I paid little attention. The duties of a wife elude me as much as the duties of a husband elude William. I suppose we will muddle through together. As far as I'm concerned, the house can fall to ruin so long as we have each other.

"I love everything about this place," William cried, picking me up and carrying me a few paces before dropping me to my feet again. Energy pulsed off of him. "I love everything about you. I want to take you right here in the grass."

"William!" I slapped his arm, laughing.

We did nothing as scandalous as taking our clothes off in the meadow. Instead, we made our way to the circular driveway, where eight servants stood waiting for introductions.

CHAPTER 4

Berkeley, California, 2006

Abby stepped out the back door. Moisture settled on her flushed cheeks, and the bluestone was slippery underfoot as she walked the path to the guesthouse. It was just one room, with a bathroom and a loft where she slept. It used to be Grandpa Carl's office. When she turned eighteen, he replaced his heavy oak desk with a plush couch that overlooked the bay and said the place would be put to better use if someone lived in it.

Growing up, Grandpa Carl had been a distant figure, coming and going on the periphery of Abby's life. He worked for a consulting agency that required late nights and business trips. There were traces of him: a tie left on the bed in the morning, an empty Scotch glass on the coffee table, shiny black shoes in the hallway. On rare weekends, when he was home, Grandpa Carl would ruffle her hair and ask, "How's it going, missy?"

"Good," she always said. Grandpa Carl was not a person of many words.

After he moved the couch in, on clear days when he happened to be home, he'd come and sit with her. They said almost nothing, and this suited them both. They found comfort in the silence of each other's company. They'd put their feet on the coffee table and watch the boats press their sails into the wind, rounding the tip of Tiburon, insignificant under the massive crest of the Golden Gate.

Tonight, there was nothing but a wet blanket of fog. Abby wrestled with her key in the lock before muscling the door open. She switched on a light, sat on the couch and opened Evelyn Aubrey's sonnets.

TO THE NIGHT

Now whilst the night mantle rests upon me,
Oh, come the words that hold me still in sleep
And rest the demons that never cease to be,
The ones who whisper longings never reaped,
Of passion unfulfilled in youth gone by.
As moon and shadow play upon the hill
A restless notion pins me where I lie
Of fraud perpetrated against my will.
Oh night, to be as cold in heart as you,
To boldly extinguish all that is light
Yet illuminate the mind to its true,
Tempestuous nature in lonely flight.
Therefore, take my charactery from me
And with it take the truth that is my right.

Abby read the poem again, trying to make sense of the words, puzzling out the tortured, defeated tone as she opened her laptop and typed Evelyn Aubrey's name into the search engine. There wasn't a single image of her other than the photo from her sonnets, and almost nothing of her life, other than that she was the wife of the writer William Aubrey. There were numerous photos of him, an uncomfortably handsome man staring out from light, squinty eyes.

In earlier photos, his hair was worn slightly long and swept back revealing a hairline that dipped into his forehead like the tip of a heart. He had a head-on, arrogant look, his aquiline nose and plump, unsmiling lips giving the effect of a man who knows exactly what he's after.

Abby scrolled through various academic websites, most of them filled with comparative analyses of his novels. Scholars seemed to be fixated on the disparity between his work, using "lens" comparisons and detailed arguments weighing the divergence of language, structure and word choice from his first novel to his last. Reading it reminded Abby of her Brown days, where she'd suffered Rhode Island winters, gained the "freshman fifteen" and finally found that getting up at 4:00 a.m. to row crew was the only thing that would keep her sane. How she got through four years and graduated with an arguably useless degree in Modern Culture and Media still eluded her. At least, she thought, it gave her the ability to dig her way through tedious academic research.

It was in an excerpt from a biography on William Aubrey written in the late 1940s where she finally found some information on Evelyn:

> *Aubrey and his wife were rarely seen together in society and there is no mention of her in any of Aubrey's interviews. We piece together what little we know of Evelyn Aubrey from the volume of sonnets she left us... Aubrey refused any interviews regarding his wife's disappearance and the accusations made against him... He became withdrawn and secluded, residing at Abbington Hall until his death on the 5th of December, 1922.*

Abby was deep into an archive of old newspaper articles when there were two sharp raps on her door. "Come in," she said, her eyes fixed to the glowing screen.

The door opened and Abby looked up as Josiah walked in. "You came." She smiled.

He shoved his hands into his pockets in a gesture of honed

offense. "Did you have a sudden urge to study for the GREs on our anniversary?"

Abby couldn't help noticing how attractive he looked in his black cashmere sweater pulled over a white collared shirt. "I promise, it's a much better excuse than that." She got up and wrapped her arms around his neck. He carried a scent that reminded Abby of water, crisp and clear and refreshing. She loved pressing her face into his bare chest and breathing him in. "I'm *really, really* sorry." She had slept with him on their first date. He hadn't thought it was a good idea, but that was Josiah. Practical, patient. She liked to get to the sex right away, not waste any time if it wasn't going to work out.

Josiah relaxed, but kept his hands in his pockets, his arms barring the way between their bodies.

She pulled away and picked up the book of poetry. "Check this out."

Josiah didn't look at it. "What is this really about, Abby? You standing me up tonight?"

"I'm trying to tell you."

He dropped onto the couch, running a hand through his damp hair, spiking it along the top of his head. "I assumed this was your passive-aggressive way of breaking up with me."

There was a tug in Abby's chest, then a clamping down. "Why would you think that?" She rounded the couch, resting her hands on his shoulders as she lifted her legs and straddled him. "Did you eat?" She ran her hand under his shirt.

"I did. I made the reservation months ago."

She rolled off him, took the photograph from her pocket and handed it to him. "I found a picture of my father."

Josiah sat up straighter. "You did? Where?"

"In my gram's underwear drawer."

"That's weird." He smiled. "What were you doing in your grandma's underwear drawer?"

"Looking for granny panties to wear for you tonight." She

raised a single, seductive eyebrow. "Seriously, I was looking for some decent earrings. Proves I wasn't planning to stand you up."

"I'm not totally convinced." Josiah looked down at the photograph. "This is your father?"

"I'm pretty sure. Gram said she didn't want to get my hopes up about finding him since there's no name or location on the photo, but it has to be him. The date on the back coincides with when my mom would have gotten pregnant with me."

"They're not in California." Josiah pointed to a cluster of trees behind the smiling couple. "It's too lush."

"It looks like the East Coast."

"Or Midwest."

"I can't believe Gram never asked my mom about this. Or showed it to me."

"Maybe she found it after your mom died."

"Either way, she shouldn't have kept it a secret." Abby let out an exasperated groan. "When I asked her about it, she played dumb, like there's no reason this photo would mean anything at all. I also found this." Abby got up and brought back the book of poems, showing Josiah Evelyn Aubrey's picture.

He held it under the lamp on the end table. "Holy shit, that's amazing."

"Right? She looks just like me."

"She really does."

"Her name's Evelyn Aubrey. She's the wife of William Aubrey."

"The writer?"

"You know him?"

"I read something by him in an undergrad English class."

"How is it that I went to Brown and never heard of him?" Going to her desk, Abby leaned over and clicked her computer keys. "There's almost no info on his wife, but I found out she disappeared eight years after she married Aubrey. At that point he'd written four novels." Abby opened her bookmarks tab. "Listen to this. It's from an old newspaper article."

EXAMINER
October 22, 1906

We this day have received news of the disappearance of Mrs. Evelyn Madeline Aubrey, the wife of Mr. William Aubrey, the acclaimed author, whose novels have been extensively read by the whole of London society. We urge all persons who may have any information of her whereabouts to contact the London police.

Josiah looked like he was about to say something, but Abby held up her hand. "It gets better."

Since the printing of our last story on the disappearance of Mrs. Evelyn Madeline Aubrey, it appears the London police have found reason to suspect her husband, the acclaimed author Mr. William Aubrey, of her murder. Chapman & Hall cannot keep enough copies of Mr. Aubrey's latest novel, *The Tides*, in print since the whole of London is enamored with the fictional heroine who disappears at the end of the novel, killed at the hands of her husband. The police have accused Mr. Aubrey for having committed the crime to create sensationalism for his novel and increase its popularity. As of yet, a body has not been found.

Abby looked up. "Isn't that wild? I can't find anything else about her. It's all academic stuff on William Aubrey's books. They had one child, Henry Aubrey, but there's absolutely nothing written about him either."

Josiah looked at her over the back of the couch, twisting a loose thread on the cushion. "I'm confused, why are you interested in Evelyn Aubrey?"

"On the back of the photo, my father writes that this is his great-grandmother. Which makes her my great-great-grandmother. If I trace her lineage, I could find out my ancestry and figure out who my father is." She felt a frenzy of excitement, a sense that she was headed toward something she might finally understand.

"That's exciting, Abby." The thread slipped through Josiah's fingers. Crossing the room, he put a hand on her shoulder. It was not a gesture to draw her in, but one of constrained reassurance. "This seems really important to you."

"It is."

"Why didn't you bring this to me over dinner?"

"I don't know. I got distracted." The truth was, she hadn't thought of him at all. Abby looked down and picked at the blue nail polish chipping off her thumbnail. She could smell the wool from his sweater where it had gotten wet in the rain, wanting to press her face into it, to wrap her arms around him and hold on before it was too late.

His hand slid off her shoulder. "I can't figure you out, Abby. Half the time I have no idea what you're feeling, and you always seem to keep me at a distance."

He was right. Her emotional emptiness was too complicated, like a cracked glass she kept filling up, but nothing ever stayed inside. How could she tell him that she was still falling through the fog with her mother? That nothing was strong enough to hold her still, not even his love, as much as she wanted it to be?

She fixated on a tiny spot of nail polish. "I don't know what you want me to say."

"Nothing," he sighed. "I think you should pursue this. Find out if a father is actually what you're searching for. I just can't wait for you while you do it."

"Why?" She wanted to beg him not to do this, not now.

"This isn't working, Abby."

There was a tightening along Abby's jaw. Rebellion kicked inside her, a thump in her gut. She did not reach out and grab him, as much as she wanted to. She had taught herself not to hold on to anything too tightly. "It has been working, hasn't it?"

"Not for a while. Not for me, anyway." He looked hard at her, his eyes quizzical and searching. *It's not there*, she wanted to say. *You won't find anything you're looking for.*

"I just can't do this anymore," he said.

She wanted to explain herself, to tell him the meaning of her name, make him understand the sleepless nights after her mother's death she spent imagining her father, this parent who existed somewhere out there for her. A not-dead parent. A parent who would take her in his arms and tell her she was worth staying home for, worth living for.

But the small space of air between their bodies felt iron thick and all she could manage was, "I'm sorry."

Josiah put a single hand on her shoulder, pulled her close for a quick moment and then let go. "Me too," he said, and walked out the door.

CHAPTER 5

Burford, England, 1899

October 15

I don't know what is happening. I thought I had everything under control. I was doing what was expected.

Our first year and a half at Abbington Hall fairly flew by. We have been happy, other than a few incidents last winter when William lost his temper, but never at me. It was at the livery boy, if memory serves, and that one time with the groundskeeper for pruning the wisteria back in March, when William insisted it was to be done in April. Overreactions, that was all.

I have done my best to organize the household instructions and they are not hard to maintain. Most of the time, William has been exuberant, spending hours in his study writing, often exploding into the library—where I am tediously working on my own novel—with pages of work clutched in his hands, his hair standing on end as he waves the papers around shouting, "It's good, it's good," before kissing me vigorously and disappearing back into his room.

Everything we did was infused with this euphoric energy. We ate feverishly, wrote feverishly, made love feverishly. At times, William would draw me up from my desk and make love to me on the library rug in broad daylight. I've abandoned my reserve of our first night together, and take pleasure in the full view of our naked bodies.

Until recently, we talked for hours, on every subject imaginable—literature, music, painting, philosophy. William marvels that I have so much to say on matters of politics and culture. It still surprises him that I am his equal, and it surprises me that he would think of me as anything less. We talked of our writing, plotted our books together, agreeing not to show each other our work until we'd finished a first draft. "Critique too early spoils the creative process," William said.

I have been careful to heed his advice.

The first time I opened William's study door and found it empty, I wasn't worried. Bennett, our butler, a man who wears a long mustache and is slightly too arrogant for my liking, told me William had gone riding. It was overcast and cold, but William returned in good spirits. He said he needed to clear his head, kissed me and shut himself up in the study, where he stayed through teatime and supper.

Normally, we take our meals together, and this sudden alteration in our routine put me out of sorts. What was the point of changing out of my comfortable muslin into an evening gown if I was going to sit through supper alone? It was humiliating standing in my room while my lady's maid, Irina, helped me out of my satin dress painted with La France roses I'd worn just for William. The first time he saw me in it, he told me all he could think of was peeling those roses off of me. Now, my lady's maid was. Looking at the girl's round pink nose and small dark eyes, I realized how alone I was here. I hardly even knew the woman who yanked my corset strings and opened my curtains every morning. I hadn't bothered to ask her a single question about herself. I thought of doing so now, but she kept her eyes down and I couldn't think where to begin.

When she left, I climbed into bed realizing how little I'd thought of my parents over the last year. I was actually relieved when Mother wrote in July to say that they weren't coming for their planned summer holiday. They hadn't visited our first summer here either, but had vacationed in Bath. I met them there for a week—William wanted to stay here writing—and it was pleasant enough, but all I could think about was getting home to my husband. This year, Mother wrote saying, "Your father doesn't want to leave the city," and all I'd felt was grateful. I couldn't imagine them bursting the bubble William and I had created. *How selfish not to worry about them until now?* I thought, plumping my pillow and rolling onto my side. Father hates London in the summer. It's smelly and hot, and I can't remember a single summer season he's spent there. And what had I expected, that William would give me every second of his time forever? *You are suffocating him, Evelyn*, I told myself, remembering Gwyneth telling me before we were engaged how men liked to be kept waiting for your attention. She said my problem was that I was too straightforward, to which I'd responded, "Why muck about in confusion if you both want the same thing?"

Light rain pattered the window. I rolled onto my back and stared at the black ceiling, the darkness like a weight over my eyes. First thing in the morning, I'd write to Mother and ask why she and Father had stayed away. Then, I would send a dinner invite to the Wismers—friends of my parents over in Chipping Campden—something I should have done ages ago. I can't expect William to be my only companion.

November 1

William did not come to bed that night and it felt devastating. He slept in the adjoining room and the next morning, he skipped breakfast and went out riding, returning agitated and unsettled. I found him pacing the hallway, buttoning and unbuttoning his jacket. I asked him what was wrong, why his mood was so altered, and he snapped, "If you weren't so indignant and gave me some peace, I might be able to think properly again."

I stared at him, dumbfounded as he walked past me up the

stairs. He had never spoken to me like that before, and something shriveled inside me.

In an attempt to give William what he wanted—and out of pride, if I am to be honest—I left him alone, convincing myself this was a bump in the road, a normal slump, a mood I should have anticipated, one that would pass like a proper rain.

Instead of sending dinner invitations to neighbors, an impossibility with William in such a foul temper, I spend my days writing in the library. Only a small comfort. What I want is William, who now spends most of his time riding horseback through the hills, going straight to his study when he comes home. Sometimes he settles in the library with a book, which, until yesterday, I mistook as a sign that he wanted to be near me. At four o'clock he came in, wordless, sat down and opened his book with a great shuffling and sighing. After an hour, I was thinking how pleasant it was to be silently engaged in this way when he suddenly slammed his book shut and said, "That damnable scratching of your pen is enough to drive a person mad." He crossed the room to my desk and stared down at me as if expecting me to get up that instant.

"Then leave," I said, resuming my work.

"Why don't you take your writing to your room?"

"Why should I?" I shot him a look. "I've been writing here all summer. You can read anywhere you like."

If space was what he wanted, why was he in the library with me? And why wasn't *he* writing? I anticipated a fight. I welcomed one, anything to get him talking to me, but he just sank in on himself, looking silently defeated.

Putting down my pen, I stood up and slid the book from his hands. I didn't want him to leave. I wanted him to talk to me, to touch me, to draw me close. It had been weeks since we'd made love. He no longer slept in our marriage bed, but in the adjoining room. Thinking I might seduce him, I began slowly unbuttoning the front of my blouse as he watched, expressionless, but not stopping me. It was when I reached for him that he winced and pulled away as if I'd touched a wound. "This—" he waved his hands at me "—is not becoming of you. It's desperate."

I flushed with humiliation as he left me standing in the middle of the room with my blouse undone.

That night I lay in bed, berating myself. How stupid of me. I knew nothing of these things. When the door adjoining our rooms creaked open, I was filled with longing as William climbed into our bed. Only, he did not touch me in his usual way—no fingers graced my stomach, or the curve of my breast. He just pulled up my nightdress, climbed on top of me and fumbled his way in as if performing a duty. When he was done, he went to sleep in the adjoining room, leaving me wide-awake and filled with anxiety. Was he disgusted with me, or did I just bore him now?

November 5

William has begun inviting his friends up from the city, mostly men who come with the occasional wife, or sister, none of whom I know. In their company, William is animated again, but it is garrulous and strained, his vivacity almost hysterical. When he drinks, he becomes startlingly loud and he is so rapacious with his conversation that others can't get in a word. Everyone is disquieted. As the evenings wear on, the company becomes increasingly ill at ease, the women excusing themselves with exaggerated smiles, the men whispering to one another.

No one ever stays long.

December 3

The visitors have stopped altogether. The leaves have fallen and the air has taken on a chill. William is sullen and silent, his attention to me increasingly inconsistent. He will spontaneously kiss me, or crawl into bed and make hurried love to me, his tenderness forced. At other times he shouts at me if I so much as speak to him. It is maddening, living for the moments he gives me his attention, sick to my stomach at the thought that he is no longer pleased with me. I have stopped writing. I cannot concentrate. I wander the house aimlessly, yelling at the cook and ordering the housemaids about. It startles them since I have not taken interest in their performance before. I think of Mother always trying to please Father, and Father remaining forever unsatisfied. I wonder if this is how marriage turns out, if real love is fictitious? I suppose all those romantic poets never made it to the end of a summer.

December 7

The wind has rolled in over the hills and the air is swollen with the pitch of it.

I don't know what has happened. I have sat for hours trying to convince myself it was a phantom moment, a delusion. *You are too sensitive, Evelyn,* I tell myself, *paranoid*, and yet I feel as if I have been slapped awake from the dream of my marriage.

Earlier, William and I were in the drawing room where I sat reading a letter from Mother. The fire burned hot, warming the tops of my knees and flushing my cheeks.

"Your parents missed their chance for a summer holiday in the country," William said. He stood by the sideboard swirling his drink, the light catching in the etched glass and dashing against the amber liquid.

"I'm afraid so." I folded the letter back into its envelope. "I asked for an explanation for their absence, but Mother refuses to give me a believable one. All she says is Father is *busy*. Busy? My father is a gentleman of leisure who lives off of his inheritance. What could he possibly be doing?"

William finished his drink, reached for the bottle of sherry and poured himself another. "Why doesn't your mother come on her own?"

"She'd never do that. Even when I was young and Father would go off for one reason or another, she always went with him."

"An unnatural attachment." William gave me a playful grin that I didn't know how to read. "Like someone else I know."

"Oh?" I smiled. He seemed agitated, but in a way that might be to my benefit. "Did I forget to mention my trip to Paris? I know how you hate beautiful, bustling cities and fabulous food, so I thought I'd go on my own," I teased.

"On your own?" William circled my chair and pressed his hand to the back of my neck, the gesture softly seductive. "What would I do without you?"

"You'd think of something." His palm was damp and warm and I leaned into it, breathing in the smell of dried musk the housekeeper hangs in William's wardrobe to keep his clothes smelling pleasant.

I sighed. "I suppose I am stuck here entertaining the likes of Mrs. Tippings, although she would rather be entertaining you."

William laughed. "God help me if we ever have her back here."

Mrs. Tippings was the wife of one of William's old school chums. Openly smitten with William, she'd taken his arm the moment she stepped out of the carriage, hardly letting him out of her sight and talking incessantly to him until the moment she left.

William and I had laughed about it, and yet a possessiveness had coiled through me watching her. "It's a good thing her husband turned a blind eye," I said.

"Or I'd have a black-and-blue one."

"You would if he wasn't such a pleasant man."

"Pleasant in what way?" William slid his hand to the back of my head, his fingers in my hair.

"In every way."

"You were looking at him?"

I had taken no notice of him, but envy can be an arousing game. "Only when you allowed him in the house. I'm surprised I saw him at all what with the hunting you forced upon the poor man. Keeping him away from me, were you?"

"Most assuredly." William moved in front of me, nudging a knee between the folds of my skirt and pressing my legs open. "You are beautiful." He drew his thumb along my lips, lightly, the touch as sensual as if he'd run a hand over my nipple. I tilted my cheek into his palm, his fingers caressing my earlobe. "Will you read something to me?" he said, and I laughed, startled.

"That is not what I thought you were going to say."

"You never know, your work might be equally as exciting as a romp in bed."

"My work?" A log snapped in the fire. I hadn't spoken of my writing to William in months. The idea of sharing it made my stomach drop. "I don't have a first draft."

"So what? Neither do I." He pulled his hand away and stepped back, leaving my skirt bunched over my legs.

This unexpected seduction, then withdrawal, disconcerted me. "It's not worthy of your attention. Anyway, it's up in my writing desk," I said, as if that would put an end to it.

"Go fetch it. I will wait." He pulled me up, spun me around and gave me a little push toward the door.

Upstairs, I gathered my work, anxious, but also excited for whatever new chapter this was. My father is the only person who's read my writing, and his opinion doesn't hold nearly the weight of my novelist husband's. Clutching the pages to my chest, I told myself that I should be grateful William wanted to read it.

When I entered the drawing room, he was seated with his glass perched on one knee, his fingernail making a soft chiming sound against the crystal. His mood seemed fragile. I held out the pages, but he said, "I'd prefer you read it to me."

The wind slammed against the glass. I turned up the gas lamp and sat down. "This is torture, you know. If you don't like it, I may never be able to confidently take up my pen again."

"I promise to be kind."

"How much shall I read?"

"All of it."

"All of it? That will take hours."

He leaned his head against the back of his chair and made a show of settling in. "Go on now, stop making excuses."

Once I started, I am embarrassed to admit how caught up in my own words I became, my characters galvanized by my voice, living and dreaming and dying on the page. When I finished, I was so sure William would be pleased that when I looked up and saw his hostile expression, I was stupefied. "William, what is it? What's wrong?" He leaned forward, his face feverish, his fists balled over his knees as if he meant to smash something. "William?"

His bottom lip was white where he bit down on it. Unclenching his jaw, he said, "Your character sounds an awful lot like Peter Emsley."

This was ridiculous. "In what way?" I demanded.

The wind tore at the windows, trying to claw its way inside.

"Edmond? Emsley? Your Mr. *Edmond* is a lawyer, lives in London, was jilted by a girl." For a horrible moment I wondered if he was right. Had I unintentionally written about Peter? "Does he get the girl?" William stood up, coming at me through air that seemed blurred, his movements slowed in time as he stood over me, his anger huge and unpredictable. For the first time, I was physically frightened of him. "Does she leave her husband for him? Are you writing fact or fiction?"

My chest heaved, but I kept my voice steady. "William." I said his name slowly, hoping to calm whatever beast had been set loose. "I promise you I never think of him. It's fiction. Pure fiction. Of course it is." Then I made the mistake of saying,

"You hardly knew Mr. Emsley. How would you know what his character might look like?"

William's hands shot out, pinning my arms to the armrests. His face was so close I could see the veins in the whites of his eyes. "Don't you dare tell me what I do and don't know."

We stared at one another. He did not hurt me, but I could see that he wanted to, not physically, but somewhere deep inside me, which made it worse. He wanted to make me suffer.

What terrified me was that I knew he could.

"Why are you doing this? I love you," I said, as if this admission would stop whatever ruthless things he had in store.

All at once, the tension left his body. His grip loosened and he looked at me with eyes so cold they seemed inhuman. "In the end, it won't matter," he said, and left the room.

CHAPTER 6

Berkeley, California, 2006

When the door shut behind Josiah, Abby's entire body sank as if a plug had been pulled. Instead of returning to Evelyn's poems, she took her Canon Super 8 camera off the shelf and pressed it up to her eye, shifting the world into a grainy black-and-white box.

After her mother died, she walked around all day filtering everything through her grandpa's camera. He told her she could use it as long as she didn't scratch the lens. Film was expensive, he said. "Don't go around recording things willy-nilly. Think carefully, and choose your shot." She didn't tell her grandpa that the recording part didn't matter. All she needed was to see the world through a viewfinder. It allowed her a comfortable detachment, turned her into a silent observer in a detailed universe she got to be outside of, instead of in.

The first time she held down the record button was in the kitchen doorway, capturing her grandparents mid-fight. Maggie's arms were crossed tight over her chest as she fired epithets at Carl, who tossed his hands around as if trying to catch them and hurl them back at her. At least, that's what it looked like when the film came back and they all sat in the living room watching Carl's swinging arms and Maggie's silent, snapping mouth projected onto the wall for a full minute and a half. When the reel ended, Abby could tell from the compressed corners of Maggie's lips, and the way Carl was holding on to the arms of his chair, that they were upset. Their emotions pleased Abby. They had paid attention. She had affected them, and this made her feel significant.

The next day she found a stack of color negative film on her bedside table with a note from Grandpa Carl saying this would give her finer grain footage than the Ektachrome film she'd been using.

She'd been using color negative film ever since.

Behind the lens, Abby reduced the day into a single image, zooming in on the photograph of her mother and father, then passing briefly over *Poems of Solitude*, by Evelyn Aubrey, the word *solitude* miserably accurate. Lifting her finger from the record button, she set down her camera and dropped onto her back on the sofa, a familiar emptiness expanding through her as she thought of all the things she could have said to make Josiah stay. How much she loved him, how much she needed him. How this was, ironically, the longest, healthiest relationship she'd ever been in. Why had she said none of these things? She pictured his face, the bow of his lips and the way his eyes turned down at the corners, squinty and brown, how he always shoved his hair up off his forehead.

The first time he invited her to his loft apartment in an old brick building in the Mission District, the chic cleanliness of it had amused her. The water pipes running along the high ceiling were exposed in that intentionally fashionable way, with pale wooden floors and recessed lighting. She'd teased him about it and he'd told her—justifying its hipness—that it was rent-controlled. "You'd better like it," he said, "because I'll be here until the day I die." Which was probably true. Josiah had never lived outside of San Francisco. His parents were still tucked up in their house on Filbert Street, schoolteachers, stable as they come. Abby had tried to find some dark, untoward secrets in their family, but Josiah's older sister and younger brother were as steady and put together as Josiah was. They were abnormally normal, Abby had decided. All three had gone to college in the Bay area. Josiah had gone to UCSF and had been on the swim team. He now worked for the university as a biomedical engineer, doing laps in their Olympic-sized pool before work in the morning.

In the beginning, their relationship had felt casual and fun, but lately, Josiah's steadiness had begun to terrify Abby. A week after her thirtieth birthday, when they were curled on the couch about to start a movie, Josiah commented on the number of wedding invitations he'd gotten that spring. All their friends, having slipped over the line into their thirties, were getting married. Some were even having babies. For a horrible moment, Abby thought he was about to propose. He didn't, thank God, just started up the movie, but the bewildering commitment of marriage and babies made Abby want to gather her things from the apartment and run.

Normally, she dated damaged men—capricious and erratic, men who wore their internal scars like fashion, a sexy handicap. *Look how fucked up I am.* Men who used sex like she did, eyeing her as if she was edible, then watching the door as they came inside her, timing their escape before they were even finished. Abby's therapist had told her these destructive relationships were her rebellion against her dead mother for not being there to teach her differently. A solid assessment, Abby thought, remembering the first guy she slept with, how she'd watched him pull his hair back with a red bandanna before having sex with her in an alley. She couldn't remember the boy's face, just his thin hands gripping her ass, the sound of cars swooshing past, the clank of dishes from an open restaurant door and the low rumble of voices. She had tried closing her eyes, but found she couldn't make herself float away with those bright spots behind her lids like she learned to do after her mother died. The act was too physical and painful. It caught her in midair and pulled her down to earth. It was the first time since her mother's death that she felt real. She got a reputation, but she didn't care. She wanted to be pulled down over and over again.

Sex still did that for her, jarred her into existence.

Abby sat up, picked up her cell phone to call Josiah then set it back down. What was she doing? The photograph of her mom had set everything loose. She could feel herself slipping.

Opening the trunk she used as a coffee table, she pulled out her mother's white purse that had been tossed from the car the night Eva died and found in a bed of dried eucalyptus leaves. From it, Abby took the tube of red lipstick, Cherry Berry, and went into the bathroom. She set it on the vanity and undressed, staring at her naked body in the mirror. The window was cracked open and salty ocean air slithered in, tightening her nipples and raising goose bumps over her skin. Outside, the gardenia bushes rustled in the breeze. She had picked a single, firm, white blossom this morning and put it in a small vase by her bed. The toughness of that small flower, the power of its scent, always astounded her. Turning sideways, she inspected her hanging breasts, her pale soft stomach and wide hips, remembering her mother's reflection in this mirror, her thin, sharp bones, her small breasts and permanent tan lines. Her mom had worn bright lipstick and shirts with no bras. At thirteen, Abby had wanted to look just like her.

But she grew up to look nothing like her. Or either of her grandparents.

She looked like Evelyn Aubrey. She looked like her father, whoever he was.

Opening the tube of lipstick, the color still a vivid red, she drew the worn-down tip along her mouth, hearing her mother's voice, *Right, left and bottom.* Leaning over the sink, her stomach pressed up against the cold brass faucet, she kissed the mirror, looking at her lone lipstick mark and remembering that night, the earsplitting bang, the jolt so violent it sent her sprawling on the floor. The room had tilted sideways, hairbrush and jewelry box and makeup kit sliding off the bureau, the framed poster of George Michael crashing to the floor. Abby's thoughts had slid out of her head like the objects off the bureau. She hadn't been able to make sense of the movement and noise and chaos. It seemed to her that the world had suddenly sprung open, walls and floors and ceilings defying universal laws of immobility.

And then everything was still and her grandma was rushing into the room, pulling her from the floor with flour-dusted hands, the fine white particles floating between them.

For hours, she and Grandma Maggie sat watching the maelstrom on *Channel 7 News*, a woman in a purple blouse with yellow hair and fat, gold earrings gesturing to a dark room behind her, saying something about the magnitude of the earthquake and losing power and the World Series. There were aerial views of smoking buildings, leaking water mains, fires in Oakland, the collapsed Bay Bridge, a section fallen in like a Lego structure bumped with a shoe.

Abby couldn't watch anymore. Going upstairs to her mother's room, she picked a red high heel up off the floor and pressed it into her chest, branding a small circle below her clavicle. Out the window, the city was terrifyingly dark. For her entire life, that view had held tiny, sparkling lights. Abby rested her forehead against the cool glass, her fear a tight ball around her heart. What if her mom was on the bridge? In one of those burning buildings? Trapped in an elevator? Under a collapsed roof? There was so much space out there to get lost in.

Abby climbed into bed, buried herself under the covers and fell asleep with the shoe in her arms.

When the overhead light switched on, she squinted, pulling herself out of a thick dream that disintegrated in the glare. Grandma Maggie perched on the edge of the bed with an arm clasped around her middle, one hand tugging at her quilted bathrobe.

"Abigail?" Her breath was sour. "Are you awake? You need to wake up."

Abby's eyes were fully adjusted now. Grandpa Carl stood just outside the bedroom door, his thick arms crossed over baggy pajamas, his legs firmly planted. His lips were moving, but no sound came out, and his eyes darted around as if afraid to settle on something solid. Abby bolted into a sitting position and her mom's shoe fell to the floor with a thud.

She looked frantically from one grandparent to the other. "Where's Mom?" Her heart leaped in her chest.

Her grandma's eyes were bloodshot eyes. Abby dug her nails into the sheets and balled her hands into fists, squeezing her whole body against the news Grandma Maggie delivered in an aching voice, the words shattering inside Abby's head.

Eva had been going to a party at Stinson Beach. There were six of them in the car. When the earthquake hit, it sailed off a sharp corner on Route 1 without leaving any skid marks. They all died. Eva had been sitting behind the driver's seat, by the window.

It was this last part Abby would always think of, her mother looking out the window. She knew the road. The hairpin turns made her carsick, but she loved it anyway, especially when the fog sucked them in, the moisture pressing against the windows, her body pinned to the door as they rounded another curve. Then the sky would break open, the road bringing them high above white clouds that touched the edges of the earth. Abby would picture the ocean turning beneath them, the massive power of it, the waves worked up under a blanket of fog so thick and soft it was hard to believe it wouldn't hold her if she leaped out into it.

Had her mother seen the fog as she sailed out above it? Had she thought it thick enough to hold her too?

After her mother's death, Abby's whole world felt like that fog. It took on the illusion of solidity, when, really, there was just empty space and she was falling right through it.

She had been trying for years to fix herself, to heal, to stop falling. Nothing was working.

Impulsively, Abby leaned over and kissed a second set of lips onto the mirror.

Climbing into her loft bed, she wrapped up in her blanket, her mind flipping through images of the past. It was all boiling over, spilling out. She couldn't go on like this, living in her grandparents' guesthouse, wandering through jobs and men. Somehow, she had to find a way to stop kissing mirrors and lying in the arms of her dead mother.

CHAPTER 7

Burford, England, 1899

December 10

A few nights after the dreadful incident with William, we were in the dining room finishing up dinner when Bennett came quietly to William's side and said, "Sir, I am sorry to interrupt your meal, but there is a motorcar coming up the drive."

I rose from my seat. "We don't know anyone who owns a motorcar, and one driven at this hour could only constitute bad news."

"No need to excite yourself." William stabbed his fork into his meat. "Bennett, see who it is, and if it's not an emergency, show them into the drawing room until we've finished our dinner."

Glaring at William, I left the room, hurried down the hall and out the front door, with Bennett scrambling to keep up. Through the cold, clear night, I saw a dim light bobbing in the distance, coming slowly closer. A monstrous contraption rounded the circular drive and roared to a stop in a puff of smoke. Bennett reached up and helped a small figure—buried in a hat, coat, goggles and gloves—remove the blanket from her lap and step out of the motorcar.

"Mother?" I rushed forward and threw my arms around her. I am much taller and fuller figured than my mother and the embrace practically knocked her over.

"Good gracious, Evelyn!" She pulled away, never one for affection no matter the occasion.

Regardless, I held her hand. "Why are you here at such an hour, and without notice? And when did you get a motorcar? How is it you're motoring at night? You can barely see the road with that silly lantern. Is everything alright? Is it Father? Is something wrong?"

"We're fine." Mother took back her hand, yanking at the bottom of her suit jacket. "Just frozen to the core."

I was astounded to see my father come around the front of the motorcar, his goggles perched on his head, his freckled face so familiar it felt like my own. Tears sprang to my eyes as he swallowed me in an embrace. "My dear girl," he said. "How we have missed you."

The warmth of him melted me. I pulled away, laughing. "When did you learn how to drive this thing? And don't you look a sight in your modern motoring attire. You could have killed yourself getting here in the dark. Why in heaven's name did you do it? Is everything alright? Father, you look terribly thin. You're not sick, are you?"

"At least let them through the front door, my dear." William came from the house, his shoes crunching over the gravel as he extended his hand to Father and said, "Mr. Wilkins," then kissed Mother's cheek.

My parents greeted him warmly, even Mother, who hasn't gotten over my rejection of Peter. She manages to bring him up in every letter, something I have made sure to keep from William.

"We don't have a room made up," I said, frenzied, watching Bennett inspect the motorcar for luggage he couldn't find.

"Not to worry." Father patted my shoulder as we walked into the front hall. My parents appeared to have aged in the short time we'd been apart. Father's features seemed sharper and thinner, Mother's softer and plumper, her hair paled to a mousy gray. "I will call for the housekeeper," I said. "You must be famished. We were just finishing dinner, but I can have the cook prepare more food. How long have you been traveling? You must not have eaten for hours."

William put a stilling hand on my shoulder. "You would think she had not spoken to a soul in months. Your ebullience is charming, my dear, but let them catch their breath. Come—" he opened the drawing room door "—warm yourselves by the fire. I will instruct Bennett to have more food brought up."

Mother and Father moved stiffly into the room, looking cloddish in their motoring clothes as I flitted about, not sure what to do with myself. I'd never had my parents as guests before and I wanted to make a good impression.

"Please, sit," I said, but neither did.

Mother walked around the room, taking stock of the tufted white chairs and gold threaded sofa, the massive floral rug. The house is a mix of the ages, delicate Queen Anne side tables, gold Rococo picture frames and ornamental Elizabethan desks.

"How strange to be back in this house after all this time," Mother said, looking up at the row of framed ancestors staring out from the peach-colored wall. She had grown up in this house.

"Who is that?" I asked, standing beside her, looking at a stern-faced, white-bearded man in a green velvet jacket.

"My great-uncle Geffrey. To think—" Mother squeezed my arm "—you were only eleven years old the last time we were here. Can it have been that long, Gilbert?"

Father was looking out the dark window. "What? Oh, yes, that seems about right." This house held little nostalgia for him. They'd summered here for Mother's sake, and he easily gave it up when she decided Bath was a more fashionable location.

"We apologize for coming unexpectedly." Mother stripped off her coat and laid it over her arm. "I tried to get your father to send a message before roaring out into the night, but you know how he is when he gets an idea into his head."

Father's goggles were still propped on his head. He slid them off and tucked them into his coat pocket with a flashing smile. "It was high time for a visit."

"Shame on you for not coming sooner," I scolded. "I've been wickedly insulted."

Just then William came in, Bennett close on his heels.

"Do you hear that?" Father said to him. "I've insulted my daughter."

"You've insulted both of us." William slapped his shoulder good-naturedly and the butler promptly took Mother's coat and gloves.

To William, Mother said, "I was saying to Evelyn you must excuse our abrupt arrival. We would have sent a message ahead, but Gilbert was determined to get away in his new motorcar immediately. What a whirlwind! It took over seven hours, bitter cold ones at that. Gilbert kept stopping to refill the paraffin and we almost got stuck a dozen times on the rutted roads."

"It's a fantastic machine, from the looks of it." William smiled, the delicate lines around his eyes stretching to his temple.

Father beamed. "She's a beauty, a Geering. Manufactured by an engine company. There are three forward speeds, a reversing gear and a friction clutch. It's absolutely brilliant. You'll have to take her out tomorrow."

"I'd be delighted."

"How long are you staying?" I asked.

"Just the weekend," Father said.

"That's it? You must stay for Christmas," I pleaded.

"Yes," William said, "make it worth your travel." My husband was acting surprisingly amiable. Normally, he doesn't like his routine interrupted. I couldn't tell whether he was putting it on, or if my parents' arrival had genuinely picked up his mood.

Mother wrapped her arm around Father's. "We don't even have a change of clothes! There was no room, what with the water jugs."

"Water jugs?" I asked.

"For cooling the cylinders," Father answered.

"Honestly," Mother said. "It's the most ridiculous form of travel."

"You can have your things sent by train." I was already clinging to the idea of them staying.

"Could we afford three weeks?" Mother looked at Father.

I couldn't help saying, "What on earth do you have to return for?"

"Nothing." Father peeled Mother off of him. "Absolutely nothing."

"I guess then, if you'll have us?" Mother gave William a terse smile. I could see it was an effort for her to ask his permission to stay in a house that was still, technically, hers and Father's.

"We'd be delighted." William poured two glasses of sherry and handed Mother one, giving her a look that made my mother, usually rigid as bone, soften just a little.

He handed the other glass to Father and the four of us stood in awkward silence until the dinner bell summoned us to the distraction of stuffed quail.

I talked a stream of dialogue as my parents ate, making them tell me every detail of their latest engagements, whose house they'd dined at and what operas they'd seen. Mother laughed at my enthusiasm and told me I was sorely missed. Father was reserved, but thoughtful, asking William questions about his latest work. William answered evasively.

That night I lay in bed and thought of home, of the buzzing city streets and the life I had so suddenly left behind, of my old bedroom at Coniston House and the carriage rides to Berkeley Square for pink ices. I thought of Peter Emsley, benignly, but without nostalgia. We had been good friends before our engagement, and I wish I hadn't ruined things. I still had Gwyneth, a tried and true friend, saddled with three children under the age of three, but as social as ever, by the sounds of her letters. I wondered if I could convince William to move back to London. Then, at least, I could distract myself with society life again.

December 19

Oh, dear God, there has been a tragedy. I don't want to write of it. This detailed penning of my life was Father's idea. Did he know I would be sitting here, writing this? How could he, and yet, I think of the sadness on his face when he handed me this journal on my wedding day. I thought it was at losing me, but now, I know it was something more.

Therefore, I will write as I have been, for Father. I will bleed my pen on these pages and feel the pain as I do it.

The next few weeks went by quickly. Mother and I spent hours in the drawing room talking of all the things I had missed since leaving London. Father spent most of his time reading in the chair he used to occupy when I was a child. I hadn't touched the piano in months, but Mother begged me to play, and when I did, the music was inspiring and I promised myself I'd keep it up.

William's pleasant mood did not last. The morning after my parents arrived, he was as sullen as ever, and since then, has made himself scarce. I told my parents not to take it personally. "William keeps to himself when he's deep into a new novel," I said, an acceptable explanation I am still trying to convince myself is true. I couldn't bear for my parents to think that my marriage was an unhappy one.

The only time we were all together was at dinner, where Father and Mother tried to engage him in conversation, to no avail. William ate silently, ignoring all of us. Father was also subdued and melancholy, which worried me. Unlike William, my father is rarely ill-tempered.

I asked Mother about it one afternoon as we sat repainting the faded wings of wooden ornaments the housekeeper dug out of a trunk in the storage room. "Your father is fine," she said, her hands engaged, her dark eyes peering through wire-rimmed bi-focals. "Things are as they have always been. Seems to me—" she lifted her angel to the light, inspecting it "—it's your own husband you should be worried about."

I stiffened. How dare she? She hardly knows William. "He's busy. His work consumes him," I said, dipping my brush aggressively into the pot of paint, a spray of silver showering my hand.

Mother touched the tip of her paintbrush to a wing, edging it in a delicate line of gold. "Our husbands do as they please and we let them, don't we?"

"You're the one who told me a wife's responsibility was to support her husband through thick and thin," I said, drawing a sloppy line along my angel's skirt.

"And I meant it." She set her ornament down, her design on each wing symmetrical, precise. "The sanctity of marriage is the highest in God's eyes. *'Man shall leave his father and his mother and hold fast to his wife, and they shall become one flesh,'*" she quoted.

I tried not to grimace. It used to be that *one flesh* was all I could think about. I did not, however, say this to my mother.

If I could go back, I would hold on to everything tighter. I would pay attention, say something meaningful to Mother instead of silently finishing up my ornament and leaving the room. On the evenings when I sat up with Father, I would have listened wholeheartedly instead of letting my thoughts wander to William, worrying over his jealousy, his anger. It was obvious the close relationship I shared with my father upset him. Once, when I was about to retire to the drawing room where Father waited, William made a snide remark about how childish I was, always following my father around.

Bristling, I responded, "It's not childish to sit up talking with someone who's clever and witty and entertaining. I think you'd enjoy Father's company if you took it. Why not join us?"

William refused, mumbling that he was tired.

Secretly, I was grateful. Sitting up with Father reminded me of all the hours we spent at my studies when I was a little girl. Learning under his tutelage had felt empowering, knowing I could bundle up knowledge and carry it through life. Father still enjoyed imparting and gathering knowledge as much as I did, and together we batted ideas around, discussing art and literature and music. It was during our evening talks that he was his old self again, relaxed and jocular. I hadn't realized how much I needed this mental stimulation. Father even convinced me to read to him, which took all of my courage. I had not picked up my novel since that dreadful night with William, but Father was thoughtful and constructively critical. He said it was excellent, solid, my characters believable and my plot well devised, but that I should work on my transitions, and that my metaphors were trite, at times.

It was during one of these conversations that the drawing room door flew open so forcefully Father and I leaped to our feet as it banged against the opposite wall. William stepped into the room, his face in shadow, his hands at his sides.

"Is something the matter?" I asked.

"No." William folded his arms across his chest and stared at us.

With an embarrassed laugh I said, "Well then, you should join us." In an effort to cover up our discussion of my writing, I said to Father, "Do your impression of Balfe's *The Bohemian Girl*."

"No." Father gave a short laugh. "William doesn't want that."

William didn't move from the shadow of the doorway.

I hated Father seeing me humor my husband in this way, but I went on. "William, we really ought to take a trip to the city to see it. It has been so long since I saw an opera. Wouldn't it be fun? Come, sit with us. I'm sure Father will humor you with an impression."

I went to William, but he jerked away so forcefully my father raised a hand as if stilling a bucking horse, and said, "No need to be upset, William."

William ignored him. He hooked an arm around my elbow and said, "It's late. You should be retiring to your room."

Rebellion rose in my throat, and shame. If Father hadn't been watching I would have ripped my arm out of William's and told him I'd go to bed whenever I pleased, but the concern buckling my poor father's forehead forced me to behave. I didn't want him worrying.

"How right you are." I smiled, falsely.

Father is no fool. I could see, in the alarmed way he watched William drag me from the room, that he wanted to interfere, to defend me, but this was a domestic matter, one we both knew was no longer his place to defend.

William and I now sleep in separate rooms. When he entered his, the light of the full moon spilled bright and cold through the window. There was no fire, and no lamp lit. I sat on the edge of the bed watching him pace in and out of the blue chips of moonlight, feeling a mix of arousal and rage. The skin of my upper arm burned where he'd held on as he dragged me up the stairs, but the truth was, I wanted his attention, no matter what it looked like, which made me wonder what kind of shameful woman I was turning into.

He came toward me so abruptly, I flinched.

"You are frightened of me," he said.

"No." I reached for him. "I just… I don't know what you expect of me."

William sat heavily on the bed, his shoulders sinking. "Forgive me." His voice was shallow, tired. "I don't know what is wrong with me." Curling up like a child, he suddenly laid his head in my lap and I felt a shock of tears on his cheek as I brushed his hair from his face. I had never seen a man cry. It was not an emotion I could comprehend. This show of anguish was as confusing as his anger. He'd never apologized, or admitted anything was wrong, ever. My throat felt thick with my own need to cry, from confusion, or relief, or fear, I didn't know which.

Kissing his forehead, I said, "Oh, my love, it's going to be alright," but I was not at all sure that it would be.

"It destroys me to see how happy you are with your father." His voice was muffled in my dress. "I can never make you that happy."

"Nonsense, you make me perfectly happy."

He sat up and looked at me, his eyes bloodshot. "That is a lie," he said, and lay down with his back to me.

I kicked off my shoes and curled on the bed against him, wrapping my arm over his. "It is I who ought to be making you happy," I said, believing, as I had been taught all my life, that this was true. My husband's happiness was my responsibility.

William didn't answer, and after a while his breath deepened and I knew he slept. I did not undress, or crawl under the covers. I lay next to him, drifting in and out of sleep until the gray light of dawn filtered through the room, at which point I slid my feet into my shoes and crept away, worried he would be embarrassed by his tears from the previous night.

I did not bother to go to my room and change out of the gown I had worn to supper, a thin, beaded thing that was much too cold for the morning. With the chill of the house in my fingers and toes, I made my way downstairs, sliding my hand along the banister, reminded of a moment as a child when I leaned out of a rowboat and skimmed my hand over the water. What simplicity there had been in that moment, what innocence and trust for my own well-being. My father had told me not to lean too far out or I'd go overboard, and I had told him it wouldn't matter because he'd rescue me. I wanted Father to rescue me now.

Wandering into the dining room, I found the scullery maid violently raking at the coals from last night's fire. "You're up early, ma'am." She barely glanced at me as she worked. "The fire'll be lit in a few. Will ya be wantin' a early breakfast called up for ya?" She hooked the coal bucket over her forearm.

"No, that won't be necessary."

"A pot of tea then?" She was halfway out the door.

"Yes, alright, that would be nice."

I went to the window and ran my fingers through the tassels of the fitments watching the sun filter through the mist, offering itself to a dusty, morning sky.

When Father entered the dining room, I was sitting with an empty cup of tea and the weekly edition of the *Morning Post*. Breakfast had been laid out, as it was nearly ten o'clock, and the smell of smoked bacon and eggs rose from the silver urns on the sideboard. Father did not mention the evening dress I still wore, or my messed hair. He nodded and sat down, his face drawn. I said good morning, poured him a cup of tea and went back to my paper. I did not want to speak of last night, or explain my husband to him. He kept clearing his throat, making little puffing sounds with his breath as he stirred his spoon vigorously in his cup. I tried to ignore it, pretending deep interest in an article on Lord Kitchener's defeat of the Mahdist army in Sudan.

Dropping his spoon onto his saucer with a clatter, Father said, "Evelyn," as if about to make a declaration. I looked up, but he only said, "You have color in your cheeks. That is good to see," picked up his spoon and resumed his noisome tapping.

"What is it?" I folded the paper and placed it on the sideboard. "There is something that presses on your mind." I was certain whatever it was had to do with William.

"It is obvious then?" He frowned.

"I'm afraid so."

Father hung his head so low I thought he meant to lay it upon the table. When he looked up, there was such torment on his face it unnerved me. "I have something terrible to tell you. It was my intention to tell you when we first arrived, but then I changed my mind, and now I feel I must."

At that moment William burst into the room as he had the previous evening, only this time he was fully dressed, wearing his newly purchased cord breeches and a bright red riding coat.

"Look at this day!" he cried with too much enthusiasm. "We had better eat a hurried breakfast if we are to capture the best of it." He filled a plate of food, slapped a kiss onto my cheek and pulled out his chair. "Are we waiting on your mother?"

"She takes breakfast in her room." I was baffled at his changed temperament. It seemed impossible to imagine this affable man crying in my arms the night before.

"Right, of course. Where is Bennett? Did you send him away again?" William dipped his knife into the marmalade and scraped it over his crisp toast.

"There was no one to serve but myself. I saw no point in the poor man standing at my attendance."

"My independent wife! That is your doing, Mr. Wilkins. She refuses to take breakfast in bed, like most wives, yours included, and is constantly sending the servants away. It confuses them, but no matter. Can I serve you myself?"

Father shook his head, mustering up false bravado. "No, thank you, William. You eat up. It is a splendid day. I think an early walk is in order."

"A walk? Why, sir, the horses are being readied for us as we speak, and the hares are not likely to be caught on foot."

"Father doesn't hunt," I interjected.

"No?" William balanced his knife on the edge of his plate. "Did you not grow up in this splendid countryside? Whatever did you find to do with your days as a young man if not hunt?"

"Read," Father said, with a note of vexation. "Something I would expect to occupy more of your time than mine. Evelyn told me that Chapman & Hill will be publishing your next novel. How is that coming?"

I cringed, unsure what this question would do to William, but he seemed utterly at ease. Taking a large bite of toast, he said, "Not at all, sir, not at all. I am afraid I wasted my summer and now I can't seem to get started again. It's your daughter's fault. She is a terrible distraction." He did not look at me when he said this, and I was not sure whether to take offense or not. "Winter is upon us and the cold is bound to set in. I figure I ought to enjoy the outdoors while I still can. I will leave dirtying my hands with ink to the long and dreary months ahead."

Watching him, I wondered if he was acting false for my sake, to make up for the tears.

"About this 'not hunting' business," he continued, brushing crumbs from his fingers. "I insist you come along if for no other reason than my desiring your company. There is a gentleman by the name of Samuel Godall that lives at Rickart House. He enjoys a hunt as much as I do. I thought we might see if we can't get him to come along. Three is a luckier number than two when chasing after small game."

"Father really does not hunt," I persisted.

"Well, we shall see if we can't find a way to change that. How about a try, sir?"

Father looked out the long windows, sunlight ribboning into the room. "I have never understood why one would want to destroy the beauty and silence of this good county with the sound of a shotgun. That said—" he thumped the table as he stood up "—it is rude to refuse an invitation. Where will I find a riding habit?"

"A sporting man we will make of you!" William waved his hand at the door. "There is a habit, as well as a pair of breeches, upstairs in my wardrobe. Ask one of the servants to direct you. I will finish up my breakfast and meet you at the stables."

I trailed Father into the hallway. "You despise hunting. Let's wait for Mother to come down and the three of us can walk out together. Or you and I could walk alone. What was it that you wanted to tell me? You've made me anxious."

Father squeezed my shoulder. "Nothing that can't wait until tonight. Your husband has been less than hospitable over these last weeks. It might be my only chance to get to know the man."

He looked at me for a long moment before saying, "It's going to be alright, you know, whatever comes of it."

I thought he was referring to William and me. I shook my head and smiled. "Of course it will be."

Standing in the gravel drive, I watched Father clumsily mount his horse, his boots barely finding their way into the stirrups. I was annoyed at William for cajoling him, but Mother said it would be good for him. "Men have ridden horseback for centuries, which is more than can be said for the abominable automobile. That, my dear, is a danger," she said, gathering her coat around her as we watched them crest the hilltop.

I was in the drawing room absorbed in a copy of Macaulay's *History of England* Father had brought with him when I heard shouting. The book slid from my lap to the floor as I jumped up, rushing to the window where Mr. Godall, a man who has lost all of his agility to younger years, was galloping at full speed across the field, holding the reins in one hand and waving his other high in the air as if summoning an army.

Mother hurried in from the hallway and we flew out the side door, the cold hitting me so hard it took my breath away. I froze for a split second before sucking the biting air into my lungs and running to meet a florid-faced Mr. Godall, who was struggling to dismount his horse. When he finally landed on the ground, he pitched forward with his hands on his knees, trying to catch his breath. "Mr. Wilkins... He... It's... Mr. Aubrey said to send for the doctor...but..." He choked and sputtered. "I think it might be too late."

In the distance, I saw William ride up over the hill, his horse at a walk, a limp body dangling across his lap. I pressed a hand over my mouth, afraid I might be sick. Mother screamed, a gut-wrenching sound, and ran toward them. She tripped on her dress, caught herself and stumbled into William as he slid from his horse, holding Father in his arms. I stood paralyzed, the sun glaring overhead, the cold eating at me under my clothes.

Through the shimmering, bright day, William moved toward me. From the unhurried pace he took, and by the hard expression on his face, I was afraid Mr. Godall was right. It was too late for the doctor.

Too terrified to look, I did not even turn my head as he passed. I should have at least gone to Mother where she'd fallen to her knees in the frozen field, but Mr. Godall was with her. As for myself, I barely managed to get back to the drawing room, where I sank into a chair, staring at father's disfigured book on the floor, "From the Library of Gilbert Wilkins" displayed in bold letters across the exposed flyleaf.

By the time the doctor arrived, the vicar had been summoned. He sat with Mother, Mr. Godall and me in the drawing room, waiting for William and the doctor to return from the upstairs bedroom where Father had been laid. The vicar was not a stranger to me since I went regularly to divine service. He was a young, impressive-looking man with disappointingly dull sermons. Putting a hand on Mother's arm, he said, in a hushed voice, that one must not question God's decisions. Heaven was surely open to Mr. Wilkins, even though he had not been able to give a last confession. Mother did not respond. She sat stunned on the sofa with her head at an odd angle.

I felt numb with disbelief.

Within the hour, Dr. Grousman came downstairs and sank wearily into an armchair. He was a small, weathered-looking fellow with beady eyes placed deep in the folds of his sagging skin. "Terribly sorry for your loss, Mrs. Wilkins," he said to Mother, who gasped and pressed a hand to her stomach. The confirmation of death sent a wave of nausea through me. Tears threatened, but I forced them back, trying to stay calm for Mother's sake. The doctor went on, "It may be a comfort to know that there would have been nothing I could do for him. It appears he died quite instantly from the fall."

"The fall?" I cried, shooting a look at William, who had

come in with the doctor and stood rooted at the far end of the room, his arms pinned across his chest. "How did it happen?"

"I don't know." William looked helpless. "It was the smallest hedge; any horse could take it. But somehow, he lost his balance and when I looked back, he was lying on the ground."

"He was sick, was he not?" I turned to the doctor. "He was so changed, so thin. He tried desperately to tell me something this morning, and now I am quite certain it was that he was unwell. He must have fallen ill on horseback and had not been able to keep his balance. He should never have gone out with you!" I erupted at William, who clenched his arms tighter over his chest and looked away.

"Now, now," the vicar soothed in a temperate voice. "You have no right to place blame, young lady. It is God's will and we must see it as such."

Young lady? The tears I had held back all afternoon sprang forward. I hated to be reproached in this way and it made the absence of Father, who would have defended me, unbearable.

The doctor wiped his brow. "Mr. Wilkins appeared to be in perfect health."

How would he know? I thought, brushing away my tears with the flat of my hand. Out loud, I said, "That simply cannot be. Mother, was Father seeing a doctor in London?" Mother stared at me in confusion. "Was he seeing a doctor in London?" I repeated.

"I don't know… Maybe… He never told me if he was."

Dr. Grousman narrowed his eyes. He was not used to being questioned on his diagnoses. "Mrs. Aubrey, your father's neck was broken upon impact. It's a fairly open-and-shut case."

"I am not questioning the cause of death," I exploded. "I am simply suggesting the cause of his fall not be overlooked."

Everyone was annoyed. The vicar's knuckles were clenched white, my recalcitrant nature clearly more than he could take. The doctor glared at me, wiping his perspiring brow, and Mr.

Godall, who had been silent through the entire discourse, shifted uncomfortably in his chair, uncertain of how he had become involved in such an intimate family affair. William stood stonily by the window.

Mother turned to the doctor. "You will kindly excuse my daughter; she is always questioning things that should be left alone. Evelyn was never very good at knowing her place." My skin prickled at her words, those tiny needles of betrayal. To me she said, "Your Father was in perfect health. He simply lost his appetite, as of late, and he was never very good on horseback." She stood up, looking small and fragile, her face ashy white. "I am going to lie down," she said, and left the room.

It was then that I understood what I'd really lost. Not just my father, but my autonomy, the right to express my opinion, to be valued and listened to as an equal. My mother deferred to men on all things, and the men staring at me in that room expected me to do the same. It did not matter that one was a gentry, one a writer, one a medical man and one a religious man; they all expected me to be gracious and obedient. I was not to question them, or anything they said.

Anxious to take their leave, these men buttoned their coats and secured their hats with unapologetic efficiency, offering appropriate condolences on their way out.

Alone with William, I felt wretched. He did not touch me or comfort me or say he was sorry for what had happened.

After he left, I curled up in my chair and wept.

CHAPTER 8

Berkeley, California, 2006

In the bathroom, Abby wet a piece of toilet paper, wiped the lipstick stains off the mirror, threw her necessary toiletries into a leather makeup case and went into the front room to dig her suitcase out of the closet.

This morning, she'd woken with a crazed impulsivity. Using her almost maxed out credit card, she'd booked a wildly expensive one-way ticket to Gatwick, England, that left this evening.

Now, she packed two pairs of jeans, a cotton sweater, three blouses and a sundress into her suitcase. Stuffing her underwear and bras into the side pocket, she crammed her bulky Super 8 camera case on top and zipped the thing closed. Turning off her cell phone, she set it on her desk next to a note for her grandparents: "Leaving for a while. I don't know when I'll be back, but don't worry about me. Abby." Not telling them where she was going was a heartless thing to do, but she wasn't going to risk being reasoned with, being told she was wasting her time. She was thirty-one years old. She could do whatever she damn wanted without checking in with her grandparents.

Making sure she had her passport, the book of poetry and the photograph of her father, she hooked her bag over her shoulder and hauled her suitcase out the door, where a cab waited to take her to the BART station. Getting off the train in San Francisco, she walked to Hill Street wishing she'd worn something warmer than her jean jacket. The fog had rolled in and the city was freezing. Leaving her suitcase in the front hall of Josiah's apartment building, she climbed the two flights of stairs to his door. He was at work, which was the only reason she'd risked coming. She told herself she was just going to give his key back; but when she got inside, she made herself a cup of tea and sat on the couch, looking out at the thickening fog. It was so delicate, those misty wisps, and yet gathered together, powerful enough to block out everything in sight. Her mother was that fog, she thought, this beautiful floating thing blinding her to her future.

She looked at the mug Josiah had left on the coffee table, and then at the photograph of them in Hawaii, Abby freckled and pale, wearing a big sun hat, Josiah shirtless and just as pale, but willing to risk a sunburn. She missed him already. She didn't want this to end. She wanted to find a way to commit, to fight harder. At the very least she should wait until he came home and give him his key back in person. There was time for that—her flight didn't leave until 8:00 p.m.—but she knew she wouldn't. Just like she knew she wouldn't call the coffee shop where she worked and quit properly. She hated confrontation. In her head she had good reasons for doing things, but as soon as she started explaining herself, they didn't seem logical anymore. She was uncommitted, bad at making decisions, bad at her jobs, at her relationships. She knew this, and yet, what no one seemed to understand was that it wasn't because she didn't *want* to be good at these things. There was a restlessness inside her, an uncontrollable energy that nothing satisfied. It had always been there, even before her mother died. She asked too many questions, talked too much, wanted too many things. She couldn't sit still, couldn't relax. For years, her therapist had been trying to get her to meditate, but it made her want to scream. When her ten-minute timer went off, she'd get up feeling itchy and breathless and panicked, like the stillness was going to devour her.

Feeling a little panicked now, she went to the window and

opened it, breathing in the damp city air, reminding herself why she was really leaving. It wasn't just to try and find her father, or escape the memories of her mother. Abby had lived her life in regret, always bemoaning the things she hadn't done, or could have done differently. For once, she'd acted quickly and decisively, and she wasn't going to turn her back on that for a boyfriend, or a job.

She was also angry with her grandma. Furious with her. All these years there had been a photograph of her father, the details of his freckled face, his young, lanky body, his bright eyes, right there in the house and she had kept it from her. How could her grandma not have known how much it would mean to her? To have something to hold on to after her mother's death? It would have made all the difference.

Abby thought back to the day an artist told her the meaning of her name, picturing the hard expression on Grandma Maggie's face, and how she'd hurried her along, refusing to talk about it.

Her grandma had said they were going to have a girls' day out. They had gotten their nails done at Zen's, went for hot chocolates at Ghirardelli's and ended up at the farmers market, where Grandma Maggie filled her bags with green beans, kale, tomatoes and lettuce. She let Abby pick out the oranges and apples, peaches and plums.

It was early and the street vendors were just setting their wares on foldout tables. The sky had been washed clean by the wind off the bay, the pavement buffed with sunlight. There was a woman slicing samples of gingerbread with sugar crusted on top; a man securing the leg of a chair; tables of pottery, carved wooden animals and silver jewelry. Abby looked at things and tried to feel something, but the fog of her mother's recent death lay like a veil over her eyes and everything came at her through a haze.

The young woman with the paintings sat at the end of the street next to a man with dreadlocks hanging under his Rasta hat. He was making jewelry with the tiniest tool Abby had ever seen, twisting the end of a metal ring around a piece of abalone. The woman next to him was tilted back in her chair, her eyes closed, her face lifted to the sun.

Maggie picked up an oil painting from her booth, the canvas stapled to a piece of wood, the brush strokes showing a sloping green hillside dotted with purple flowers. "This is beautiful," she said.

The young woman opened her eyes and dropped the legs of her chair on all fours. "You like it?" She sounded skeptical. Getting up, she walked around the table to inspect her own work. Abby thought she might be the most beautiful woman she'd ever seen with bright, narrow eyes and a mound of black hair coiled high on her head. Her skin was rich and dark, her body lean and angular.

"It's stunning, the way you capture the light," Maggie said.

"Thanks." The woman shrugged, her youth revealed in the gesture. "My mother's disappointed with my work. She doesn't think it's original enough. *'Nouveau réalisme,'* she says, 'is original art.' She's French. She loved the '60s."

Maggie smiled. "Well, whatever style this is, it suits you."

"I'm still studying. For now, it's just landscapes and bowls of fruit. It's boring."

Abby could see that her grandma didn't know what to say. Maggie liked landscapes and bowls of fruit.

The woman turned to Abby. "What do you think?"

"It's fine," Abby said, not caring one way or the other.

The woman stuck out her hand. "Phoebe."

Abby took it. "Abigail."

"Nice to meet you, Abigail. That's my sister's name. It means *my father's joy.* Are you your father's joy? My sister was a bit of a terror."

Abby sucked in her breath, feeling like the wind had been knocked out of her. The painter said, "I got into the meanings of names for a while. In some cultures, they say a name holds all of who we are in its meaning."

The city hummed with noise and yet Abby felt as if she was being held in a cool pocket of soundlessness. A longing filled her, so huge and desperate she felt she'd burst in two.

Maggie snapped open her purse, returning to practical matters. Words were exchanged, but Abby didn't hear them. Her grandma took her hand and pulled her away, the bag of plums Abby carried bumping her knees.

The sun was bright, the people on the street close and suffocating. Abby kept her eyes on the ground, on the cigarette butts and scraps of newspaper plastered to the gutters. She focused on the homeless man sleeping on the sidewalk, his skin rough and worn as cowhide, his hair springing out in gray patches, revealing pink scalp. Even he had a dad, she thought, somewhere.

Only once had Abby dared ask her mom about her dad. She was six years old. They were sunbathing in the front yard, wearing matching sunflower bikinis and smelling like the coconut oil they had rubbed on their bellies, her mother's skin crisp and brown, Abby's blistered pink and threatening to peel.

"Who's my daddy?" Abby's eyes were closed, her face tilted to the sun the way the ladies in the magazines did it. "Max at school says I have to have a daddy, even if I don't know him. He says everyone has a daddy."

Eva was quiet. Abby kept her eyes closed, not sure if this would make her mom mad.

"Max is wrong," Eva said finally. "There is no daddy."

Then her mom's arms were around her, lifting her up, their greasy stomachs sliding together.

"You know why, baby?" Eva brushed Abby's hair off her sweaty forehead. Abby shook her head *no*. "Because there are only daddies for kids who need daddies. We don't need a daddy, do we?" Abby shook her head again. "It's just us, baby doll. All we need is each other."

Abby tried not to look at the painting under her grandma's arm as her name sloshed around inside her. Her mom had given her a name instead of a father, which is precisely the thing Eva would have done, expecting the name to fill in the empty space where a father should have been. *There is no daddy. We don't need a daddy.* Had Eva known there would be a day when there was no mommy either? Had she given Abby her name with that in mind? An emergency name, in case things didn't work out as planned?

In Josiah's apartment, the same anguished longing Abby had felt all day washed over her again. Shutting the window, she turned to the empty room trying to hold her unutterable loneliness at bay. She was her father's daughter, only her mother had failed to tell her who he was, and she had become no one's daughter.

She did not leave Josiah's key on the coffee table, but slid it back into her pocket. Finding a pad of paper, she wrote a note explaining that she was not leaving because she was angry with her grandma, or because she thought their breakup was a good idea—which she didn't—but because she'd lived her whole life with this huge, unanswerable question hanging over her.

"This," she wrote, *"might be my one chance to answer it."*

CHAPTER 9

Burford, England, 1900

January 19

The night of Father's death, William came to my room and I let him. We made love in our grief and anger with a devastating urgency, clinging to whatever shred of affection we had left.

William has come to my room every night since, but our desire is painful, like food hitting a stomach that has been empty for too long. It is with a stubborn stoicism that we keep at it, trying to convince ourselves we can settle into something enduring, at the very least habitual, but there is madness in it.

As we claw at each other, the house mourns. The shutters are kept open and the drapes drawn shut to show that death has come. We ignored Christmas, and the New Year. Mother wanders aimlessly around the house in her widow's weeds of twilled sarcenet. She refuses to speak of the accident. I often find her sitting up against a window with her forehead scrunched as if she is working through some complicated thought. I wrap blankets over her so she won't take ill from the cold, and have ordered the fires to burn as hot as they can, which frustrates the servants as they cannot be left unattended for long. Mother's returning alone to London is unthinkable, so I have made arrangements for her things to be sent here. It is a comfort having her around, even in such a state. Despite her grief, there is a reckoning in her expression I have never seen before, as if she is trying to make sense of who she is without Father.

January 27

I am pregnant. I had suspected, but the doctor I sought out in Bibury—I refuse to see Dr. Grousman—has confirmed it. A little over three months, he said.

Returning from the appointment, I had the coachman stop the carriage so I could walk the last mile home. William, who thought I'd gone to the milliners, told me to take the car. I flat out refused, angry with him for even suggesting it. No one has driven Father's car since his death.

I am often angry with William these days, despite my best effort. The doctor, a young man with a spare, cold office, told me women sometimes experience hysteria during pregnancy. If I find myself out of control, I am to keep to bed and avoid any physical or mental activity, he said. This made me laugh. No mental activity? Was I to stop thinking? I wanted to ask if the same cure would work for my husband's hysteria. I did not.

The day was cold and overcast, but the air felt refreshing as I walked away from the carriage. Wrapping my scarf tight around my neck, I ducked off the road along a path that leads through the woods to the river. The news that I am carrying a child does not excite me. It feels overshadowed by grief. How does one lose and embrace life in the same moment? I am not even sure I want a child. Am I to write with a child clinging to me? And what does one do with it until it is old enough to speak? The idea of a baby seems wildly foreign, which does make me wonder if there is something wrong with me. Women are expected to mother. They do it all the time without instruction. Why do I feel like I can't manage it?

I stood at the river's edge, watching the icy water ripple over the rocks and remembering how I used to sit here as a child making stick figures out of twisted grass, dropping them over the embankment and sending them floating away. I was so absorbed in thought that when I turned and saw a boy sitting on a large rock watching me, I jumped, startled. He was so close I could reach out and touch his arm, and so silent it seemed unnatural. His knees were tucked up, his breeches exposing bare, dirt-stained calves above his scrunched-down socks. His boots were muddy, but well-made, and he had on a proper wool coat.

"I didn't mean to frighten you," he said.

"Well, you have done," I answered sharply. There is something unnerving in thinking you are alone and discovering you are not.

"Sorry," he said, so lighthearted I couldn't avoid softening a bit.

"That's alright."

"Do you need help?"

"Do I look like I need help?"

He shrugged and slid off the rock, regarding me with the clearest, palest blue eyes I'd ever beheld.

"You could be lost," he said.

I clasped my hands. "Your concern is chivalrous, but I am not lost. I am on my way home, as a matter of fact."

"To Abbington Hall?"

"Do you know it?"

"No, but it's the only house in this direction."

"Clever, aren't you?"

He grinned, revealing a row of crooked teeth. "Sometimes. Mostly I do things that get me into trouble." Bending down, he picked up a flat rock, then he walked to the river's edge and skipped it over the foaming water.

"How old are you?" I asked.

"Ten."

"And where do you live?"

"On Orchard Rise." He picked up another rock. "With my grandfather. My parents are dead." Instead of skipping it, he tossed it up and down, walking over to me as he asked, "Do you like stories?"

This seemed an odd question. "Who doesn't like stories?"

"Not everyone—you'd be surprised." He let the stone drop to the ground and retrieved something from his pocket, holding up another stone unlike anything I'd ever seen. It was the size of a large coin, oval and opalescent, its opaque whiteness turning an iridescent blue in the sunlight as he held it out to me.

"It's a moonstone." He flashed a proud smile. I took it, the stone cool to the touch and soft as a rabbit's foot. "The ancient Romans say it captures the moon inside itself. In East Asia, they believe the tide washes it up on shore every twenty years for good luck, and in India they say if you put it into your mouth on a full moon, it will clear your mind to wisdom, and you'll see the future. Don't worry—" he shoved his hands into his pockets "—I've never tried it. I couldn't give a lady a spit-covered rock."

"I should hope not." I laughed. "Thank you for showing it to me, it's beautiful."

I tried to hand it back, but he kept his hands in his pockets and said, "You take it."

"I couldn't possibly. It must be valuable."

He shrugged. "Once it's passed on, it's bad luck to return it."

"Goodness." I wrapped my fingers around it, the weight satisfying. Who was this odd boy to give me such a treasure, watching me with eyes so like the stone?

"There's a novel called *The Moonstone*," I said. "Have you read it?"

"No," he said. "Who is it by?"

"Wilkie Collins."

"Haven't heard of him."

"He's an accomplished writer. My favorite is *Armadale*, but *The Moonstone* is worth a read. I'll bring you a copy."

"I'd like that." He flashed a genuine smile. "I'd best be going. My grandfather will give me a lashing if I'm not home by nightfall. Goodbye, miss," he said, and dashed off into the trees like a nymph. I stared after him, turning the stone over in my hand and thinking of the stories I'd heard as a child sitting in the kitchen listening to the servants. They'd talked of healers who lived in the woods, witches and hags. They were always women, but why not a grandfather or his grandchild? Maybe the boy was a healer, a seer. Not that I believed in that sort of thing.

Tucking the stone in my pocket, I continued on my way, keeping my hand wrapped around it, the sensation, when I ran my fingers over it, palliative as a balm.

Part Two

THE HUNT

CHAPTER 10

Burford, England, 2006

The rain had stopped by the time Abby stepped off the double-decker bus. She was grateful since the five quid umbrella she purchased that morning in Oxford was already broken. She shifted her floppy leather bag higher on her shoulder, yanked up the handle of her suitcase and watched the bus pull away.

No one else had gotten off and she felt instantly stranded. There wasn't a house or building in sight, just towering elms. She walked in the direction the bus had gone, the wheels of her suitcase catching on loose gravel. Eventually, the trees cleared and she found herself at the top of a steep hill overlooking a town so old it was as if time had tucked it in and smoothed out the edges. Stone cottages abutted the sidewalk, tipping into each other, lush, green vines climbing their ancient facades. Shutters had been thrown open and the window boxes were stuffed with flowers: petunias and geraniums and nasturtiums blooming in unabashed, mismatched colors.

Jittery and slightly nauseous, Abby made her way into the center of town, deciding food was what she needed, convinced her shakiness stemmed not from nervousness, but from an empty stomach and a caffeine-induced high from her double espresso in Oxford. She passed a teahouse, the tiered trays in the window brimming with neatly arranged scones, clotted cream and finger sandwiches. It was crowded, the waitress barely able to maneuver between the crammed tables. Abby kept walking. Down a side street she saw a restaurant with a sign hanging over the doorway, The Angel at Burford. It was quiet and empty. Sunlight pierced through the dense windowpanes, casting squares of light onto the tables. A young waiter with a toothy smile took her order. The food arrived quickly, homemade fish cakes and a portion of granary bread with thick pads of unsalted butter.

Abby ate slowly, her stomach pulled taut as rope. It had been about twenty-four hours since she stepped off the airplane in London, and she'd hardly slept or eaten. She squeezed a wedge of lemon on her fish cake, guilt settling in with the food. She should find a pay phone and call her grandma. Did they still have pay phones in England? It was stupid to leave her cell phone. This was exactly what Eva had done to Maggie before Abby was born. Left her home in Berkeley without a trace. Never called. The only difference was Eva was seventeen when she took off, showing up a year later pregnant and desperate. At the very least Abby wouldn't be going home pregnant. Desperate, she wasn't so sure about. Still, she felt like a teenage runaway, not a thirty-one-year-old woman on a trip to England. How was she going to pay for all of this? She hoped her credit cards kept working or she was screwed. The last thing she was going to do was call her grandparents for money.

In the empty restaurant, with its quiet washed sunlight, Abby imagined her mom sitting across from her. They were searching for her dad together. She always aged her mom appropriately in these fantasies. Eva would be forty-nine. She would have highlighted the gray out of her hair. Her bangs would cover the wrinkles in her forehead from all her sunbathing. She would be wearing a tasteful, slender top. Reaching across the table, she'd squeeze Abby's hand and tell her how brave she was to come all this way. Eva wouldn't smell like cucumber lotion anymore. She would have moved on to something sharper, like the Noir 29 Abby wore.

They finished lunch. Abby ordered dessert. Eva was watching her figure. *It's harder the older you get. Enjoy the sweets now.* Abby paid the bill. Eva smiled and said they would use their credit cards until they didn't work anymore. What choice did they have?

At the door, the restaurant manager retrieved Abby's suitcase from behind the desk. "Everything satisfactory, ma'am?" he asked.

No. She was dining with the dead.

"Yes, thank you." Abby hooked her purse over the handle of her suitcase. "Could you direct me to Abbington Hall?"

"Across the bridge, over the River Windrush." He had one of those impossibly thick English accents. "There's a footpath to the left, at the bottom of the hill."

She thanked him and left, having considerable trouble with her suitcase over the cobblestones. When she reached the narrow bridge, she paused, looking into the water at the leaves sailing in clusters down swirling patches of sky. She pictured Evelyn Aubrey resting on this same bridge. This was the town she disappeared from, was possibly murdered in. This was the river she'd looked into, the cobblestones she'd walked over, the buildings she'd entered. Maybe she'd sat in the very same restaurant eating her own bread and butter.

Dining with the dead indeed, Abby thought, gathering up her suitcase as the sky clouded over again. Rain began to spit down and she wished she hadn't ditched her umbrella in the garbage bin.

She took the footpath up a steep hill, the wet grass soaking through her sneakers and wetting the bottom of her jeans. When she reached the grove of yew trees at the top, a manor came into view with a mass of dark clouds moving swiftly behind its myriad of chimneys. It made Abby think of a Hitchcock movie. Dropping her suitcase in the grass, she opened it and took out her camera. In the misty drizzle, she captured the clouds and the house, the tall grass and the sheep on the hillside taking shelter under a yew tree, the branches swaying, the sound like rushing water. She put her camera back and snapped her suitcase closed, lugging it over a stone wall and into the yard, tramping gracelessly through spiky weeds, hoping no one was watching from a window. English ivy climbed up the stone siding of the house, reaching like fingers through the cracked windowpanes. With a momentary clutch of disappointment, Abby wondered if the place was abandoned, but then she saw a half-filled glass of water on a metal table next to two lawn chairs covered in plastic cushions. The glass was clean, the cushions new. Someone was here not too long ago.

She made her way along the gravel driveway to the massive wooden front door. Clouds tumbled overhead. Abby's heart raced and her palms were sweaty. What did she think was going to happen? Her father would open the door? That would be ridiculous, and yet she'd pictured it, envisioning an older version of the man in the photo. He would have grown a beard, but his hair would still be red and he would still look like her. She needed him to look like her, to claim her in his DNA.

She pressed the buzzer and waited. Nothing. She pressed it again. After what seemed an eternity, the door made a groaning sound and slid slowly inward.

A plump, red-faced woman stared up at her. "Blimey!" She clasped a hand to her chest, breathing heavily. There was a glisten of sweat on her brow. Behind her, Abby could see an enormous, empty hallway. "No one uses this entrance anymore. I thought there was some sort of emergency the way you kept on about it. Is something wrong? Are you in trouble?" The woman looked at Abby's suitcase. "Are you lost?"

Abby fumbled for words, startled by the woman's many questions. "I'm so sorry, I didn't mean to bother you. I didn't see another entrance."

The woman puffed out her lips and pointed. "It's just there

around back," she said as if anyone with a brain would know where the proper entrance was. "Did you not drive here?" She peered past Abby at the empty driveway and then back at the suitcase.

"I walked," Abby said.

"Through the field?"

"Yes."

"It's awfully wet. Where are your Wellies? No one goes traipsing around the countryside in trainers."

Abby looked down and gave a small laugh. "Clearly, I'm unprepared."

The woman stared at her, waiting for some further explanation. Abby, seeing that she had no intention of inviting her in, reached into her bag and pulled out *Poems of Solitude*. "I'm trying to find the descendants of Evelyn and William Aubrey."

The woman backed away, clucking her tongue. "No, no. We don't do tours anymore. I stopped letting people in here ages ago."

"I'm not a tourist," Abby said quickly, pressing a hand to the outside of the heavy door. "I never even heard of William Aubrey until a few days ago when I found this book." She scrambled to make sense of her intentions. "This is going to sound crazy, but my father gave this book to my mother, a man I have never met and am trying to find."

The woman crossed her arms. "I don't see how this has anything to do with me."

"My father writes that Evelyn Aubrey—" Abby opened the book to the photograph of Evelyn, hoping the resemblance would help her case "—is his great-grandmother."

The woman glanced at the book before reaching into her skirt pocket and pulling out a pair of tortoiseshell glasses. Fixing them behind her ears, she gazed down at Evelyn's round, unsmiling face. With a grunt of approval, she slid off her glasses, dropped them into her skirt pocket and stuck out her hand. "Sally O'Conner."

Abby shook it. "Abigail Phillips."

"Not Aubrey?"

"I was given my mother's maiden name."

"I see." Sally paused, a troubled look crossing her face. "I apologize if I wasn't more courteous. People used to knock on our door all the time. Mostly research professors and nagging college students. Can't say I've had a person claiming to be a missing relative. Especially not one who looks like she stepped out of the paintings on the walls. It took me a minute to see it, what with that short hair." She waved a hand in the direction of Abby's hair. The humidity had tightened it into a frizz of curls. "I've never seen that book. I don't read much. Pathetic, seeing as I live *here*, but that's the truth of it." Sally stepped aside, letting the massive door swing open. "We've had our trouble with tourists. Disrespectful lot." She grinned. "You look harmless enough. Would you like a spot of tea? I was just having mine."

"That'd be lovely, thank you."

Abby followed Sally into the house, past a marble staircase and down a long hallway with flat, tightly woven carpeting that muffled their footsteps. Wood molding, mellowed with age, circled intricately carved, closed double doors that flanked them on either side.

"It's beautiful," Abby said.

"A mess is what it is. I can't keep up with it anymore. My mother scrubbed every inch of this house herself. Keeping up appearances. No money at all, my parents, just the house. My mother spent every last quid throwing parties she couldn't afford and we'd be left eating potatoes for weeks." A series of short, breathless hiccups came out in a laugh. "Oh, the stories I could tell you. Thomas, that's my brother, gets sick of me telling them. What else do we have to talk about? I ask him, but

I know, my mouth's a bit of a nuisance at times. You just hush me up if I get to talking too much."

"I want all the stories I can get," Abby said, trying to make out the portrait paintings on the walls. It was too dark to see the faces clearly.

"Too many of them here if you ask me. The walls will whisper to you if you're not careful, trying to give up the secrets, summon the past." Sally marched along, her pale green skirt swirling around her ankles, her cardigan stretched tight across her back. "For years we made money opening the house to tourists. Put my grandmother Eliza into a fit of anxiety. She'd trail behind making sure a finger didn't wander onto a painting, or a trinket into someone's pocket. Rooms are just like they were in the 1890s, you know. Not too many folks are interested in William Aubrey anymore. He only attracts the real literary types, professors and English majors and such. They got so pesky wanting every last detail, I couldn't be bothered with them anymore. Go to the library, I told them! Plenty of facts in there."

They came to a door lined in green baize that opened into a room blooming in gaudy floral decor, couch, chairs, rugs, one bright blossom bleeding into the next, the curtains billowing like prom dresses over the high windows.

"What do you think?" Sally beamed.

The room gave off an overwhelming smell of artificial potpourri. "It's lovely," Abby lied, letting her bag slide down her arm. She had left her suitcase at the front door.

"You fancy it?" Sally clasped her hands. "I had it remodeled five years back. Thomas hates it. My brother. Did I mention him already? He lives with me. Come, sit." She folded herself onto the couch, the petals swallowing her. "How do you take your tea?"

"Black."

"Black?" Sally balked, reaching for the pot and pouring a

stream of dark liquid into a china blue teacup. "No cream and sugar?"

"If you insist." Abby smiled.

"I do!" Sally spooned in a heap of sugar and poured a hefty portion of cream before handing the cup over.

"Sit, sit." Sally flapped her hand at Abby, who eased herself onto the edge of a firm chair upholstered in a sleek, black mohair that made her feel like she was sitting atop a horse. It was the only unadorned piece of furniture in the room. Even the rug under Abby's feet was a pattern of pink roses bordered in pale green, the wallpaper a similar design. Behind the sofa where Sally sat was a row of bookshelves, and to the left, a flat-screen television on the wall above an extraordinary stone fireplace. A small fire crackled behind the grate, fingers of smoke curling through it. Near the window was a desk with an enormous computer, and Abby thought how strange it was to live in a house where the present butted right up against the past.

Resting the tiny arrangement of cup and saucer over one knee, Sally commented that the chimney was in need of a cleaning. "I had everything reupholstered instead of paying for a chimney sweep. Priorities! I suppose you don't want to hear about my redecorating. I hate to disappoint, dear, but my brother and I are not blood relatives of the Aubreys. We're related by marriage. My grandmother Eliza's sister Clara married Henry Aubrey, William and Evelyn's child. Are you following?"

"I think so?"

"Eliza and her sisters were Irish. There were six of them. Eliza always said Clara was the loveliest, which was how she managed to snag herself a posh English husband. 'Me on the other hand,' she'd say, 'plain as paper.'" Sally sank into the pillows. "But that's my side of things, which you don't want to be bothered with. I don't know any of the good stuff, like what happened to Evelyn, or if her husband did, actually, murder her. That, on top of my not being a direct descendant of the Aubreys, has disappointed a lot of scholars, let me tell you. I've always said it's a blessing, not to be directly related to the likes of them. It's not my curse, thank the good Lord." She adjusted her skirt over her knees as if to emphasize the rightness of this statement. "How are you related again?" Sally narrowed her eyes at Abby, trying to place her in the family line.

"Evelyn Aubrey would be my great-great-grandmother."

"But you don't know who your father is?"

"No. My mother never told anyone his name."

"You can't ask her?"

"She died."

"Oh, sorry, love." Sally glanced out the window.

"What did you mean by a curse?" Abby sipped her tea, the sweetness as indulgent as this loquacious woman dishing up stories.

"Bugger." Sally shook her head, pooh-poohing her own words. "It's just a story."

"You have to tell me now." Abby laughed, feeling giddy and loud and overly excited.

"Well..." Sally directed her gaze upward, as if the story was to be found in the ceiling. "People said Clara Aubrey's death was the beginning of Evelyn Aubrey's revenge, but my grand-mother Eliza said Evelyn cursed this house long before Clara came along. My grandmother was a bit—" Sally made a swirl-ing motion with her finger by her head "—if you know what I mean. A staunch believer in ghosts and spirits, that sort of thing."

Outside, the trees shifted in the wind as Sally explained how Clara died the summer of 1931, on a hot summer day when cousins and aunts and uncles had piled onto the shore of a lake for a picnic. The wind was blowing that day too, sending frothy waves sailing over the water. Clara had taken the boat out and gone for a swim off of it, leaving Henry and their five-year-old son, Nicholas, on the shore. It was Eliza who saw the boat drifting away, and the dark, bobbing spot on the surface of the water. They all heard the cry that was torn away on the wind. Henry plunged into the water after her. The boat drifted to the opposite shore. The wind got stronger; the waves frothier.

Henry swam for over an hour before they managed to coax him in, everyone worried he'd drown out there too. They found Clara's body floating in the reeds later that night. Sally said she'd heard the story a million times, how Eliza sat with Henry on the hard, stony sand, watching the beam of light from the police boat move over the water in long, slow sweeps like a stage light. When the boat returned with Clara's body wrapped in a sopping blanket, Eliza couldn't watch. A policeman, white-haired with a soft voice, guided her to her car, where she sat on the sticky leather seat with her hands on the wheel, watching Henry walk toward the bundle being lifted over the side of the boat. A Clara bundle, a grown body wrapped like Eliza had wrapped her baby earlier, arms and legs tucked in. Eliza looked away. She watched the moon rise over the lake, full and greedy, taking up a portion of the sky it didn't deserve.

Sally paused her storytelling, dropping her chin to her chest. "My grandmother Eliza always ended the story on the painful sight of the moon. She'd say, *'Nothing justified that kind of beauty on a night so tragic.'* And if she was in one of her darker moods, she would add, *'Life will hurt you one way or another. So, you'd better watch out. You'd better be prepared.'*"

The wind had died down and the room was very quiet. There had been a child, Abby thought. A child named Nicholas.

"After that, my grandmother Eliza went a little batty. She said her sister's drowning was no accident, said it was Evelyn Aubrey out there holding her sister's head underwater. Her ghost was angry, my grandmother claimed, enraged." Sally slapped a pillow into place as if snapping herself into the present. "It's nonsense. Dramatic notions from a generation that believed Ouija boards were the dead talking to you. Grandmother Eliza held séances straight into the 1950s. I remember her sitting right here in this very room with a gaggle of old ladies hovering around that board, the silence so thick you could drown in it. She had a box of candles she reserved for the occasion. Wouldn't let us turn on a single light. Terrified me, all those seemingly reasonable adults gone temporarily mad, believing ghosts were talking to them."

Sally fell silent. Abby sank back in her chair, her teacup empty. She'd been conjuring ghosts her whole life. Maybe here, inside these ancient whispering walls, they'd finally tell her something.

CHAPTER 11

Burford, England, 1900

January 28

I did not tell William of the pregnancy right away. I should have, but I got it into my head that a child would either settle our love into something manageable, or else ignite more chaos. William has started writing again, and I thought it crucial that I find just the right moment to break the news to him.

A mistake.

Peter Emsley arrived today.

Peter's father, Hubert Emsley, was my father's lawyer, and has always handled his financial affairs, so when Bennett announced Mr. Emsley, I naturally assumed it was the senior. When Peter stepped into the drawing room, I was so undone I stared dumbly at him, thinking of my drab skirt and blouse and wishing I'd put on something more flattering. Why would I think that? I had no need to impress him, and yet I wanted to. One does like to appear attractive to those they've jilted.

Poor Peter stood shifting from one foot to the other, hat and bag clutched in his hand. Thank goodness Mother was there, rising to my aid with an extended hand. "Mr. Emsley, how good of you to come."

"However unexpected," I said rudely, glancing out the window, my appearance less worrying than William returning from his ride and finding Peter in his drawing room.

"I will be as brief as I can," Peter said, with a kindness I did not deserve.

Regaining a semblance of hospitality, I smiled. "Please, do sit down."

He perched uncomfortably on the sofa. His hair had grown out and it curled in tight waves over his head. Looking at his good-natured face made me sorry that we were no longer friends.

"My father sends his condolences." Peter looked from me to Mother. "He would have come himself, but he is not in London anymore. I have taken over the bulk of his work as he spends most of his time in Brighton." Peter's tone was businesslike, efficient. His good character would never allow him to abandon my father's affairs, no matter how wretched a visit this was for him.

Unclipping his bag, he slid out a stack of papers and handed them to Mother, who immediately laid them aside and said, "How is your mother getting on, Mr. Emsley? I hope she has not worsened?" Peter's mother had been a grande dame of society, considered an eccentric before she went stark raving mad. During our engagement, Peter's father had tried to put her in an asylum, but Peter wouldn't allow it.

"As well as can be expected. I found her a house in the north. She is cared for. I see her when I can. It's kind of you to ask, and brave." Peter smiled. "Most people are too uncomfortable to broach the topic."

Mother patted his arm, looking more herself than I'd seen since Father's passing. "She was a lovely woman in her day. You send her my regards the next time you see her."

"I will, thank you."

"Well then," she sighed, glancing at the intimidating documents. "What needs settling?"

"The first order of business is whether you plan to stay on at Abbington Hall or return to Coniston House."

"I don't see how I could return to London. Not without Gilbert."

It struck me that the social life my mother had always known and clung to had come to an abrupt end. I couldn't imagine what she would do with herself in the country, but the idea of her staying on permanently, especially with the baby coming, was a relief.

"You'll see here—" Peter reached over and drew out a piece of paper "—that your husband chose to leave all of his property, and the remainder of his assets, to you. Normally, the Dower Act of 1833 entitles widows to one-third of their husband's estate, and requires that a percentage go to the nearest male heir. In your case there are no male heirs, and it wouldn't have mattered if there were, because of the jointure assignments that Mr. Wilkins signed."

Mother looked bewildered.

"The most urgent matter is that of Coniston House. I would advise selling the property and investing the capital in funds that would provide a greater income than you would receive if you were to let it."

"Sell Coniston House?" I had not thought any of the properties would be sold.

Peter looked at me. "I'm afraid it's necessary."

Abruptly, Mother gathered the papers and shoved them at Peter. "I have never handled this sort of thing before, property and all the rest of it. Gilbert should have known it would be too much for me. The financial matters would best be turned over to William. Where is he?" She looked distractedly around the room. "Never mind. Evelyn, dear, you instruct Mr. Emsley, for now. You've always had a better head for such things." She stood up. "I'm afraid I'm useless. I'm sorry you've traveled all this way and I am of no help."

Peter took my mother's arm. "Don't you worry about a thing. We'll sort it out."

She patted his sleeve. "Never mind me. I'm just... I'm tired is all. I think I'll lie down. You've come all this way. You must at least stay for dinner."

"Thank you kindly, but I'm afraid I have to catch a train back tonight."

"What a shame. I would have enjoyed your company." She rose onto her tiptoes and whispered, "You are a good man," as if he were the last good man on earth, and left the room.

Peter sat back down, keeping his eyes in his lap. Alone, he could not look at me.

"I must confess, I know little of my father's financial affairs," I began, in an effort to put him at ease.

"There is something I must tell you," he said, in so personal a tone that for a wretched moment I thought he was going to speak of our engagement. "When your father died, he was no longer a wealthy man. All that is left are his estates. This house, I am afraid, takes more money to maintain than he had coming in, which forced him to dip into his capital. I advised him to cut household expenses, but he didn't want to worry you. May I be direct, Miss Wilkins—pardon me, Mrs. Aubrey?" He looked at me.

"Of course. I've married, but I have not changed in manner. You were always direct with me in the past, and I would wish for you to maintain that with me now."

My reference to the past made the tips of his ears redden, but his voice remained unaffected. "There were enormous sums of money withdrawn from his account in the last few years. It shows here—" he tapped his finger on the document "—that your father set up payments for Abbington Hall when you married, but the sums of money that were withdrawn prior started in the spring of 1897. I inquired about it when his funds became dangerously low, but he wouldn't explain himself. I feel it my obligation to be as honest as possible since this concerns the entire family, financially."

Was this what Father had tried to tell me? "Could it have been for doctor's bills, those withdrawals?"

"I don't know." Peter shook his head. "It's far more than doctor's fees, and I don't see why he'd hide it."

"Well, what does this mean for us?"

"It means you have no choice but to sell Coniston House, and it must be immediate in order to set up funds that will allow you to maintain Abbington Hall."

I stood up and went to the window. It distressed me to sell our home in London. Looking out at the expansive countryside, I thought how trapped I'd become in all that open space. Abbington Hall was never meant to be our permanent residence. The plan was to return to the city when William's next book was published. "Can we not sell the Essex estate instead?" I asked.

"It wouldn't bring in enough to maintain you. Unless Mr. Aubrey is bringing in something."

"I don't know what *The Beaumont Man* brings in. Chapman & Hall are waiting on his next book. We could sell Abbington Hall and move back to London permanently, but I am sure William would not agree to that. Could Mother sell it on her own?"

"She could," Peter said. "But if she doesn't plan to return to the city, I'm not sure why she would."

The hillside was still empty and I wondered just how outraged William would be to find Peter here. If I was smart, I would hurry this up and send Peter on his way.

"Not that this matters much, since you and your mother seem to agree on most things, but you should know," Peter said, "that your father was setting up a separate dowry where pin money would be put into a trust that would provide you with your own income. In this case, it would be an estate that you would possess and use for your own purpose. Your husband would have no control over this property, legally, and you could do with it what you wished. Your father told me he felt concerned about your future and planned to leave Abbington Hall to you, only he never signed the new will."

Until that moment, I had never thought about having an income of my own. I hadn't needed one. Father had always taken care of me, and now William was supposed to, but I was uneasy with him these days. I wondered if I should get Mother to sign the estate over to me. Not that it would matter. We would have to sell Coniston House anyway, and having Abbington Hall in my name would only insult William. I suppose Mother controlling our assets was as good as Father.

I turned to Peter with a strained smile, hoping I did not sound sarcastic. "What reason would Father have to be concerned about my future?"

"Since I am no longer a part of that future," Peter said, gently, "I wouldn't know."

The intimacy of his statement startled me. I felt exposed standing in front of him, reminded of a time before my marriage when life was mine to mold, an innocent, easy, hopeful time. Peter had adored me. I wanted to be adored again. Recklessly, I sat next to him and took his hand. He did not pull away. "Goodness, Peter, can we drop all this nonsense? We have been friends forever. I'm being beastly to you. I'm sorry. I've always been beastly to you."

"No." He shook his head. "Just honest. Something I have never been with you."

"In what sense?"

"Evelyn…" He laughed uncomfortably. "Don't ask this of me now. It's not the place, or time." Carefully, he took his hand back, politely refusing to give in to whatever I was doing. "This is not why I came. There is nothing more to be said about the past. What we need to do now is decide about the estate."

He was right: best to suppress the demons rising up to plant regret in my heart. Restraining myself, I went to the door and said, "You are absolutely right. William is out on a ride. I will speak to him and we will come to an agreement about selling the property. I am sure he will do what is best, and then we'll have Mother sign the necessary documents."

"Very good, I'll leave them for you to look over." Peter set the papers on the desk.

"Thank you for your trouble," I said.

"No trouble."

Peter settled his hat on his head and we stepped into the hallway, startling William, who was wrestling to undo the top button of his coat. I hadn't heard my husband come in. Both men froze, staring at one another as if they'd stopped moving through time. I noticed how skinny and pale William looked, how much smaller in stature he was than Peter, who drew himself up and said, "Good day, Mr. Aubrey."

"Good day, Mr. Emsley." William's voice was as crisp and cold as the air that trailed in after him.

Dread laid itself over me. Without a glance in my direction, William walked down the hall and up the stairs. I forced a smile and opened the front door. Peter came toward me, standing so close I could smell the scent of cedar on him. It was a new smell of aftershave or cologne. I wanted to know what new things he used. What I had missed.

"I will be in contact by post with all further transactions," he said, the words formal, but his voice as soft as if he was caressing me. He started to say something else, stopped, took my hand for a quick moment and said, "Well then, I'm off. Goodbye," and walked swiftly out the door.

After he left, I sat in the library and scribbled out a poem, trying to rearrange my emotions. It was silly how Peter's presence had affected me. I'd never felt like that with him before. It was the pregnancy making me vulnerable, I decided.

Vulnerability is not an emotion I can afford with William's door locked against me. Things will not be good with him, this much I am sure of.

CHAPTER 12

Burford, England, 2006

Sally leaned back on the couch, one hand resting on her ample stomach. The words of Eliza's story had ironed her face smooth and serious, cleared the laugh lines around her eyes. The fire sulked, dying to embers, the cheery flowers wilting in the dampness descending on them.

Abby sat perfectly still, her empty teacup perched on one knee. The bottom of her jeans were wet from her walk through the field and her arms were freezing under her thin silk shirt. "What happened to Henry and Nicholas?" she asked.

Sally tugged at her cardigan, sighing. "After Clara died, my grandparents Eliza and Jacob moved into Abbington Hall with them. My grandfather didn't want anything to do with a cursed place, but there was no arguing with Grandmother Eliza. Nicholas needed looking after, she said, and she wasn't going to abandon her sister's only son. He needed a mother, family. It was their duty. My father, Patrick, was... I think...eleven years old when they moved in? Told me his parents were never the same again, fought like the dickens, throwing their Irish voices about the place. My father, Patrick O'Conner, was a good egg, always caring for others, even as a child. He made himself guardian of Nicholas, which was partly his doing and partly his mother, Eliza's." With a great rustling of fabric, Sally hoisted herself forward and reached for the teapot. "More, dear?"

"No, thank you." Abby was buzzing, her stomach a bundle of nerves.

Sally poured tea into her own cup, took a sip and settled the cup back on the tray. It seemed, all of a sudden, as if she no longer wanted to talk.

"How did you and your brother end up with the house?" Abby was still puzzling the pieces together, aware that Sally had not answered her question about what had happened to Henry and Nicholas.

"Oh, well, we don't own it, not exactly." Sally fiddled with the tea tray, dotted a finger over an empty plate of crumbs, collecting grains of sugar and rubbing them off again. "When Nicholas moved away, he left the house to Eliza. Let me think what year that was…1963? I was sixteen. What with the money it took to keep up this old place, and everything that had happened, my father begged Eliza to sell it. Most of these grand old houses had been sold, or fallen into ruin, but my grandmother flat out refused. We still can't sell it, or anything in it. She put every bloody object into a trust. The whole lot of it. My aunts and uncles and cousins want nothing to do with the place. Not after the string of tragedies. No one even visits anymore. My brother and I just use this room and the kitchen. Our bedrooms are in the servants' quarters. There's no heat in the rest of the house." She paused, her eyes flicking around. "It's been a long time since I talked about Clara. Tourists only ever wanted to hear about William Aubrey and his books and his missing wife."

"Do you believe in the curse?" Abby asked.

She leaned forward, clearly avoiding the question as she said, "You could be Irish, what with those green eyes and freckles. You're as pale as any Irishwoman. A natural beauty is what you are, and so like the painting in the upstairs hall it gives me the chills. It really is an uncanny likeness."

Questions boiled up. What tragedies? What happened to Henry? Where did Nicholas go? Was he alive? Did Sally know him?

But Sally stood with an abrupt slap to her knee and said, "It's getting late. I'll see you out."

Abby was startled to her feet. She'd come so far. She was so close. Grasping, she said, "I'd love to see the painting. The one of Evelyn."

"Sorry, dear. Thomas is due home, and he'll be wanting his dinner. For another time." She took the empty teacup from Abby and lifted the tray, the porcelain items clattering.

"Here, let me." Abby reached for the tray, Sally's shoulders rising and dropping in a gesture of surprise as she released the silver handles. A cup slid in the transfer and Sally gasped. "Hold it with two hands. Grandmother Eliza would roll over in her grave if you broke something."

They exited through a door at the back of the room and descended a narrow flight of stairs into a large kitchen with stone floors and small paned windows. Sally took the tray from Abby and set it on a thick wooden table, scarred from use.

"They liked to keep the servants far away from the rest of the house." Sally swatted her belly. "I'd be fatter than I am if not for these long walks to and from the kitchen. Truth be told," she leaned in, confessing, "I'd go mad in my friends' homes with their quaint little rooms all butted up together. No space at all. Everyone on top of each other."

Abby took her cup from the tray and set it in the deep porcelain sink. She looked out the window at a car parked in the driveway, an impossibly small thing with shiny silver hubcaps. Outside, the light was fading. "Can I wash up for you?" she asked Sally. The thought of walking away down that gravel drive, when she was so close to something tangible, felt torturous.

"I wouldn't hear of it." Sally heaved herself into a chair, looking elfish at the massive table. "I'll do the dishes later. Later is always my motto. I'm an awful housekeeper, and cook. There you have it. My mother was brilliant. Catered all her own parties, and here I can hardly boil an egg."

Abby sat across from her on a wooden bench, smiling at how distractible Sally was. "I'm no cook either. My grandparents eat out a lot."

"So, there are grandparents, thank goodness. I thought you were a ghost of Grandmother Eliza's imaginings. Evelyn come to haunt us in modern-day clothing!" Sally laughed.

"I assure you I am quite real."

Abby pulled her hands into her lap, listening to the settled ticking of a clock and the wind whistling through the cracks in the windowpanes. She imagined the kitchen a hundred years ago, the servants hollering at each other, dishes clattering, the smells and the warmth. There was a boarded-up fireplace where a cast-iron pot must have hung, flames licking at it while a soot-faced child scraped at the coals spitting onto the hearth. A maid would have sat on this wooden bench with her sleeves rolled up as she shelled peas. There was the cook in a white apron chopping onions, shouting orders, Evelyn standing in the doorway giving instructions for dinner.

There were oddly dispersed modern items around the kitchen that seemed dropped in temporarily, as if the house was waiting to spit them back out. Round, frosted-glass light fixtures hung from the ceiling and a four-burner gas stove butted up against the wooden counter.

"After all this time and still, no one knows what happened to Evelyn," Abby said, her voice disturbing the silence.

"Evelyn knows what happened." Sally chuckled. "But she's not talking."

Getting up, she flicked a wall switch, and stark light flooded the room. There was a startling bang as the back door flew open and a short, round man walked in puffing heavily, his red cheeks blown out, gray tufts of hair sticking up on top of his head. He had a pink, smooth-shaven face and a chin that disappeared into his neck.

"Ferocious wind out there," he said, hooking his bag on a peg by the door.

"Thomas? Gracious. Where does the time go? I was about to start dinner." Sally took a glass from the shelf and held it under the tap.

Thomas walked past Abby into the pantry without a glance.

"He's painfully shy," Sally whispered, placing the glass of water in front of her and yelling after him, "This is Abby! She's from America. Distant relative of the Aubreys." Abby liked how decisive that sounded. Sally pulled a loaf of bread off the counter. "Stay for dinner? Sandwiches." She waved the bag in the air. "I warned you, I'm no cook."

"That's kind of you," Abby said. "I'd love to. Can I help?"

"No, you just sit there and keep us company."

Thomas appeared with a jar of mayonnaise, mustard, lettuce, a pack of ham, and sliced cheese balanced in his arms. He dumped it all on the table and they worked deftly, Sally spreading the condiments, Thomas layering on the ham and lettuce. Sally ripped open a bag of chips and shook them onto the plates as Thomas popped the tops off three bottles of Hoskins Brothers Ale, handing one to Abby.

"Thanks." She tipped the bottle in a cheers motion. Thomas dropped his eyes and sat down.

"It's bloody cold in here, Sally," he said, biting into his sandwich.

"Is it? Should I turn the heat on?"

Abby said, "Don't do it on my account."

"Please," Thomas interjected. "Do it on her account." He chewed with his mouth open, pink pieces of ham between his teeth.

"Thomas thinks I'm cheap." Sally tucked the lettuce under the corner of her bread. "He's always forgetting the television set I bought him for his fiftieth birthday."

"I might be able to forget if you didn't bring it up all the time."

Abby bit into her sandwich and kept quiet, not wanting to insult either side.

Thomas met Abby's eyes for the first time. "It's uncanny, how much you look like that painting in the upstairs hall. Gives me the willies it does. No offense to you, just saying. Have you seen it?"

"No," Abby said.

"How are you related?" He seemed interested in her now.

"On my father's side, but I don't know him."

Thomas gave Sally a raised eyebrow. Sally ignored it, stuffing a bite of sandwich into her mouth. No one said anything else and Abby realized she would have to bide her time with these two. There was definitely something they were not telling her.

When they finished, she helped Sally clear the plates while Thomas tossed their empty beer bottles into a paper bag by the door. "Where are you staying?" he asked.

Abby hadn't thought past this afternoon. "I'm assuming there's an inn in town?"

"The walking tours of the Cotswolds usually book everything out this time of year," he said.

Sally ran hot water into the sink and said nothing.

"I can take a bus back to Oxford if I have to. I'll find something."

"Sally?" There was a hint of reprimand in Thomas's voice.

Sally plunged her hands into the soapy water. "There aren't any beds made up."

"Easy enough to put sheets on a bed," Thomas said.

Despite how much she loved the idea of staying here, Abby said, "Oh, please, don't worry about it. I wouldn't ask you to put me up."

Sally kept her back to them, attentively scrubbing a plate. "I've not been into the guests' rooms in an age. They're probably covered in dust, or mouse droppings." Then, slowly, "It does seem impractical to spend money on an inn."

"I'd be happy to pay you," Abby said.

"No, I wouldn't hear of it," Sally said. Thomas started to say something, but she cut him off, pointing a dripping plate at him. "Not a word. I only charged that couple because they were highfalutin graduate students who had the gall to drive out here in a Rolls-Royce." She handed the plate to Abby. "Here, rinse and dry this and we'll call it even. Thomas, go fetch her luggage from the front door and bring it up to the room across from mine."

Thomas's mouth twitched into a smile and he gave Abby a quick, victorious wink before ducking out to fetch her bag.

Abby finished rinsing and drying the plates and Sally peeled off her gloves and laid them over the sink. "He's shy, but he likes the company. Poor Thomas, works as a driver for the Swindon Borough Council. Hates his job, although I don't know why. He buggered about in theater when he was younger. I think he feels cheated, living here with me, like he never had a chance." She paused. "Truth is, you being here makes me nervous."

"Does it? Why?" Outside, the wind howled. Somewhere, a door banged open and shut.

Sally laughed. "My grandmother Eliza's getting into my head. We kids were always scared of that painting. We thought Evelyn would curse us just for looking at her. The funny thing is, we never knew anything about her other than her disappearing. It's her husband that was accused of murder, and yet Evelyn's the one blamed for cursing things." Sally shook her head. "Come on, you look tuckered out. I'll show you to your room and stop gabbing nonsense."

Abby's resemblance to Evelyn Aubrey had felt exciting, despite the dark story surrounding the poet, but suddenly Abby wasn't so sure. She felt uneasy following Sally up the winding staircase. What had happened in this house? To think possibly a murder was slightly unnerving.

Entering the neglected, musty room she was to sleep in didn't help things. The coverlet on the twin bed, the rug and curtains were a chalky gray, as if impermeable dust had settled over them. The dresser pitched to one side from the slope of the floor, looking like it might send the green glass lamp set on top of it tumbling off at any moment. On an end table, next to the bed, sat a clock encased in dark wood, the hands stopped at midnight.

Sally muscled open the dresser drawer, took out a stack of sheets, handed them to Abby and left, telling her she'd be across the hall if there was anything else she needed.

It was early, but Abby was exhausted. She put the sheets on the bed, dug her pajamas from her suitcase, wiggled out of her jeans into warm flannel and crawled into bed. A burnt smell came from the baseboard, along with a dull popping sound. The bed was lumpy, but the sheets were clean and soft, the coverlet warm. Abby set all notions of ghosts and curses aside. There was something foreign and exciting here, an expectation outside of her predictable, restless life. Who could she become if she was no longer the person tethering her grandparents to Eva? If her identity was no longer as "the one who had survived"? If she wasn't this damaged adult who couldn't get her life together?

The air in the room felt alive, as if the darkness had a pulse. Abby found herself whispering into it, asking her grandparents to let her go, asking her mother to let her go, asking her name to let her go. All she wanted was a small, undamaged space to open up inside her, a space where she could feel who she might be without the weight of her mother's death, without the weight of her name, or even the need to be her father's daughter.

CHAPTER 13

Burford, England, 1900

February 2

I have not discussed selling Coniston House with William because he has refused to see me since Peter's visit. He takes his meals in his room and no longer goes to his study, as it would require walking past me through the library. When he goes riding, he makes sure to leave out the kitchen door so I won't stumble across him in the hallway.

It is all very humiliating and childish.

I also haven't told him I'm pregnant. Mother knew just by looking at me. We were finishing up lunch when she set down her spoon and said, "I think congratulations are in order, my dear. You've filled out nicely. When is the child due?" I was relieved she'd discovered it on her own. Telling her before William hadn't seemed right, but I didn't like keeping it from her.

"July," I said, and she smiled and remarked that July was the perfect month for a baby.

"We'll fill his room with roses," she said.

"He?"

She smiled and gave a quick, decisive nod. "He."

It was the first time I'd seen her smile in a long time, and it made me wonder if a child would be good for all of us.

I have not brought up selling the London estate, or the idea of her turning Abbington Hall over to me. She still seems fragile, and I am worried it will upset her. Tomorrow, I will write to Peter and ask how much time we have before a final decision must be made.

February 6

This evening, as Mother and I were sitting down to dinner, William suddenly appeared, taking his seat at the head of the table. He was clean-shaven, dressed in a white shirt, waistcoat, jacket and tie. "Braised ham and peas," he observed as Bennett served him from the sideboard. "Lovely." He gave me an unsettling smile, picked up his knife and fork, and dug in.

I ate with a knot in my stomach, not knowing what he was playing at, but certain he was playing at something. When the meal was over, Mother retired to her room and William, very casually, slid a piece of paper across the table to me. When I looked down, I saw that it was my application for access to the Reading Room at the British Museum Library.

"Why do you have this?" Picking it up, I saw, written at the bottom, *"I think not, my dear."*

"What is the meaning of this? I posted it weeks ago? How do you have it?" I demanded.

"You left it in the hall for Bennett to post. I saw the address and have saved you the humiliation of rejection."

"Rejection?" I was furious. How dare he!

"Only real writers are given access to the Reading Room. You cannot prove you are in need of any research. You are unpublished."

I stood up, tingling with anger. "That is for them to decide, not you," I said, and fumed out of the room before I said something worse.

Upstairs, I slammed the application into my desk drawer. If it had been accepted, I would have had an excuse to go to London. I would have been able to meet other writers, to discuss my work with like-minded artists. William was sucking away my creativity, my ability to think.

I was not sure how much longer I could stand it.

February 20

My skin tingles with anger and my hand shakes as I write this.

For the past few weeks, William has been perfectly cordial and things appeared normal, except for the fact that normal is not normal—for William.

Today, my patience gave out. I was not going to sit around waiting for him to reveal his hand any longer. I still hadn't told him of my pregnancy, a thing he'd notice if he ever really looked at me.

Before I went to his room, I took the moonstone from my jewelry box. It seemed easier to confront William with its small weight of reassurance in my pocket.

He was sitting up in bed when I walked in, fully clothed with one hand pressed over his eyes as if they ached. Drawing his hand down, he looked at me, calm and questioning. I climbed onto the bed next to him. I wanted him to be excited about a child. I wanted him to believe in us again.

"What are you doing?" he said.

"What have I done to anger you?" I tried to touch him, but he caught my hand in midair and shoved it away.

"I am not angry," he said, his eyes cold, blue flecks of sky.

"Why are you dismissing me then?"

"I am not dismissing you. I am simply not taking you to my bed anymore." There was something final in the way he said it.

"You hardly speak to me."

"I am tired of your opinions."

This pierced me. "I thought you liked my opinions."

"You are very self-assured, aren't you?" His tone was sinister. "I did like your opinions. I found them refreshing. But I must admit, it is harder to be married to those opinions than I anticipated."

My stomach turned in on itself. How much insult did he expect me to take? I slid off the bed. "I don't know what you want from me."

"Nothing," he said cheerfully, his unfettered dismissal the worst kind of rejection.

I wanted to fight back, but I was so tired of this endless push and pull. "Just tell me that this has nothing to do with Peter Emsley's visit. That this is just one of your moods again."

"This is entirely because of Mr. Emsley's visit."

"Why? Where is the logic in that?" William didn't answer. He just stared at me with his disconcerting smile. My voice rose. "Mr. Emsley was here on business. You know that. It had nothing to do with me."

"Oh, I know he was here on business," he said. "But he was also here for you."

"William!" I wanted to shake him. It was impossible to have a reasonable argument with him. "He came because of Father's death, because there are important matters that need settling. Matters we haven't spoken of because you won't talk to me! Why are you so stubborn about Peter? He means absolutely nothing to me. Don't you believe that? Why do you think I married *you*?"

William shrugged, the gesture so maddening I'd rather he had struck me.

I spit out a desperate "I love you," but he only replied, "I don't care," like a spoiled child.

"Why are you saying that?" I held back tears. He had completely severed himself from me. I could feel it as plainly as if he had taken a knife and cut the air between us. "Answer me?"

"Don't tell me what to do." His voice soured. "How is it you have none of your mother's decorum? You could learn a thing or two from her."

"What on earth do you mean?"

"Your mother simply does as she's told."

Nausea rolled through me. "What has my mother done?"

He paused, triumphant. "She's put Coniston House up for sale and has given me the deed to Abbington Hall."

"Given you the deed?"

"Yes, well, put it in my name."

"It's done? The papers are signed?" I'd been too distracted to write the letter to Peter I'd intended. How had it all been done without my knowing?

William smiled. "Yes, my dear, and if you were more like your mother, you'd see it was for the best. Why would she want to be burdened with running an estate?" He stared at me, taunting, reveling in how defeated I was.

Why did it matter? I wondered. He was my husband. It made sense he'd own our estate, and our assets, but it frightened me to be totally under his control. "I'm pregnant." I blurted the words at him, hoping for some reaction, but he remained unaffected. "Do you have nothing to say? Do I repulse you that much?" Something smoldered in me. I thought, *Why this devotion and servitude to him? What am I sacrificing myself for?*

I backed toward the door, my hand in my pocket, holding the stone to keep myself from doing something I would regret. My exhaustion was gone. All I felt was impulsive, outraged.

"You don't repulse me, Evelyn. I simply don't trust you. When Peter was here, I saw you as a woman capable of wanton dishonesty. Which I appreciate in a whore, but not in a wife."

I swiped the nearest thing at hand—a vase of hummingbirds and pink flowers—and hurled it at him. He ducked as the vase sailed over the bed and crashed to the floor. "Damn you to hell," I said, and left, the shocked look on his face only remotely satisfying.

In my bedroom, I touched my stomach and paced like a feral cat. Of course Mother had turned everything over to William. I remembered what she said about me the day Father died. *Ev-*

elyn was never very good at knowing her place. William had remembered too. He knew exactly what he was doing. He used Peter as an excuse to keep me away until he could go to Mother behind my back.

The stone sits on my desk, dark as the sky out my window. What I understood tonight, watching William, is that he intends to hate me as much as he loves me. He will build up our love with the very purpose of tearing it down. It is impossible for him to hold the intensity of one without the other. Both emotions feed him, fuel whatever keeps him going. This is the real game he's been concocting, the one he expects me to continue with him. It is more than a mood. Something wicked is at work in him, a self-satisfied glee at my suffering, and the monstrous power he finds in it.

CHAPTER 14

Burford, England, 2006

"Rise and shine!" Sally called through the bedroom door. "Toast and tea are on the table. Meet me in the front hall in half an hour and I'll show you around the house."

Abby rose stiffly. Sunlight filled the room, and the view out the window was magnificent. Today, her surroundings felt normal, antiquated, but winsome and cheerful in the morning light. Abby went to the kitchen, still in her pajamas, ate two slices of toast, drank a cup of lukewarm tea and hurried back upstairs to shower. She dressed in jeans and her cotton sweater, grabbed her Super 8 camera and met Sally in the front hall.

Sally wore tan trousers and a bulky cardigan with round leather buttons done up to her neck. "Sleep well?" she asked, swirling the feather duster in her hand.

"I did, thank you." Abby had slept exceptionally well.

"Good, good." Sally smiled. "I thought a tour would be fun. I haven't been in some of these rooms in years. Hopefully Rags has kept the rodents away."

"Rags?"

"Our cat. He's a mangy-looking thing, but a proper hunter."

The house was enormous. Full of long, echoing corridors and softly carpeted, bleakly lit hallways that led into massive rooms with elaborate wall hangings and rugs the size of small ponds. Abby held the camera up to her eye, recording whatever struck her—vases set atop mantels covered in dust so thick a finger could make a track through it, a stack of books, a quill pen, a chess set, a globe. Sally had given her permission as long as she wasn't in the shot. "No one wants to have to look at this," she'd cried, sweeping her hand up and down her middle.

There were numerous portraits of William Aubrey. In some he was young and handsome with thick hair and striking eyes. In others he had aged into a plump man with pasty skin. There was a painting of his son, Henry Aubrey, a scrawny boy with pale hair and a sour expression. The portrait of Evelyn was in the upstairs hall. She sat stiffly in a chair with her hands placed one over the other. Her bare arms were creamy white, the fabric of her green dress falling in soft folds around her legs. Her eyes were bright and excited, her lips parted in a slight smile. She looked young and happy.

"How old was she when she married William?" Abby asked.

"I don't know," Sally said. "The family only spoke about the things that happened *after* she went missing."

"Which was what? Clara's death?"

Sally moved on down the hall, acting as if she hadn't heard. Her ability to completely ignore a question was impressive. "Not everything's original," she was saying. "Fabrics have been replaced, curtains and bedclothes, new upholstery to match the era."

She opened a door and Abby followed her into a large room with a canopy bed, the bed-curtains extravagant in yardage and yellowed with age. There was a small desk, a vanity, an armoire and a chaise lounge, the green velvet still opulent under a visible skin of dust. "The mysterious Evelyn Aubrey's bedroom." Sally raised a single eyebrow.

"Might she curse us for walking in here?"

"I think we're alright." At the window, Sally threw open the green brocade curtains, the diffuse, milky light catching in the etched glass bottles on the vanity and sending rainbow prisms over the papered walls.

Abby touched the scrolls and grapevines carved into the top drawer of Evelyn Aubrey's desk. On the airplane, she'd read *Poems of Solitude* like she might a textbook, trying to decode the meanings, find some secret messages, but they were just sonnets of love, loss, death, birth—the same torments every poet encapsulates.

"I have to leave for work soon." Sally came around the side of the desk and swept the duster over the wood. She'd done this in every room, leaving a cloud to settle behind them.

"Where do you work?" Abby went to the armoire and opened the doors. It was empty. She'd hoped for a row of elegant gowns.

"At the flower shop on High Street, Pick a Lily. Did you notice it?"

"I didn't."

"Well, small place, really." Sally was at the bedside table, scattering more dust. "I love my job. Arranging flowers all day, the smell of roses and lilies, curling ribbons for weddings, or birthdays. Makes me happy, contributing to people's lives in that way. There's a lot that can be said with a flower." She sounded like a slogan. "I don't make much money, but I like what I do. No use wasting one's life doing what you hate. Could be dead tomorrow." She laughed, lightly. "What is it you do?"

Abby went to Evelyn's bed, the eyelet lace coverlet looking like it might disintegrate if she touched it. "Nothing," she said.

"Oh phooey, that's not possible. You just haven't found a name for it. You could be an observer of life, a thinker. The world doesn't have much to say for people who wander around thinking anymore. They used to be called philosophers, now we call them unambitious." Sally began slapping the curtain, the air filling with particles so thick it was a wonder they could breathe. "Who says you have to do something with your life? Isn't living it enough?"

"It should be." Abby sat at Evelyn's desk, the spindle-backed chair uncomfortably hard.

"It can be here, if you like." Sally unlatched the window and swung it out, the festering scent of disuse replaced with the sweet smell of grass. Reaching in front of Abby, Sally slid open the desk drawer and pulled out a small stack of newspapers tied up in a brown satin ribbon.

"You might find these interesting. They were found in Evelyn's desk after her disappearance. Nothing else of hers remained, not a letter, an original poem, a piece of clothing, nothing. Just these reviews of William Aubrey's books. People said he got rid of everything of hers, but the one thing that propped up his ego. Apparently, this room was shut up when she went missing and no one dared use it again. Once a year my mother cleaned in here, out of respect, she said, but she didn't like doing it. Said it gave her the heebie-jeebies."

"What year did Evelyn go missing?"

"1906, exactly one hundred years ago in October."

Abby touched the top piece of paper. "It's okay if I handle them?"

"If you're careful. They're delicate." Sally stuck the duster under her arm. "I have to run. I'll be back around six. Feel free to roam the house, read the library books, do what you please, just be respectful. Toodle-oo," she called, heading out the door.

Sunlight slanted across the desk and the birds chattered loudly through the open window. The room did not feel bleak or forgotten, but quite alive. A breeze rustled the papers as Abby peeled a filmy square of newspaper from the top of the pile.

SPECTATOR
June 5, 1904

Aubrey is one of the most successful writers of the day. His characters are complex, impossible, revolting, and many, like our beloved Samuel in *Mr. Winthrop*, ingenious.

She picked up another, the layers thin as pastry dough.

ATHENAEUM
September 3, 1904

Mr. Winthrop is endearing, exquisite, and the end of this marvelous book, an utter delight.

QUARTERLY REVIEW
August 13, 1902

Aubrey is sagacious enough to convince us of the lowliest of crimes committed by highly civilized criminals who move quietly through parlors, attend the opera and drive in carriages. It shows the power of an author who can make us profoundly interested in the lives of the ones we despise.

Abby read every review, twenty-seven in total. When she was done, she tied them back up and returned them to the desk. The birds had stopped chattering and the room was quiet. There was not a single review of *The Tides*, but Evelyn had disappeared the day of its publication. Was that a coincidence? Abby thought about the articles she'd read online, how people believed that the fictional wife in William Aubrey's final novel, *The Tides*, was written as an exact portrayal of Evelyn Aubrey.

Intensely curious, Abby left the room, making sure to tuck the chair back under the desk and latch the window before making her way to the library. She'd only peeked in with Sally. Now, she stood in the center of the room and took in the walls of bookshelves reaching the ceiling. Somewhere, in these hundreds of books, must be William Aubrey's novels.

Starting at one end of the room, she began searching the bindings. If all trace of Evelyn had been erased from the house, there might be something left of her in *The Tides*.

CHAPTER 15

Burford, England, 1900

February 21

This afternoon, I took a copy of *The Moonstone* from the library and walked to town with it in my handbag. It felt good to watch people going about their daily business, women hooking baskets over their arms and marching their children forward, a blacksmith smashing his hammer in an open doorway, the sound ringing out, sparks flying. It made me long for an ordinary life full of straightforward, necessary tasks like beating steel into a horseshoe. Through a window, I watched a shopkeeper weigh out a hunk of butter, wrap it in brown paper and hand it to a girl who couldn't be older than seven. How useless I was in my wealth, I thought. I'd never purchased a hunk of butter in my life.

Hats, on the other hand, I'd purchased.

Going into the milliner's, I greeted Mr. Oxley and asked if he knew of a boy who lived with his grandfather on Orchard Rise.

"I do, your ladyship."

"Could you point me in that direction?"

"It's the third cottage on the right. No garden or nothing in front, but there's a gate that goes round back. You can't miss it."

I thanked him and found my way to the cottage, a single-story stone house with two small windows and a heavy wooden door that opened onto the sidewalk. When I knocked, I was greeted by the boy's keen eyes and carefree smile. "You came," he said, delighted.

"I promised."

"You didn't promise."

"Saying you're going to do a thing is as good as a promise." I extended my hand. "We've never properly met. I'm Evelyn Madeline Aubrey."

He shook it. "Lesley Jacob Wheelock, pleased to meet you, ma'am."

"Likewise."

Lesley widened the door. "Come in." Over his shoulder he called, "Grandfather, we have a visitor."

I entered a low-ceilinged room with heavy beams. The smell of wood smoke and cabbage filled the small space, and the mote-filled light came through the densely paned windows as if through a cloth. A man crouched in front of an open fireplace, poking at the hot coals.

"I'm sorry to bother you." I addressed myself to his back. He didn't turn, or answer.

Lesley said, "It's no bother," and pulled out a chair for me. The small table was laid with a gingham cloth, two bowls, spoons and napkins. "We were about to eat. Would you like to join us?"

"She won't be wanting the likes of what we have." The man stood up, brushing a hand down the front of his pants. He was tall, long limbed and thin as a reed. His hair was white, his face clean-shaven and deeply lined. He looked at me with eyes the same astounding blue as his grandson's, pale and clear as water.

"Evelyn Aubrey." I extended a hand.

He ignored it. "I know who you are," he said, taking a pewter bowl from the table and ladling soup into it.

How boorish! I was not used to being insulted by the lower classes. My servants never spoke to me like that. Although, I thought, they worked for me, so they wouldn't dare. This man clearly didn't care who I was. From the look on his hard face, he was a man who worked for no one but himself. I set the book on the table and said, to Lesley, "I've brought you *The Moonstone*. I'll just leave it here and go."

"You must stay," he said, unconcerned with his grandfather's effrontery. He took the soup bowl his grandfather handed him and passed it to me, pointing at the floating bits in the broth. "Those are ramps I picked by the river. Right where we met. You must try them."

"Do ramps grow this time of year?" I asked, dutifully taking a seat, careful not to spill the broth as I set my bowl down.

"No," Lesley laughed, sitting in the chair opposite me and dipping a spoon into his soup. "The ground's frozen if you hadn't noticed. I dried them."

"How resourceful," I said, feeling stupid. I knew ramps didn't grow this time of year.

We ate the watery mix of cabbage, ramps and carrots in silence. There were only two chairs at the table so Lesley's grandfather sat in the rocker by the fire with his bowl in his lap, keeping an eye on me as he spooned soup into his mouth. It was nerve-racking to be stared at like that and I ate as quickly as possible and took my leave.

At the doorway, Lesley thanked me for the book and waved me cheerfully off. I wondered why Lesley's grandfather was so put off by me. We didn't know each other, so it couldn't be personal. Maybe it was because I'd dropped in unexpectedly. I should have sent a card requesting a visit. Next time, I'd do so, I decided.

Walking home, my fingers habitually finding the stone in my pocket, I felt a strange connection with Lesley, one I can't explain, but feels vital that I find a way to keep.

CHAPTER 16

Burford, England, 2006

Abby gathered up her leather bag and left the house, taking the gravel drive to the main road. The sun felt good after the drafty chill of the house. It was amazing how little warmth penetrated those thick stone walls.

It had been four days since she arrived at Abbington Hall, and Sally and Thomas hadn't said anything about her leaving. They'd quietly eaten dinner together, watched television and all gone to bed as if this was a perfectly normal arrangement. A few times Abby had tried to bring up Nicholas and Henry Aubrey, but Sally had quickly changed the subject.

This morning, Abby had finished *The Tides*. She'd found the book easily, the Abbington Hall library being organized alphabetically by author, but it was a first edition and she hadn't dared take it out of the room. Instead of reading in bed like she usually did, she'd sat at the desk in the library with the book laid open in front of her, delicately turning the pages. She could see why people thought the story was real. For starters, the main characters were named William and Evelyn, different surname, Hastings, but still, naming the character you're murdering off after your wife, and the murderer after yourself, seemed like a psychotic thing to do. Even if William didn't kill her, something must have been going on for him to write a scene, in gruesome detail, where a husband holds his wife's head underwater until she drowns.

Walking into town, Abby couldn't shake the story. It had left her feeling gutted and sad. For one thing, the description of Evelyn was the exact description of her, which was creepy, but more than that, it was how skillfully William Aubrey had written the slow unwinding of the couple's love. What started off passionate and beautiful had slipped into a feverish hatred so believable, and with such subtle accuracy, murder seemed an inevitable outcome.

Abby couldn't imagine loving, or hating, anyone that much.

She found the Burford library on High Street in a two-story stone building. The bookshelves abutted small bay windows and the overhead lights flickered irregularly. The place was empty, save for the librarian at the front desk, a young woman with pulled-back hair and a terse, unsmiling face. Abby found *The Life of William Aubrey: A Biography* on the second floor and took it to a chair by the window. The book was worn, the binding cracked, the pages dog-eared. She opened it to a sentence underlined in pencil:

...best-known, best-loved, and for a time, best-paid Victorian writer. Aubrey's range from high society romance in The Beaumont Man, *to the life of an impoverished family in* Mercer Corner, *illustrates the unique skill with which Aubrey masterfully crafted his works.*

She skipped ahead.

The Tides *is a Sensation Novel at its finest. Aubrey gives us dangerous women who generate social instability because of the knowledge and secrets they possess. He exposes hypocrisy in polite society, gives us adultery, extreme emotionalism, hidden illegitimacy, and the astute but aberrant Mr. Hastings, a villain with gentlemanly pretensions. Aubrey adds twist upon twist in the most lavish profusion and throws an air of mystery over every event.*

Abby read for over an hour. She didn't like the biographer's tone. He glorified William Aubrey, and only dedicated a single chapter to Evelyn's disappearance, describing her as

a pale, red-haired wallflower who kept to herself and rarely accompanied William anywhere.

He touched on the details of the murder in *The Tides* that coincided with real events: Evelyn Aubrey going missing the day the book was published, her bicycle that was found by the side of the road with blood on it, and the most shocking coincidence—because that is how the biography framed it all, as a coincidence—the knife found in the river. Yes, the cook at Abbington Hall had confirmed it was a knife from her kitchen, but that was it; there was no proof of murder, and the knife, at least in the novel, wasn't used to kill "Evelyn" Hastings anyway.

If the book chronicled events as they happened, her body would have been found in the house, as it was at the end of the novel. The biographer, Daniel Dillard, speculated that Evelyn Aubrey had mental health problems and most likely suffered from undiagnosed depression. *"Suicide was far more likely than murder,"* he wrote, lamenting—or so it seemed to Abby—more than the death of Evelyn, that William Aubrey's final book, despite the success of it, ultimately ruined his reputation and career.

Good repute was everything back then, honor, character, scruples. After The Tides *was printed, William Aubrey was never seen in society again. He died at Abbington Hall in 1922, and never published another book.*

Abby shut the biography and brought it back to the shelf. It seemed far more likely to her that William Aubrey never wrote again because he suffered from guilt. Did he seriously care about society at that point? The crashed bicycle, the blood, the knife, it was exactly as she'd read it in the novel. Even if William didn't commit murder, he had some hand in what happened.

On her way home, Abby bought a notebook and stationery and stopped at the grocer's for beer, meat, cheese, pickles, bread and biscuits, taking the initiative to have dinner ready for Thomas and Sally on neatly arranged plates when they arrived home from work.

"Well," Sally exclaimed. "How thoughtful."

"It's the least I could do."

Thomas stuffed his hands in his pockets. "How did you know custard creams were my favorite?"

"A good guess," Abby said.

It was a warm evening, and a proper summer breeze came through the open window. Thomas stacked his bread with prosciutto, cheese and pickle while Sally gabbed about her day at the flower shop, telling them who was getting married and how the soon-to-be mother-in-law had ordered an extraordinary number of flowers for the wedding. Eventually she asked Abby about her day, and Abby told her she'd spent it at the local library.

"We have more books in our library than they have in theirs," Thomas said, sounding insulted.

"Ancient books no one can be bothered with." Sally swatted his arm. "She doesn't want to read any of those."

"Actually, I've already read one." Abby spread mustard on her bread and set a hunk of cheddar over it. "*The Tides.* I hope that's alright?"

"Of course," Thomas said.

"Don't bother us none," Sally added.

"Have either of you read it?"

"Nope." Thomas kept eating.

"I'm afraid I've become rather obsessed with what happened to Evelyn Aubrey," Abby said.

"You and everyone else," Sally said.

"I photocopied this review I found at the library. Do you want to hear it?"

Sally bit into a pickle and nodded yes, but looked disinterested.

Abby got up and found the review in her bag. Coming back to the table, she read,

"The Tides is a mystery of rare artistic merits, and evincing powers of narrative. It gives us Mrs. Hastings, one of the greatest characters of all times. She is an exquisite sketch, eccentric, lovable, kind and innocent. The end of this marvelous book is almost unbearable."

Abby looked up. "Isn't that so twisted? To make her *'lovable, kind and innocent'* and then kill her off, possibly in real life? He could at least have made her unlikable. Why would he write himself the villain? Even if he did it to create sensationalism over the novel, as everyone suspected, he must have known it would ultimately ruin him."

"Bloody hell. He drowns her in the book, right?" Thomas asked.

Abby gave him an earnest look. "You really ought to read it yourself, Thomas O'Conner."

"Oh, come now! I know he drowns her, what with our grandmother Eliza's going on about it."

Sally said, "We haven't talked about curses and murders in this house for years. It all died with Grandmother Eliza."

"Give it to us." Thomas slid his empty plate to the side and rubbed his hands together, preparing himself.

"Alright." Abby propped her elbows on the table. "Mr. Hastings loved his wife as passionately as he hated her. After drowning her in the river, he carries her body up the hill, like he did the day he married her." She paused, dramatically.

"What does he do with her?" Sally propped her elbows on the table.

"You're not going to like it."

"Go on," Thomas said.

"He buries her body under the floorboards of one of the un-occupied servants' bedrooms. Every night, after the house is asleep, he leaves his room and goes back to her, sleeping in the bed he's pushed over the boards."

Abby expected them to be horrified, but Sally simply said, "What nonsense."

"Hogwash." Thomas picked up a slice of meat and began rolling it into a little log. "Sensational is right. People really suspected Aubrey of that? Absurd. It would have stunk to high heaven."

Sally thumped her fist on the table. "Downright implausible. He might have drowned her, but that last bit is far-fetched."

"I suppose," Abby said, still convinced it could have happened. "I did read that William Aubrey had an erratic personality and people speculated he might have had bipolar disorder, or severe depression, which doesn't make for a murderer, but still."

Thomas said, "That's what everyone's got now. Depression."

"It's a real thing, Thomas," Sally said. "Our father suffered from it."

"And he wasn't an Aubrey, my point exactly."

"Your father was Nicholas's cousin, right?" Abby said, clutching the opportunity to move the conversation in this direction.

"That's right." Thomas nodded. "But they were more like brothers. They grew up here together, married within a year of each other and stayed on with their wives and us kids, for a time."

Scraping her chair loudly over the floor, Sally cleared her dish to the sink, the plate clattering.

Undeterred, Abby pressed her. "What happened to Henry Aubrey, Evelyn's son?"

"Died alone in London in some opium den," Sally snapped. "He abandoned his son, Nicholas, a year after his wife died. The boy was only six years old. Our grandmother Eliza raised him like he was her own, and what did Nicholas do? Grew up and abandoned her in return. Maybe that's the damn curse, running away from the people who sacrificed everything to care for you."

"He was in pain, Sally," Thomas said, softly.

"That's no reason to abandon your family."

"He moved away is all," Thomas said. "You always make such a fuss about it."

Sally tossed her knife into the sink. "Because you didn't watch Eliza suffer at the end of her life. You were off with that theater troupe while I was stuck here, day in and day out, listening to her moaning on about where Nicholas had gone, and why did he never write to her and what had she done to deserve it? The worst of it was watching how it affected Daddy, loyal as the day is long, her *actual* son, who never left her side, and she didn't give a hoot about him. He suffered for that. That's the damn thing about this place, always making people suffer." Sally leaned against the sink, her chest heaving.

Thomas got up and put an arm around her. "We're doing alright," he said. "There's no suffering where we're concerned."

"Speak for yourself." Sally shoved him, gently, smiling a little.

Abby held very still, feeling sorry she'd pressed Sally this far, but wanting every detail. Sally looked at her. "Nicholas had a son. He took the boy with him when he left. You being here means Nicholas's son, Little Willy, grew up. It means Little Willy had a daughter. It means time passed and I didn't do a damn thing to find him." There were tears in her eyes and a tightness around her mouth. She slid out from her brother's arm, went into the pantry and came out with two cold beers. Setting them on the table, she said, "You two sit for a while," and left the kitchen.

Sally's words washed over Abby as she listened to the thud of her shoes going up the stairs.

Thomas sat down, wrapping his hand around the neck of the

beer bottle. "Sally doesn't like to talk about it, but she wants me to. Otherwise, she'd never let me have another beer." He grinned and took a swig. "It doesn't bother me like it bothers her. I was away at school when the accident happened. And then Nicholas took Little Willy away. I hardly knew the boy, but Sally loved him. Losing that boy broke her heart. I don't think it's ever fully healed."

Abby waited, silently. Nicholas had a child, a son. Little Willy. A child who grew up and stood beside her mother somewhere in a lush, green field.

Thomas took a long hard drink of his beer and rubbed his chin, the soft, pink skin reddening. "Our father died of a heart attack ten years ago. Sally was his pride and joy. Me, I was a disappointment. But that's of no importance." He glanced around the room. "There were a lot of us here, once, all living together. Seven kids we had in our family. Sally and I were the youngest. Then there was Nicholas and his wife, Rose, and Little Willy. Even Grandmother Eliza stayed on until she died. Now, the place just gets lonelier. Sally won't admit it, but I'm sure it was the accident, and then losing Little Willy that stopped her from marrying and having a child of her own. She had suitors, back in her day, but never settled on any of them." Thomas took a long breath, finding his words.

"Nicholas's wife, Rose, was killed in 1962. Sally was the one who found her drowned in a cow trough. Our father and Nicholas were farming the land, or trying to. There was hardly any money left and this place took more to run than they had. Rose and our mother cleaned the barns as well as the house. No one knows how it happened. People said she must have tripped, hit her head or something. Her son, Little Willy, was only six years old. Another lost mother, is what Eliza said, and hadn't she warned everyone? She never wanted Nicholas to marry. We all thought it was her obsession with him, wanting to keep him for herself the way some mothers get about their precious sons, even though he wasn't her real child. After Rose's death, Eliza went around raving like she did after her sister died about how Evelyn Aubrey was haunting us, and how no Aubrey woman would live if Evelyn had a hand in it. In her last batty days, she looked me right in the eye and said, 'Just you watch, every Aubrey woman from here on out will meet her death by drowning.'" Thomas finished his beer, watching Abby. The sun dipped behind the hill and the light slid out of the room. He shook his head. "Bunch of malarkey if you ask me."

"What year did Rose die, again?" Abby asked.

"1962."

"If Little Willy was six, he would have been born in…1956?" That would make him eighteen when Abby was born. He looked eighteen in the photo. She pressed a hand to her chest, stilling the part of her that wanted to laugh, or cry, she couldn't tell which. Her father had a name. He had a birth date. He had a history, a home, people who loved him, whose hearts had broken for him.

"What happened after the accident?"

"Well." Thomas's words had slowed, but they were still coming. "Everyone thought Nicholas would go the way Henry did, depression, drugs, abandon his son. Instead, he got angry. Said he was leaving, taking the boy and getting out of this cursed house. He and Eliza had a huge row. I was home from school that week and remember it well. Screaming bloody hell at each other. She begged him not to go. But Nicholas was as stubborn as the Aubreys before him. Said Little Willy would be better off far away. Somewhere they could start a new life together, get away from England." Thomas gave a dry laugh, as if that were absurd, the idea of getting away from England.

"Sally was as broken up about it as Grandmother Eliza. She loved Little Willy. It's funny—" Thomas leaned over the table "—she gives our grandmother a bad time of it for loving Nicholas more than her own son, but what Sally won't admit is that she loved Little Willy more than her own brothers. Not that I mind." Thomas spread his palms open on the table. "We're good to each other, and I am sorry she never found Little Willy. On her deathbed, Grandmother Eliza said she regretted Nicholas's leaving as much as her sister's death. Don't know if tragedy followed them. None of us ever heard from them again."

Tragedy had followed them, Abby thought, all the way to her mother.

They sat in silence, finishing their beer, the kitchen darkening around them. To Abby's surprise, instead of upsetting her, this tragic history gave her a sense of relief, as if the current she'd been riding her whole life had just dropped her on solid ground. Her past was a thing handed down over time, inevitable. All the what-ifs about the night her mother died—*What if she'd stayed home? What if she'd been going to a different party? What if she'd left five minutes later?*—wouldn't have mattered. Not if the curse was true.

CHAPTER 17

Burford, England, 1900

March 23

Father's secret has been revealed to me. If I write it down, there will be proof of his sin, but I must unburden myself. That said, I will take extra precautions to lock this journal in my desk and make sure it falls into the hands of no one.

A horse-drawn wagon arrived a little past noon today. Thank heaven Mother was out. She went to call on a neighbor, which I believe was God's will, since this was the first time she's left the house since Father's death.

The man's name is Simon Gray. When he stepped into the drawing room, I took one look at his red-rimmed eyes and felt a prickle of uneasiness. His coat was worn thin in several places, and much too large for his slight frame. He refused to give it to Bennett, and as he sat, something bulged in the front pocket. "Mr. Gray did you say your name was?"

"Yes, your ladyship." He removed his hat, circling the crushed, misshapen brim in his hand. He was ill-kempt, with a face that stretched to a prognathous chin, an imprint the size of a large thumb stamped in its center. His ears stuck out like sails snapped taut in the wind and his hands trembled violently.

A small fluttering started in my womb, a gentle reminder of the life inside me, and I pressed a hand to my stomach, which has begun to swell visibly.

"Where have you come from, Mr. Gray? It looks as if you've been traveling for some time."

Struggling to sound authoritative, he said, "I came up from London. Is Mr. Aubrey in? I asked to sees the both of you."

William was writing in his study and I had no desire to disturb him. "Mr. Aubrey is indisposed. You were not expected, Mr. Gray, and did not send notice of your arrival. Are you an acquaintance of Mr. Aubrey's?"

"No, ma'am." He offered no further explanation and I waited, wishing Bennett had had the decency not to leave me alone with this man. His eyes combed the room as he said, "I am afraid I must sees the both of you. It is a matter of great importance. A financial matter that Mr. Aubrey is sure to want to concern himself with."

"Very well," I said, not because I believed this "financial matter" was of any real concern, but for the excuse of summoning Bennett, who entered promptly when I rang. "Would you please tell Mr. Aubrey that a visitor is here on important business that cannot be disclosed without his presence."

"Yes, my lady." Bennett backed out of the room, and Mr. Gray and I sat in uncomfortable silence until William arrived.

"This gentleman has come from London about a *financial* matter," I said.

William, annoyed at being interrupted, said curtly, "This is not a good time for a donation, if that's what you're after. We have had a death in the family and are still sorting out our financial affairs."

Emphatically, Mr. Gray reached into his bulging pocket and pulled out a bundle of envelopes. "I knows all about the death—that's why I'm here. I suppose, if you want, you could look at this as a donation of sorts." His tremulous hands worked at the tattered string until it fell away. Plucking a letter off the top, he handed it to William, who read it, his face shifting from annoyance to astonishment.

"What right do you have to this?" he asked, his voice threatening.

"It was written to my daughter."

"And what is your purpose in bringing it to our attention?"

"She's been receiving money from Mr. Wilkins and I don't see why, with his death, she's no longer cared for."

I thought the letter had something to do with William's past that I was not privy to, but at the mention of Father, I snatched at it.

There, in black ink, in the familiar, scrolling handwriting of my father, was a letter written to a woman named Marion Gray. The words were adoring, the tone intimate, as if he had known this woman for years.

My scalp tingled. "How has this come into your possession?" I said, my voice steady and cold.

For all his conniving, Mr. Gray looked like a trapped animal. "I took it from her," he said.

William put a hand on my shoulder and slid the letter from my fingers. "I suppose there are more letters like this one?" He pointed to the bundle in Mr. Gray's hand.

"Yes, sir. And these is only some of 'em. There are loads more, but I thought it best not to bring them all on the chance you tried to take them from me by force."

"You have thought this through."

"Yes, sir."

"Does your daughter know you have taken them?"

Mr. Gray dropped his eyes to the floor. "No, sir."

"What exactly do you want from us?"

"Money, sir."

"Or else?"

"Or else I will have these letters made public along with all the rest I got. That would be very bad for you, soiling the family name and all. Mr. Wilkins is an honorable figure in society, and I imagine you would be wanting to keep this from Mrs.

Wilkins as well. I figure that all equals out to you paying me something to stay quiet."

An honorable figure in society. I pictured my stolid, generous father, the man I'd spent my life adoring, writing numerous passionate love letters to a woman who was not my mother.

"He's right," I said. "Mother must never find out. It would destroy her."

"What are you after?" William went to the desk. Money was tight. Coniston House hadn't sold yet and we'd had to get rid of three servants.

"One hundred pounds a year dispersed monthly."

"That is an enormous sum!" William looked as if he might pounce on the man.

"I will take the first payment before I depart and leave the one letter with you for good measure."

"How thoughtful." William glowered, taking the ledger from the top drawer. "If anyone finds out about this, the payments stop immediately, so you had better keep those letters shut up tight. Is that clear?" He slid the book to the edge of the table and said, "Leave an address where the money is to be sent. I will have it to you on the first of the month. As long as the payments come promptly you are never to contact us, or be seen here, again."

Mr. Gray scribbled down his address, looking up at me with a sympathetic smile. "I am terribly sorry to upset you, your ladyship. Your father was a good man. Don't think badly of him for his weakness. My daughter is an extraordinary woman."

As if this was supposed to make me feel better! "If she's anything like you, I find that hard to imagine."

"She's unlike me in every way," he said, snatching at the money William handed him and scampering out of the room.

Sickened, I picked the letter up from the desk and threw it into the fire. I wanted it to burst into violent flames, but it just smoldered, the edges curling in as I stabbed the poker at it until it was a little heap of ash behind the grate. William offered no sympathy, no comfort. I was not surprised given the manner in which he treated me these days, but for a moment, when he touched my shoulder, I felt myself weakening to him.

"Promise you will tell no one?" I looked up. "We have to protect Mother, and the family name and reputation. Promise me." I didn't care a wit about reputation. What I could hardly stand to admit, even to myself, was that I was protecting my father. I couldn't bear to have his name ruined.

"I don't want a scandal any more than you do," William said, and left without a glance in my direction.

I sank into a chair, picturing my thin and distracted father. Could he not eat because he was in love? Was he actually going to confess this to me over breakfast? I could not imagine it, or the idea of Father depleting his funds to indulge a mistress. I wondered what he had bought her, what she looked like and where they had gone together. I always knew Mother was not the woman Father wanted her to be. He wanted her strong and independent. These were the women he admired. It was why he had educated me.

When I was sixteen, he brought me copies of *Hermsprong* and *A Vindication of the Rights of Woman*. Mother read them first and an argument followed. She told Father the books were full of ideas that would confuse a young woman. If there were no clear rules on how women should behave, then how would one know right from wrong? Father said the point was women should not be held to such rules of conduct and submission in the first place. I was to read the books and decide for myself. "Knowledge is strength," he said.

Is it? I wonder. These days it seems to me that a weak-minded man has more power than the strongest-minded woman. I feel trapped in my inability to fend for myself.

A new moon hangs out my window as I write, a sliver of yellow, bright and fine as thread. On my desk, the light appears in the moonstone like a strand of hair beneath the surface. Lesley said the stone would clear one's mind to wisdom. Is wisdom the same as knowledge, or truth? *Tell the truth at all costs*, my father always said. The one person I trusted has turned out to be a hypocrite. A liar. What good is truth, or wisdom?

CHAPTER 18

Burford, England, 2006

Abby sat in the library at Abbington Hall composing a letter to Josiah, her hand cramping. Writing by hand was not something she did much of anymore, but it seemed fitting, considering her surroundings, and she found she liked the physical act of pen to paper, how easy it was to express herself. He was the first person she'd thought of after learning her father's name, the first person she wanted to tell. It should have been Grandma Maggie, but that was too complicated. Josiah had no stake in this, nothing to lose. He would be excited for Abby, and she wanted to live in that excitement for a while.

She filled five pages of stationery describing Abbington Hall, Sally and Thomas, and the stories she'd heard. *"Somewhere,"* she wrote, *"another William Aubrey roams the world."* She told Josiah that she wished he was with her, but that it was better he wasn't. Then she licked the metallic envelope seal, addressed it, set it on the bureau and, in a ridiculous, romantic gesture, spritzed her Noir 29 on it.

When he wrote her back, she felt like a giddy teenager crawling into bed with his letter. She'd slept with it under her pillow, waking the next morning with an urge to get on a plane and go home to him.

She didn't. Instead, she wrote another letter.

Josiah,

Well, it's been over a month since I arrived, and despite knowing my father's name, I am no closer to finding him, or solving any murders. I have no idea what I'm still doing here, other than waiting to see how the past I've fallen into fits into the present.

My days are strangely routine. In the mornings, I drink a cup of tea, eat a slice of toast with marmalade and head out to walk the hills. October is beautiful here. Sometimes I follow the sheep. Mostly, I am alone. There is a stillness in the hills, the grass bending beneath my feet, the sky opening overhead and the birds settling into the tops of the trees. The leaves have already turned yellow, which makes me feel like time is passing quickly. I often imagine Evelyn walking with me, picturing her so vividly I can actually feel her quiet presence. There is something desperate and unsettled in her. It makes me want to know who she was, and what she suffered.

Sometimes I go into town and meet Sally for lunch at The Angel at Burford. I'd love to take you there. Mack, the man who showed me to my table the first day I arrived, knows me by name, which makes me feel oddly special. Even in the bustle of the restaurant, surrounded by modern people in modern clothing, when all possibility of ghosts seems absurd, Evelyn's presence feels as palpable as breath to me.

I spend my afternoons in the library at Abbington Hall, reading and perusing the endless shelves of books. I've read all of William Aubrey's novels. I don't know which one you read in college, but The Beaumont Man, his first, I found boring and tedious, riddled with historic detail and high society dinner parties. My favorite of his books is Mr. Winthrop. It's about a man who abandons his wife and children for his mistress. The wife, Emily Winthrop, ends up killing herself, leaving Mr. Winthrop free to marry his mis-

tress, while the son plots revenge on his stepmother, who he blames for his mother's death. You should read it, if you haven't already.

I sit in the library now thinking how much you'd love the ancient vibe of this place. It's like landing in my own novel. I have been keeping my stationery in the top drawer of the library desk, along with your return letter, which gives me a sense of ownership over this desk. My plan is to start a wildly romantic letter exchange with you, so you'd better be prepared.

You will be happy to know I took your advice and sent a letter to my grandparents. I gave them no specifics, but I let them know I was safe. I don't know why I can't tell Maggie about any of this yet. I'm not ready to let her in. This might be the first time I've ever felt truly independent. No Maggie or Carl, no dead mother, no meaningless job, no late nights in the city. Writing to you is the closest thing I have to the outside world. Mostly I'm with Sally and Thomas, whose dinner conversation consists of town gossip and sibling bickering, which I find adorable. I've started doing all the cooking. Simple things, like grilled chicken and rice, or pasta with veggies, but you'd think I'd served a five-course meal how grateful they are, and not once have they asked how long I plan on staying.

It's only at night, in the pitch-black of my bedroom, that I feel restless. I haven't brought up Nicholas or Little Willy to Sally, and she hasn't offered any more information. When I asked Thomas why no one in the family had tried to find them, he told me it wasn't the leaving that angered the family, it was the fact that after all Eliza had done for him, Nicholas never sent a single letter, or made a single phone call home. He just disappeared. Listening to Eliza cry out for him on her deathbed was more than anyone could take. After she died, no one wanted anything to do with Nicholas Aubrey.

Little Willy just got lost in all of it.

I do have a fascinating discovery to tell you. I had the town librarian dig up old articles for me, not on microfilm, but on actual yellowed paper pulled from boxes she brought up from the basement. They all repeated the same story about Evelyn Aubrey's disappearance and the facts that corresponded with The Tides, *except for the one from* Oxfordshire Weekly News. *It featured a letter, written by a man named Lesley Wheelock, which, clearly, no one took seriously because it was published between an article on an auction in Swinbrook and an account of a meeting of the Church of England Men's Society.*

In the letter, the man pleads that the police not give up the search for Evelyn. It claims the only reason Aubrey was released from prison was because he was a wealthy society man. A commoner would hang, he wrote. He goes on to name a woman who reported to the police that she had seen bruises on Evelyn Aubrey's arm in church shortly before she went missing, and that the postmaster said she came in with her wrist swollen the size of a melon. How is this not evidence that she was being abused? According to the letter, after she disappeared, the house was searched by a single policeman, and the grounds weren't searched at all.

It's infuriating that there's evidence of Evelyn Aubrey's abuse right here and not a single biographer, or scholar, has mentioned it in anything I've read! They're more interested in Aubrey's literary genius than his being an abusive husband. All the brushed-aside conclusions are that Evelyn Aubrey committed suicide, a frustratingly sexist assumption. Victorian writers love to kill off their women to suicide. Much better than having a woman live a sinful, happy life. Death or virtue, one had to choose. And from the sounds of it, Evelyn wasn't even sinful. She was a devoted wife, just a little withdrawn. I think people chose suicide as an easy answer.

This Lesley Wheelock didn't seem to think it was suicide, and neither do I.

I guess this is why I stay. I'm not ready to give up on finding her truth, however unlikely.

I miss you, and hope you'll keep writing. Otherwise, I'm afraid I might vanish into history myself.

Abby

CHAPTER 19

Burford, England, 1900

March 30

I no longer sleep. My nerves vibrate and my body feels as if it is racing through time. My pregnancy confuses William. He is uncomfortable around me and keeps his distance, the baby a new barrier between us. Once, he came to my bedroom as I sat brushing out my hair and said, "You are so changed."

"Am I?" I raked the brush through my curls, looking at my full face in the mirror, my cheeks flushed from a heat I seem unable to cool, my freckles blotchy and darker than before. William wavered in the doorway, uncommitted, his hand on the knob, his feet barely over the threshold.

"A child will be good for us, I think," he said, and I could see that he believed this might be true.

I said nothing, gave him no encouragement. It was too much, the amiable way he stood there making hopeful declarations after all the horrible things he's said to me. Everything feels out of control, my capricious husband, my changeable body, the teetering, volatile life I have stepped into. I want to believe William, to fall at his feet, to give in to whatever compassion he offers, but I know better than to trust him. It will weaken me, and weak, I will never survive.

Mother is my sole comfort. Since Father's death, all of her edges have softened. When I touch her hand, instead of pulling briskly away, as she used to, she squeezes it back. She is happy about the baby, and I think she understands that William will not care for us as Father did, that we must rely on each other.

Something has opened up in her, and she talks of Father ceaselessly now, retelling stories as if we hadn't lived them together. His memory brings such joy to her face, her tone so full of reverence it splits my heart. I will do whatever it takes to keep his secret from her. It would destroy her, and I need for at least one person in this house to stay unadulterated and blameless.

We sold Coniston House, and with it any hope I had of returning to London. I miss the city, and fear, without our home there, that I will be stuck in this dreadful countryside forever. The quiet of Abbington Hall unnerves me. After my sleepless nights, when dawn finally crawls through my window, I can no longer stand the wretchedness of the house and I take myself out of doors. Mother says I could catch cold and compromise the baby, but I don't care. I roam the hills with the sheep, take in the expansive countryside and try to find some peace in nature.

One morning, returning from my amble, I found Mr. Wheelock on my doorstep, arms crossed, his hair standing up in the breeze, thick and white as the clouds.

"Good morning." I pressed a hand to my chest to catch my breath. He nodded a silent greeting, his light blue eyes moving out over the horizon. His phlegmatic presence made me nervous, and I babbled, "Would you like to come in for a cup of hot tea? I'm afraid the weather has not been kind to us, what with all the storms. At least the sun is trying, today."

He glanced up at the clouds and then back at the house, scanning the windows. "I'll not stay for tea, thank you. I came to ask that you stay away from my grandson."

His blunt insolence galled me. I had done absolutely nothing to deserve it. Tightly, I said, "Your grandson approached me. I was simply returning the favor."

"I'm sure he did." Mr. Wheelock's eyes locked on mine, the

intensity immobilizing. "He's the type to take pity on a wild animal and lose an arm trying to save it. Do you get my meaning?"

I pulled myself up as straight as was possible with my enormous stomach. "Are you implying I'm a wild animal, or a woman in need of saving?"

This cracked a small smile out of him, the lines around his mouth deepening. "Depends on your opinion of wild, and your opinion of a woman, I suppose."

"I am not up for riddles, Mr. Wheelock. I loaned Lesley a book, nothing more."

I began to walk past him, but Mr. Wheelock stepped in front of me, raising a finger in my face. "You didn't loan it—you gave it. A loan means a return, and I'll not let my Lesley come to this cursed place."

"Cursed?" I barked a laugh, wanting to get away from this man.

He dropped his hand. For the first time he looked apologetic, but still determined. "What goes on here is none of my business, but I won't have it being my grandson's either. You just leave him out of it." With a curt "Good day," he stepped around me and headed down the drive, his boots thudding away over the gravel.

I watched him go, shaken, wondering if this was about the stone. Did he know Lesley had given it to me, and did he think I was taking advantage of the boy? I could return it, but I know Lesley won't take it back. He told me as much already, and I can see he is a boy of his word.

The idea of not seeing Lesley again upsets me. It is unnatural for a grown woman to look to the friendship of a ten-year-old child, and yet some part of me feels inextricably drawn to him. Maybe this is because he is so pure of heart, a child such as we all once were, such as William once was.

I have tried to picture William as a boy, before he became a man who needs to prove himself, who must be adored and admired and told that he is brilliant in order to feel worthy. He had a meager upbringing, at least in the beginning before his father had some success with bonds, and I sometimes wonder if this isn't what makes him so hungry for success. He told me he was nothing before he became a writer. This was early on, and I had kissed him and said I would have loved him even if he'd been a fishmonger.

I would have been better off with a fishmonger, I think now. William is insufferable.

A few days ago, I was writing in the library when a tremendous crash came from his study. Heaving my exhausted body from the chair, I went to the door and called, "William, are you alright?" When there was no response, I pushed my way in. Paper was scattered on the floor and the inkwell had been tipped over on the desk, causing a pool of ink to seep into the fine grains of wood. I placed the bottle upright, but there was nothing at hand to mop up the spill, so I left it to make its mark. William stood by the window, staring out at the frosty landscape.

"William?" He did not turn around.

Leaning over my bulging stomach, I gathered up the scattered paper.

"My father was right," he said, pathetically. "I am a failure."

I placed the paper safely away from the spilled ink. "I am sure your father did not believe that."

"He did. When I presented him with *The Beaumont Man*, he didn't even open it. He slid it on the shelf and said, 'Your success will be short.'" William sounded defeated. "He was right."

Maybe it was the pregnancy gnawing away at me, but I had no patience for his indefatigable self-indulgence. "You are lucky to be as successful as you are," I said.

William charged at me with a fist in the air. "Get out! Let me be. I have told you to just let me be!"

With a glare, I did just that.

CHAPTER 20

Burford, England, 2006

Abby found the letter by accident.

It had been raining for three days and she was housebound and bored. She'd considered taking the train into London, but that seemed daunting in the downpour. Instead, she took out her camera and wandered onto the ground floor of Abbington Hall, curious what lay behind the closed doors that ran from the kitchen to the back of the house. They were the only rooms she hadn't been in.

When she peeked inside, she discovered they were storage rooms, crammed with so much stuff Abby could hardly walk between the antique furniture, rolled-up rugs and endless boxes. There were shelves of crockery and crystal mixed with shoe polish and dirty rags, old metal tools, stacks of newspaper and books and magazines, modern cleaning products with bright plastic bottles next to cardboard ones with faded labels. The oddity of all this history thrown haphazardly together, each generation shoving itself up against the last, fascinated Abby.

In one room, she found stacks of suitcases and trunks, decades of differing eras, tweed canvas, lime-green vinyl and vintage leather, all piled together. For fun, she began rummaging through them, snapping open rusted clasps, forcing up hinges, the faded scent of mildew and baby powder released from the cloth linings.

Some of the suitcases were empty, but most held pieces of disintegrating clothing—a threadbare blouse, moth-eaten sweaters, a tiny pair of shoes. One suitcase was dedicated solely to children's clothing and toys—pinafore dresses, slacks and nightgowns, a stuffed bunny with missing eyes and a wooden elephant.

In a trunk with gold trim around the edges, she found a navy blue cloak with a wide hood and a thick satin lining. Beneath it were white dresses stained with age, thin georgette with lace trim and hems that fell to the floor. Digging underneath the clothing, Abby's hand hit something hard and she pulled out a jewelry box painted with an English landscape, the inside lined in red velvet, the jewels pillaged. All that was left was an empty perfume bottle, some loose beads and a small card that said Marion Gray against a swirling green background.

Carefully, Abby arranged the things back in the trunk, impulsively trying on the cloak. She wished she could try on the dresses, but they were much too slender. She'd burst the seams, if she even managed to get the narrow waists up over her hips. The cloak was heavy and soft. The hood fell down her back and the wool billowed around her ankles.

It was then that she slid her hand into the camouflaged pocket that disappeared into the layered fabric and found a lumpy square of paper tucked at the bottom of the slick lining. Pulling it out, she began delicately unfolding what looked like a meticulous work of origami, anticipation winging through her. It could just be an old grocery list, she told herself, eggs and sugar, a reminder to pick up a dress from the haberdashery—a word she'd picked up from Aubrey's novels.

What she found was a letter, the elegant cursive crossing through the many folded boxes.

Abbington Hall,
October 20, 1906

Dearest Lesley,

I put pen to paper under a glorious sunset on this October eve from my writing desk where I have spent most of my days these last six years. The sunshine is an unusual visitor after our extraordinarily wet fall. Things seem to be looking up for me already. If the sky can hold on to its desiccate state, I will be able to leave this house by way of the road on my much beloved bicycle. If the rain had been pouring down, I would have been forced to take the footpath around back, and I do so long for one last view of Burford from the hilltop.

I missed you earlier today. I do hope nothing too distressing kept you from our meeting. It troubles me to do it, but I am leaving you my journal as you have proved yourself worthy of keeping a secret. I have no one else to trust. If William knew this journal existed, he would stop at nothing to destroy it. I considered leaving it with Marion Gray in exchange for the destruction of my father's letters, but her avaricious desires feed on just that sort of bribery, and I am sure she'd find a way to keep those letters tightly in her clutches regardless, self-preservation being the one quality I admire in her.

If there is a future where you know my son, I beg of you to find a way to give him this journal when he is old enough to make sense of it, if sense is to be made of anything anymore.

I am sorry, after all I have confessed to you, that I cannot tell you of my final deception. For your own good, do not read it in these pages. I know you would lie for me if pressed to do so, and you must honor your promise to your grandfather—and yourself—and not lead a life of lies as I have. You are the most decent person I have ever met. Pure of heart. Stay pure of heart, my dearest Les-

ley, as you grow into a man. You will be a rare gem in a sea of misguided stones.

Which leads me to the moonstone. Giving it to me was a kindness I never deserved, but like your friendship, it has allowed me to see clearly. It continues to remind me of what is precious and pure and true, and for that, I owe you everything.

Already, night descends. The last bright spots of sun melt down the crooked slopes of the hillside, illuminating the gray poplars whose leaves have fallen to the ground. Foolishly, I bend over my writing, as if I cannot let it go. I must put down my pen and follow the light from the room, as it will not last much longer.

Regards, and forever in your debt,
Evelyn Madeline Aubrey

Abby's hands shook as she folded the letter back up, scurrying to replace the bones of Evelyn's unearthed voice. Her presence, the pulse in the air, was suffocating.

Matching the lines was like trying to refold a map and Abby made a mess of it before sliding the lumpy paper back into the pocket. Taking off the coat, she shut it all back into the trunk and sat on top of it with her head in her hands. Here was Evelyn, her handwriting, her words, evidence that she left Abbington Hall on her bicycle. *"One last view of Burford,"* she had written. Had she committed suicide after all? Was she being pursued by an abusive husband? Either way, her leaving by choice coinciding with *The Tides*'s publication made little sense if William had plotted her murder. Maybe it was a crime of passion, and her leaving and the timing of his book publication a coincidence?

The sun slunk away from the windows, and Abby had the sense that time was vanishing, day blurring into night, the past into the present. She wanted to read the letter again, but something prevented her from opening the trunk back up. Instead, she went upstairs to the library and stood scanning the hundreds of books bedded down in their shelves, settled for lifetimes. Could Evelyn Aubrey's journal possibly be in this house? If Lesley had given it to Henry, it seemed unlikely that Henry would have taken the journal with him when he abandoned his son. Or maybe Lesley never had a chance to give it back and it was lost to history.

Going to one of the shelves, Abby drew an arrow in the dust with her finger. Why did Evelyn leave her journal behind? Where was she going? Lesley must have thought something bad had happened to her to write that letter to the newspaper. And who was Marion Gray? Abby felt more confused than ever. There were too many questions, questions that could only be answered with Evelyn's journal.

CHAPTER 21

Burford, England, 1900

April 13

Spring is here.

The crocuses have poked their purple heads up around the house and the primroses bloom yellow over a ground still dusted with frost, their red centers blazing. The air is filled with the anticipation of warmer days, and despite my cynicism over the winter months, I am hopeful spring will revive our spirits. William has written ceaselessly over the last few months, and he is calmer and more even-keeled than I have seen him in a long time.

I have allowed myself to think that a child will bring happiness to this house, temper the storms, brighten the rooms.

May 13

William has, at long last, finished his book.

I had gone out for my morning walk, leaving through the kitchen and rounding the house by the garden. Mist covered the hillside and the sky hung low. It was chillier than I anticipated, and when I turned back to get a coat, I saw Father's two-seater parked in front of the carriage house, shiny and bright as the day he drove it here. No one has driven it since his death, and I moved forward as if the car were an apparition. Father would step from the house, smile, wave, pull his goggles down and climb into the driver's seat. Time would erase.

It was William who came barreling from the house, rounding the motorcar so quickly he fairly smacked into me. Halting, he pulled himself up and cried, "Evelyn?" as if I were a stranger.

"You were not expecting me?"

"I was not." He stepped around me. "I need to get an early start."

"Where are you going?"

"London."

"London? Why?"

"To bring my book to Chapman & Hall." He spoke with defiance, as if I might stop him.

"You finished your book?"

"Yes." He mounted the seat, tucking his coat around him. "I should only be gone a fortnight."

"Do you know how to drive this thing?"

"I do." Gripping a funny-looking stick in one hand, he cranked a lever with the other and the engine chugged to a start with a raspy groan. "Your Father took me out, remember?"

I did not remember. "What does it run on? What if it breaks down?" I was stalling, envious he was heading off without me. It would have been impossible in my condition, but oh, what I wouldn't give to be in the city again.

"Not to worry. I'm only taking it to the train station," he cried, and with a jolt, the motorcar bounced forward and puttered away in a cloud of smoke.

Standing in the chill of the dusty morning, the baby pummeling at my womb as if it were sport, I burst into tears. I had not cried in so long. I had not let myself, refusing to give in to the hysterics the doctor warned me about, refusing to give in to William's wounding words, his cutting looks, the loneliness closing over me. Only, these were not tears of sorrow or loneliness or hysterics; they were tears of blinding envy.

My writing was shoved useless in a drawer upstairs. I had held on to this idea that when William finished his book, he'd dash into my room, reading madly to me like he had in the beginning. With its completion, his confidence and pride would return, and with it his confidence in me. Our work was what kept us both going. Our writing was the one real thing that united us. The only thing. Why did he get to have it and I didn't?

June 12

My husband has been gone for a month. He has not written a single letter or bothered to send word of his return. I am huge with child and sick with jealousy thinking of him celebrating his accomplishments, dining in London, going to the theater, of all the women he's seeing. In my condition, I feel fat and useless and bored.

Mostly, I sit in the library writing silly sonnets, indulging my emotions. I should go over my manuscript, but what would be the use? It's probably rubbish anyway.

June 15

It is early morning. Rain sputters outside. I can barely sit up and my eyes are heavy from the laudanum the doctor gave me last night.

Last night.

Last night Mother retired early. Alone, I circled the library like a broken horse, my ankles swollen, my legs cramping. When I'd tired myself, I sat at the desk reworking a poem that had been giving me trouble for days.

I didn't hear the motorcar drive up, and William opened the library door so quietly that I had no idea he was there until he said, "Hello, love."

I looked up, disoriented, my head in a sea of words.

He stood on the other side of the desk, cheeks flushed, eyes brilliant. This was the longest we'd been apart since we married, and I was overcome seeing him again. He looked like he had our first night at the inn. He'd called me love. I wanted to feel him again, to have him brush the hair from my forehead and kiss the insides of my wrists.

"I was not expecting you." I reached a hand across the desk, sure he'd never take it, but he did. He squeezed his fingers around mine and said, "I wanted to write, but I couldn't. It's all too exciting. I wanted to tell you everything in person." The publication of his book had revived him, brought back his vibrancy.

"I can't wait to hear all about it. Shall I ring Bennett? You must be hungry. You can tell me over dinner."

"No, no." He shook his head. "I ate at the inn."

"Ah, well, that's good. How was your journey?"

"Excellent." William brought my hand to his lips and kissed it before going over to the bag he'd dropped by the door, bounding back with a package in his hand. I laughed, reminded of how he'd bounded over the fields the first day we arrived here. Dropping the package on the desk, he said, "Open it." Unable to contain himself, he reached over and untied the string for me. "I got three thousand pounds for the copyrights."

I smiled. "What an enormous sum. You should be pleased with yourself."

Rolling back the stiff brown paper, I held up his book, beautifully bound in a deep reddish brown with gold letters etched into the cover. *Mercer Corner*, by William Aubrey. I stared, speechless, the reality not wholly sinking in until I cracked the book open and cut the first page, then the second.

There were my words, typeset and laid out exactly as I had written them.

I looked up. The shadows from the fire danced along the stenciled walls, licking their way over the deep green floral pattern.

"Where did you get this?" It was a betrayal beyond anything I could imagine.

William backed away, standing in the center of the room, putting distance between us. "From your desk."

"When?"

"The morning I left. You'd gone out for a walk."

The fact that it had been gone all this time without my noticing was as unfathomable as my words printed in front of me. "But the manuscript was written in my hand," I said, still not quite believing what he had done.

"A simple matter of dictation." William's face lit up, as if expecting a compliment for this extraordinary feat.

Anger prickled my throat. A diligent wife penning her husband's novel for him; what could be more believable. I stood up, nauseous, swaying to one side as a sharp, physical pain shot through my abdomen and straight down my legs. I slammed the book shut, looking at my title etched in gold with my husband's name standing boldly underneath it. The room moved around me, the dark bookshelves undulating like tenebrous trees. William looked small and insignificant against them.

"How could you?" I gripped the desk as one might grip the rail of a ship.

He looked insulted. "You should be pleased."

"Pleased?" Was he out of his mind? My voice shook, my emotions quivering to the surface. "This is the most cowardly thing a person could do."

"Cowardly? I've gotten your work published, haven't I?" The dazzle had gone out of him. He looked crushed that I wasn't thanking him. He was insane, I decided. Utterly out of his wits. He went on, "Chapman & Hall were expecting something, and we needed the money to pay off your father's mistress."

Furious, I heaved myself around the desk, teetering as the pain seared through me. The room swirled, the lamps bright and glaring. The room was much too hot. "How dare you use my father's folly as an excuse to further your own interests. Chapman & Hall would have given money for the copyrights no matter whose name was on the cover."

"They wouldn't have given as much, if they'd published you at all, which I doubt."

"Why? Because I'm a woman? Women publish books all the time, in case you hadn't noticed."

"Most of it trivial, sentimental babble. Your work is good, Evelyn." He dared to tell me my work was good, now? "The good ones use pseudonyms for the very purpose of saying what they like. You told me yourself how often writers like Christina Rossetti fall prey to didactic fiction. Your female characters aren't exactly virtuous." He came near me, imploringly, as if expecting I'd come around to his rational thinking. "This way you don't have to censor yourself. Isn't that what your beloved father told you to do? Write boldly?" He said it with such confidence I had the urge to spit at him.

"As a woman! As myself! What century are you living in? Women are being published more than ever and it's hardly sensational babble." A pain surged through my abdomen so sharp it was all I could do to stay on my feet. "The truth is you had nothing to give them, and you couldn't admit it, so you stole something to save face and made up this ridiculous story to justify it." My words came fast. I was riding the waves of pain now. "What have you written the past twelve months? Anything?"

"I've written."

"What? Show it to me!"

William ran a hand through his hair, yanking at the ends. "You have no right to speak to me this way. I will show you nothing."

"Because you have nothing. Your father was right. You are a failure." I wanted to wound him as he had wounded me. "And now you are a liar and a thief as well. Is this why you intercepted my application to the Reading Room? Did you plan it the first night I read you my work?" I welcomed the idea that I could make him that angry again. "Mr. Emsley was just an excuse, wasn't he? You couldn't tolerate my being a good writer. You hadn't planned on that when you married me. That I might turn out better than you."

"That's enough!" William slammed a fist into the palm of his hand, his eyes narrow, their glare like shards of glass.

I felt almost hysterical as the pains of labor swept through me. There was no way out of any of this.

"I did you a favor," he said, his arrogance more than I could stand.

I flew at him, my arm raised. I meant to hit him, to smash everything he'd smashed inside me. But even in this I failed, doubling over, the pain of my child about to tear its way out of me dropping me to my knees.

Henry was born in the middle of that night.

Dr. Grousman and Mother sat with me into the early hours. It was a quick, excruciating experience, dulled by the laudanum the doctor gave me. The baby is a month early, but the doctor says he is healthy, if not on the small size. When it was over, Mother took the child from me. I told her I was not well enough to feed him and Dr. Grousman said he would send the cook for evaporated milk. He left the drops for my pain, and they make me sleepy and temperate.

I feel numb looking at my child asleep in his bassinet, a child who has the blue eyes of his father. I prayed for a girl and God mocks me with a son that looks nothing like a Wilkins and everything like an Aubrey.

CHAPTER 22

Burford, England, 2006

They started in the library—Sally, Thomas and Abigail—reading binding after binding, pulling out the books that had either no printed titles on the spines, or unreadable ones, for inspection. Abby had convinced them to scour the rooms of Abbington Hall. This house was filled with history, and clearly no one had thoroughly dug through it. What questions had been asked? What had anyone tried to uncover? Consumed with their own stories, the family had never bothered to find out what really happened to Evelyn Aubrey. Instead, they'd dehumanized her, turned her into fiction, just like her husband did in his novel, created a myth, made her into a ghost tale. The reality was harder to live with—a self-aggrandizing, abusive man who either killed his wife for fame or drove her to suicide. It was easier to put the curse on Evelyn, blame the woman for her own demise, and for all of their troubles that followed.

The injustice of it made Abby angry, and that anger propelled her to action.

Intent on giving it everything she had, she charted their course through the house. She'd told Sally and Thomas about the letter. There seemed no doubt it was a thing of value, but none of them were sure what to do with it, and if they had the journal, well, that had to be worth a lot more than a single letter.

Abby stuck to the high bookshelves because Thomas was

afraid of heights and Sally's knees were too "cranky" to climb the ladder. She liked looking down on their bobbing heads, the two of them working close together. The ladder rolled a little to the left and Abby steadied herself, amazed at how high up she was. Hundreds of books surrounded her, stacked floor to ceiling like vertical bricks fortifying her from the outside world. It seemed impossible Evelyn's story wasn't among them.

Exhausting themselves in the library, they moved on to the drawing room, opening cupboards and drawers, looking behind pictures and inside tall, painted vases.

At one point, Abby admitted to herself that she wasn't just looking for Evelyn's journal; a small part of her was searching for some evidence of her dad, hoping for a hint at where Nicholas had taken him, a letter sent to Sally's father or other family. Even if Nicholas had never reached out, wouldn't Little Willy have wanted to contact his family at some point? He had lived here until he was six years old and must have had memories of the place. Abby had always been so eager for family, the idea of having all these cousins and history and not coming back for it was unfathomable.

Two days in, Abby stood in one of the upstairs bedrooms inspecting a photograph of William Aubrey, who leaned jauntily against a mantel. "What the hell did you do to her?" she said out loud, his haughty silence making her want to hurl the picture across the room. Next to it, overwhelmed by a heavy, ornate frame, was a photograph of a boy with his arm wrapped around the neck of a rocking horse. The boy must be Henry, she thought. He looked just like his father, William. Pulling out the metal pin that held the back in place, Abby slid the photograph from its frame, but there was no name or date written on the back, no hidden message.

Within the week, the three of them had gone from the library to the smoking and billiard room, the drawing room, dining room, and morning room, and then on to the upstairs bedrooms and dressing rooms. They looked under mattresses and rugs, felt around for loose floorboards, looked for secret compartments in dressers or inside the walls of armoires. No one was willing to admit the journal may not be there. Its existence was too promising.

At one point, Thomas suggested ripping open the furniture, and Sally cried, "Have you lost your marbles? Grandmother Eliza would haunt us for the rest of our days. Nothing is worth that." Brushing the whole business away with a slap of her palms, she said, "I, for one, give up. I'm too old for this."

Which left Abby and Thomas to finish the last of the upstairs bedrooms.

Eventually, Thomas gave up too, but Abby couldn't. They'd spent a week of bullish, eager searching and she wasn't ready to quit. While Thomas padded back to the living room, Abby went and stood in William Aubrey's study, watching the rain slide down the windowpanes. It seemed like an uninspiring place to create. On one wall was a row of bookshelves; on the other a huge painting of hunting dogs and horses and men with rifles. The windows overlooked a weedy garden with no view of the hills, and at the far end of the room was a glass cabinet displaying Aubrey's original manuscripts.

Abby traced her finger over a large ink stain on the desk, the spot darkening as she rubbed the dust away. The room felt oppressive, as if William Aubrey had sucked all the air out of it.

From the top drawer of the desk, Abby pulled out a large leather notebook. It was a ledger she'd already looked through, full of figures and calculations, meaningless numbers written in neat rows next to lists of names. This time, as she looked through it again, something caught her attention.

Abby found Sally and Thomas in the living room having their tea. She squeezed onto the couch between them, opening the ledger in her lap. "I discovered something. I don't know what it means, but it seems important."

Sally set down the teapot. "That is very old, and it's supposed to stay in the desk. It's part of the archive."

"I'll put it right back, I promise. Just tell me what you make of this name first." Abby angled the book toward Thomas, who picked up his wire-rim glasses and hooked the loops behind his ears. "Simon Gray?" he said.

Abby ran her finger under the big, scrawling print. "The first time his name appears is on March 23, 1900, for a payment in the amount of 16 pounds, 5s, 1d. I don't know what *s* or *d* means."

"Five shillings and one sixpence," Sally said.

"Was that a lot back then?" Abby asked.

"I suppose," Sally said.

"You'd think that was a lot now." Thomas chuckled and Sally rolled her eyes at him and handed him his tea.

Abby thumbed through the pages. "There were six more payments in the exact same amount. The last one is in September 1900. His name never appears again after that. It's funny a ledger doesn't say what the person was being paid for. Maybe he worked here? Either way, I'm guessing he's a relation of Marion Gray, unless it's a coincidence. Was Gray a common name?"

"Sounds common," Sally said.

"I also found this." Abby took out a sheet of paper she'd found stuck between the pages. "It's an application for a ticket to the Reading Room in the British Museum Library."

Thomas looked carefully at it, dunking a biscuit into his tea. "It's an application for Evelyn Aubrey."

"The interesting thing is what's written here." Abby pointed to the bottom of the page where someone had written, *"I think not, my dear."*

"Bloody hell." Thomas lost half his biscuit into his teacup and began digging it out with a finger. "Controlling bugger, wasn't he?"

Sally sat down in front of her monstrous desktop computer. "Why would Evelyn Aubrey want to apply for the Reading Room? Does one do research for poetry? Let's see..." She typed with a single index finger, searching and plunking away at the keys. "Ah, here we are. It says the Reading Room opened on 2

May 1857…blah, blah, blah…those wanting to use it had to apply in writing and were issued a reader's ticket. Among those granted tickets were: Karl Marx, Lenin and novelists such as Bram Stoker and Sir Arthur Conan Doyle—"

"There's something else in here." Thomas had taken the ledger and was carefully turning over each page. Between two blank pages in the back, pressed tightly into the spine, was a newspaper clipping. He pulled it out. "It's like we're in an Agatha Christie mystery. I'm a right Professor Poirot." He laughed, peering at the faded print while Abby looked over his shoulder.

"Good Lord, read it out loud," Sally said.

Thomas shifted the page to catch the light from the window. "September 22nd, 1905…says it's written by a journalist named Edward Garnett, who, according to this, *'attended a gathering of Thomas Hardy's at Max Gate along with Aubrey, Kipling, and Yeats the poet.'*" Thomas looked up. "Never heard of any of these fellows."

"Just read the article, already." Sally looked like she might tumble off the edge of her chair.

"Don't get your britches in a bunch." Thomas cleared his throat, drawing out his moment of reveal as he scanned the page to find his place.

"Hardy and Aubrey had a falling-out due to the stringency with which Hardy enforced his method, sending the writers off during breakfast and luncheon. Aubrey brought a proof of Mr. Winthrop, but refused to work. Hardy took great offense when Aubrey settled himself to reading instead of taking up his pen along with the other literary guests. Aubrey did, however, heartily partake of the orange brandy offered before dinner, and had his fair share of the hot gin punch after. Hardy himself made the punch and the enthusiasm that Aubrey showed for this 'nightcap' allowed Hardy to forgive the daily neglect of his regiment."

"He was a drunk," Sally said. "No surprise there."

"Look, look at this." Abby leaned over Thomas, pointing to something written in the margin of the article. "It says, '*Careful, dearest.*'"

"Someone likes writing in margins," Thomas said.

"But the handwriting is different." Abby put the papers side by side. *"I think not, my dear"* was written in big, looping letters, *"Careful, dearest"* in tiny, scrolling print.

Sally jumped up, her sweater flapping open. "Come with me, you two, and bring all that along."

Flicking light switches as they went, Sally led them down the hall and through the library into Aubrey's study. There, she clicked on a floor lamp, took a key from Aubrey's desk drawer and fitted it into the door of the glass case. Lifting out the hefty bulk of a manuscript, she set it on top of the case with a thud that shook the glass.

"You keep the key right in the desk drawer?" Thomas cried. "What good is that going to do if we get burgled?"

"Shush. Bring that article over here."

The three of them gathered around as Sally held the article over the first page of the manuscript.

"I see." Thomas's face lit up.

"Do you see it?" Sally looked at Abby. "The handwriting in the margin of the newspaper article matches Evelyn's handwriting."

Sally had told Abby it was a well-known fact that William Aubrey dictated his novels to his wife. The handwriting on the manuscript, and the handwriting in the margin of the article, *"Careful, dearest,"* did look the same, the way the *f*'s looped at the bottom, the slant of the *l*'s, and the *s*'s.

"That's definitely Evelyn's handwriting," Thomas said, deliberately authoritative. He was loving this.

Sally pulled off her glasses, snapped them shut and dropped

them in her sweater pocket. "Why would any of these things have been kept?"

"What do you think Evelyn meant by it," Abby said. "'Careful, dearest.' Do you think she was looking out for him? Protecting him?"

Thomas shook his head. "I have no idea."

Sally crouched down, putting the manuscript back into the case.

"What about the application?" Abby asked. "Can we assume it's William Aubrey's handwriting in the margin, and if so, why wouldn't he want Evelyn to do research in the British Museum Library?"

"Control." Sally slid shut the glass door and locked it, using the cabinet to pull herself up. "Keeping a woman at home in her place."

"Why keep the application? The date is 1900, years before Evelyn went missing."

Thomas said, "Reminds him of her, maybe. Whether he killed her or not, doesn't mean he didn't love her. Like you said, the Mr. Hastings in the book loved his wife, even after he killed her." He tugged at a tuft of hair. "Tomorrow we'll start over. We're going to find that bloody journal. I can feel it in my bones."

"Oh, you feel things in your bones now, do you?" Sally dropped the key back into the desk drawer.

"I don't think we're going to find it." Abby hated to admit it. "I wanted to believe it was here, but we've looked everywhere."

Sally sighed. "It does seem unlikely."

The disappointment sank in as they replaced the ledger and documents. Sally clicked off the light and they hustled back to the living room, the bright garishness a comfort. Thomas threw a log on the fire, and Sally and Abby settled on the couch, the silence holding their deflated hope.

"On another subject." Sally tried to sound cheerful. "Abby

has been getting an awful lot of letters. I didn't think young people wrote letters anymore."

"Oh?" Thomas gave a final nudge to the logs, set the poker in its stand and eased into his chair.

Abby pulled a wool blanket from the back of the couch and laid it over her knees. "I've discovered the joy of old-fashioned handwriting."

"Who are you writing to?" Thomas probed.

"A *Josiah*." Sally raised her eyebrows. "Not snooping. I've just seen the name on the envelopes."

Thomas looked annoyed. "You never told us about a Josiah?"

"We broke up, just before I left."

"People who break up don't generally write letters to each other," he said with a grumble, shifting his buttocks in his seat.

Sally reached for the remote control. "Don't pester her, Thomas. She'll tell us when she's ready."

Abby smiled, remembering how giddy she'd felt receiving that first letter from Josiah. "There's nothing to tell."

"Alright then, whatever you say," Sally said, and clicked on the television.

CHAPTER 23

London, England, 1900

July 16

The morning William and I departed for London, the sky was a pale blue, the air soft and warm. As we drove away from Burford, I thought of sitting on the bench in the churchyard when we first arrived. How deliriously happy and in love I had been.

What blind ignorance. What naivety.

Other than severe headaches, I have recovered completely from Henry's birth. The doctor told me I was well enough to travel and that my head would be eased if I took my drops regularly. William tried to prevent my going. He said I should stay home with the baby, but Henry is better off with the nurse and Mother, who adores him. I told William if he tried to stop me, I would go on my own. That would be more difficult to explain, so he has let me come along. No need to let London society get a whiff of our marital discontent at this particular, glorious moment in his career.

Mercer Corner's first impression has sold exceedingly well and the *Quarterly Review* spoke so highly of it that the name William Aubrey is on the lips of every Londoner. William's vivacious energy is back, but with a nervous edge of deceit.

The fact that he does not know why I want to come to London, or what I am planning, gives me a certain power over him.

The weather was clear and pleasant when we arrived, the air

full of rich, ripe odors. It was my first time in the motorcar, and I was covered in a layer of dust. It would have been faster, and more convenient to take the train, but William likes the prestige of driving one of the few automobiles on the road. We slowed in the thickening of omnibuses and street vendors, and I took off my goggles and pulled my scarf away from my face. I had forgotten how much I missed the smells, the noise and commotion, vendors shouting from every corner, the carriages creeping along. I watched the Dutch biscuit seller pushing her barrow with arms thick as logs and wondered what it would be like to be a woman with that much physical strength. What one could do with those arms! Much more than pick up a useless pen, I imagine.

William let a place on Belgrave Square, and when we arrived, I went straight to the servants' quarters and made inquiries after Simon Gray and his daughter. None of the servants knew them, but they promised to ask around for me.

I waited a week, fulfilling my social obligations, making the appropriate round of visits, caring about none of it. The hardest thing was seeing my friend Gwyneth—bright, cheery Gwyn—arriving in a flurry of soft fabric, hugging me as if nothing had changed, her figure twice what it used to be. I listened as she babbled about her husband and three children and their villa at Fulham, just two miles west of Hyde Park. Mind you, she said, they could afford to live in fashionable Bloomsbury, but they preferred the suburb. "And how is your little one? Henry, isn't it? Babies are just delightful, aren't they? I simply want more and more of them. And Mr. Aubrey's book! What a thrill. I couldn't put it down. You must be so proud of him."

I smiled, feeling a headache coming on. I wished she'd go away. I didn't want to be reminded of a time when I was engaged to Peter Emsley, and Gwyneth to Alexander Farley, of all the plans we made, hers coming to fruition, mine ruined by impulse. Watching her chatter on, so sincere and content, I realized how different we'd become. Despite how happy she seemed, and how grand her life sounded, it was not a life I wanted. It was not a life I had *ever* wanted. Contentment was a close companion to apathy, I realized with a small smile that Gwyn took as encouragement to keep talking.

I stopped listening and instead paid attention to the darkness uncoiling inside me. How satisfying my anger suddenly felt, how empowering the pain. Blackness was not empty space; it was thick and full and motivating. Maybe this is what William had been getting at, where he'd been pushing me to. Only my lightest self could find darkness, and only my darkest self the light. And only in this could my writing be truly great.

By the time Gwyn left, my head felt as if it would split open. I had the housemaid bring a cooling wash of salt, vinegar and brandy to my room, took a dropperful of laudanum and fell into a heavy slumber.

I woke to someone pinching my arm. "Stop that," I cried, pulling my arm out of the housemaid's grasp.

"Sorry, my lady, but I got a note here from the livery boy and he says you'd be wantin' it straight away on account of the Miss Gray you was inquirin' after."

"Well, you don't exactly need to tear my arm out of its socket to give it to me." I snatched at the note.

The girl was scrawny, her eyes saucer wide. "But I was tryin' to wake yous for a good long while and you wouldn't budge. I was startin' to get a fright that you was dead."

"Clearly, I'm not dead." I scrambled out of bed. "Hush up now, and have the car readied for me."

She squeezed her hands. "My lady, you're not lookin' well, and it's almost the dinner hour. Won't Mr. Aubrey be wonderin' after ya?"

"Stop pestering me and do as I say. Hurry up now—I haven't much time if I am to go before William returns home."

"Won't you be needin' my assistance in dressin'?"

"No, I will do it myself," I said, throwing open the wardrobe.

"Yes, my lady." The housemaid nodded and ducked out the door.

Bleary-eyed from my drugged sleep, I mused over what to wear. I did not want to dress too grandly and yet wanted to show authority in my appearance. I chose a flounced, knife-plaited skirt of royal blue with a gathered bodice and lace-trimmed sleeves that took great pains to get into on my own. Pulling my hair into a severe fashion at the back of my neck, I pinned a hat squarely atop my head and pinched my cheeks, hoping my sickly appearance would not weaken my stance.

I was shaky climbing into the carriage and wished I had put some food in my stomach as we rolled along. We were headed to Brompton, the abode of workaday artists and theatrical people. Not a proper place to be seen, but no one would know me there.

The driver stopped at a street corner that was busy with foot traffic, and I told him to wait for me. The address I had been given belonged to a draper's shop. A bell chimed as I opened the door, but the plainly dressed woman who sat winding a spool of orange ribbon did not look up.

"Excuse me?" I said, but she took no notice of me.

I was about to repeat myself when an elderly gentleman stepped from the back, wiping his hands on his trousers.

"She can't hear ya, ma'am. She's deaf."

"My apologies."

"No need to be sorry. Happens all the time. What can I help you with?" He was eyeing the carriage parked outside. "I got a lot of lovely lace, and some new silks have just come in. Could I interest you in—"

"No, thank you," I said, stopping him. "I am not here for linens. I am looking for a Miss Marion Gray. I was given this address."

The man's smile dropped. "She lets a room upstairs."

He motioned to the deaf woman, who led me into a dark

hall and up a narrow flight of stairs to a closed door. She gave it a violent thump and then pressed her cheek flat against the wood. A thump came back and she pulled away and trudged back down the stairs, leaving me alone on the landing. I thought to knock again, but figured I would only get a thump back, so I turned the handle.

The room was grander than I expected above a draper's shop. It faced south, and warm light filtered through the high windows. The shutters were open, and the gossamer drapes rippled in the breeze like something alive. A gold, upholstered settee angled toward the fireplace next to a colorful brocade chair and a round table where someone had placed a fine hair comb.

It was not until I stepped all the way in that I saw a woman by the window. She was tall, with astoundingly white skin and fair hair that she wore loose and long. She had on a dress of muslin as soft and airy as the curtains. The beauty of it struck me, the shades of whites blending together, her yellow hair falling over her shoulders as she plucked dead leaves from a plant.

"It is early yet for my dinner, Mrs. Whittaker." She looked up, a handful of brown leaves clutched in her fist.

She did not appear as one easily startled and remained poised, her eyes flicking momentarily to the door, and then back at me before leaning out the window and tossing the leaves into the air.

"Here you are," she said, brushing her hands together. "Please, sit. Shall I have something brought up for us? Tea? Sherry? Mrs. Whittaker makes a lovely tea cake if you are hungry." A seductive breeze ruffled her dress. She was younger than I expected, and slender in figure. She would have appeared childlike if not for the bold, strong lines of her face.

"I am quite alright, thank you."

I held myself rigid by the door as she draped herself across the settee, kicking off her slippers—ivory silk, pointy-toed things I couldn't help noticing, wondering if Father had purchased them for her. No wonder he'd gone broke.

"Sit, please," she said, pulling her stocking feet under her. Propping an elbow on the armrest, she stuck a fist under her chin and stared at me unwaveringly. "You don't look as I imagined."

I forced myself into a chair and pressed my hands into my lap, her cool confidence disarming. "I don't know what you mean. How could you have been expecting me?"

"Oh, I wasn't. Not exactly." She smiled. "Things simply happen. You happening here does not surprise me."

"How do you know who I am?"

She let out a trickle of laughter. "My dear, you are so like your father I would have known you in a crowded street. But, sneaking into my room as you have, makes the similarity all the more obvious."

My face grew as hot as if she'd slapped it. "I did not sneak anywhere. I asked after you and was led here by the woman downstairs."

"Yes, of course," she said in a slight mocking tone.

I felt provoked by her smile, her beauty, her bold mention of my father. "If you don't mind, I would like to get directly to the business at hand."

"By all means." Now she was absolutely mocking me.

"I know all about your affair with my father." I expected some reaction, but she just looked at me, waiting for me to go on. "Your father, Mr. Gray, is in possession of the letters my father wrote to you, and he has been demanding money from us to keep them secret." Not the slightest show of emotion. Nothing. My jaw tightened. "It is a most distressing matter for our family, and I have come to you with the hope that you will find a way to retrieve those letters and destroy them."

Miss Gray swung her legs off the settee and leaned into her hands, looking at me without saying a word.

I tried my last tactic. "Father would have wanted those letters destroyed. If you loved him at all, you would do this for him."

"How naive you are," she said. Hate rose in my throat like

a bitter aftertaste. "Did you not notice my father's abominable appearance? Would a man dress like that if he were to have money? The man cares for nothing but the bottle. It is not my lowly father who has been demanding money from you, but I." She was unflappable. "As a matter of fact, my father doesn't approve of the whole scheme. He seems to think he can teach me something now. It's a little late, I told him. The fool refuses a new hat, but he will take the money for a drink." Miss Gray stood up with a bitter laugh. "I suppose we both have to pay for the sins of our fathers."

Blood pulsed in my ears, thrummed through my body like a current. I wanted to run from the room but her eyes held me frozen to my seat. Was everything a betrayal?

She crossed to the window, and I noticed a slight limp. "And yes, I loved your father. You can think me cruel, but it is simply a woman's survival. Gilbert, of all people, would have understood."

I hated her for saying that. Hated that she called him Gilbert. I could see now that she wore no corset and wondered if this was the woman Father had wanted Mother to be, the woman he had wanted me to be. Miss Gray began talking and I couldn't stop her. I couldn't tell her I had not come to hear her story. I was transfixed, rooted to my chair, her sole audience pinned down by my own stupidity and the seductive quality of her voice.

"I was an opera singer." She looked out the window, directing herself to the street. "I was set to open Meyerbeer's *Le Prophète*. During dress rehearsal, I tripped and fell off the edge of the stage, shattering my hip bone. There was no doctor in-house and one of the musicians ran into the street and asked a passerby to send for one. The gentleman went straight away and escorted the doctor to my quarters. That gentleman was your father. I asked him to stay while the doctor set my broken hip."

She began plucking leaves from her plant with methodic attention. "Your father asked if I had anyone to help me, and I told him that I did not. He would come to me here—" she gestured to the room, a brown leaf crumbling between her fingers "—bring me flowers and baked delicacies. He was very honorable. He told me he was just coming to help until I could walk again, but we both knew that wasn't true. I didn't think much of him at first, but I needed the help, so I let him come. Then I found myself waiting for him, watching out the window for his carriage. He had these wild ideas, your father, magnificent ideas. I loved those ideas." She fell silent. I could hear the street noise outside, and the sound of children laughing. "We lay together before I could even walk. It was wonderful. Have I shocked you? You look terribly pale."

I was shocked, sickened. It was unimaginable her speaking this way to me about my own father. I could not move. I couldn't speak.

"He was going to come to me for good." She gave me a fierce look. "After I broke my hip, the theater replaced me with Johanna Gatski. She was brilliant. Received magnificent reviews, and I never performed again. No one wants a limping opera singer. Your father knew my career was over. I told him I would not be taken advantage of and kept like a common mistress. If he wanted me, he had to leave his wife and move us somewhere respectable."

She paced in front of the windows. There was such elegance and grace to her movements that one hardly noticed the slight shifting of her hip. "If it makes you feel better, it was not an easy decision for him. In the end, he said he couldn't live without me. We were to go abroad when he returned from his trip to the country." She looked at me. "You know the rest. I never saw him again. Now you ask that I destroy his letters? The only memory I have of him? How terrifically horrible of you."

Shaking, I somehow managed to lift myself from the chair. "I was mistaken in coming."

"Oh, no, not at all. It's been lovely to meet you. Your father spoke very highly of you."

"Father would hate what you are doing."

"Yes, he would have. Despite his unfaithfulness, he was a good man. I am not that good. I have never even tried to be."

For one wretched moment, I imagined how it would feel to push her from the window.

I fled from the room, stumbling on the top step and catching myself on the rail as I groped my way out of the draper's shop to the waiting carriage. I told the driver to hurry. "I'm going to be sick," I said, and he cracked the whip and the horses charged into traffic.

Looking back, I saw Marion Gray at the window. She lifted a hand to the glass and gave a small wave. I jerked my head around and reached into my reticule. Finding my bottle of laudanum, I took a dropperful, letting the bitter relief slide down my throat and into the hate in my gut.

The carriage slowed in the crowded street and the noise of the city reached me as if in a dream. Sunlight exploded in little bursts in front of my eyes, and I felt as if I was sinking, melting into the muck below the carriage wheels. William had threatened to stop payment and tell Mother about the letters if I so much as entertained the idea of exposing him. Destroying those letters was my only hope for freedom. "My words are no longer my own," I whispered to the empty air. "My words are no longer my own!" I shouted out the window, laughing, wildly, at the few who turned their heads to stare as I rolled by.

I have lost my writing. I curse my father. I wonder if it is a sin to curse the dead. I do not care. I will curse the dead, and the living.

CHAPTER 24

A week after giving up the search for the journal, Abby was in one of the upstairs bedrooms with her Super 8 camera. She had decided to shoot each room starting with a wide angle that slowly narrowed in on a single item that felt symbolic of her time here. A time she felt was coming to an end, as much as she didn't want it to.

Sometimes the item was obvious to her, a painting of William Aubrey, the scrolls on Evelyn's desk, the binding of *The Tides* from the library or the floral armchair Sally sat in. At other times, she had to invent something meaningful, a vase with painted English roses, a map on a wall, a fountain pen in a drawer.

She looked around thinking a picture of Henry, or Nicholas, would do nicely. Better yet, Little Willy. She hadn't found a single picture of her dad in her searching. There were surprisingly few photographs in the house, and none to be found in this room. Abby sat down on the bare mattress of a wrought iron bed that looked like something out of *Mary Poppins*. This had been a child's room. She'd searched in here, but distractedly, not really looking at the things around her. Now, she took in the rocking horse and dollhouse pushed up against the wall, the shelves arrayed with stuffed animals and toys and books. On the top shelf by the window was a solid row of books, the title of one standing out in red lettering against a blue binding, *The Moonstone*. Reminded of the moonstone Evelyn had referred to in her letter, Abby took the book off the shelf and laid it on the windowsill to videotape.

Getting her shot, she set her camera aside and picked up the book. It was large, bound in blue linen with an intricate border of small stones on the cover. When she opened it, there was the blank flyleaf, the title page and then, nothing. She stared at the empty rectangle in the center of the book where someone had neatly and meticulously cut out the pages. Abby turned the book over, looked at the red-and-gold stamping on the spine, opened it again. The center cut clear through to the back binding, but whoever had done it had cleverly left the edges of the pages intact so that when the book was closed, you wouldn't notice the mutilation.

Placing her hand inside, Abby felt the pulse of the missing pages. The journal had been here. What else could have been set inside this hollow book?

Closing it, she slid the book back on the shelf, devastated at getting this close and having nothing. Going to the window, she looked out at the slate sky and remembered standing in Josiah's apartment the day she left filled with expectation. Even here, in her seemingly peaceful solitude, she'd been driven by the need for answers.

She felt homesick. She missed Josiah and her grandparents. She missed the hot, dry air of California and the smell of eucalyptus. If the journal couldn't be found, maybe her father couldn't be found either. Maybe the point was for her to accept this unknown, and to learn to move forward anyway.

The next morning, Abby woke early. The room under the gables at Abbington Hall was cold. She kicked her legs out from under the covers and pulled on the hand-knit, Irish sweater she'd bought at a wool shop in town. It was mid-November and

Burford was freezing. She used the heat in her room sparingly since Sally and Thomas wouldn't let her give them any money, which was a good thing because she had exactly three hundred and twenty-two dollars left in her checking account. By some miracle her credit cards were still working.

She didn't tell them about finding the cutout book—it would only disappoint them—but the night before, she'd looked up *The Moonstone* on Sally's computer and found out that it was published in 1868 by Wilkie Collins. It was considered the first English mystery novel ever written. Fitting, she'd thought.

In the kitchen, Sally had already placed a tea bag in the pot and a sliced English muffin on a plate. Abby struck a match and held it over a burner that clicked to the smell of gas before bursting into blue flames. There was no toaster, so she heated the muffin face down in a pan. The edges always burned.

When Abby entered the floral living room, Sally was crouched on the floor placing strips of newspaper under an unfinished chair. A can of wood varnish the color of tobacco was open next to her.

"You're not going into work today?" Abby stood in the doorway, coffee and muffin in hand, the smell of varnish toxic and uninviting even though the fire was lit and the room was warm.

"I took the day off," Sally said, not looking up.

"Did you have breakfast?"

Sally shook out a piece of newspaper. "Already ate. You go ahead." She waved her hand, the paper crinkling. "Don't mind me. Sorry to stink up the room. It's too bloody cold to do this anywhere else." Her voice had an edge.

"Everything alright?" Abby asked.

"Yup." Sally stuck the newspaper under the leg of the chair. "Just need to get this done. Thing's been sitting around for months."

Abby set down her tea and muffin. "Sally, what's wrong?"

Sally sighed, dropping the newspaper to the floor. She gave

Abby a helpless look. "Nothing's wrong, dear. I actually have good news, which doesn't make sense given how cut up I am over it."

A worrisome feeling crept over Abby. "What do you mean?"

Sally smiled weakly. "I never had any company other than Thomas, and I never knew I wanted any until you arrived. Having another woman around, a young one like yourself, has made me sorry I never had children of my own." She flicked away a tear. "I'm being ridiculous, but Thomas will be crying when you leave us too."

"Am I leaving?" Abby said, even though leaving had been on her mind all week.

"You will be after you hear my news." Sally pulled her shoulders back. "I didn't say anything before because I didn't want you getting your hopes up, but there was a cousin on my mother's side, Grant Tanner, who was good friends with Nicholas. One Christmas, Grant out and asked why none of us had ever tried to find Nicholas. We were all so damn stubborn and loyal to Eliza, we didn't give him a straight answer, but Grant said it was a right shame we were blaming Nicholas for abandoning us after all he'd been through, losing his mother and then his wife so tragic and sudden. 'He's the one who's been abandoned,' he said. Went on to tell us it was no wonder Nicholas didn't want to come back to a family who held a grudge like that, and stormed out. Grant didn't have much to do with us after that, but I got to thinking, if anyone had tried to find Nicholas and Little Willy, it would have been Grant."

Abby's heart began to thrum in her chest.

Going to her desk, Sally plucked an envelope off a stack of mail. "I didn't even know if Grant was still alive. I couldn't find a telephone number for him, but I tracked down an address in Crosby. I wrote a letter the week you first arrived and had pretty much given up on hearing from him." Sally handed the envelope to Abby, who drew out a small piece of paper.

Dear Sally,

Excuse my penmanship. My eyesight is poor. I should have my wife write this, but I am a stubborn old man and like to pretend I still have all my faculties.

I did find Nicholas, years ago. We wrote a few letters, telling what we could of our lives. Then we stopped writing. I don't know why. Time and life getting in the way, I suppose. The last letter I received was eight years ago. I hadn't heard from him in a long time. I'm not sure why he thought of me again, but he sounded lonely, said he didn't think he was going to live much longer. Maybe that's why he wrote. We look to someone in our last days on earth. I can only assume he died. I wrote him back, but never heard from him again. I tried ringing the number he gave, but my calls never went through.

Nicholas's letters came from the USA, a town called Granville, in the state of New Hampshire. 23 Wicket Road. I had to have my wife read the postscript, because I've misplaced my address book, but I am pretty sure we have spelled it correctly.

Hope this helps.
Grant

Abby slid the letter back into the envelope. The panic she felt must have shown all over her face because Sally said, "It's frightening to come right up to the thing you've spent your life desiring. What if it doesn't solve all the problems you thought it would?" She took Abby's hand. "You can't stop what you've set in motion, love."

The lump in Abby's throat made it impossible to speak. She wrapped her arms around Sally, not letting herself cry, afraid of what might open up inside her if she did.

When they pulled away, Abby said, "Come with me."

Sally's face was bright red with emotion. "It's too late for all that."

She went back to her chair, dipped her brush into the open can of stain, letting it drip for a minute before painting it lightly over the leg of the chair.

"Nicolas might not be alive, but Little Willy would be about fifty years old," Abby said. "Don't you want to see him again?"

"Oh, Abby." Sally straightened, the brush dangling in her hand. "I was sixteen the last time I saw him, and he was only seven. Now, I'm old and he's old. What would be the use? We would have nothing to say to one another."

"There's a lifetime of things to say."

Sally shook her head and crouched down, returning her attention to the chair. "Speaking of things to say, have you called those grandparents of yours?"

"Not yet."

"You'll have to face them eventually. Dead family members are the only ones you get to avoid, and sometimes—" she raised her brows "—not even those."

"Ha," Abby laughed. "I'd say the dead ones are the most persistent."

"Well, they do have an advantage, what with their ability to stick around forever."

Impulsively, Abby said, "Thank you, Sally, for everything."

Sally's cheeks flushed. "Get on you," she waved her brush, splattering drops of stain onto the newspaper. "You'd better book a flight to New Hampshire before I start charging you rent."

Abby smiled. "I'm broke, so you'll have to kick me out."

"Being forced into a thing is sometimes best."

"But I can't force you to come?"

"Nope. I'm too stubborn and old."

Abby took her muffin and tea and sat at the computer. She would miss drinking beer over tasteless dinners with Sally and Thomas, miss watching ridiculous British comedies, the two of them snorting away with laughter, miss trying to uncover Evelyn Aubrey's mystery.

The computer keys clicked softly as she searched for flights. "Maybe I can convince Thomas to come with me," she said.

Sally kept her eyes on her work. "He'll be beside himself you're leaving. I think he fancied you would be here forever."

"I think I fancied that myself."

"You'll move on with your life." Sally's brush made a soft slapping sound over the wood. "This house has never moved on, never will. But you—" she nodded "—you're already on your way."

And with a click of a button, Abby purchased a one-way ticket from Manchester, England, to Manchester, New Hampshire.

CHAPTER 25

Burford, England, 1900

August 16

After my visit with Marion—and sleeping off the laudanum—I woke to a blue-sky morning and a feeling of revenge.

If I give up, they win—Marion, my father, William.

I will not give up. I will start something new. I will begin again.

Everything I loved about the city, I suddenly hated. The noise, the smells, the way everyone hurried about. I wanted to get back to the fields that begged no attention and the trees that did not ask me to speak to them. I wanted to go back to my room, to my writing desk, to a sense of self I recognized.

The morning William went to see an aeronautics exhibition at the Crystal Palace, I used the money left for household expenses and took a hackney to the train station, where I rode third-class in the railway carriage to Oxford. From there, I found a ride to Burford in a wagon with a kindly farmer.

Mother was shocked when we pulled up, but I explained that William was busy, and I did not want to bother him with money matters. She pressed Henry into my arms, and I diligently kissed his soft baby cheek before handing him back.

It is impossible not to admire the boy's tiny hands and feet, his little chin and button nose, but I don't feel attached to him as I think a mother should. When he is not in the room, I hardly think of him. What I think of is my writing, of my need to pick up my pen, which is far greater than my need to pick up my child.

At home, I practiced touching the dark place inside myself that I first recognized in London, mentally pressed it like one might test a bruise for its tenderness. From that place, I have begun a new novel, one that speaks to this wounded tenderness in all of us, because it is not a matter of whether we are bruised, but whether or not we take pleasure in the pain. We either let ourselves heal, or continue to beat ourselves black and blue.

Like William, I now see the usefulness in both.

August 20

Mother has bought me a bicycle for my twenty-first birthday. William did not even send a card. He wrote a single letter the day I departed asking why it was so abrupt and hoping there was nothing the matter with Henry. *"I trust you are all well?"* he wrote. *"And that you are feeling yourself?"* Which I took as questioning whether I'd spilled any dirty secrets, Father's or his. I responded saying we were in good health, and he should stay in London as long as it pleased him.

The house is almost pleasant without him. Especially now that I have my bicycle.

Mother was standing in the driveway with it when I went out for my morning walk. "Happy birthday, dearest." She beamed. I was speechless as she wheeled it over to me. "It's a Rudge-Whitworth. The salesman said it's the latest model."

It was gorgeous, with white tires and a black frame. "Mother, you shouldn't have." I stroked the soft leather seat and gave the bell attached to the handlebars a ring. "What made you think of it? You always said bicycles were unfeminine."

"Times are changing, dear," she said in a tone that implied *I* was the one behind on such matters, which made me smile. "Bicycles for ladies are getting more and more popular, and when

I saw it, well—" she touched the shiny frame "—I imagined it was something your father would have gotten you, and figured, why shouldn't I be the one to do it now that he isn't here?"

It was the first time she'd ever purchased something like this on her own, without Father's approval or opinion, and the proud look on her face made me throw my arms around her. I hugged her hard. "Thank you, thank you, thank you."

She batted me away, laughing. "Don't thank me yet. If you break your neck, I'll be the one to blame."

"Don't you know how sporting I am?" I hiked up my skirt and swung my leg over the seat, keeping my feet planted on the ground.

"Don't go flying off this instant!" Mother held on to the handlebars. "I read about this condition called Bicycle Face in the *Literary Digest*—flushed skin, bulging eyes, clenched jaw. It can affect anyone, but women are especially prone. They say it's due to the upright position and the effort to maintain balance, so don't overexert yourself."

"I'll be sure to take it easy," I said, and she let go as I pushed off with one foot, propping my boots on the pedals as the bike wobbled over the gravel. I looked a sight, and Mother and I laughed so hard it was a miracle I didn't fall flat on my face.

It took a few days to get the hang of it, but once I figured out how to balance, and tie up my skirt so it wouldn't get caught in the spokes, it was the most exhilarating thing I'd ever done. The speed flying down hills makes my stomach drop. The sensation of pedaling fast, the heat rising in my face, my heart pounding furiously, is intoxicating. My mind goes completely blank. I can think of nothing but holding on to the trembling handlebars and keeping the wheels straight.

I return exhausted, and yet with a zeal. My appetite has never been so good, and for the first time since Henry was born, I am able to sleep at night without my drops.

September 6

The most unfathomable thing happened today. I had intended to go out for a bicycle ride, but the clouds had rolled in and a thunderstorm threatened on the horizon, forcing me to stay in.

I was seated with Mother in the drawing room when the carriage pulled up. Going to the window, I saw a veiled woman in a crisp white coat step out. "Who on earth is this? Have you invited someone, Mother?" I asked, watching the woman instruct the footman who was unloading her trunks from the boot.

"No." Mother joined me at the window. Swift, dark clouds rolled overhead and fat raindrops began to fall. The woman hurried toward the house, shielding the rain with a hand on the brim of her hat. It was in one brief second when she looked up that I saw her face through the mesh.

Marion Gray's arrival was like witnessing something precious and fragile slipping through your fingers and shattering to the floor. There's that moment when you think you can stop it, and then realize, tragically, that it's already out of your control.

She must have pushed past Bennett because she stepped into the drawing room unannounced and rushed at me with open arms. "Evy, dear, how good of you to invite me." I recoiled, practically shoving her off me and stepping back so abruptly I tripped over the hem of the curtain.

Pretending not to notice, Marion unpinned her hat and pulled it from her head. She looked different than she had in London, rigidly corseted in a bone-colored traveling dress, her hair done up in soft swoops around her face. "This weather came out of nowhere. It was sunny and then boom! Streaks of lightning across the sky. What a relief to have arrived safely." She looked me up and down, holding her hat under one arm as she unhooked her suede gloves from her fingers. "You look ever so much better than the last time I saw you. And this must be your dear mother." In one swooping motion she'd crossed the room and wrapped her arms around Mother, who stiffened visibly. "Evy has told me so much about you I feel as if we are already friends. Haven't you, Evy?"

She pulled away, leaving poor Mother stunned. No one hugs my mother, and no one calls me *Evy*. "I am afraid Evelyn has forgotten to mention you," Mother said, her face tight with suspicion.

Panic set in. The flow of deceit had taken a course I couldn't stop. Mother was staring at me as if she could sense something unbearable coming. Left with no other choice, I stepped to Miss Gray's side and forced a ridiculous smile. "How foolish of me. Mother, this is Marion Gray." The name soured on my tongue. "I ran into her in London and completely forgot I'd invited her."

Marion threw an arm over my shoulder, and it was all I could do not to shove her away again. "It is not surprising Evy never mentioned me. We met in Bath three summers ago." She put a humble hand on her chest. "I am an opera singer, you see, not of your society, and Evy thought you would disapprove of our friendship. We haven't seen each other for quite some time, but, as luck would have it, we ran into each other in the tearoom at the Langham, of all places. Evy said it was so lonely out here, and that you rarely receive visitors, and as I could use some time away from the city, I thought this would be the perfect place to holiday."

The dread of this unfolded over me.

"I see." Mother relaxed a little. "Evelyn, how silly to think I would disapprove. I'm sure Miss Gray is suitable company, and how good of you to come all this way in such weather. I am afraid, since the death of my husband, we haven't sent a single invite. I haven't been up for it, but I do miss London. You can tell us all about the theater. Mr. Wilkins and I attended regularly. We were fans of the opera."

It took everything I had not to lunge at Miss Gray as she said, soberly, "My condolences for your loss. I have recently lost someone I loved dearly as well."

"Have you?" Mother said. "I am so sorry."

I didn't move, afraid I might hurl something at Miss Gray if I so much as lifted an arm.

A cooing sound came from Henry's bassinet that turned quickly into a cry. Mother picked him up, smoothing a hand over his bald head and shushing him against her shoulder. "You must be tired from traveling," she said. "I will bring this little one to the nursery and have a room readied for you."

"I am much obliged." Miss Gray brushed at the front of her dress and smiled deeply.

Mother moved toward the door, Henry quieting in her arms. "You can have a rest before changing into your dinner attire. I will let you girls catch up. Lovely to meet you, Miss Gray."

Silence followed her departure. Marion flung herself onto the sofa with a sigh, tugging at her corset.

I stood where I was, determined to meet her in battle.

"You're a stubborn one, aren't you?" Her voice took on a lazy tone. "Your father always presented you as such. I think he would have wanted us to be friends."

I shot forward, grabbed Marion's arm and yanked her into a sitting position. "You will never speak to me of my father again," I hissed. "It is one thing you have come into my home. It is quite another if you think you will have your way here."

It was clear I'd startled her, but also that she was not going to be pushed around. She yanked her arm back, looking amused by my display of emotion, but not attempting to make herself comfortable again.

"You are not welcome here, Miss Gray." I sat across from her, steadying myself. "You are no friend of mine, despite your lies, and I advise you to be more discreet with your words. If my mother finds out who you are, all is lost to you. There will be no more money, and I will have you thrown out of this house swifter than you entered it. Henceforth, you will not so much as breathe my father's name to me, or to anyone else in this house. The servants have ears in places you could not imagine. I have not protected my mother this long to have her scarred by an ignorant woman who is unable to keep her mouth shut. Furthermore, my health is none of your concern, and if you are to remain here for the rest of the summer you will stay out of my personal affairs. Lastly, I have never been called *Evy* in my life and do not intend to be called so now. You will address me as Mrs. Aubrey, and respect that this is *my* home and you are an unwelcome guest in it."

There was a pause before Miss Gray clapped her hands and said, "Well done, my dear. You are absolutely right. It was careless of me to mention any past relations that could jeopardize our delicate situation. I will heed your good advice and not mention your father's name again." She pressed a hand to her bosom. "I guess I'm going to have to get used to this wretched corset." She gave a sharp laugh. "Are we not to become friends then? I thought maybe there was hope of that, but clearly you are much too loyal a daughter." She dropped her voice to a whisper. "I appreciate your directness, *Mrs. Aubrey*. It will make our situation much easier. I might as well tell you now that I have no intention of leaving at the end of the summer."

I felt the air leave my lungs.

"Don't look so dismayed," she went on. "I couldn't stand that dreadful draper's shop, what with a deaf woman endlessly banging around. Country life will suit me much better. It is wonderfully quiet here." She leaned back with a winning smile and stuck her legs out, crossing one ankle over the other like a man.

My control was slipping away. I would lose to this woman like I had lost to my husband. "Do you care about no one but yourself?"

She laughed. "Not anymore. Love is weakness. So is sorrow. Resilience is best."

"Resilience is not an emotion."

"The less emotional we get, the better for both of us."

"What makes you think I will agree to your staying on? And do you think it's even up to me? What about William? When he hears you are the one taking his money, do you think he will let you stay?"

She straightened, shifting to the edge of the sofa. "Trust me, your husband will not be a problem. With the success of his book, I think we can all agree this would be a very inconvenient time for scandal. It is evident your care for your mother will prevent you from selfishly ridding the place of me, which is very noble of you. She is clearly a fragile woman, and as you said yourself, the news would destroy her, and any honorable memories of your father the family hopes to hold on to. Who knows—" Marion stood up, her dress brushing my knees as she walked past my chair "—I might end up being good company for her." Opening the door to the hallway, she said, "I will be in my room resting until dinner."

"You don't know your way," I said.

"I will find it."

September 14

William returned this morning. The weather is fine and he is vibrant and soaring. It did not trouble him to find Marion Gray in his home, just as she predicted. Nothing can bring him down when he is like this. He said her arrival only means that he no longer has to dole out the monthly allowance to her father.

"It will be cheaper to provide for her under our own roof," William replied to my hushed protests. The three of us stood in the drawing room negotiating Miss Gray's terms as if this were all very civilized.

"Which means she's living with us permanently now?"

William glanced at Marion, who stood by the door, her arms crossed over her chest. "Is that your intention?"

She shrugged. "If it suits me."

William took my hand—an intimacy I hated in front of Marion. When I'd first seen him step out of the car, I was filled with desire, which demoralized me. How could I want anything to do with him, much less long for him? I pulled my hand away, reaching inside for the inky bruise of hate he'd hammered into me. "How dare she get to set her own conditions."

"I do have the advantage," she said, lightly.

"You said yourself she's been discreet," William said, his voice palliative, as if I could be reasoned with. "Your mother won't find out. Miss Gray is obviously not going to compromise her situation, and a companion might be good for you."

His stupidity was astounding. "I don't need a companion," I said.

Marion unhooked her arms and stepped toward me. "She's already refused my friendship. I tried, but she's too stubborn to let bygones be bygones."

"Bygones?" I looked from her to William.

"Evelyn has yet to learn how to make the best of a situation," William said, and my own stupidity hit me. They were cut from the same cloth, these two, courteously wrapping up their dealings in extortion, Marion needing William's security and money, William needing Marion to keep his hold over me. How perfect for them.

I stormed from the room, set on fighting both of them if I had to.

The scene that played out that night at dinner was like a stage show, the actors lit and animated. It was hot. No air came through the open windows. The moon had not yet risen and the sky was dark. Hundreds of frogs croaked down by the river. Mother, William and I sat with the steam from our soup bowls rising under our chins. Marion was late for dinner. William took a drink of wine. I pressed a hand to my perspiring forehead.

We all turned when Marion entered, which was exactly what she wanted. She wore a dress the color of sea kelp, the shimmering green stunning against her exposed white skin, the neckline plunging to the tops of her breasts, which were pushed up high in the corset she supposedly detested. Half her hair was twisted at the back of her head, the rest falling flame white down her back. As she made her way to the table, I noticed that it was not her features that made her attractive, but her movements, her arms gliding through the air, her fingers brushing absently across her cheek, her chin tilted up, her lashes lowered, every gesture a performance, polished and alluring. William couldn't take his eyes off her. None of us could.

"Forgive me," she said as she sank into her chair. "I lay down for a rest and didn't notice the time. How thoughtless of me."

"Don't think of it." William tipped his glass and took a long drink before picking up his spoon.

"You are too kind." Marion picked up hers, dipping it gingerly into her soup.

William stared so openly I was embarrassed for him. He became garrulous, excited. A spark lit by a new woman. He spoke about London, about the aeronautics exhibition, about the dinner parties and balls and operas he attended. Soup was cleared, roast pork was served and he kept talking, describing all sorts of unnecessary details. The new cars that pulled up to Madam Cleary's door, each dish that was served, what the woman on his right said about her sister's fiancé.

Marion swooned. She smiled, each bite of food slipping from her fork between slightly parted lips. She knew exactly what she was doing. She loved how nervous and lively she was making him. Even Mother's eyes showed a glint of excitement as she listened, dipping into the conversation to inquire after her friends.

I said nothing. My pea soup went cold. The smell of roast pork stung my nose. The wine tasted sour and sharp. Dishes came and went, silver clanked, liquid swirled. Laughter broke the air into little pieces. How could I not have seen this coming? Any sensible woman would have seen this coming.

Midway through the sugared strawberries and Madeira, I set down my tiny silver fork and reached a hand to my throat. The heat was suffocating. I wrapped my fingers lightly around my neck and struggled to take a deep breath.

With a violent motion I stood up, looking from the strawberry on the end of Marion's fork, to William's gesticulating hands and Mother's napkin dabbing at the corner of her lip. They looked back, startled. *I will tell Mother the truth*, I thought. *Right now, get it over with.* We could leave. Take Henry with us. Marion and William could stay here and rot in their lies. They were perfect for each other.

Mother lowered her napkin, concern deepening a line between her brows. My hands were balled at my sides, clutching the fabric of my dress. It wouldn't do any good. We had nowhere to go. Coniston House was sold and Mother had turned all her funds over to William. Even if she hadn't, I couldn't be the one to take Father's memory from her, to tell her her life had been a lie.

"Dear, whatever is the matter?" Mother asked. "Are you ill?"

My resolve slithered away. "It's the heat," I said. "I think... I need to lie down."

It was when I looked over at William that a new confidence surged in me. There was fear in his eyes, and I suddenly realized he was afraid of what I might say. It struck me that the knowledge of his lie, of his weakness, gave me a certain control over him.

He stood up and I thought he meant to show me to my room. Instead, he gestured to Bennett, who came around the table and took my elbow. I leaned against the butler, letting myself be supported and missing my father, no matter his sins.

At the bottom of the stairs, I told Bennett I'd left my book in the library. "You needn't accompany me. I'll retrieve it and see myself to my room," I said.

The overhead lights were on in the library, and the windows were wide open, the heat pressing in. I looked around, remembering William making love to me on the rug in broad daylight, of sitting with Father the night before he died, of falling to my knees in labor pains. I thought of all the writing I'd done at that desk and felt old at twenty-one, as if a lifetime had been lived in this single dreadful year.

How to keep writing? How to keep up what I started here? Around me were shelves upon shelves of books that I adored. What had Father meant by educating me like a man? It did no good unless I *was* a man. Learning to use my femininity to seduce men, like Marion, would have been more useful.

Unless, my thoughts raced, an educated woman had the wherewithal to outwit the man, write something clever enough to bring him down. I ran my finger along a shelf, walking slowly around the room gazing at row upon row of male authors. Maybe that's what Father meant. In a world controlled by men, a woman had no choice but to be smarter.

In my bedroom, I found my laudanum on the nightstand and took a dropperful. Out the window, an enormous moon was cresting the rooftops of the town, the first visible portion a rubescent slash in the sky. Pressing my hands to the windowsill, I leaned out and watched it rise, huge and red. A blood moon. I'd heard of such a thing from the Bible, but I'd never seen anything like it. It was said that the blood moon was the beginning of the end of time.

The sun shall be turned into darkness, and the moon into blood, before the great and terrible day of the Lord come.

I went to my vanity and took the moonstone from my jewelry box. It was no longer a cool, opalescent blue, but as warm and bloodred as the moon outside.

Putting out my light, I stripped off my gown and corset and pulled my chemise over my head, lying naked on the bed. Delicately, I placed the stone on my tongue, pressing it to the roof of my mouth, hard and round and warm as skin. The laudanum made everything soft and blurry, but I did not want to sleep. I wanted to pay very close attention.

Within seconds my mind went blank as paper, exactly as Lesley said. It was then I began to see. I saw my mother climb the stairs and tiptoe to my bedroom door, pressing a flat hand against the wood before moving away without knocking. Then William came down the hall, his blue eyes turning to the darkness behind him, Marion rising from it like the tide, her pale, tendril hands reaching for him, her green dress snapping, her whisper in his ear seductive as sea spray.

I saw my future unfold as plainly as if I had already lived it: William drawing away, curling his lies around him like a second layer of skin, taking Marion with him. I stumble upon them in the hallway and they pull away, pretend innocence. This is fun for them. They make a sport of it. Henry grows, clinging to his grandmother, knowing she is the one who will guide and protect him. Marion becomes Mother's loyal companion, sits with her during the day, attends mass and visits the almshouses, pretending to be a charitable, good woman. She slips into my shadow with the grace and ease with which she does everything, and I disappear, become a witness to my life instead of a participant in it.

For a time, my days weave together like identical beads on a string. I learn to write in solitude, to ride my bicycle with fury, to prefer the bitterness of coffee to tea weakened with milk and sugar. I take my dinner alone in my room, writing through every meal, my stories the only thing left to me. They become my sole escape. I learn not to mind that William will take them from me and make them his own.

In them, I will find my strength.

And he will find his ruin.

I cannot see my own death, but I now know what I must do to plot it.

Part Three

---·---

WATER

CHAPTER 26

Granville, New Hampshire, 2006

The first thing Abby saw as she approached the house at 23 Wicket Road was a shed so pink it reminded her of a teddy bear that you'd win at a fair, its fresh brilliance staging a rebellion against the dilapidated house.

Abby pulled to the side of the road and cut the engine of her car, working up her nerve as she sipped her lukewarm coffee. Her plane had landed at 1:00 a.m. From the airport, she'd rented a car, bought a map and drove for an hour before stopping at a motel off Route 293. This morning, she'd filled a to-go cup with weak coffee from the motel lobby and climbed into her rented Chevy Impala.

The exit for Granville had dropped her onto an endless winding road bordered by thick forest, the leafless trees and tangled conifers occasionally springing open to a field or a house before snapping shut again. At one point, Abby had had to pull over, check the map and make a U-turn before turning down a road that wove deeper into the valley.

And then there was the shed springing into view, the mailbox with number 23 painted on the side, and the house, small and run-down, the panes of the attic dormer windows broken, the roof missing shingles. It was a far cry from Abbington Hall, and yet it had the same neglected melancholy, as if the burdens of the owner were carried by the house itself.

It took a good five minutes before Abby found the courage to get out of the car and cross the street, buttoning her jean jacket over her wool sweater, which was proving a pathetic barrier against the frosty air. This morning, Josiah told her it was eighty degrees and sunny in the Bay area. She'd called him from the motel room, forgetting it was 5:00 a.m. in California. When she'd first heard his groggy morning voice, her chest had tightened with misgiving. There were a few uncomfortable moments of silence, each starting and stopping, trying again, cutting each other off laughing, until she managed to tell him she missed him. He said he missed her too. "It's good to hear your voice," he'd said.

Her heart pounded now as it had when speaking to Josiah, but for entirely different reasons. Walking past the Honda Civic parked in the gravel drive and up the porch steps, Abby had the urge to turn around and go back to the motel. This felt grittier and more real than walking up to Abbington Hall. This time, there was proof her grandfather had lived here, and when it came down to it, Abby was petrified: of rejection, of disappointment, of coming this close and still not finding her dad. She stood for an interminable amount of time looking at the cluttered porch—an old freezer, a broken fan, empty boxes and black garbage bags shoved up against the railing. Unquestionably, an old person lived here, a person trying to deconstruct a lifetime of possessions. She calculated that Nicholas Aubrey would be eighty-one, and Abby was so prepared for him that when she finally rang the bell and a young woman answered the door, she stared dumbly at her.

The woman looked to be in her late twenties. She was painfully thin, with pallid skin and inky black hair pulled into a tight ponytail. "Yes?" she said, her expression guarded through the mesh barrier of the screen door.

Abby tried for a smile. "I'm sorry to bother you, but I'm looking for a man named Nicholas Aubrey. Does he still live here?"

The woman folded her arms and didn't answer right away. "Nope," she finally said.

A heavy exhaustion washed over Abby. "Does William Aubrey live here?"

The woman squeezed her arms tighter. "What is this about?"

"I think he's my father," she said bluntly, not wanting to explain any of it to the circumspect stranger in front of her.

The woman stiffened. "You've got the wrong house," she said, and shut the door.

Abby went back to her car, her tires spinning on loose gravel as she pulled away. She cranked up the heat and drank the dregs of her coffee. Why had that woman lied to her? Aubrey was written on the god damn mailbox. She'd seen it on her way back to the car. It was a mistake to come, she thought, turning down one road and then another, every inch of the forest surrounding her looking exactly like the last. It didn't seem possible she could be related to anyone in a place this remote and incongruous with the city world most familiar to her.

Eventually, the road dropped her at a four-way intersection, the parallel street sporting a white church, a bar, a used bookstore and an antique shop. A little farther down the road, Abby saw a gas station with a bakery jutting off the low side of the building. She pulled into the parking lot and went inside, a blast of warm air hitting her. The woman behind the counter pushed her silver hair up off her forehead and said, "What can I get for you?"

Abby ordered a raisin-walnut muffin and an Earl Grey tea. Pulling her credit card from her wallet, she asked, "Do you by chance know if a Nicholas or William Aubrey live anywhere around here?"

"Randy!" the woman shouted, securing the top on the to-go cup. A heavy bearded man appeared in the doorway behind her. "Is the guy who does the furniture named Aubrey?"

"Yup. Bill Aubrey."

The woman put the muffin in a bag. "I don't know about a

Nicholas. But there's a Bill Aubrey off—what's that road where his sign is?"

"Temple Road."

"Temple Road." The woman nodded and handed over the bag. "It's a dead-end dirt road—you can't miss his sign."

In the car, Abby settled the tea in its holder and took out the photograph of her mom and dad she'd carried all these months. William Aubrey, Little Willy, was called Bill now. She tried to match the lush, green trees in the photo with the leafless ones out her window. Her mother had been here, in this tiny town in New Hampshire. Her father had been here. Was still here.

The sign, Furniture for Sale, faded and chipped, was painted on a block of wood nailed to two posts with an arrow pointing Abby down a rutted dirt road. It was the first house she saw, nestled in a grove of trees, with gray siding and a steeply pitched roof. There was a stone wall and a dirt path that led to a front door painted a deep red.

Too nervous to pull into the driveway, Abby eased the car to the side of the road and kept the engine running, hesitant after her encounter with the woman behind the screen door. What if Bill was as cold, and rude, and wanted as little to do with her? Before Abby could quiet her nervousness, the front door opened and an older, skinnier version of the man in the photo walked slowly out. He was medium height with broad shoulders hunched forward in a way that made him appear uncertain. He wore jeans, a heavy jacket and brown boots with a splatter of white paint over the toes. Seeing him in his environment, the slightly beat-up truck, the house on the edge of the woods, the sawdust clinging to his jacket, made him so real.

Climbing into his truck, he backed out of the driveway, and Abby eased her car onto the road and followed, not wanting to lose sight of him. They drove through the center of town, took a left and then another left before the truck turned into the parking lot of a small grocery store. Abby parked three cars down and watched Bill get out of his truck and go in, the glass doors opening and shutting behind him. After a minute, she got out of her car and followed, hooking a basket over her arm and pretending to inspect an apple as she watched her dad place three bananas into his basket. Spying on him had not been her intention, but she liked observing him without having to interact, absorbing the details, his hair, red and thin as dandelion floss, his sallow cheeks with a fresh growth of patchy, white whiskers sprouting from them, his wide brow and deeply lined forehead.

He moved down an aisle and Abby moved with him. There were only a few customers in the store and she felt painfully obvious, but Bill didn't seem to notice her. He took a box of saltines from the shelf and went to the dairy section, musing for a moment before deciding on a package of tiny yogurts. He ate saltines and yogurt, she thought, holding these insignificant facts close to her heart. She should say something, anything. Would he recognize himself in her? In her red hair and green eyes and freckles?

He put an orange juice in his basket and went to the checkout, greeting the cashier as if he knew her, a young girl with roots showing through her dyed blond hair. Abby moved behind Bill and heard the girl say, "You take care now, and tell Lillian I said hello."

"Will do, Clover."

Who was Lillian? A wife? Daughter? The woman who shut the door in her face?

Abby paid for her single apple and stood in the grocery store window watching her father get into his truck and drive away.

Instead of following him back to his house, she drove to her motel, a run-down place with rooms that opened right into the parking lot. The rug was threadbare, the bed hard and flat, the pillow thin. Everything stank of stale cigarettes and citrus cleaning products, but the heat was cranking and Abby felt a feeling close to joy as she peeled off her sweater and stood in front of the blowing hot air.

When she was warm, she put her sweater back on and lay down, thoroughly drained. Saying goodbye to Sally and Thomas just yesterday, talking to Josiah this morning, and now seeing her dad, made her feel stretched thin. England and Abbington Hall were already a world away. Rolling up in the blanket, Abby closed her eyes and pictured the view of Burford from Evelyn Aubrey's window, conjuring the breeze, the smell of the grass and the rustle of paper as she drifted slowly to sleep.

In her dream, she floated in a pool of dark water. Overhead, the sky was flat and bright with moonlight. She was naked, buoyed on her back, her breasts bobbing to the surface, her soft stomach and freckled legs visible in the light of the moon. At first it was peaceful, and then she felt the horrible sense that she was sinking. Her head slipped under, her eyes open, the water stinging her sockets, the moon a ball of blurred white light above the surface. There was a pressure in her chest that grew tighter and tighter, like a vise squeezing her lungs.

This is it, she thought. *I'm dying. I didn't survive, I didn't escape the curse.*

Panic set in and she tried to scream, but only water came out of her mouth.

CHAPTER 27

Burford, England, 1905

October 6

These past five years have dragged on. I've kept myself occupied writing, forcing some sort of unnatural contentment upon myself.

But today I found out that my mother is dying, and so my end begins.

When the doctor told me of the cancer inside my mother's stomach, I felt the ironic surge of promise. Here again the shadows play with me. Hope peeking behind death and sorrow.

The idea of losing Mother frightens me, as does the idea of losing myself. I thought there would be more time, that I would write more books, see my son grow into a man.

That cannot happen now.

I have plotted my revenge as carefully as I have plotted my novels, and I will not back down. I will see this through.

After the publication of *Mercer Corner*, William made it perfectly clear that I was to keep writing for him. If I did not, he threatened to cut me off financially, take away my son, reveal Marion's identity to my mother. I already knew I'd do it, but I strung him along as I wrote my second novel, revealing nothing of my intentions. Once, when he thought I might try and publish it under my own name, he told me he'd tell the publishing house *I'd* stolen it from *him*. A violent argument ensued, but in the end, I gave in to him.

In a way, I have William to thank for the books I have written. I wrote content much too scandalous to come from a woman's pen. I wouldn't have dared publish them under my own name, and no publisher would have touched them if I'd tried. Critics questioned the morality even with William's name on the covers, but that did not stop people from reading them. It made them all the more appealing.

In this, I have been free. Under my husband's name, I write what I please. I have learned to hone my power as men do, to manipulate my readers. It was seeing how easily they believed my false identity that first gave me the idea to use their gullibility against them. I am in full control of my fictional world, and in this space, I, like the moonstone, can make people see what I want them to.

Even William.

I felt almost sorry for him yesterday. I had broken from my routine and gone for a walk instead of my usual bicycle ride. The sun was high in the sky, ducking in and out of the clouds. I had stopped to rest on the stone wall that runs along the bottom of the hill when I saw William walking toward me. Over the years, his temper has become increasingly unpredictable. I can take his physical violence, the occasional bruised wrist or the brandy thrown in my face, but he is verbally cruel to the point of exhaustion. At times, the things he says makes me wonder if he is not actually capable of the murder for which I will frame him.

Landing on the rock beside me, his feet splayed out, he looked aged beyond his years. He has grown weary in his darkness. I have not let myself grow weary. I cannot afford to be tired.

The swallows called to each other as they settled into the treetops, a few stragglers dipping and diving before joining their mates, their last notes lingering. At first, William didn't say anything, just sat knocking the mud from his boot with a walking stick he'd carried through the field. He never rides horseback anymore and has grown lazy over the years. The short walk from the house, downhill, I may add, had taken his breath away.

After a few minutes, William looked into the sky and let out a long whistle. "Splendid day." A fresh flock of birds rose from the river and dipped in unison through the air.

This is what our conversations have come to, talks of the weather, or what's for dinner.

"Yes," I replied. "Splendid."

It was temperate, like William's mood, but would become severe as the winter set in, and I wondered, when I left, how my husband would survive without me. He and Marion remain cordial, but spend little time in each other's company. William spends most of his time in London. I have accompanied him to social events over the years, but the mendacity of our life takes so much energy to maintain that I prefer to stay behind.

William is obsessively attached to me. Not in any normal way a husband should. He hasn't taken me to his bed since Henry was born—Marion still satisfies that desire for him—but he believes I am the one who keeps him from going completely mad in his darkness. When he is in good spirits, I see nothing of him. He stays in the city and becomes wildly social and entertaining, but things always take a turn, and when they do, he returns to Abbington Hall. Berating the women here seems to improve his spirits. We have learned to keep our heads down. Mother and Marion stay out of his way, and for the most part, he leaves them alone.

I have not been so lucky.

Looking over at me, William smiled and drew something from the inside pocket of his coat. "A gift," he said, with pride.

It was a book, bound in yellow with a rose embossed under gold lettering: *Poems of Solitude*, by Evelyn Aubrey.

What was this? Penance? His attempt to make amends? Redeem himself after all these years by having one lousy book of poems printed in my name? How big of him, giving me credit for something I had actually written.

I opened it and read:

TO THE NIGHT,
Now whilst the night mantel rests upon me
Oh, come the words that hold me still in sleep,
and rest the demons that never cease to be.

I snapped the book shut. No grand gesture can ever undo what he has done to me.

"Where did you get these?" I demanded, instinctively touching the moonstone around my neck. I had it made into a necklace years ago and do not remove it even to sleep.

"From your desk." William kept knocking the stick against his boot even though all the mud was gone. "I had them printed for you."

"Yes, I see that." He'd stolen them just like he's stolen everything else. I looked toward the house. It was getting cold and I wanted to go in.

The sun hit the top of William's graying hair. He looked at me as I stood. There was something in his eyes that made me remember that brief time when he sincerely loved me, and in an instant, I leaned down and kissed him. It was foolish. It was what he wanted, a sign of forgiveness, but I couldn't help myself. His lips felt rough and cold, not at all as I remembered. When I pulled back, my cheeks were hot, and I wanted to laugh at my impulse. Instead, I dropped the book in his lap. "I've read them already," I said, and walked away.

October 20

I saw Lesley today. We meet once a month by the river, always on the twentieth, which was Lesley's idea, taken from the stories of the moonstone washing up on shore every twenty years, and by the coincidence that it was the twentieth of September when he came to see me.

A week after I held the moonstone in my mouth, Lesley threw a pebble at my window. It was early dawn and I was still in my nightclothes. Laughing down at him, I asked if he thought he was Romeo. He said no, I was much too old to be Juliet and he had no intention of playing a harp.

"My grandfather has forbidden me to come here," he called up, "so you'd best meet me by the river, which he hasn't forbidden, but only because he hasn't thought of it." He grinned, his gap tooth making him look younger than his ten years. He is just a child, I thought, rushing to get dressed.

He was waiting where we first met. When he saw me coming, he stood up and bowed to the rock as if it were a throne. I thanked him and sat down, not caring that my skirt fell into the dirt at my feet.

"How did you know which window was mine?" I asked.

"Lucky guess." He dropped to the ground, crossing his legs and looking out at the river. "Did you see the moon last night?"

"I did."

"I thought the world might end, like the Bible says, only it didn't."

"Here we are," I said.

Bugs skittered over the water, leaves swirled, a dragonfly landed on a leaf. I waited for him to ask about the moonstone, but he didn't. I wasn't sure why he had come, or why I had followed. After a long silence, Lesley stood up with an earnest expression on his honest face. "All I have is my grandfather. Who do you have?"

"I have a whole family. Husband, son, mother."

He picked up a stone and threw it clear across the water, hitting a tree on the opposite bank with a soft thud. "You seem lonely."

"I am."

"My grandfather says your house is like a bucket full of holes—the bad things stick and the good things seep out." He squatted down, sifting for stones in the dirt. "Maybe that's why you're lonely?"

I squeezed my fingers. "Your grandfather likes metaphors, doesn't he?"

Lesley rolled his eyes. "Most often, I can't make sense of them."

"Well, I appreciate them, but that's only because I'm a writer." It struck me that it was the first time I'd ever called myself a writer.

"What do you write?"

"Stories."

"Like *The Moonstone*?"

"Similar. Did you enjoy it?"

"Yes, ma'am." Lesley inspected a stone, dropped it and picked up another. "I'd like to hear your stories. Would you read them to me?" He smiled, all boyish charm. It was strange, how wise and innocent he was all at once.

"Your grandfather said I was to keep away from you."

Running his fingers over the stone's flat surface, Lesley stood up and skipped it across the water. "He didn't tell me to stay away from you, just from your house, so if you come to the river, and I happened by..."

"It's a bit of a stretch," I said.

"But worth it." He smiled.

I didn't know it then, but in the end he would become the one person who knew the truth.

Over the years, his visits have sustained me. We meet by the river no matter the weather. I often read aloud to him. Wilkie Collins is a favorite, but at times I have read portions of my own work. Lesley listens attentively, eating the tea cakes and scones and finger sandwiches I bring. Mrs. Bartlett, the cook, a snappish, unsmiling woman, sets a basket by the kitchen door each month without question. Once, she said she noticed the raspberry cakes were a favorite and did I want her to make more of those? I said she was very observant and that yes, those were a favorite.

The servants and I have a silent understanding. They know what goes on between my husband and Marion—they are the ones, after all, who change the sheets and open the bedroom curtains in the morning—and refuse to acknowledge her as anything but a mistress. They dismiss her orders, always saying they must check with the lady of the house, which infuriates Marion. It's a small pleasure, but one I enjoy.

When I first brought *Mercer Corner* to Lesley, after telling him a portion of the truth a boy might understand, he looked at William's name on the cover and said, "You wrote it?"

"I did."

"Why does your husband claim it?"

"Because it is easier than finding the strength to write it himself."

"Do you do it out of kindness?"

"No."

"Am I not to tell anyone?" he asked.

"You are not."

He looked thoughtful before saying, "I'll keep your secret if you like, but I can't outright lie. I've promised my grandfather I'd never lie." He pulled his shoulders in and whispered, "I don't necessarily tell the truth either. It's a matter of being sneaky."

"It all comes down to your choice of words."

"Precisely."

Lesley is no longer a boy, but a man of fifteen, lanky and youthful, with eyes so vivid and clear and kind they'll melt a young girl's heart one day.

It saddens me that I cannot tell him of my plans. If the police question him, I know Lesley would lie to protect me, despite his vow, and I will not make a liar of him. It is bad enough I have asked him to keep my secrets all these years.

December 18

Mother is still able to get out of bed and sit with me in the library, but for shorter and shorter stretches. Death reveals itself in her pallor and shrunken bones. I am a grown woman, a mother myself, and yet the idea of being parentless makes me feel adrift. I cannot help but think, *Who am I without my parents? Who have I ever been?* Father was not entirely lost to me while I had my mother. We spoke of him often, remembered him together. Without Mother, I will be truly alone with my memories. Already, they skitter away like wisps of smoke. I can only hope that one day this house, my son and husband, Marion, will become wisps of memories too.

I am worried for my boy. Mother has been his whole world. Already, there is a sadness that pinches his mouth and slows his movements. The other day I found him circling Mother's room, tracing the wallpaper with his fingers, his eyes on his feet.

"What are you doing?" I asked.

He stopped short. "Counting."

"Counting what?"

"The minutes I have left with Grandmother."

This broke my heart. From the bed, Mother said, "None of that, now. I have ever so much longer to scold you. Come here this instant and recite a Shakespeare sonnet to distract me from the intolerable pain in my side."

Henry went to her, wide-eyed and obliging, a small, relieved smile on his face to hear her old, sharp self. I watched them from the doorway, keeping to the perimeter, sticking to my role of mother as silent observer.

The next afternoon, I stole away to the library when Marion had gone to visit the new family in the cottage down the road. Mother was too sick to get out of bed and William had gone to

Oxford. I don't go into the library when Marion is home, but I knew she would not be back for hours and I had an urge to write at the desk where I first began. I have written furiously since Mother's diagnosis, adding to the pages I have secreted away all these years, hiding them in a box at the back of my wardrobe under my folded chemises even though William would not think to look anywhere but my writing desk for my work.

Engrossed, I was startled to hear the clearing of a small throat. Looking up, I saw Henry sitting in the overstuffed armchair by the fire. It swallowed him in its enormity, his little legs sticking straight out over the cushion. I was struck by how much he resembled his father, his blue eyes fiercely confident.

"What might I help you with, young man?" I asked.

"You are my mother," he said in a clear and deliberate voice, "and I do not know you at all."

It was a reasonable statement. One Lesley might make. I set my pen down. "That is not surprising, for I do not know myself."

"Why not?"

I reflected for a moment and a memory sprung into my mind. It was of a day in spring when Peter Emsley took me for a carriage ride to Gunter's for the first ices of the season. I remembered the sweet scent of cherry blossoms that hung all along Regent's Park's southwest end, and how Mr. Emsley ordered the barouche to stop so he could purchase a bundle of flowers from the flower girl. As she stood on her tiptoes to place them in his arms, the string came untied and the delicate blossoms spilled to the carriage floor. Peter had laughed and said, "Never mind, you were meant to walk on flowers anyway." Where had the years gone? I had once been so sure of who I was.

"I lost my words," I said finally.

Henry scooted to the edge of the chair. His small legs didn't even touch the ground. "Did it happen when I was born?"

"The very night."

He got up and came around the desk, standing so close I could smell the rose scent of his laundered clothes. "Is that why you do not like me?" His voice quavered, but he held himself strong and upright.

Any good mother would have drawn the lad to her, kissed his soft cheeks and smoothed his curly hair. I did none of these things.

I spoke to him truthfully, as he deserved. "I do not know."

Reaching up, Henry touched his small finger to the moonstone around my neck. "It's alright," he said. "I suppose it can't be helped." He dropped his hand. "I am not sure I like you either."

I felt a tingling of emotion toward him. "I suppose that is because I am not very likable, not anymore."

Henry studied me for a moment, and said, "Why do you always wear that necklace?"

"Because it reminds me of what is possible."

"Where did you get it?"

"From a good friend."

He cocked his head. "You and I might be friends, if we got to know each other."

"I'd like that," I said. "Where do we start?" I could not bear to tell him it was too late. There wasn't enough time.

"You could read to me." The similarity to Lesley was striking. How well they would get along, I thought. After I am gone, maybe Lesley will become to Henry what he has been to me.

"This drivel I am writing would bore you."

"Not that." Henry went to the bookshelf and, without hesitating, pulled *Mercer Corner* from it and handed it to me.

I glanced at the book and then back at my son. He couldn't possibly know, and yet climbing into the chair by the fire, he looked as if he was challenging me, daring me to refuse him this truth. I opened it to the first page and felt a ripple of leftover shock. Reading these words to Lesley by the river wasn't the same as reading them at this desk, in this very room where the extremity of William's deception was first revealed to me.

"You haven't read this yourself?" I asked.

"No. Grandmother said I was only to read Shakespeare until I was seven."

"She got that from my father, you know."

"My grandfather Gilbert?"

"Yes. He taught me as Grandmother has taught you. Shakespeare first and everything else to follow."

"Who taught *my* father to write?"

"He learned from other great writers."

"Is that why he's so good?"

"I suppose." I looked at the book on my desk. Would my son ever know the truth?

"Go ahead," Henry said. "I'm ready." He closed his eyes, and it was eerie how like William he looked, how similar the gesture.

Steadying my voice, I forced myself to read to him. I owed him at least that much.

CHAPTER 28

Granville, New Hampshire, 2006

Abby gasped for breath, choking in sobs as she peeled her eyes open. Her throat was tight and her sockets painfully dry. Untangling herself from the blanket, she lay panting on her back, sweat dripping down her sides. *It must be ninety degrees in here*, she thought, dragging herself up and turning down the heat, which was still blasting. She sank back onto the bed, the dream clinging to her, the air charged with sparks that made the hair on her arms stand up.

Outside, the sun was setting, casting a red glow around the motel curtains. Abby sat up, reorienting herself. Falling asleep in the middle of the day always made her feel as if the world had shifted out of place. It was just a dream, she told herself, getting up and going into the bathroom where she splashed cold water on her face, patted down her unruly curls and gathered them into a messy ponytail. Putting on her jacket, she grabbed her bag and left the dank motel room, telling herself it was ridiculous to be avoiding what she'd been after all along.

This time, she pulled into her father's driveway, walked up to his door, took a deep breath and knocked. Darkness settled around her, the trees a mass of shadows, the light from the house bright and startling as the door suddenly opened. Bill stood in front of her, his flannel shirt untucked over a pair of faded jeans. "Can I help you?" There was a note of surprise in his voice, and what sounded like embarrassment. "Do I know you?" He peered at her with guarded curiosity.

"You don't know me," Abby said.

"Oh." He sounded confused.

"We've never met." She reached into her jacket pocket, took out the photograph and handed it to him. "But I believe you've met my mother."

Bill took a step back, his face becoming very still as he angled the picture into the light. They stood for so long Abby's feet grew cold, and when he finally raised his eyes, there were tears in them.

This open show of emotion startled a lump into Abby's throat, and for a long moment they just looked at each other as silent tears fell down Bill's cheeks. He did not try and stop them, or wipe them away as they collected under his chin and dropped to his shirt.

Handing the picture back, Bill cleared his throat and said, "Come in. It's cold out."

Abby stepped over the threshold onto wide pine boards polished to a shine. Bill was in his socks and she asked if she should take her shoes off. Pulling a tissue from a box on the hall table, he blew his nose and said only if she liked. Leaving her sneakers by the door, Abby padded in her socks to the kitchen while Bill filled a kettle of water. She looked around at the open space, the kitchen and living room separated by a woodstove with a chimney that went straight out the ceiling, the dry crackling heat filling the house.

"Hot chocolate?" Bill asked.

"That sounds great," Abby said. "Can I help?"

"No." He was direct, but not rude. "Where are you coming from?"

"I live in Berkeley, but I was in England for a while." Abby watched him for signs of recognition, but his expression stayed fixed.

"Sit, if you like," he said.

Abby sat at the table, noticing how it narrowed at one end with faint yellow lines painted down the middle like a road fading into the horizon.

"This is unusual." She touched the pale line in front of her.

"A joke." Bill took a mug from the cabinet. "Like the road I should have taken, but didn't."

"You made this?" she asked.

"Yup."

There was so much to take in. The dark cabinets and butcher block countertop, the maple tree out the window with a trunk so large Abby imagined three people could stretch their arms around it. The chair she sat in was shaped like a swan, the bookshelf in the living room carved at the top like a tree. Bill was an artist, she realized, wishing she had brought her camera to capture this moment. She wished her grandparents could be here. To know this place where Eva had been all those years ago. Maybe not this house, but this town, this man.

The teakettle whistled and Bill ripped open a package of Swiss Miss, dumped it into the mug and poured the hot water over it. Setting it in front of Abby, he took a seat across from her. His chair was shaped like an eagle, the bird looking away over his shoulder.

Bill coughed into his hands. Abby stirred the undissolved pockets of cocoa powder around in her drink. "Where do we begin?" she asked, feeling suddenly embarrassed.

"We could start with your name," he said.

"Abigail."

Bill smiled a little, his green eyes wet around the edges. "That's pretty."

"It means *my father's joy*."

"Does it?" He shook his head. "Just like Eva to go and do a thing like that. She never did make any sense, but I hardly knew her. I thought I did, but only with age do I see how little

I knew." He went quiet, his eyes in his lap, his thin hair exposing patches of scalp.

"She died," Abby said, and saw what she thought was a flicker
of pain cross Bill's face.

"When?"

"Seventeen years ago."

He nodded, slowly, taking this in. "How?"

"During the San Francisco earthquake of '89. Her car went
off a cliff into the ocean."

"She drowned," he said, not as a question, but a confirmation. How much did he know about his past? Abby wondered.

Bill glanced out the window, the overhead light reflecting in
the glass. "I'm sorry," he said. "Must have been hard. Did she
tell you about me?"

"Not even a name."

He let out a long, loud breath. It hurt to think of all Eva had
deprived them of, and for what?

"Who raised you?" Bill asked.

"My grandparents."

"Decent folk?"

"Very."

"That's good."

A log fell in the fire, and they could hear the hiss of burning wood.

"You look nothing like her," Bill said.

"I never have." Abby laughed a little. "I look like you."

He raised an eyebrow. "A much better version of me."

She expected him to tell her about her mother then, how they
met, what Eva was doing here, but he said, softly, "I'm so sorry,
Abby, but I am dying too."

At first, Abby wondered if he meant metaphorically, like *We're
all dying*, but the agonizing way he was looking at her left little
room for misinterpretation.

"I'm sorry," he said again, and there was a lurch in Abby's

chest, a clamping down on her lungs like in her dream. She stood up, panicked, looking around the room as the air pressed in on her. She went to the sink, gripping the cold metal and trying to catch her breath.

She heard the scrape of Bill's chair and felt him standing behind her. "Lousy timing," he said.

She turned around with a laugh that came out as a sob. "On my part or yours?"

Bill shrugged. "Both." Then he asked, "Can I give you a hug?"

Abby was fully crying now. She nodded, unable to speak, and Bill put his arms around her, his hug clumsy, his chest lumpy and hard as a sandbag. She held on, her hands clasped around the body of this stranger she didn't want to let go of. He felt brittle, thin, and she realized just how little there was of him hidden under his large frame. They pulled away and Abby wiped her cheek on her sleeve. Bill looked as helpless as she felt, his hands at his sides, his face full of concern.

Abby sat back down at the table and wrapped her hands around her mug, trying to pull herself together. "How?" she asked, unable to say *Are you dying?*

"Cancer. Pleural mesothelioma."

The word *cancer* was so real. Tears sprang to her eyes again. "What does that mean?" She forced herself to take a sip of hot chocolate, the liquid sweet and watery.

Bill eased himself into his chair. "It's a cancer in the lining of my lungs. I never smoked. Maybe I should have. Might have enjoyed it. It's from asbestos. It can live in the body for over forty years before it shows up. So, really, I've been dying since I was in my twenties. I just didn't know it." He turned his palms up and shrugged. "Probably a job I never even got paid for."

Abby felt unanchored, as if the smallest breeze would knock her off her feet. Her heart beat quickly and her throat constricted as if the water in her dream was drowning her in the kitchen.

Bill was saying, "The doctor said surgery might give me a year." A year? A single year? "Chemo would only slow it down at this point. I'm not going to get the surgery, or do chemo. I might have six months, if I'm lucky."

There was a fast fluttering in Abby's chest as if her heart was trying to find a place to settle. She had done the impossible, only to have this other impossible thing happen. She'd waited all this time to know him, this broad-chested man with his green eyes and soft voice and patchy, white beard. They had so little time now.

Bill coughed, a hacking sound that made Abby's whole body hurt. She got up and poured him a glass of water. He took a slow sip and the fit eased off. His face had gone very pale.

"You should lie down," she said, and he nodded and let her put an arm under his.

"I'm not too weak to climb the stairs yet," he said, but leaned on her as they went up them anyway.

The shades were drawn in the bedroom and there was a sterile, pungent smell in the air. Prescription bottles littered the bureau and an oxygen machine was set up by the bed. Bill let go of Abby's arm and sat down on the mattress, propping his back against a pillow.

"How did you find me?" he asked.

"It's a long story," Abby said.

"Is that why you were in England?"

"Yes."

"I remember almost nothing of my childhood, but just now, I remembered this painting of some relative that used to hang in the house where I was born, and by God if you don't look like the woman in it." He wiped his hand over his lips. "There was a story my cousins told of her murder. Said the body was hidden somewhere in the house, that her ghost haunted the place. Terrified me. I'd stare up at the painting of her for so long my feet would go numb."

"I've seen the painting," Abby said. "I've stood in front of it."

Bill pushed himself up with one arm. "You have?"

"I've been to Abbington Hall."

"Where?"

For a moment, Abby didn't understand the question. "To Abbington Hall. You don't know the name of your childhood home?"

"I do not." Bill sank back. "I don't even know the name of the town where I was born. My father never told me."

"Burford," Abby said.

Bill shook his head. "It's a shame I'll never get to go back there. I would have liked that. I remember fragments of my mother, but there's no place attached to her. Tell me what it is like."

Sitting on the bed, Abby described Burford to him, her first impression the morning she stepped off the bus, Abbington Hall rising from the hilltop, foreboding and beautiful. She described the hallways and paintings and rooms, the antique furniture and the things she'd dug from ancient trunks. She didn't tell him about the letter or her obsession with unearthing the truth of Evelyn's story. Instead, she told him about Sally and Thomas, and the things she'd learned about his father and mother. Bill listened, nodding and smiling, his eyes closing. Eventually, his breath deepened and Abby realized he'd fallen asleep.

In that quiet room, the walls white and pictureless, Abby looked around trying to absorb who her father was. The headboard of Bill's bed was carved like a mountain peak, or the curve of a woman's hip; it could be either, depending on how you looked at it. His dresser was built to fit perfectly under the pitched eave, the handles carved into different-shaped animals— a bird, a mouse, a chipmunk and a lizard. Each creature replicated with care. It reminded her of being behind her camera, focusing on a simple object and giving it meaning.

Getting up, she went to the window and opened the shade.

Looking down into the dark, wooded yard, she tried to imagine what her life would have been like if she had grown up here, if her mother had stayed, if Bill had been her father when she needed one.

When he stirred, she went to him and lightly touched his shoulder. "Bill?" His lids fluttered and opened. "I should go," she said, but he grabbed her arm, his hand strong and calloused. Not long ago, he'd been working hard at something.

"Don't go yet. I want to get to know you," he said.

Her heart ached at these words. How much time did they have to get to know each other now?

"You should sleep," she said, and he shook his head *no*, holding his lids open like a defiant child. "There's a notebook." He motioned toward a closet door. "In there, on the shelf."

In the closet were his paint-splattered boots, a pair of slippers, a few shirts hanging next to a row of empty wooden hangers. On the top shelf, in between a cardboard box and a stack of folded sweaters, she found a Mead composition notebook.

"This?" She turned with it in her hand.

"I wrote it for my daughter Lillian." Bill's eyes closed. "But I think…" He paused, his breath shallow. Abby thought he'd dropped off to sleep again, but then he said, "Read it."

"What is it?"

"It's the story of your mother and me."

"You want me to take it?"

"Only if you come back," he said.

CHAPTER 29

Burford, England, 1906

September 6

The early morning light has begun to ease its way through the cracks between the heavy drapes as I write. It is very quiet.

Mother died at three this morning. She held on for almost a year after her diagnosis. Somehow, summer passed and autumn is upon us again. The vicar and doctor were with us, but left shortly after her passing, reassuring me that they would be back with the first light of day to lay her out in the parlor. I have spent the last month in a haze, writing and caring for Mother, sleeping little, eating only to sustain myself, imagining Mother's last breath and the last page of my book would be one and the same.

I am nearly there.

The end frightens me. I feel as if I am cursing myself with my own words, but I cannot stop what I have started. I strove for light, but the darkness triumphs, and the water closes over my head.

Henry was with Mother when she died, holding her hand, her sour breath still lingering in the air. He has been so strong for a child of six, watching his grandmother fade and weaken, her cheeks sinking, her eyes huge and startled. He has spent the last week pressing warm dock root poultices to her shrunken abdomen, a remedy the doctor said wouldn't do a lick of good, but Mrs. Bartlett insists eases pain. Sometimes, I'd catch him crying, his small wet cheek pressed to Mother's, or else he'd be asleep, slumped over on the bed from his chair, his grandmother finding what strength she could to stroke his hair, murmuring to him as if he were an infant.

She has been his mother and he will mourn her as such. He will not even notice when I am gone.

I am sorry for the way things turned out between Mother and me. Keeping Father's secret drew me away from her, numbed my affection. I protected her more than I loved her, but at least I gave her peace of mind at her death. She thinks Father is waiting for her, that his love is pure and unadulterated, and in this, her death comes as a relief. All this time, I managed to keep Father's sin from her without lying. It was a simple withholding of truth, an arrangement of words, as Lesley would say.

Now, I am creating the lie of a lifetime. A lie that will carry through the decades, possibly centuries. William wanted fame, and so he shall have it. It will follow him to his grave.

It will follow me to mine.

I will leave as soon as my book is complete and Mother's body has been laid beside Father's. I will not take a single belonging. Dead people do not take their possessions with them. I will write a letter to Marion telling her how violent William has grown and that I am afraid for my life. My hope is she will take the letter to the police fearing for her own life and thus help build suspicion against him. I have watched her carefully over the years, learned from her deceptive ways. She is a master pretender, cunning in her ability to get what she wants, and ruthless in the face of almost anything except William. His erratic behavior unnerves her. When William is at his worst, she keeps to her room. Locks her door. She's not privy to the coldhearted things he says to me, or his imploring, groveling weeping. She does not see how he uses me.

What I did not foresee is the newfound tenderness I feel toward my son. Caring for Mother with him, being side by side in this intimate task, has endeared me to him in a way I had not anticipated. Henry will pay for what I am about to do. This cannot be helped, and yet, I worry I'm setting him up for a life of misery. If it is in my power to tell him the truth, I must. Not now—he is too young to be trusted with such a secret—but someday, when he is a grown man.

Which means, as risky as it is, I must find a way to leave him my journal.

September 16

My book is finished.

This morning, I took the brass paperweight to my wrist, gave it a good smashing, put on my black blouse and skirt, long gloves and jacket, and went to church. I have not been to church since Mother's death and I made sure to arrive a few minutes late, squeezing into the front pew next to Elizabeth Amesbury, a woman always ready to spread a rumor. She smiled at me, patted my arm and whispered how sorry she was to hear of my mother's passing. My wrist throbbed. After the service, Elizabeth asked how Henry and William were getting on, and I said as well as could be expected, considering the recent loss. Thanking her for her concern, I pulled off my gloves and fanned my face with them, saying how dreadfully hot the furnace was this morning. Her eyes went to my wrist, swollen to the size of a lemon, a ghastly bruise blooming up my hand.

"Gracious, Evelyn, what on earth have you done?"

"Oh, nothing." I feigned embarrassment, pulled my glove back on, mumbled my apologies and hurried from the church.

Crossing the River Windrush, I touched my sore wrist with pleasure, wondering if even Marion would go to such lengths. I will keep my gloves on at dinner so William does not see what I have done. But I will be sure to bear my wrist in the library tomorrow when I go to ask Marion about a certain book I'm missing.

September 17

Today, I bound the pages of my novel in twine, sealed it up with brown paper and brought it to William's study. He still works in there, or so he says. What he produces I have no idea. When I entered the room, he was at the bookshelf thumbing through a copy of Sir Walter Scott's *'Tis Sixty Years Since*.

I set the package on his desk. "It's finished."

"So quickly?" He shut his book and slid it back on the shelf.

"Yes." Poor man has no idea how long I've been working on these hidden pages.

"You haven't let me read a single word." He walked over and thumped his knuckles on the sealed book.

"That was our agreement."

"Yes," he said, so complacent, so trusting.

I have played my part well.

Picking up his pen, he addressed the package to Chapman & Hall. His waistcoat was pulled tight around his paunch, and he smelled of the pomade he uses to keep back his thinning hair. I pictured him as he had been our first night at the Yately Inn, all lean muscle and bushy curls. I missed him, not the youthfulness of his body, but the life that has gone out of him. There was so much possibility, and so much lost. The lie he lives dampens even his better moods, and there is always a disoriented look about him, as if he has no idea how he arrived at this place of self-deception and folly.

I would like to hate him, but I do not, despite what I am about to do to him. I feel only pity.

September 20

I paced the whole morning. Chapman & Hall have only had the manuscript for a few days, but I'd begun to panic. What if they don't like it? What if they want to discuss this or that chapter with William, as they did with the last book? What if they send it back for changes and William insists on reading it?

I changed my clothes three times, my wool skirt too hot, my muslin too cold. Settling on heavy, striped silk that made me feel weighted to the ground, I put on a hat and went for a walk. When I got back there was a note on the hall table:

They love it. Sticking to The Tides *for a title. It's set to be published on the twenty-first of October. Gone to Newmarket Heath for the horse race.*

W

I laughed out loud, standing in the hallway, the door open behind me. I had done it. *The Tides.* The twenty-first. How perfect. I wish I could tell Lesley. How delighted he would be.

"Well, well," I heard, looking up as Marion came toward me, stunning as ever in a pink silk tea gown that trailed to the floor. I was surprised to see her. She has made herself scarce since Mother's death, uncertain if her bribery fails now. "Another book. How does he do it?"

She had obviously seen the note before I did. "Sheer genius, I suppose," I said, sarcastically.

"Genius or madness." She took a step closer, dropping her voice. "There's something I've been wanting to ask you."

"Oh?" Nervousness tingled my spine. The last thing I needed now was Marion poking around in my business.

She looked at me for a long hard moment, the lace sleeves of her dress fluttering in the breeze from the open door. "No. Never mind," she said, her manipulation as vexing as ever.

"Ask it already, Marion," I said.

She squinted her eyes as if trying to put me into focus. "It's just that it's always seemed odd to me how happy William's publications make you. You should see your face! It's lit up with pleasure. I'd be bitter with resentment if I'd spent as many years as you have writing and never being recognized. I wonder how you stand it?"

"Didn't you hear?" I smiled, my voice mockingly sweet. "I published a book of poetry."

"Did you, now? Well, that's brilliant. Congratulations." She moved close enough for me to see the bitterness in her eyes.

"But, it's ever so kind of you to be concerned," I said, moving past her up the stairs to my room, where Irina had drawn me a scalding bath.

Putting Marion out of my mind, I stepped into the claw-foot tub, my calves tingling from the heat, my pale skin reddening as I eased into the water and lay my head against the slick, porcelain rim. I looked at my breasts bobbing to the surface, my soft stomach and freckled legs. My body in water exactly as I had written it. I slid my head under, keeping my eyes open, my vision blurred as in a dream, the water stinging my sockets.

CHAPTER 30

Granville, New Hampshire, 2006

Abby sat in a diner eating a grilled cheese sandwich and fries with the notebook lying on the table in front of her. She hadn't opened it. She wanted to. Eva was in that notebook, a young Eva. The Eva who might finally explain herself, but this confession, or whatever it was, wasn't meant for her. She felt no loyalty to Bill's other daughter, and yet something compelled her not to betray Lillian by being the first to read it.

Twirling a single fry around on her plate in a pool of ketchup, Abby pictured the thin, guarded woman who opened the door to her earlier. It felt strange to be all alone and have no one to share the news of finding her dad. On one hand, she wanted to celebrate, on the other, mourn. Life had given her this man, only to take him away. She wanted to call Josiah, but putting all of this into words felt impossible. She should be sharing the news with Grandma Maggie, only it didn't feel right to do that over the telephone. So much had happened since Abby left, she wouldn't know where to begin. It was Sally and Thomas who would understand, but they were definitely asleep by now with the time difference in England.

Not ready for her impossibly lonely motel room, Abby paid her bill and drove a few blocks to the local bar, a single-story, run-down building with a Bud Light sign shining in the win-

dow. A proper drink felt like a good idea, a wallowing, cele-
bratory drink. Was there such a thing?

Inside, the bar was noisy and smelled of beer and cafeteria
food. A function was going on and people gathered around tables with paper plates and plastic cups. At the bar, a thin woman
with a butterfly tattoo on her upper arm was wiping the counter
with a dirty rag. Abby tried to order, but the woman ignored
her, looking busy and pissed off.

"She's impossible when she's in a bad mood," the man next
to her said, setting his empty glass on the bar.

Abby said, "Is she in a bad mood?"

"Wouldn't you be?" He nodded at the group of twentysome-
things gathered around a buffet table drinking pitchers of beer
and eating little sausages wrapped in dough, their pink ends
sticking out.

"What's the occasion?" Abby asked.

"Going away party for Sandy Tilson. Moving to LA to model,
or be a movie star, or some other bullshit." He grinned. "I hope
you're not a model or a movie star."

"Not even close."

He stuck out his hand. "Sam." He wore a brown leather
jacket unbuttoned over a T-shirt and jeans, his shirt so spank-
ing white Abby imagined he had drawers full of them still in
their plastic wrapping.

"Abby." She shook his hand.

"You from around here, Abby?"

"No. California."

"What are you doing in New Hampshire?"

"Visiting family."

The bartender tossed her rag into a sink and came over, picking up the empty glass. "Another one, Sam?"

"I'll have a shot of whiskey." He looked at Abby. "Join me?"

"Why not."

The bartender filled two short glasses and told Sam to settle up with her later. He clinked his glass to Abby's and shot his drink back. Abby did the same, the whiskey hot in her throat. She had the sudden urge for a cigarette as Sam took a pack from his pocket and tapped it against his palm. She hadn't had a smoke since she was sixteen, but this guy was like a walking ad campaign for cigarettes: white T-shirt, buffed arms, endearing grin.

She leaned onto the bar. "Got an extra one?" she said, knowing exactly what she was doing.

He slid one out, flipped it up and placed it between her lips. A U2 song played, Bono moaning, *"My hands are tied, my body bruised."* Adrenaline, or alcohol, or both, ran through Abby. Finding her dad and simultaneously learning that he was dying had upended her, thrown her off the cliff right when she was finding her footing. It brought back all her ghosts. Now, she just wanted to lose herself.

"You can't smoke in here." Sam raised two fingers to the bartender, who refilled their shots. Abby hadn't had hard alcohol in months and the second shot made her feel instantly drunk. She followed Sam toward the back door, the room blurring, the people like objects behind frosted glass. Outside, the cold sucked them in like a vacuum. Abby pulled her jacket closed, remembering climbing the stairs to Josiah's apartment in this jacket, how cold she'd been from the San Francisco fog, how much she'd regretted breaking up with him. What the hell was she doing?

Sam stepped up to her, so close she could see the tiny lines around his eyes and the slight chip in his front tooth. He was frustratingly good-looking. "You smoke?" he asked suspiciously, lighting her cigarette for her.

"No." She inhaled deeply.

"Me either." He grinned and blew a smoke ring, leaning against the wall, his hand brushing lightly against hers.

Abby pressed her back to the wall, the smoke curling around them under the streetlight. She glanced down at her untrimmed nails, her fingertips blue from the cold. She and Josiah had never officially said they were no longer broken up, she thought, just to find an excuse.

"You think she'll make it?" Abby flicked the ash off the end of her cigarette.

"Who?"

"That girl headed to Hollywood. You think she'll find the thing she's looking for?" Abby watched a stray dog sniff the trunk of a tree, its fur tangled and torn away in spots. "Will any of us?"

Sam said, "I don't know," as if he knew exactly what she meant.

Abby tossed her cigarette on the ground and dug her heel into it, peeling herself from the wall. It felt as if cement had been poured through her limbs.

"Thanks for the smoke." She reached a hand out to steady herself and Sam caught her around the waist. A tingling sensation gathered under her ribs and rippled up her back.

"You alright?" His voice was soft, and something about that softness made her want to crawl inside it.

"I'm fine."

"Okay." He let go and leaned back against the wall, propping one foot up as he finished his cigarette.

She wanted to kiss this stranger, to take him back to her motel room, to fill in the emptiness. But she knew the person she really wanted was Josiah. She ached with wanting. "Thanks for the smoke," she said again, and hurried inside, intent on leaving before she changed her mind.

Angling her way through a cluster of people toward the front entrance, Abby suddenly recognized Lillian standing at the bar. A hefty blonde sat on a stool next to her. "Carla!" the woman shouted in a gravelly voice. "Another cosmo if you would be so kind." Leaning over, she said something to Lillian, who shook her head, put her hands up in a gesture of refusal and turned around, looking directly at Abby. The two of them stared at each other across the room. Someone turned the music up, the guitars grinding like lawn mowers over the bad speakers.

Emboldened by the alcohol, Abby walked over. Lillian wore bright pink lipstick and a baggy sweater over a pair of skinny jeans. "Lillian Aubrey? I'm Abby." She stuck out her hand, forcing Lillian to take it.

Lillian shook it, giving a faintly amused smile.

The blonde heaved herself off her stool, her breasts bulging, her bold, black liner laid down like pavement around her large eyes. "I'm Dorine." She smiled, shaking Abby's hand.

"Nice to meet you, Dorine," Abby said.

Dorine looked from Lillian to Abby. "You two know each other?"

"Nope," Lillian said, openly amused now, waiting to see what Abby intended.

The strings from the San Francisco Symphony screeched to a crescendo in a Metallica song. Above them hung a stuffed deer head, its antlers reaching out, sharp as knives. Abby wished she'd only had one drink instead of two. It made everything thick and slow. "I have something of yours," she said.

"Oh?" Lillian said. "What?"

"A notebook."

Lillian looked around with a sardonic smile. "Where is it?"

"In my car."

"Perfect. I was just leaving."

"No," Dorine moaned. "Nick has the kids and I finally have a night out. Don't leave me yet."

"You'll be fine." Lillian pulled a puffy jacket up over her shoulders. "I'll get you next time," she said, slapping Dorine's arm, and walked out, leaving her friend pouting at the bar.

Heading out after her, Abby regretted what she'd said. She should have taken the notebook back to the motel, read it and returned it to Bill.

Too late for that now. Abby took the notebook from the back

seat of her car and looked around for Lillian, who leaned against her car, waiting, her keys dangling from one hand.

Abby walked over and held out the notebook. "It's from your dad."

Lillian frowned down at it. "Confessions from the dying. Why do they always ambush you with this shit?" She didn't take it. "Why'd he give it to you?"

"He said it was the story of my mother."

"Then why are you giving it to me?"

"Because he wrote it for you."

In the blue glow of the streetlight, Lillian looked at Abby long and hard. "How'd you know my grandfather's house?"

"A whole lot of searching."

Lillian shoved her hands into her coat pockets, her face fixed. "You look just like him, my dad." She paused, letting out a breath of air. "So, you're like his long-lost daughter? Is this some romantic end-of-life reunion? You show up now because he's dying?"

Abby shivered in the frigid air. "I don't know how romantic it is, but yes, I am his daughter, and I didn't know he was dying."

"Yeah, well, that makes two of us." Lillian pulled open the driver's door of her car. "He's known for four months and just told me a week ago. You want to go somewhere?" Abby hesitated. "Don't worry." She grinned. "I'm not as much of an asshole as I seem, I swear."

Reluctantly, Abby got into the car, holding the notebook in her lap as Lillian pulled onto the dark road.

CHAPTER 31

Burford, England, 1906

October 20–21

The time nears, and already things have not gone according to plan.

I woke to a perfect autumn morning, bright with sunshine and cool air. Taking my journal with me, I left early, riding my bicycle all the way to Stow-on-the-Wold, where I treated myself to a breakfast at The Porch House, and then rode the ten miles back to Burford, where I was to meet Lesley by the river, only he didn't show. It has happened before that his grandfather has kept him at some task, preventing him from making our usual time. Normally I'd wait for him, but after an hour passed, my nerves got the better of me. I was in no mood to explain myself if someone found me prowling along the river's edge. I felt crushed walking away without this final goodbye. My plan was to leave my journal with Lesley and ask that he keep it hidden until Henry is old enough to be given it. I don't know what I'm to do now. There is no one else I can trust, and it feels like bad luck having it still in my possession.

Nevertheless, I keep writing.

By early afternoon, I was a bundle of nerves, restless and excited, a current of expectation and fear soaring through me. Hoping the second part of my plan would be better executed than my first, I went into the garden and waited until Mrs. Bartlett left the kitchen on her daily trip to the market. Watching her round the corner of the drive, I hurried through the kitchen door, only to find Samantha, the kitchen maid, chopping vegetables at the counter. Startled, the poor girl dropped the turnip she was holding, and it rolled to the floor with a thump.

"Gracious!" she cried, bending to scoop it up. "Is something the matter, my lady?"

Yes, I thought, *you*. The last thing I needed was a witness. "There's a mouse in the front hall," I lied in a rush. "Would you see to it?"

Impudent and practical, she said, "But you've come from the garden."

"I saw it earlier."

"Do you wish me to see to it now?" she asked, looking worriedly at the vegetable in her hand.

"Yes, now," I said, wondering if this brash young girl was going to be the ruin of everything.

Setting down her turnip, she gave me a quick curtsy and left the kitchen at no hurried pace. I had the mind to have Mrs. Bartlett fire the girl before remembering that this arrogant kitchen maid would, very shortly, no longer be my problem. I waited until I heard her open the hall door at the top of the stairs before making a quick dash for the cutlery drawer, where I found a long knife Mrs. Bartlett was certain to notice had gone missing. Hiding it in the folds of my skirt, I left out the back door.

It is 9:06 p.m. I sit and wait. I am not hungry, but I ordered dinner to my room and forced down the meat pie and potatoes. I will need my strength. I have written Lesley a letter telling him what I wish him to do with my journal, and have slid it into the front pages. The letter I wrote to Marion Gray sits folded on my desk.

Abbington Hall,
October 20, 1906

Miss Marion Gray,

You may well wonder why I write to you. I can say that I do so out of no respect for your person. There are two individuals that I hold entirely responsible for the ruin of my life. You, and my wretched husband. You cannot know what has gone on between us, and I will not write it here. I do not put pen to paper seeking sympathy, but because I fear for my life. William has grown frighteningly volatile and erratic. I leave Abbington Hall tonight in an attempt to escape him, and I write this as a warning to you. He is not to be trusted, and you would do well to look out.

Regards,
Evelyn Aubrey

I am afraid it's a bit too obvious, since I have no real reason to write to her other than planting this evidence, but so be it.

After William retired to the sitting room with his cigar, I sneaked into his study, found his ledger and slid in my old application for a ticket to the Reading Room in the British Museum Library as a symbol of his attempted obstruction and my ultimate success. For extra spite, I also slid in a scathing article about the time he was invited to Thomas Hardy's, and his noticeable inability to write. I hoped he'd stumble on these one day and be reminded of how much I had achieved, and how tremendously he had failed.

A few hours later, I lay in my room under my bedcovers fully clothed, listening for William. At ten fifty, I heard him go into his room. I heard the door shut and the lock click into place. I pictured him undressing, climbing into bed and putting the light out. When sufficient time had passed, I climbed out of bed in my stocking feet, my heart beating so hard I felt it pulsing in my neck. Putting my journal and the knife into my skirt pocket, I eased my door open as slowly as possible, holding perfectly still as I listened for any sound of my husband, or Marion, who has a habit of prowling the house at all hours. Hearing nothing, I crept into the hall with my boots and hat clutched in one hand. No light came from under Marion's door. I slid the letter under it before tiptoeing to Henry's room. His curtains were drawn and it was so dark I could hardly make out his small form in the bed. I was glad I could not see his face clearly as I put my farewell poem under his pillow, my heart shattering.

DEAR CHILD, DEAR BOY

Dear child, dear boy, one whom I call my own
Whose first affections thou showed to me
Before ever I, could show it to thee
Entwine all of thyself in the unknown
Then you will tremble not when truths awake
The tempted soul to find, not grief but strength
In wakened hearts that go to many lengths
To seek the love we tried so hard to break
From slumber deep I wake to take my flight
In haste I flee for new fledged hope is near
Grieve not when I have gone away, my dear
As colors wane and darkness takes the light
Look to find sweetness in the passing
For something tells me love is everlasting.

Moving swiftly and silently down the stairs and out the front door, I crammed my feet into my boots, tied my hat strings under my chin and went to the carriage house for my bicycle. My coat was draped over the seat where I'd left it that afternoon. I put it on, checking the pocket for the coin purse, pocket watch and bottle of laudanum I'd put there earlier. Holding my breath, I eased my bicycle out, every sound magnified—the creak of the carriage door, the metal lock banging against the wood, the wheels of my bicycle crunching over the gravel as I walked it down the drive. The moon was full and bright and I could see my way as if lit by a lantern.

Reaching the road, I pulled up my skirt cords so my dress wouldn't get caught in the spokes, climbed onto my bicycle and took a final ride down the hill, the air cold and invigorating. I was tempted to let go of the brakes and soar, but I knew to take care. I couldn't afford a real accident. Midway down the hill, I squealed to a halt and got off. It gutted me to do it, but giving the leather seat a final loving pat, I shoved my beloved bicycle forward, watching it careen and wobble and crash sideways near the bottom of the hill.

Taking the knife from my pocket, I tore the cuff of my blouse, ripping the fabric clean around and letting it drop to the ground. Standing over my bicycle, I rolled up my sleeve, took a deep breath, and cut a swift, clean gash across the inside of my forearm. It stung painfully, but I felt victorious watching the blood burst to the surface and drop onto the mangled frame, red as the moon that night I put the stone in my mouth.

Still bleeding, I stepped off the road into the woods.

I had imagined this day for years, escaping into the dark, the night swaddling me like a baby. I would not look back as I ran away. In my imagination the moment would be full of elation, of pure joy. But I did look back, and when I saw the dark shape of Abbington Hall rising from the hilltop, I hesitated. I pictured William stumbling into my room in his robe and bed slippers with his fierce eyes and lascivious, drunken smile. He never touched me anymore, but it was there, under the surface, our desire, despite the disgusting nature of it, and his power over me. I hated that smile, the smell of cigars and wine that lingered after he left, and yet, I had needed him. He had become my wretched muse, one whose misery I wrote with.

I closed my eyes and touched the moonstone around my neck. It felt as if numerous little trapdoors had sprung open inside me, and everything was leaking out. I pictured Henry, trying so earnestly to love me, making such a gallant effort. Maybe I should go back for him? A sob escaped and I tightened my throat against it, opening my eyes to the rutty road in the light of the swollen moon. I was not going to cry. That was foolish. I was not going to relive all the mistakes that had been made. I jammed the feelings back down, slammed that door shut and hurried into the woods.

My arm throbbed as I felt the sticky blood running down my wrist. The wind picked up, tearing the dead leaves from their branches and flinging them into the air. My life was like the seasons, I thought, the time after my marriage a brief, brilliant summer, and then the autumn of my father's death, of William's darkening, a time when everything began to fall. The last six years have been my winter. I have been frozen underground, dusted with snow, cold to the core. This is my spring, a time to uncurl and lift my center toward the sun.

I only pray that William does not find me.

CHAPTER 32

Granville, New Hampshire, 2006

They drove in silence. Abby looked out the window and tried to sober up. Lillian kept her eyes fixed to the road, the head-lights illuminating the tall trees that flashed past. Before long, they pulled onto a narrow turnout. Lillian cut the engine and flicked off the headlights. The darkness was astounding. There wasn't a single streetlight and the trees blocked out most of the star-sprinkled sky. Without a word, Lillian got out of the car, shoved her hands in her pockets and plunged into the thick, black woods. Panicked at being left alone, Abby jumped out after her. "Lillian?" she called, terrified at the idea of being left behind by the side of the road.

"This way," Lillian shouted, and Abby took off into the woods, not at all sure what she was doing, or why.

The quarter moon barely lit their way down a short path that went quickly uphill, the incline so steep Abby had to put her hands out to scramble up it. Back home, the redwood for-est, in its staggering grandeur, felt open and spacious, whereas this dark wood had a weight to it, as if the trees might close in and devour her.

When the hill finally plateaued, Lillian parted a section of low-hanging branches and said, "Watch you don't fall."

They were standing on the edge of a rock cliff overlook-ing an expansive body of water, a ribbon of moonlight rippling down the center like someone had thrown out a bolt of satin. Plopping down, Lillian dangled her legs over the rocks as if she'd done this a million times. Intimidated, Abby eased herself into a sitting position, sliding carefully to the edge, her stomach dropping. She'd never been afraid of heights, but the black expanse below made her feel as if the universe had tipped upside down.

"I used to come here as a kid," Lillian said. "After my mom died. Now, I come here whenever my life feels out of control."

The confession surprised Abby. She stared into the emptiness, not knowing what to say, the night blanketing them in frost, everything wet and heavy. They sat quietly listening to the forest, the scurrying of creatures in the underbrush, branches creaking, the gentle lapping of water, and then out of the silence, Lillian began talking. "Ever since I found out my dad was dying, it's like I can't catch my breath." She looked into the sky. "I feel like the world is happening without me, like I'm this solitary planet orbiting further and further away. My life is playing out in a time where I don't exist. Maybe never existed." She laughed. "Why else would I curl my hair, put on this ridiculous lipstick and traipse out to a bar with Dorine? Dorine, a nurse who wears too much perfume and drinks martinis with blue-cheese-stuffed olives in dimly lit bars with her cleavage showing. If anyone could make you feel real, it's Dorine."

Lillian's cold honesty, her affecting words, made Abby think that everything she'd assumed about this woman was wrong. "How did your mom die?" she asked.

"She drowned, right here. No one even knows what she was doing out here all alone."

A tingling sensation began in Abby's feet. "Mine died too. Drowned in the Pacific Ocean."

"They were cursed," Lillian said, and Abby looked at her, startled.

"How do you know that?"

"My grandpa Nicholas told me. I hardly knew him even though he lived five minutes down the road. My dad didn't want anything to do with him. My grandpa was a drunk, always had been, or so I was told. A few weeks after my mom died, he came over when I was home alone. He'd never stepped foot in our house, as far as I knew. I remember he had this massive red nose and smelled like pickles. My dad always made him out to be this mean old man, but I felt sorry for him. He just looked sad, to me. He said he'd come to warn me, to tell me I was cursed." She rolled her eyes. "Not exactly something you should tell an eight-year-old kid right after their mom dies, but I actually remember thinking it was cool, like I was this girl in a fairy tale. He told me his mother had drowned, and then his wife, and now his daughter-in-law, that they were all cursed. He said he left home hoping to escape it, but it hadn't done any good. Then he hugged me. My dad was pissed when he found out, but I thought it was nice of my grandpa to warn me. If someone had warned my mom, she might have fought back. No one even gave her the chance. That's why I come here." Lillian jumped up, stripped off her jacket and kicked off her shoes.

"What are you doing?" Abby scrambled to her feet.

"Swimming."

Abby remembered her dream, the dark water, the moon, her head slipping under. "You can't be serious. It's like thirty degrees out."

"I am absolutely serious." Pressing a finger into Abby's breastbone, Lillian said, "You have to fight back," and with a whopping cry, she hurled herself off the cliff.

Abby felt her entire body plummet, as if she was the one who had jumped. There was a splash, and then silence. "Lillian?" she screamed, looking over the edge. The water was still and dark. She was completely sober now. Grabbing Lillian's shoes and jacket, Abby scrambled down the hill, tripping over rocks and roots and sliding halfway down on her butt. At the bottom, she tore off in the direction of the lake, stumbling from the trees onto a rocky shore as Lillian made her way out of the water, breathless, her clothes dripping wet.

"Holy shit, it's freezing," Lillian sputtered, shivering uncontrollably.

Abby wrapped the jacket around Lillian's shoulders and they stumbled back to the car, where Lillian stood squeezing the water out of her hair as if she'd just come in off the beach. Abby climbed into the passenger seat feeling shocked. Getting in after her, Lillian slammed the door and started up the engine. "Next time, I'm pushing you off," she said, turning the heat up full blast.

Abby lifted her cold hands to the vent. "That was insane," she said.

"Trust me, I've done much stupider things."

"The sad thing is, I always thought of myself as someone who would go night swimming. Especially after two shots of whiskey."

"Don't worry." Lillian slapped her knee. "I'll give you another chance."

Abby watched the trees rush past, her hands starting to warm up. "I had a dream this afternoon that I was drowning in a place just like this. I woke up soaked in sweat feeling like I couldn't breathe."

Lillian kept her hands on the wheel, her eyes on the road. "I've had that dream a million times," she said.

They sat there feeling the shared fate between them, powerful, but breakable.

Instead of taking Abby back to her car, Lillian turned onto Wicket Road and pulled into her driveway. Without discussing it, Abby followed her into the house, helped her make up a bed on the couch and listened as Lillian sloshed up the stairs in her wet clothes to take a warm shower.

Abby was grateful to climb under the wool blanket Lillian

had brought down for her. She'd been so obsessed with finding her father, she'd never stopped to consider a sibling. Tucking up her knees, she looked out the window facing the dark street and let the idea of a sister settle over her.

CHAPTER 33

Seaton Carew, England, 1907

March 3

Astoundingly, my journal has come back into my possession. My past haunts me no matter how hard I try to leave it behind. Possibly my father is haunting me, daring me to keep writing what I started.

Or, just the indomitable Marion Gray, who is as efficient at finding a person as she is at everything else.

I suppose I will start where I left off.

Finishing up what I thought was my last entry by the river, I bound my cut arm with a torn strip of my petticoat, tossed the knife in the water as plotted and made my way into town with my veil pulled down over my hat, an unnecessary caution at that ungodly hour as the streets were empty and the cottages dark. I approached Lesley's house quietly, lifting the latch to the side gate and stealing around back. I meant to find Lesley's window and ease it open, but when I saw the chicken coop, I remembered him telling me how he liked to read in there. "If I'm in the house, my grandfather will find something for me to do, but if he can't see me—" he'd winked, thinking himself very clever "—I can read for hours."

The hinges of the coop door groaned loudly as I opened it. The roosting hens ruffled their feathers and clucked at me, but stayed where they were. The small, square space had a peaked roof that allowed just enough room to stand inside. In the moonlight through the open door, I placed my journal on the shelf next to a settled hen, checking to make sure that the note I'd left Lesley was still tucked inside. It was not a foolproof plan. There was the risk of his grandfather finding my journal, but I was fairly confident Lesley was the one who collected the eggs in the morning. I had intended to give him back the moonstone, but when I removed it from my neck, there was such exquisite beauty in the milky opal I found myself unable to part with it. Plus, I thought, this was no time for bad luck. Clasping it back on, I tucked it inside my bodice and slipped out the door.

Keeping to the tree line, I followed the road out of Burford, walking the nine miles to Ducklington, arriving at the train station at 4:39 a.m., my feet aching and my toes pinched in my boots. The station was empty and I sat alone on a bench until the 5:00 a.m. train pulled up. Boarding with my veil down and my coat sleeve hiding my shoddily bandaged arm, I took a seat in the back. A few passengers moved down the aisle and took their seats. Out the window, the sky turned a pale pink as the train pulled from the station.

We arrived to a bright, wakeful London, people rushing every which way getting to their respective destinations. On the platform at Euston Station, I stepped into a sea of men in tailored suits and women with ballooning rumps, parasols tucked under arms, hats bobbing along like seals in a current.

Grateful for the heavy veil over my face, I followed the crowd out onto Cardington Street. My timing was not ideal. It would have been much better if I'd arrived in the city at dark. I could not risk going anywhere familiar, so I spent the day wandering sections of the city I'd never stepped foot in, Stepney and Ratcliff and down to the docks where boats were being hauled up on the shore, where men shouted as they lifted and stacked boxes. My legs were so tired that I wanted to sit down on the rocks, but I was afraid I'd be noticed and kept moving, my arm pulsing where I'd cut it, my stomach empty and grumbling.

By midday, I could walk no more and stopped at a café on Tilney Street near Hyde Park. I ordered fillet of brill and a cup of tea and sat for so long the waiter asked if everything was alright. I had not removed my hat and brought my food up under my veil, which I'm sure roused suspicion. I finished my tea, paid him quickly and left.

After that, I sat on a bench in the park and waited for nightfall, so exhausted I could barely keep my head up. I could not risk dozing off in public, so I counted feet as they passed by, keeping my eyes fixed to the gravel path.

Darkness came slowly, the air cooling, the park green dimming behind my veil. The people walking past with baby carriages and parasols and packages thinned until there were only a few straggling lovers with linked arms and an old man walking his dog. I lost count of feet. The lamps came on and the stars came out. I checked my pocket watch: 9:15 p.m. I wondered what was happening at Abbington Hall. Had William contacted the police? Had anyone found my bicycle? Were they searching for me yet?

After a while, the park emptied completely. The moon rose over the chimney tops and bathed the grass in blue light. Clouds tumbled in. By the time Big Ben tolled midnight, a fog had settled over the city, the streetlamps diffuse, floating bubbles in the mist. As the bells faded, I stood up, my first day of disappearing accomplished.

I walked to Piccadilly; the few people I passed took no notice of me. At Hatchard's Bookstore, I stopped and boldly lifted my veil. Visible through the display window in the hazy streetlight, bound in olive green, stood my book, *The Tides*, the title embossed in gold. I knew today was my publication day, and yet it felt astonishing to see it. All those years of planning and plotting and here it was. It didn't matter that my name wasn't on it. This time, it was meant to have William's.

It was almost one in the morning by the time I arrived at Peter Emsley's gate. He lived in a modest house on St. James Street with a small front garden gone to weed. Walking to the door, I dropped the knocker with confidence. It gave a resounding crack, but no one came. I knocked again. My face was damp from the fog and my toes were cold. At last, I heard footsteps coming down the hall. The bolt slid back, and the door opened just wide enough for me to see a candle flickering in the papery hands of the housekeeper. She wore a nightcap and a shawl pulled over her shoulders. Eyeing me, she asked what I wanted.

"I need to speak with Mr. Emsley."

"Do you know the hour?" She was highly irritated.

I did not present her with a calling card or remove my veil. "I must speak with him immediately. It is a matter of great urgency." My voice did not falter, even though I suddenly felt weak at the prospect of seeing him. What if he turned me away? What if he refused to be disturbed?

The housekeeper scowled, the skin under her chin wobbling as she widened the door and stepped aside so I could enter. She shut the door, slid the bolt back into place and narrowed her eyes at me. "Wait here. There's no fire in the sitting room anyway." Grumbling, she mounted the stairs, her robe dragging behind her.

There was no lamp in the hall and I was left standing in the dark, the candlelight fading with her receding footsteps. I heard nothing save for the ticking of a clock on the stair landing, and then the click of a latch and the shuffle of heavy feet overhead. I did not remove my veil for fear the housekeeper would return, but Peter descended the stairs alone, fully dressed, his night-clothes properly discarded. It was so like the man I remembered, respectfully receiving his visitor no matter the hour.

"May I help you?"

He stood at the bottom of the landing, one hand resting on the rail, his voice full of concern. He carried a candle, and the light illuminated his soft face, unchanged to me—his dark eyes, his lips pressed into his teeth, his eyebrows drawn forward.

"Would you be so kind as to speak in private," I asked, fearing the housekeeper might hear us in the hall.

"Evelyn?"

I was surprised he recognized my voice so quickly. Taking my arm, he guided me into a room, fastened the door behind us and lit a lamp, adjusting the wick as I removed my veil.

I don't know what came over me, but tears welled up in my eyes. I felt completely undone. "Forgive me." I pressed my gloved hand to my cheek, a silly laugh escaping.

"What has happened?" Peter stepped toward me. "Evelyn, what is it?"

"Why do you not call me Mrs. Aubrey?"

"I have never been able to say the name."

Maybe it was the bewitching hour, or being wakened from a deep sleep, or maybe time had changed him, but I had never known him to look so sincere.

"I have left William." It was exhilarating to say it out loud.

Peter looked startled. "What do you mean? How?"

"How does anyone leave a thing? They simply do it." My tears retreated, replaced by familiar bitterness. "I have compromised you by coming here, but I had nowhere else to go."

Peter rubbed a hand across his forehead, taking stock of the situation. "This is about the worst place for Mr. Aubrey to find you."

"He will *not* find me." I reached for Peter's hand, but he pulled away.

His rejection exhausted me. I did not have the energy to reason with him. I had been awake for almost forty-eight hours and everything hurt—my eyes, my cut arm, my feet and hips. I had counted on Peter's loyalty. My plan would not work without it.

"Your absence will make the papers, your sudden disappear-ance," he said. "It will be gossip to no end. If anyone finds out I am housing a woman, it won't take much for the authorities to figure out it is you."

He had no idea the gossip that was about to erupt. "No one will find out. Keep me locked in a room until the news dies down, and we have time to figure out where I should go." I intended to leave England, but there was no need to tell Peter this just yet. I'd lead him there, make him think he'd come to it on his own, that he was the one saving me. Men needed that sort of heroism to feel in control.

Peter went to the window, untied the sash and dropped the curtain.

I took this as a silent gesture of agreement. "I'm sorry," I said. "To put you at risk. I only need a place to get my bearings and then I will go." Peter did not answer. I had an urge to rest my hand between his shoulder blades, to feel the strength of his spine. "I was a fool." I could not stop myself. "A fool to choose William. If I could go back, I would do everything differently." This was not true. I was using Peter, telling him what he wanted to hear and convincing myself in the process. A simple life with him sounded pleasant enough, whether I could have borne it forever or not.

"You were a fool. You have no idea how the loss of you has made me suffer." Peter kept his back to me, his hand on the curtain.

"I am a fool still."

He turned with a sad smile. "I see how a life with me would have bored you. Much better a husband to run from, yes?"

The disturbing truth of this made my stomach clench. "Pos-sibly," I said. "At the moment, boredom sounds wonderful, and sleep. I am so very tired."

"You must be." Peter took my elbow, guiding me into the hallway. "I have only the one bedroom, and a room in the attic where my housekeeper sleeps. I'll sleep on the sofa, but I'll have to be discreet about it or Miss Evans will get suspicious."

A single lamp was lit in Peter's room, next to the bed he had hurried out of, the covers tossed aside, the impression of his body in the sheets. We stood inside the doorway, feeling the strangeness of being along together in his bedroom.

"You have no change of clothes?" Peter asked.

"It's no matter. I can sleep in my undergarments."

Embarrassed, Peter stepped quickly into the hall. "Keep the curtains drawn and lock the door," he said, easing the door shut behind him.

The latch clicked and silence fell. I realized I was terribly thirsty and wished I'd asked for a glass of water. It was too late now. I closed my eyes, not quite believing I wasn't in my bedroom at Abbington Hall. Nothing felt real. The truth of leaving William was just beginning to sink in and I couldn't fathom that I was no longer beholden to him.

From my coat pocket, I took my coin purse, pocket watch and bottle of laudanum and set them on the night table. It struck me that these were the only items left in my possession, besides the moonstone around my neck and the clothes on my back. Shoddy clothes at that, what with my torn blouse.

Locking the door, I removed my coat and inspected my makeshift bandage, crusty with dried blood. I thought to clean the wound, but was too tired to do anything other than sit on the edge of Peter's bed. There was something so personal in the tossed-aside covers, the indent in his pillow, the warm crumpled sheets. Turning off the lamp, I lay where his body had been and closed my eyes.

I thought I'd drop off immediately, but a disquieting sensation coursed through me and I launched into a maelstrom of worry. What if Lesley's grandfather found my journal and exposed me? What if none of this worked? What if William came for me and dragged me back? What if Peter turned me in? How did I know I could trust him after all this time? The clock in the hallway chimed two in the morning, and then three. When it struck four, I sat up and groped for my bottle of laudanum in the dark, the bitterness on my tongue instant relief, drops of erasure, sweet numbness. I closed my eyes, sleep rising like smoke.

I woke to the sound of heavy boots and a deep voice that did not sound like Peter's. The curtains cast an eerie glow about the room, and I couldn't tell what time it was, or how long I had slept. I looked at my watch, but I had forgotten to wind it. Dragging myself out of bed, my eyes leaden, I went to the window, itching to pull aside the heavy brocade. I did not, knowing that by now, anyone could be watching the house.

My mouth was dry as sand. I went to the washbasin and drank from the palm of my hand, the water ice-cold. Splashing my face, I dabbed water over my hair and fastened the loose strands into place.

The drops had left me groggy. I paced the room, listening to the voices below with increasing anxiety, hating how dependent I was on Peter. I wished I was more like Marion, a woman who managed to master everything on her own. She was probably sitting in the dining room right now, laughing as William seethed over his food and barked at the servants, contemplating which was worse, my presence, or my absence. At least she detested children and would not bother Henry. Maybe they would send him away to boarding school. I felt a flood of compassion toward my son that angered me. I had never loved him properly when I had the chance; why was I doing so now? He would be fine. He was a strong boy who would grow into a strong man.

Men do well in the world. It's the women who have to look out.

Finally, the door opened and Peter entered. He turned on the gas lamp, and the room softened in the warm light. I hadn't realized I was pacing in darkness.

"I'm sorry I couldn't get away sooner." He took my hands as if this were a normal intimacy between us. "Have you been terribly worried?" I did not tell him I'd drugged myself and slept most of the day. "Your blouse?" he said suddenly, turning my arm over. "Good God, you're hurt."

"It's nothing. I crashed my bicycle getting away and cut myself."

He touched the torn fabric. "You'll need to clean it, and get a proper bandage on so it doesn't get infected."

"Never mind for now. Tell me of your day. Who was downstairs? I heard voices."

He drew me to the chair by the dark hearth. "You should sit. Are you hungry?"

"I'm not hungry." I remained standing.

"You need to eat." Peter knelt on one knee, striking a match and putting it to the coals. "We must put the housekeeper in our confidence. I am certain Miss Evans can be trusted. You will need a new blouse, for starters, and someone to bring you food and drink and to keep the fire lit. I can have her bring you some dinner now. I have taken mine in the dining room and couldn't think how to get any food up to you without her noticing." The flames sparked as he slid the grate back in place.

"I am not hungry," I said again. I should have been, but my stomach felt twisted inside out. For a moment, I thought I might be sick. *It's the laudanum wearing off,* I told myself.

Peter took me by the shoulders and eased me into the chair. "A policeman paid me a visit."

My heart leaped. "Why?" How were the London police looking for me already? And how had they known to come here? I thought I'd been so clever.

"It's alright." Peter kept his hand on my shoulder. "He has no idea you're here. He only came because he knew I had been the family lawyer. Evelyn—" he sank to his knees, taking my bandaged arm in his hand "—did William do this to you? If he has wronged you, or hurt you, you have reason to be removed from his home."

"I don't want to talk about it." I pulled my arm into my stomach, feeling defensive and angry.

The lies. So many lies. How could I keep track of them anymore? Peter must not know what I had done to William, or what he had done to me. He must believe the book publication and my disappearing were a coincidence. The true depth of my deception would repulse him, and I needed him to keep loving me. He did still love me; I saw it in his eyes, in the way he knelt and held my arm, in the way he was trying so hard to understand.

"If you were expecting the girl I was at nineteen, you will be sorely disappointed." I heard the irritation in my voice, but couldn't stop it.

"I expect nothing of you," he said.

Agitated, I got up and went to the nightstand for my bottle of laudanum, but decided against it. I needed to be clear minded. I needed to stick to my plan. I turned, calming myself. "No one will believe I had good reason to leave William. It is his word against mine, and he is admired and adored. There are no laws in my favor." I did not say that the laws wouldn't matter, that I needed to stay hidden to keep the story going. "My only chance at true freedom is to leave England. To go where no one will know who I am. To start over."

I sat on the edge of the bed. Peter stayed on his knees, watching me.

My journey was just beginning, but already I felt bone weary and doubtful. The fire hissed and spit smoke at us. I wanted Peter to touch me, to lie naked against me and ease the weariness from my limbs, breathe life back into me. I wanted to drink my fill. To forget.

I waited, hoping he would come to me without any more talking, without any explanations.

"I don't know what you want from me, Evelyn." He looked so confused.

I didn't know how to tell him, so I said, "To pretend I am someone else."

"I don't want you to be someone else."

"Why not?"

"Because I am in love with you, Evelyn."

Hearing those words from him now, felt tragic. "You are in love with who I used to be. You would despise me, if you knew what I've become."

"Tell me what you have suffered."

"You wouldn't believe me."

"I would believe anything you said to be true."

"William is a horrible man, but I played my part. Come, let's not speak of him." I beckoned with an outstretched hand, thinking of Marion Gray, of how she would have seduced him, gracious and determined, her skirts snapping behind her as she rounded a corner, her head turning to show the curve of her long neck, the line of her jaw, her lips parted as if about to say something remarkable. Reaching up, I drew the pins from my hair, letting it fall thick and heavy down my back. From the bed, I saw Peter's hands tremble.

This was how I would leave my old life behind. This was how I would become a different person. I closed my eyes as Peter crossed the room to me and whispered, "Is this really what you want?"

I knew he was asking if I was willing to no longer be a respectable woman, if I was willing to give up my place in heaven and join the ranks of sinners.

I smiled, and nodded *yes*.

My plan worked; *The Tides* was a sensation. All of London was talking about it. I'd like to take credit for the writing, but it's my disappearance that ignited the frenzy, my plotted revenge going better than expected. When the news first broke, Peter came home with a newspaper in hand and a look of suspicion on his face. He asked if I knew what William had written. "Did you plan it?" he demanded.

I was tempted to tell him everything—this is what happens when you get close to a person, you want to reveal yourself— but held back. "Of course not." I took the newspaper from him and sat down, trying to hide my excitement.

The headline read,

NOVELIST WILLIAM AUBREY ARRESTED
FOR WIFE'S MURDER

Since the printing of our last story on the disappearance of Mrs. Evelyn Aubrey, it appears the London police have found reason to suspect her husband, the acclaimed author Mr. William Aubrey, of her murder. Chapman & Hall cannot keep enough copies of Mr. Aubrey's latest novel, *The Tides*, in print since the whole of London is enamored with the fictional heroine who disappears at the end of the novel, killed at the hands of her husband. The police are investigating Mr. Aubrey for having committed the crime to create sensationalism for his novel and increase its popularity. As of yet, a body has not been found.

The article went on to tell how a schoolteacher named Connie Scuttle found my bicycle on her way to the schoolhouse. It was the police who alerted William, knocking on the door to ask if anyone was injured. According to the reporter, William did not seem concerned. He told the police he had no idea his wife had gone out for a ride, but that I was probably in my room. Not finding me in the house, a search party was formed, and the hills and forests and town were scoured. William did not become a suspect until the following day when a copy of *The Tides* was sent to the Oxfordshire police from a reporter saying they'd better have a read on page 223. The article, warning readers that they were about to spoil the book, went on to tell how Aubrey's fictional character Mrs. Hastings crashes her bicycle attempting to get away from Mr. Hastings, who is pursuing her on foot. Convinced her husband is trying to kill her, Mrs. Hastings limps away into the woods. At the river's edge, her husband catches up with her. There is a struggle, and the knife Mrs. Hastings carried to defend herself slips from her hands into the water as Mr. Hastings holds her head under until she drowns. Incidentally, the characters given names are Evelyn and William.

It was when the police found an actual knife in the river only a few yards from the bicycle crash that they promptly arrested William.

I set the paper in my lap, suppressing a smile. Picturing William in a jail cell filled me with reprehensible pleasure. I had done it. I had fooled everyone, almost.

I could feel Peter hovering doubtfully over me. Keeping my face as serious as possible, I pretended to read the article again as I thought through what this meant. I hadn't imagined it would go this far. I'd only thought to ruin William's career, his reputation, his position in society. I should have realized arrest was possible, but I am not, after all, dead, so I don't see how they could prove anything.

"What do you intend to do now?" Peter said, his tone of sympathy replaced with caution. It was clear he did not believe this was all a coincidence.

"I don't know," I said, beginning to wonder if my plan had been executed too well. If this went to trial, and William was convicted, he'd hang. No matter how horrid he'd been, I couldn't let that happen. I might be revengeful, but I am not a murderer myself. I couldn't leave Henry without a father, or have the death of William on my conscience. I'd have no choice but to reveal myself. What then? A sense of panic started in me.

I'd be forced back to Abbington Hall, or worse, convicted of a crime myself. Was faking one's death illegal?

"It is not safe for you to stay here," Peter said. "What with the shades drawn night and day. Someone will suspect something."

I stood up, afraid he meant to turn me out. "Where am I to go?"

Peter looked at me, inquiring and cold. "Has William been unfaithful?"

"Yes."

"Has he abused you?"

"Yes."

This allayed Peter's suspicion a little, but he remained businesslike. "In that case, you could file for a divorce under the Matrimonial Causes Act. There has to be adultery and at least one other offense: bestiality, incest, bigamy, sodomy, rape of a third party or two-year desertion." He did not censor these horrific things, but said each deliberately, gauging my reaction.

I didn't flinch. "His abuse does not fall under any of these categories. I guess adultery on its own is a permittable offense," I said, with mock cheer.

Peter raked his fingers through his hair. "What has he done then? Why would he write such a book and why did you flee with a bloody arm? It makes no sense, Evelyn."

I couldn't tell him. The truth was too complicated, and he wouldn't understand my own complicity. How could I explain what William had stolen from me without implicating myself? "You are better off not knowing," I said. "Trust me."

Exasperated, Peter went to the side table and poured himself a glass of brandy, drinking it down in a single gulp. "Am I only a stop on your way to whatever you've got up your sleeve? Do you care at all for me, or is this just part of your little plan?" He swept his arm toward the bed.

"No." I went to him, took the glass from his hand and set it down. I could see how desperately he wanted to understand.

Maybe in time I would tell him everything. "I knew you would help me, as you would help anyone in need, but I didn't know if you still cared for me, and I never expected to care for you. I didn't think I was capable anymore of caring for anyone."

Peter wrapped his arms around me and bowed his head over my shoulder. "Damn you, Evelyn," he whispered. "Why do you do this to me?"

"I'm sorry," I whispered. "It was not my intention to do anything but get away. Should I turn myself in? Tell the police I am not dead so they release him?"

"No." Peter straightened. "You would be charged with desertion."

"And adultery." I smiled, finding his hand with mine. I did not feel a shred of remorse. "What am I to do then?"

"Wait, and stay hidden. It is highly unlikely William will be convicted. There is no evidence against him other than a novel he wrote himself. I am surprised they can hold him at all. I imagine he'll be out before the end of the week."

"Right." We were convincing ourselves to leave a man jailed. Thinking of my pampered husband sitting for a few days in a cold, damp cell eating gruel hardly seemed the worst thing to happen. "You do realize this scandal will ruin him. He will stop at nothing to find me now, even if only to clear his name."

Peter slid his hand to the small of my back and pulled me closer. "Then we must make sure he doesn't find you." With the other, he traced a single finger over the stone around my neck. "Let's go to America together."

My skin tingled under his touch. The thought of starting a new life with Peter, in an entirely new country, was thrilling. "How soon could we book passage?"

"We'll have to wait until the news dies down. Not everyone is convinced you're dead. The *London Evening Post* claims you fled on your own to ruin William. A shrew, they called you."

"Goodness, I like the sound of that."

"You would." Peter kissed me, softly, and then harder, drawing me down on the bed, where we stayed, without any supper, until morning.

Two days later we departed London and arrived in a town on the North Sea, between Hartlepool and the mouth of the River Tees. I am to stay in the house of Peter's mother until arrangements can be made for our departure to America. We didn't dare take a train for fear of being seen, and the carriage ride was long and tedious. When we arrived, Peter insisted on walking into Hartlepool. I agreed even though I had no desire to. I hate the sound of the ocean pounding away, the gray sky, the spit of rain and the wail of the wind. The sea frightens me with its dark expanse of swallowed space. I was heavily veiled and if anyone asked, I was to pretend to be his sister, but no one asked. People here know he is the son of an insane woman and keep their distance.

We walked along the headlands where a massive wall extended out to the ocean and the waves crashed so loudly a scream would not have been heard against them. I wanted to turn around, but Peter said the air was good for us, that it would wash away the soot and rot of London. I feared it would only wash away what time we had left together, wash away the sound of our breath as we made love in the tiny bedroom of his mother's house, the rhythm of the waves audible above the cries of the wind.

I hardly left the house after Peter departed for London. The only person I spoke to was the hired nurse, Miss Granby, a wiry woman with a shock of white hair and wrinkles that pull at her mouth. She looks ancient, but she is as strong as an ox. She dumps the laundry water out the door as if it's a bucket of goose feathers, and lifts Mrs. Emsley out of her chair with ease. Peter says she knows nothing of London society, so I need not be afraid of her recognizing me. I told her I wanted no visitors. That I was looking for solitude.

"What ya do with yourself don't concern me none," she replied with a splintered voice and a vigorous sweep of her broom.

Mrs. Emsley doesn't seem to care who I am either. She rarely speaks. Her iron-gray hair and skin have not seen the light of day in years, but her eyes look just like Peter's. Only hers are fiercer and plunged deeper into her face and it frightens me to look at them. Peter's father agreed to keep his wife out of the asylum if Peter housed her far enough away that he never had to see her. Maybe those eyes frighten him too. All day long she sits in her chair, rocking to the sounds of the ocean. She refuses to go outside, but she is always opening the windows to "smell the sea," and Miss Granby is constantly slamming them shut and yelling at her to keep the draft out or she'll kill us all with the chill that blows in off the water.

Mostly, I keep to my room, reading or writing. I have tried to start a novel, but it reminds me too much of William, so I've stuck to poetry, which stacks up around me. The days are slow and endless, and I have no sense of myself. I feel as if I am melding with the tides, rising and setting with the sun; except, unlike the cycles of nature, I have no purpose. Things will go on in this house, in this town, as they are, with or without me. This is what I wanted, to disappear, and yet it frightens me to have the whole world think I am dead. If only William believed it and would give up the search. A terrible fear of my own death has taken hold of me, as if I've willed it to happen by my own ambition.

Sometimes I walk after dark, but I hate the wind that tears at my clothes, the taste of salt on my lips and the smell of rotting fish and seaweed. I prefer to stay indoors, waiting by the window for the weekly letters Peter writes, rain streaking the glass, the sky dark even at midday.

Peter told me they released William, and there has been no

further investigation into the murder, but that the police are still looking for me. He promises we'll leave England as soon as possible, but I feel desperate and lonely and can only be soothed by the laudanum Peter refills for me. I did not need my drops when we were together in London, when my nights of sleep were undisturbed by the weight of his arms around me, but the solitude in Seaton Carew is unbearable. I try and remember the feel of Peter's skin against mine, how his hands stroked the small of my back and his lips brushed my shoulder. I try to remain hopeful, but it is hard to have hope in a place where the sun never shines and a madwoman stares out the window and moans with the sea.

If I stay here much longer, I am sure to go mad myself.

CHAPTER 34

Abby woke startled and disoriented. She'd dreamed she'd drowned again, and the weight of her dream pinned her down, made her mind feel warped and uneven, the room cracking around her. It was freezing cold, and yet somehow, the sheets were a sticky pool of fuzz under her sweating body. She ran her tongue along the inside of her mouth. Her empty stomach left a sour, rotten taste. Rolling onto her back, she stared at the ceiling fan, the blades covered in a thin layer of dust.

It was early, the light barely visible through the window. From the kitchen, Abby heard the sounds of a coffee grinder, running water, dishes clanking. It reminded her of when she was little and she'd wake to the sound of her mom in the kitchen. She'd smell coffee and hurry down in her Holly Hobbie nightgown—the one she'd worn until it was so small her knees showed—knowing her mom would have foamed her cup of milk and honey.

Abby pulled herself into a sitting position as Lillian came in with two cups of steaming coffee.

"Cream, no sugar?" Lillian said.

"How did you know?" Abby took the mug gratefully, wrapping her hands around it.

"You seem like a no-sugar kind of woman. Scoot over." Lillian shoved the blankets aside and sat down. She wore a baggy

T-shirt and a pair of mesh shorts. Abby couldn't figure out how she wasn't freezing. It felt like there was no heat on in here.

"What time is it?" Abby asked, noticing the books that filled the room, stacked on shelves, on the floor, on the end tables and the coffee table.

"Ten."

"Really? I thought it was early. It's so dark."

"It's the house, and the cloudy day, but mostly the house. Too few windows and too many trees." Lillian crossed her legs, jiggling one foot up and down. "My grandfather thought he was doing me a favor leaving it to me. He died upstairs on a bare mattress. Drank himself to death at seventy-three years old and then left me this shithole. I know I shouldn't complain, but he left all his misery behind." She took a sip of her coffee. "I swear there's a living darkness in here, burrowed under the floorboards and behind this awful, fake wood paneling." She held her jiggling foot to the floor, a red circle blooming on her thigh where her legs had been pressed together. "Maybe that's why my husband left. The house and I both drove him away."

"Husband?" Abby asked.

"Soon-to-be ex. He moved out six months ago." Lillian patted the couch. "But he'd been sleeping here long before that. I'm not even thirty and I've already managed to royally fuck up my life."

Abby rested her head on the back of the couch. She could see cracks in the ceiling like spider veins showing through the house's skin. She thought of William Aubrey's study, of the desperation people leave behind in the spaces they occupy.

Glancing at Lillian, taking in her stark complexion, her fidgeting hands, the hard-boned, sharp edges of her face and the delicate skin under her eyes, Abby said, "You're doing better than I am. I'm thirty-one. I still live with my grandparents, and I can't seem to keep a boyfriend or a job. The fact that you own a house, have been married, and divorced, is highly impressive."

Lillian grinned. "Impressive is not what I'd call it, but thank you."

"Do you read all these books?"

"Most of them. I work in a used bookstore and I often sort the inventory here. I'm a writer too," she said, with total confidence.

"What do you write?"

"Stories, poetry. I'm not published or anything. Most people don't consider themselves to be a writer until they're published, but I think you can claim to be whatever the hell you want. Success shouldn't be the reason we are, or are not, something. Don't you think?"

Abby laughed. "I wish I had your confidence."

"What do you do?" Lillian asked.

Abby hesitated. "I'm an artist."

"What kind of art?"

"Film."

"Like, movies?"

"No." Abby had never been good at putting her work into words. "I shoot images, like still photographs, but in motion, I guess. I don't know, I never verbalize it well." She took a sip of coffee. It was strong, despite the cream. "Do you have any books by William Aubrey in these stacks?"

"Who?"

"The famous writer, your great-great-grandfather?"

"Never heard of him."

"Nicholas told you about the curse, but not where it came from?"

"Sounds about right. He was hell-bent on keeping the past from my dad, which meant it was kept from me too. I knew they came from England. That was it." Lillian looked over at Abby. "It's lonely when you have no past. They left me with no history, no family, no stories. Maybe that's why I make them up. I like the sound of having a famous writer relative." She stood up. "More coffee?"

"Thanks." Abby handed over her cup, noticing a printed, framed poem on the end table. She picked it up. "Did you write this?"

"No," Lillian said. "It's by a writer named Louise Bartlett. It's one of my favorites."

Abby read the poem while Lillian went to refill their coffee.

ARRIVAL

There was a moment I remember on a day in winter,
When the snow hung from the trees like feathers,
When the ice shimmered like glass and the sky held
no clouds,
Just a pale blue, so clear I could have dived into it.
It was a day when I turned from the sky,
Curled back into my misery
I should never have looked away.
Those are the moments that make up a life
You choose what you look at and there is always
something beautiful.
That is your beginning
Notice the moments and you will find,
That you are no longer waiting for your life to begin,
You will find that you were there all along,
That you had already arrived.

When Lillian came back, Abby saw that she had Bill's notebook tucked under one arm. Setting their coffee down, Lillian sat with it in her lap. "I haven't read it yet. I don't know if I can bring myself to. Whatever he's written in here will be the last thing I have of him." She angled herself sideways on the couch and slid her feet under the blanket. "I wanted him to fight harder, to get chemo, or surgery. I wanted more time with him, but he won't do any of it." Lillian stared down at the notebook in her hands. "I used to do things to make him worry about me. Stay out all night, or when I was little, not answer when he came home just to remind him how sad he would be if I wasn't there. I had this idea that worried parents wouldn't leave you, and here he is leaving me anyway."

"Tell me about him," Abby said.

Lillian bit her bottom lip, thinking for a while before saying, "He's kind, but not affectionate. He gives terrible hugs. He doesn't say much, but when he has something on his mind, he wastes no time getting to the point." She looked around as if the objects in the room held pieces of her father. "He makes beautiful furniture, but hardly any money. People call him when their sinks won't drain, or their rotting boards fall in. If someone is low on money, he tells them not to worry about it, knowing they're barely feeding their kids. He wouldn't marry after my mom died. He wouldn't even date. He never said it, but I think he believed in the curse." She held up the notebook. "I guess we'd know more if we read this."

"I'll read it if you will."

Lillian slid next to Abby and pulled the blanket up over their laps. Side by side, their shoulders touching and their heads bent together, they opened their father's notebook.

Dear Lillian,

I know you hate all this dying stuff, and "confessions," as you call them, but some things need to be said, and as you know, I am not very good with words, so writing them here seems easier than talking them out. It's also selfish, because I find myself wanting to talk about it, to remember.

The spring I graduated from high school, three years before I met your mother, I met another woman. I was raking grass in the front yard. I remember that the lilacs were in bloom giving off the most terrific smell. A car pulled up and this girl got out. She had hair down to her waist, and I was struck by how tan she was. No one around here was tan in May. She asked me where she was, and I told her the town of Granville. She laughed and said, "Not much of a town," got back in her car and drove off.

Later that night, she knocked on my door. It's amazing what you remember when you've replayed the moment in your mind over and over. I remember I was still sweaty from yard work, that I was holding this plastic container of lasagna, and when she walked in, she took a bite right off my fork and asked if there was any beer in the house. She said she needed a place to stay and did I mind if she slept on my bedroom floor? Her name was Eva. She was outrageous, totally fearless. I'd never met anyone like her.

I gave her my bed and slept on the floor, which only lasted a few days. I won't embarrass you with the details, but I will tell you that this strange, beautiful woman walking into my life was the most astounding thing that had ever happened to me. I had no idea what she was doing here, or why she stayed. Even my dad's drunken idiocy didn't bother her. She wouldn't tell me where she was from, or anything about herself. She wouldn't even tell me her last name. She told me I was lucky she'd given me any name. I was so infatuated with her, I honestly didn't care what she was running from. There had never been a woman in our house, and Eva brought that warmth only a woman can bring, one I had forgotten existed. With it returned vague, early memories of my mother I didn't even know I had.

I felt like a frozen man thawing out.

Every night she'd wash out her dress and her one pair of underwear in the bathroom sink and hang them to dry at the end of the bed. She would slip in with nothing on and say what a shame it was she had to sleep naked every night. I wrapped my arms around her and wished I could stay awake forever. When I did sleep, I tried to keep a hand on her hip, or a foot on her ankle, just to make sure she was still there.

Her favorite place was Cedar Lake. Eva loved jumping from the rock ledge. Back then, it was so thick with eastern hemlock you had to leap blindly. Eva would get a running start and fall with a shriek. I'd never jumped from that ledge before she arrived. I was a wimp. I hated it, but I jumped with her just to prove I was as brave as she was.

It was not until I watched Eva run and disappear through those branches that I thought of the stupid curse my father told me about. The old drunk wouldn't tell me a thing about my mother, or where we came from, but when I went on my first date at fourteen years old, he told me to watch out because I'd kill whoever I fell in love with. Not being the most credible guy, I didn't take him seriously, shrugged it off as old folklore until Eva came along. She was the first girl I'd ever loved, and my father's words haunted me.

I became paranoid. I begged Eva not to jump. At first, she ignored me, but then my paranoia started to annoy her. She'd swim defiantly after dark, after a couple of beers, rock the canoe until it tipped over, jump from the slipperiest rock, hold her breath under water until she almost passed out, turn the headlights off while we were driving and hang her body out the window. Every warning or plea for her safety she took as a dare to do more.

August 22 came and went. The day I was supposed to be at Syracuse for orientation. Eva was all I thought about, and I couldn't imagine going to college if it meant leaving her. But we were careless and stupid and young, and Eva got pregnant. I was scared, but excited. I thought it meant she'd stay with me. She'd tell me her secrets. Depend on me. Need me. The curse was a joke, I told myself.

It's easy, at eighteen, to believe you can change a story.

But after the pregnancy, she became withdrawn and hardly talked to me. I didn't know what to do. I told her everything I thought a woman wanted to hear. That I'd take care of her and the baby. I'd get a job. I'd support us. None of it mattered. I think she felt vulnerable in a whole different way, and she didn't like it.

I knew she was gone before I even opened my eyes that morning. I lay in bed for hours, imagining she had just gone for a drive, that she was coming back. I didn't think I could survive without her.

When I finally crawled out of bed, I found a note:

Fall is here. I feel it in the air, and I have nothing to wear! Off to a place where I can wear my sundress forever. You had better get yourself to college, you're late. It's been grand! Eva

That was it. All she said. I cried for weeks, blubbered like a baby. I couldn't eat or sleep. I know I told you I never drank, but I started drinking then. Went to the bar, stayed until closing. I could have gone to Syracuse. It wasn't too late. Instead, I drank myself stupid. Sometimes I brought a girl home, but it made me sick to see her in the morning when I woke up sober.

Three years later your mother come along. I don't know what Cynthia saw in me. She was beautiful and patient and kind. I wanted to love her. I was a fool not to, so I tried. I tried to be all the things I'd planned to be for Eva.

We got married and pregnant and I started building this house. I told myself I was building it for her, for you, but in my heart, I imagined I was building it for Eva. I'd picture her showing up on my doorstep with our baby saying how much she needed me.

Even now, at the end of my life, I can't accept the fact that she never came back. I never wanted to believe she died, but after your mom's death, it was hard not to.

I am sorry about how things were between your mom and me. I tried to love her, Lillian, I really tried, but the fighting began as soon as you were born, huge screaming fights. When you began to walk and talk, I realized we couldn't be doing that around you. My childhood was filled with anger, my father always screaming at me. I wanted to protect you from that kind of misery and tried to stop the fighting, but that only made Cynthia angrier, as if I didn't even care about her enough to fight anymore.

She had no patience with you, and I saw that as my fault. It seemed to me the more you loved her the more she denied you her love, as if depriving you would get back at me. When she left that night, I didn't know anything was wrong. I still don't know what happened. Maybe she went for a swim, maybe she fell. It's not having any answers that's the worst of it, and I am sorry I could never give you that.

I guess what I'm trying to say here is that none of it was your fault. For years, you thought it was your fault, but you were just a kid, and your mom loved you as best as she could.

I'm also telling you all of this because I haven't given up hoping that if Eva doesn't turn up one day, our child, your sibling, might. Now that I'm dying, this hope is all I have to give you. I don't want to leave you all alone.

You deserved a much better dad.

Bill

Sobbing, Lillian shoved the notebook into Abby's lap and curled up on the end of the sofa with her head in her arms.

Gentler tears slipped down Abby's cheeks. She shut the notebook and set it on the coffee table, thinking that this was a side of her mother she knew existed, but had never fully understood. It was the reckless, thoughtless Eva, the one who had hurt her grandparents, who had hurt Bill, who had hurt her. Her mother was unsatisfied, a woman intent on pushing herself to the edge, possibly right over it. Maybe she was cursed, or maybe that was just Eva.

After a while, Lillian's crying eased up and she pulled herself into a sitting position. "Jesus Christ, it's all so tragic." She gave Abby a grim smile. "Sorry I closed the door in your face yesterday."

CHAPTER 35

Seaton Carew, England, 1907

March 3

Marion Gray arrived with a fierce wind from the north, a wind that crashed sailors on the rocks and blew fisherman to shore, their boats wedged up on the sand, the smell of dead fish seeping through the cracks in the walls.

Mrs. Emsley was unusually agitated. Earlier that morning she had opened the door of my bedroom without knocking while I ate my breakfast of toast and tea. I had never seen her climb the stairs before. "She's no good, that one, the one with the light hair. Don't let her stay the night." She leaned over me, her breath sour in my face. "I know who you are. You're no good either. You stay away from my son."

An hour later Marion arrived in my room with no announcement. Her sudden appearance was like a kick in the stomach, a lurch backward.

"The haggard woman downstairs told me I could come up," she said, drawing her fingers from her gloves before removing the hood of her cloak that flared around her shoulders.

Her hair, in my memory so luminous, looked dull and limp. She pulled the cloak from her shoulders, shook the rain from it and draped it over the back of a chair.

"May I?" She sat before I answered, her face pink from the cold. Reaching for the teapot, she poured herself a cup, splashed in a bit of cream, stirred, tapped the spoon on the edge of the china and then raised the cup to her lips. Her face had not changed, but there was nothing beautiful about her anymore.

"How did you find me?" If Marion knew where I was, then, surely, William did too.

As if she'd heard my thoughts, she said, "William has no idea where you are. He'd kill you for real if he did." She laughed. "Oh, my goodness. Jail? That was brilliant. You are so much cleverer than I thought you were. It's a shame I never realized that before."

"Why have you come, if not to expose me?"

"I come bearing good news. Isn't that worth something?"

I was not convinced. "What do you want?" There was always a price with Marion.

She waved her hand at the room. "From the looks of it, it doesn't appear that you have anything left to give." She set the teacup down hard, as if she meant to break it. "I commend your leaving. I never thought you had it in you."

I wondered if she was actually jealous. It had never occurred to me that she might also be miserable at Abbington Hall. I had envied her. In my mind, she could have left anytime she wanted. But now I understood what it was to be a woman with no money, no connections and nowhere to go.

Marion sighed. "Horridly weak tea. I prefer coffee these days. Or wine. William still likes his wine. We amuse each other, in our own way." She narrowed her eyes at me. "He has a temper, but he is not violent. The letter you wrote to me was a lie, was it not? What was your intention? That I show it to the police? As false evidence against him?"

I stared at her, silent. I was not going to give her anything.

"It may surprise you, but I care for him. Only a little, but enough. He cares about me too, in his own pathetic way."

I didn't want to hear about William. This is what I had wanted to get away from, what I had tried to forget about with Peter. This was the old life creeping back and it made me wonder if anything other than death would allow me to escape it.

"I know you have come for some purpose," I said. "Would you kindly have out with it and leave me be."

Marion could ruin everything now that she knew where I was. I took the teacup from the table and opened the window, dumping out the remains. Drops of rain flew into my face and the wind bit hard. I wanted to remind her of the day we first met, when she had tossed the dead leaves from her window. Now I was the one living on my own, while she was stuck with William. Bracing myself against the wall, I yanked the window shut and turned back to Marion, who sat as she always did, legs stretched out, ankles crossed, her pointed boots sticking out from under her heavy skirt.

She rested a finger on her chin. "Is it so hard to imagine I have come to do you a good deed?"

"It is impossible to imagine." I took my seat.

Marion brushed a strand of hair from her forehead and stood up. Pulling something from her cloak, she came over to me, her limp noticeable. She smelled of the wind, of the sea salt air. "For you." In her hand was my journal.

I stared at it. "How do you have this?"

"By no cunning on my part. I found it entirely by accident. I was in Henry's room poking about when I pulled a book off his shelf, and wouldn't you know, I found that the pages had been neatly cut out and this—" she dropped the journal unceremoniously onto the table by my chair "—stuck inside along with a note." She took a piece of paper from her skirt pocket and handed it to me.

I unfolded it, steadying my shaking hands. If Marion had read my journal, she knew everything.

Dear Henry,

You don't know me, but I have been given the task of leaving your mother's journal to you. Forgive me for sneaking into your room in the middle of the night, but your mother meant for you to have it and I can't think of any other way of getting it to you. I'm hiding it in this book, along with the note she left me so you'll know her intentions. I pray you don't find it until you're older, this particular book being so hefty and all. It saddened me to cut the pages out of The Moonstone. *It was the first book your mother ever lent me, but it's the only thing I could think to do.*

You weren't meant to have her journal until you were grown, but my grandfather has died and I'm leaving for America. I have an uncle in New York City who says there's work for me at a good wage. I thought of waiting, just to see this through, but I need to look after myself and I might never get this chance again.

If you do find it when you're young, keep it a secret, will you? I haven't read it, since your mother asked me not to, but I'm sure, whatever's in here wouldn't make your father too happy.

I wish I could tell you whether your mother were alive or not. I am hopeful she is, but I don't know if something happened to her in her attempt to get away. She was a wonderful writer, your mother. Know that, at least.

I am sorry this is so clumsy. Hopefully I haven't failed you.

Humbly,
Lesley Wheelock

I set the note in my lap. My dear Lesley, trying his best. I was sorry to hear about his grandfather, despite how little the man liked me. He was good to Lesley, and now the boy was on his own. I was also sorry I could not help him. I could have, if I had stayed Lady of Abbington Hall.

Marion watched me closely, the edge of her dark skirt a few inches from mine. "Why are you returning it? Why not destroy it?" I asked. The thought of her leafing through the intimate pages of my life made my neck hot with anger.

"It's more useful to me if you want it back." She sat down, leaning toward the hot coals as she rubbed her hands together. The fire burned low and the room was chilly. "Do you want it back?"

"Otherwise, what? You destroy it and Henry never knows the truth? Or you make it public and expose my whereabouts and everyone knows the truth?" My voice was filled with disgust. "What best benefits you, Marion? Go ahead, I'm all ears."

She looked as if thoughtfully considering these options before saying, "It's far too valuable to destroy, and I think we can both agree William would rather be remembered as a murderer than be exposed as a fraudulent writer. Best to let people speculate you're one rather than know for certain you're the other."

The house creaked as the wind hit the outer walls. "Maybe I'll destroy it myself." I rested a threatening hand on the soft leather cover.

"You wouldn't," she said, with infuriating confidence.

"Why not? It's no use to me. I wanted Henry to have it."

"Well, yes, I am sorry about that, but it couldn't be helped. The last thing I need is Henry knowing the truth. He would be at liberty to tell anyone he liked." Her voice dropped into a conspiratorial tone. "You see, William has asked me to marry him, which means I need your little scheme to work as much as you do."

A sickening feeling spread through me. This should have been good news—their union would mean my total erasure—but I knew it was William's way of sending me a message. His engagement would be in the papers. It was meant to trick me into believing he thought I was dead. That way I might get sloppy and expose myself. Cunning bastard, I thought. Keeping my face as neutral as possible, I said, "What does that have to do with me? William can do as he pleases."

"As long as you stay dead, he can."

"Clearly, that was my intention. Why come all this way for that reassurance?"

"I wanted to see for myself if you were alive. And it's very probable you'd regret your decision and come crawling back. You don't exactly have much practice in survival, and if I'm to marry William, I'll need your word you'll stay gone."

"How could you marry him, knowing what he's done to me?" I asked, truly curious.

An almost defeated look crossed her face, but was gone in an instant. She shrugged. "He doesn't get the same pleasure abusing me, and I don't know how to write a bloody thing, so that's to my benefit. It's a practical arrangement. William is desperate for some footing back into society and living with your mistress doesn't exactly help the cause. As for me, well, I guess I'll get to order the servants around now, won't I?" She laughed, a sharp cynical laugh, and I saw something flare up in her. This was what she'd always wanted, to be Lady of Abbington Hall, to have the power and respect it granted her.

She could have it, as far as I was concerned. "Fine. In exchange for my journal, I give you my word I'll stay dead."

"At least you know a good bargain when you see one." Her task accomplished, she stood up, took her cloak from the back of the chair and flung it over her shoulders. "Look at us, being civil to one another. Speaking of civility," she said as she reached into her cloak pocket and pulled out a piece of paper, "I have the note here that you wrote to Lesley, the one he returned with your journal. I brought it intending to give it back to you, but you know—" she paused, folding it meticulously into a tight, little square "—I think I'll keep it. It proves you're alive, which might be useful to me one day." She slid it back into her pocket, still so calculating and cruel. Picking her gloves up from the table, she began hooking her fingers back into them as she stepped into the hallway.

Getting up, I called, "Tell me, how is Henry?"

The dark of the hallway was swallowing her. "He's fine. He never speaks of you."

"Marion." I stepped out the door. "How did you find me?"

She turned. "You'd think you weren't so desperate to get rid of me." She gave a short nod. "An artful guess. Going to Mr. Emsley is what I would have done, and everyone knows he has a deranged mother he's hidden away. What better place to hide you? It wasn't that hard to piece together. Honestly, the police are pitiful."

At that moment the sun broke from the clouds, sending a ray of light through the hall window. Marion took a step toward me, her eyes fixed on my chest. "I've always wondered where you got that," she said, suddenly.

I glanced down at the moonstone, pearlescent in the sunlight. "A friend," I said, curling a protective hand over it.

"You never take it off," she observed, an idea forming in her eyes. "If you did, it would be just the thing to prove you were dead."

"Do you mean for me to give it to you?" This was a more gut-wrenching prospect than the idea of her marrying my husband. "I've already given you my word."

"Yes, but William won't know that, and this would be so much more convincing. There's already talk that you took your own life. That necklace would help prove it. If I were to say, find it on the grounds somewhere, William might even be convinced."

Her hood fell from her head, and I could see the hollows under her eyes. I hated to admit how right she was. I had refused to take this necklace off for any reason. William and I had even had an argument about it. If it were found, it might be just the thing to convince him I'd taken my own life. The search would die down, and I would be free to leave, undetected, with Peter. Reaching up, I unhooked the necklace, remembering Lesley saying to me, all those years ago, that once it's passed on, it's bad luck to return it. This would be a true goodbye.

I dropped it into Marion's palm, watching her fingers close

over it, thinking how ironic it was that she was to become the final player—an accomplice, no less—in my story.

"I admire you." She slipped the stone into her pocket and pulled her hood back up. I had never known her to admire anyone but herself. "To beat William at his own game. Bravo," she said, and disappeared down the hall.

I watched her go from my bedroom window, her cloak flapping open, her head bent down, her small, dark figure the shadow of something so much bigger.

CHAPTER 36

Granville, New Hampshire, 2006

Without discussing it, Abby and Lillian slipped into a temporary routine.

Abby slept on Lillian's couch, picked up prescription medications for Bill and packs of applesauce at the Super Save. Lillian taught her how to start a fire in Bill's woodstove, how to work the espresso machine and turn on his Bang & Olufsen turntable. Abby learned that Roberta Flack's *Chapter Two* and the Rolling Stones' *Sticky Fingers* were her dad's favorite albums, that he liked civil war books, and that his favorite food was Indian, one recipe in particular that Lillian first made for him when she was in high school. "I've had to make it for him ever since," she said with rolled eyes, but Abby could tell it pleased her.

Abby learned how Bill began making furniture, apprenticing with a craftsman before going out on his own, combining art and practicality that got him a write-up in the *Boston Globe*, of all the summers he and Lillian traveled around selling furniture at outdoor flea markets and summer fairs, how poor they were until he started getting steady commissions. One day, when Bill felt up to it, he took Abby into his woodshop, a converted barn out back, and proudly showed her his tools and photographs of his favorite pieces. Moving aside a pile of scrap wood, he knelt down and showed her a dollhouse he'd made for Lillian, taking out a dresser and proudly sliding open the miniature drawers, the tiny perfection making Abby want to weep. Her dad had been here all along making perfect, tiny things for his daughter.

Helping Bill to his feet, Abby led him back to the house, where he asked her to tell him everything she could remember about Eva. Abby had never spoken of her mother for so long or in such detail and it felt good, weightless, like the memories were floating away on balloon strings.

Abby did what she could to give Bill and Lillian space, but Lillian told her it was better having her around. She said that for the first time in her life, a time when it mattered the most, she had someone to help her. They took turns sitting by Bill's bed, covering him in blankets, waiting for him to need a sip of water from a straw or to ask them to shift the pillow under his head. Together, they rolled Bill onto his side, cleaned his shit from the bedpan, changed his sheets, washed him with a wet washcloth, spoon-fed him, wiped the drool from his mouth and rubbed ice chips over his lips. Abby noticed the ease between Lillian and her dad, how silly and honest and harsh they could be, comfortable and confident in their love for one another.

Abby finally called her grandparents. Caring for her dying father made her appreciate them in a way she never had before. She told Maggie this, and Carl, after Maggie put him on the line. She said she had no idea when she was coming home, but she was coming home, and her grandma had cried for so long Abby had had to hold the phone away from her ear and take numerous deep breaths.

Instead of letters, Abby and Josiah spoke on the phone now. Josiah let her hang out in long, uncomfortable silences, which sometimes ended in her saying a quick goodbye, and sometimes ended in her muddling through something tender and vulnerable.

The one thing Abby didn't talk about was her dreams. They'd gotten more intense. Night after night, she would drown in her sleep, waking up in a cold sweat gasping for breath. Here in Granville, under Lillian's roof, thousands of miles away from Abbington Hall, Evelyn Aubrey still haunted her.

CHAPTER 37

Seaton Carew, England, 1907

March 4

The night Marion left, a storm raged. I dreamed I was in the middle of the sea in a sailboat made of ice. My hair was the color of goose down, like Marion's, and the wind blew it out like a sail. I wore no corset, and my underclothes were soaked through so that every inch of my naked body could be seen by the light of the full moon. William appeared, his eyes blue chips of ice. I was the woman he wanted and his arms were warm and seductive.

As he made love to me, the heat from our bodies began melting the boat. A hole appeared beneath our legs and the water leaked around us. William leaned down and said, "Look, look what you've done." He pinned his hands on top of my breasts, pushing me down, the ice cutting into my back as the hole grew bigger. I shouted for him to stop, that he was making it worse, but he just shoved harder. As we sank, I realized he was trying to murder me after all. That he had been murdering me all along. Then I saw Peter in the sky, by the moon, so close I felt as if I could touch him, except when I reached out, there was nothing but air. I kept reaching, trying to stroke the side of his cheek, but my hand cut into ice. William disappeared and I was alone. I stood up and looked into the sky. Peter was gone too, and when I looked down, I realized I had become the sail, my body the mast, my dress the billowing canvas. *I don't know my way home*, I thought. *I don't know how to sail. I am so useless.*

I woke sobbing, my pillow soaked with icy tears, the room so cold it might have been the winter sea. I pulled the covers over my head and tried to remember where I was, but remembering only made me feel more lost. How had I gotten here? Where did I think I was going? I could not save myself: that's what the dream meant. I would always be Mrs. William Aubrey. There was no hiding. I could run from William, but he would always be pinning me down.

CHAPTER 38

Granville, New Hampshire, 2007

Thanksgiving came and went, and then Christmas and New Year's. Lillian and Abby had decided not to acknowledge the holidays, but friends of Bill's insisted on bringing them Saran-Wrapped plates of food, boxes of cookies, and socks stuffed with lipsticks, lotions and gift cards. Of these friends, Abby liked Carol Ann best. She had red-dyed hair and wore large flowered dresses. She was loud and affectionate, the kind of person who pulls complete strangers, like Abby, into warm hugs.

Lillian said, that after her mother died, Carol Ann saw it as her Christian duty to watch over Lillian, showing up at her school functions, throwing her princess-themed birthday parties, buying her dresses for homecoming, sitting next to Bill at her high school graduation, and in the front pew designated for family members at Lillian's wedding. "All the while, trying to get my dad to fall in love with her," Lillian said. "Poor woman's still never gotten to spend the night."

The first week of February, Abby set up a projector in Bill's room. She'd driven all the way to Boston to rent it and have the film processed. Bill was exceptionally alert watching the silent, grainy images move across the wall at the foot of his bed. There was the photo of him and Eva, the book of sonnets, the tip of an airplane wing and a grassy field. When Abbington Hall rose in front of them, Bill pushed himself up in bed and said, "I remember it," in an awed voice.

Each time Abby reloaded the film, the wall went white and they'd listen to the whir of the projector and the tick of the clock until the images reappeared: large, old rooms, shelves of books, a desk with paper rustling silently in an unseen breeze. There was an old couple drinking tea on a floral sofa. Abby told Bill these were his cousins. "Sally is the reason I found you," she said, wishing Sally was the one showing Little Willy his childhood home.

Afterward, Bill was quiet for a long time, but then he began talking, slowly, a breath between each word. Abby and Lillian sat on either side of the bed and listened as he spoke about hiding under the bed when his father came home drunk, how Nicholas would find him and drag him out, how the beatings became less frequent after Bill grew into his teenage body, until, one day, when he was as tall as his father, they stopped altogether. "It was as if he just wanted to beat up on something smaller than him. Like it wasn't enjoyable once I grew up." Bill turned his palms up in a gesture of weakness. "In a strange way I missed it. It was the only time he noticed me." He talked about Abbington Hall. He remembered the nursery and the church steeple out his window, how he used to pretend it was a needle and he could reach out and poke his finger on the spire. He spoke of his mother, how she smelled of vanilla, how her wool dress scratched his neck when he hugged her, of her strong arms and wide smile.

"Remember," he said to Lillian, taking her hand, "how you taught yourself to cook from that old cookbook with a red-checkered jacket? That was my mother's. What was it called?"

"Kitty's Kitchen," Lillian said, biting her quivering lip. Bill asked Lillian if she remembered starting from the first recipe and making her way to the last, and she laughed and asked if he remembered how, when she didn't have the right ingredients, she'd just leave them out, making flat cakes and watery cream

sauces. "Whenever you'd get paid for a job," Lillian said, "you would take me to the grocery store and let me pick out anything I wanted. I loved that."

Abby sat silently absorbing what she could of their life together as they talked about the lemon meringue pie Lillian made after overhearing Bill tell a flashy brunette, who was flirting with him at the pharmacy, that it was his favorite. There was the cookbook Bill bought her, *Meals from around the World*, and the *dahi baray* and *chana* she made, scented with the one dull curry they found at Super Save. Together, they talked about curling paper plates like banana leaves and sitting cross-legged on the floor, poses of Delhi, how they ate porridge made out of jasmine rice, called it congee and imagined they were walking the shores of the Li River, stone-slab paths under slippered feet, chimes in the air.

Lillian talked of all the books her dad read to her of faraway places until she swam in dreams of kimonos and swords, burkas and prayer rugs. How they listened to Joan Baez sing of brown-haired boys and Chinese gongs. "I used to tell you we'd hike the mountains of Peru one day," Bill said, his voice shallow, "swim in the waters of Tahiti, ride elephants in Morocco."

Tears rolled down Abby's cheeks. Lillian managed to keep hers at bay, holding a small smile on her face and telling her dad she'd do everything they'd ever imagined, and more.

After that, Bill slept while Lillian and Abby sat quietly watching him as the day moved toward night, and the room grew cold. Eventually, Lillian went downstairs to put wood on the fire. Abby sat holding her father's bony hand, stroking the squishy, protruding veins where his blood still ran. She noticed how his barrel of a chest had caved in, how soft and thin his arms looked. So much of him was disappearing.

She wished Sally were here. For weeks Abby had held on to the fantasy of her reunion with Little Willy, imagining picking Sally up from the airport and leading her into Bill's room, the tears and memories and apologies. But this wasn't going to happen. The last time she called, Sally said, "This was about you, Abby, not me. Take some of those pictures of yours for me, and tell Little Willy he has a cousin who is praying for him." When Thomas got on the phone, he told Abby that Sally was happy knowing Little Willy had lived a good life, and that Abby was there with him.

A few days later, sitting by Bill's bed in her bulky sweater, Abby picked up the teaspoon for the morphine and her dad pushed her hand away, grumbling, "I don't want any. I want to remember, and I can't remember a damn thing when you give that stuff to me."

"Okay." She set the spoon back down.

Skin hung from Bill's cheeks like crinkled paper, and a clump of hair was matted to his right cheek, but there was a ruddy glow to his skin. "Do you know," he said, "I feel like working on something. Would you bring me a piece of wood? Small." He held his hands a few inches apart. "And my straight-edged carving knife. It's on the top shelf in my shop."

It took a little digging, but Abby found the knife and a small piece of wood, and brought them to Bill, watching as he turned the wood over in his hands, inspecting it.

"I'm fine," he said, which she took as a hint to leave him alone.

Downstairs, Abby curled up on the couch with a book, but was too tired to read. Dropping the book to her chest, she closed her eyes and fell asleep in the warmth of the crackling woodstove.

This time, in her dream, there was no moon, just a profound darkness with the cold weight of water on her skin. The wind tore at her hair while the water tossed her like a rag, sucking her under and spitting her out until she finally sank deeper and deeper. There, at the bottom, lying in the sand, was her dad.

He stared up at her with a smile on his face and fish swimming out of his eyes.

A log fell, jolting Abby awake. The clock on the kitchen stove said 5:30, but it was already dark outside and the house was distressingly quiet. Worried, she ran upstairs, but Bill was sitting up in bed, perfectly alive, one hand curled around his piece of wood, the other working his tool in careful strokes, sliding his fingers along, manipulating it with his rasp.

"Have you slept?" she asked.

"No." Bill kept his eyes on his work.

"You didn't drink your juice. Can I bring you something else?"

"I'm okay," Bill said.

Abby hesitated, not wanting to leave him. "Rest if you need to, okay?"

"Will do."

When Lillian came home from her shift at the bookstore, Bill was still carving. They got him to drink his juice, but he wouldn't take any pain medication. There was color in his face, and he looked pleased, holding his creation under the light, telling them how lucky he was he never needed reading glasses.

That night, Abby slept on the couch and Lillian slept in her childhood bedroom. When Abby woke in the early morning, the house was freezing. Usually, Lillian put a log on before she went to bed. She must have forgotten, Abby thought, hauling open the stove door. She layered kindling over twisted newspaper and struck a match, waiting until the small sticks lit before piling on a log and securing the door shut. The room was smoky and she opened the flue before going upstairs to check on Bill.

The light in his room was still on and he was slumped over, his mouth parted, his eyes wide open. Lillian stood over him, hugging her arms to her chest. His skin was ashen, his cheeks collapsed around the bone, his pale lips curled over his teeth from his last breath. It was freakish, seeing him that way, and

Abby felt a shock of horror. He had looked so healthy last night, so alive. They hadn't even called hospice yet. How could he die so quickly?

When Lillian saw Abby, she sank to her knees by the bed. "I'm not ready." Her voice fell hard in the room. "I've spent my whole life being his daughter. I don't know who I am without him."

Not knowing what to say, Abby placed a silent hand on her shoulder. Her grief couldn't begin to match Lillian's, but she wasn't ready either.

Lillian climbed onto the bed and lay with her head on the pillow next to her dad. Abby joined her on the other side, linking arms with her sister across Bill's lifeless body. Everything felt surreal, and at the same time oddly vivid, the light from the window bathing the floor in winter sunshine, the smell of antiseptic and laundry detergent and woodsmoke, the sound of water dripping from the shower faucet in the bathroom. Abby listened to her own breath and felt the profound stillness of her father's body next to her.

Lillian got up. "I want to go to my room," she said, her voice like a little girl's.

When Abby stood up, she saw the wood carving on the table next to her. It was a man sitting cross-legged with a child in his lap, their faces round and featureless, their limbs smooth. The man's arms were wrapped around the girl's, his head resting on top of hers. "I think this is for you," she said, holding it out to Lillian, who took it, turning it over in her hand, tears rolling down her cheeks.

Together, they went into Lillian's room and lay side by side on her twin bed. Above them was a stained-glass window of an angel set into the pitched roof. Lillian traced the bead of metal connecting the amber wings. In the sunlight, the sheets of glass looked like liquid gold. "My dad made this for me after my mom died," she said. "I never thanked him. I hated everything back then. I used to lie here and listen to the rain pelting the roof and imagine God was up there with a slingshot, aiming right at me. For the longest time—" her finger circled the tip of a wing "—I couldn't see the angel. All I saw were broken pieces of glass. That's how I felt, like a person pieced together, full of cracks. I stopped playing with friends or going to dance class. I learned to use the vacuum cleaner and the washing machine. I brought in wood and stoked the fire and taught myself to cook." She dropped her hand and rolled onto her side, propping her head up on her fist. "I thought if I was really good, I could please God and he'd keep my dad alive forever."

Looking at this brave woman, Abby felt ashamed. "I didn't do anything as redeeming when my mom died. I turned into a rebellious teenager and made life hell for my poor grandparents. I still make life hell for them."

"At least you have them." Lillian flopped onto her back. "I want to remember everything and forget everything at the same time."

After Bill was taken to the funeral home, Abby and Lillian put on the record player and spent the day quietly stripping his bed and cleaning the house. For dinner that night, Lillian wanted to make the first meal she'd ever cooked for her dad out of *Kitty's Kitchen*: corn chowder, dinner rolls and a lemon meringue pie. While she squeezed lemons and measured butter and flour, Abby drove to Lillian's house for the cookbook. Lillian told her she'd shoved it in the attic years ago in an attempt to declutter. "It will be a miracle if you find it in that mess," she said, but Abby insisted it was worth a try.

The sun was setting as Abby pulled into the driveway. She paused getting out of the car, the branches creaking like old hinges as she watched the clouds turn orange, brighten, deepen and fade to purple, the darkness settling fast.

Finding the key from under the fake rock, she went up the porch steps. She had bought herself a cheap coat at a thrift store, but still had no gloves, and her fingers were freezing as she struggled to unlock the door. When it gave way, she stepped inside, the air stale and heavy. Keeping to task, she flicked on a light and went upstairs, pulling the ladder down from the hall ceiling as Lillian instructed. Groping her way up, Abby yanked the string attached to a bare, dust-covered bulb, and murky light flooded the room.

On her knees, her breath misting in the cold air, she began going through boxes. Digging, yet again, through someone else's past—old clothes, Christmas tree ornaments, rusty metal tools, frosted vases, lamps, a shortwave radio, a box of records—Abby began to wonder what it would take to truly let go of a story, not just her story, but her mother's story, the Aubrey story, the ideas carried through generations, passed on as truth to explain away loss and suffering.

Alone with her thoughts, Abby became aware of the drastic shift that had taken place in her since she started out on this trip. She had never gotten to say goodbye to her mother. Being able to say goodbye to her father, caring for him, helping Lillian, made her feel like she was filling in her own cracks, all those broken pieces of herself. Her suffering, her need to conjure her mother's ghost, was her way of loving Eva, of not forgetting her. Letting her mother go, and still loving her, seemed possible now.

Unable to find the cookbook, Abby leaned back and stuck her hands under her armpits to warm them. Looking around at the torn-apart space, she saw a trunk pushed up against the far wall under a deeply pitched eave. Inside, she found a pair of children's woolen snow pants, tea-stained with age, and a matching coat and cap. *These must have been Bill's when he was a little boy*, she thought. It was hard to imagine anyone other than a mother saving these. Maybe Nicholas had been sentimental after all. Maybe these clothes had reminded him of a time when his wife was alive, and Little Willy had played in a snowy English countryside.

Under the snow pants was a tin box with antique photographs

in it. One was of a thin, serious-looking man. *"Henry Aubrey, 1919"* was written on the back. There was another of the same man standing beside a beautiful woman in front of a fireplace: *"Henry and Clara, 1931."* The year Clara died, Abby thought. There was a photograph of a small boy standing next to a sled with long runners wearing what looked like the exact snow-suit she'd found in the trunk. *"William Aubrey Junior."* No date. The fourth picture was of two couples on a picnic blanket by a river. *"Nicholas and Rose Aubrey, Patrick and Katherine O'Conner, 1956."* Here were Sally and Thomas's parents, and here was the infamous Nicholas and his wife, long before he ever arrived in Granville. 1956 was the year Bill was born. Maybe Rose was pregnant with him in this picture. She looked happy. They all looked happy, their eyes squinted with laughter. Even Nicholas was laughing. He resembled the picture Abby had of Bill with her mother, only a little fatter and formally dressed, wearing a suit jacket and tie, the ladies decked out in flared dresses. It didn't seem possible that the man in the photograph was the same man who drank himself to death in this very house.

Under the last photograph, in the corner of the tin, was a sil-ver chain with an oval stone hanging from it. When Abby held it up, the stone caught the moonlight from the window and the opaque whiteness turned an iridescent blue. It was startlingly beautiful, and when Abby took it in her hand, warm to the touch. Impossible, she thought, setting it quickly back in the tin before taking a book from the trunk, *Mercer Corner,* by Wil-liam Aubrey, blocked and lettered in black on the dust-soiled cover. There were three other books of Aubrey's: *The Beaumont Man, Mr. Winthrop* and *The Tides.* Original, first editions, Abby thought, astounded to see them here, in this frigid, crammed attic in New Hampshire.

Abby sat on the cold floor, holding the books in her lap, inspecting each one. *The Beaumont Man,* bound in blue and speckled with mold like a robin's egg, had clearly been handled at one time, but the other three looked to be in perfect condition, the front and back covers pristine, not a crack or crease in the boards. When Abby opened *Mercer Corner*, she saw that the pages of the book were uncut. Somehow these first editions had been passed around all these years and never read, possibly never even opened.

When she opened *The Tides*, bound in olive green, the stiffened muscles of the book cracked in protest, the hair-veined, marbled endpaper, thin as a moth's wing, separating from the board. Delicately, she lifted the paper and found herself staring, once again, at a mutilated book. Just like with *The Moonstone*, someone had neatly cut out the center, only this time, tucked inside where the pages should have been, was a small leather notebook.

Evelyn's journal.

Here was the very thing Abby had searched for high and low, had insisted could be found. But in this time and place, its sudden existence seemed unfathomable. Abby tried to lift the journal out, but it was pressed down so tightly, it was as if it had grown roots. Hooking her fingers around the worn leather, soft as baby skin, she pulled. The thin paper around it tore away and the book slid into her hands like something alive.

At that exact moment there was a loud popping sound, and Abby looked up in time to see the bare bulb screwed into the ceiling explode in a shatter of glass, plunging her into darkness.

CHAPTER 39

Seaton Carew, England, 1907

March 29

At long last I have received good news. Peter sent me a letter that our plans for departure are in place. We will be taking a boat to New York in May. He knows a man whose brother lives in Brooklyn and has agreed to help us when we arrive. Until then, I will remain here. I've gotten through worse winters. With my freedom on the horizon, I can brave this last one.

Included in Peter's note were two steamship tickets on the SS *Minneapolis*, Atlantic Transport Line, the scrolling black letters on the thick, cream-colored paper holding every possibility: *"Class of Passenger: Saloon, Route: London to New York, Date of Departure: May 10, 1907."* I pictured our home in New York City, a brick building like the ones I'd seen in the newspaper. Our bedroom would look out onto the busy street. I would have a writing desk, and a small library of books. I would take Peter's name, write a few articles, publish a short story. In time, I would write another novel.

Peter's letter said he would be coming in two days on the earliest train to celebrate, that he would arrive in time for supper. I can't wait; the end of my confinement here feels within reach.

April 30

Peter did not come. Dinnertime came and went. It grew dark, and the supper Miss Granby laid out went uneaten. I sat by the window in the one dress I owned, a simple, blue muslin, one I had thought fitting for my humbler life. I sat for hours, cold and worried, convinced something terrible had happened.

There was no letter the next day, or the next. When I went into the sitting room on the third day, Mrs. Emsley turned her drawn face to me and said, "He's not coming. He's never coming," and turned back to the window.

"Did a letter arrive?" I asked, but she didn't answer.

A fortnight went by. I did not dare write to Peter in case my letter was intercepted. Had someone found out he was hiding me? Or had he changed his mind? I reread his letters. He had written multiple times a week, and in every one of them he spoke of his love for me, of his desire to go to a place where we could be happy together, where we could start over. He said he loved me more now than he had as a young man. He couldn't have changed his mind.

Another week went by before I heard the scream of a mother who has lost her child, a scream so deep and guttural it tore the sound of the waves from the wind.

Miss Granby was pinning Mrs. Emsley in her chair when I went downstairs. She had been trying to climb out the window that was flung wide open, sending an icy breeze tearing through the room. I clasped it shut and picked up a letter that lay open on the table. It was addressed to Mrs. Emsley from Peter's partner Mr. Heckle. He gave a short account of the typhoid fever that had taken Peter's life. According to the dates, Peter fell ill the night before he was to come for a visit. He lay ill for two weeks and it took another five days for Mr. Heckle to inform Peter's mother of his death. The family didn't want to risk her coming to the funeral, so they had kept it from her until after.

"Don't make no sense why they didn't inform you earlier," Miss Granby said, still believing I was Peter's sister, and too pre-occupied with Mrs. Emsley to worry herself over much else.

I didn't make it back to my room. At the top of the stairs, I sank to my knees with the letter clutched in my fist. I lay my head on the hard floor and curled my legs beneath my skirt, reaching instinctively for the stone around my neck, reminded that even that small comfort was lost to me. Closing my eyes, I tried to remember the last words Peter spoke to me. I tried to remember the way he looked at me, the sound of his voice and the feel of his hands on my skin, but all I could think of was William. William's eyes were the eyes that stared back at me, his smell of tobacco and wine, the pitch of his voice and the heat of his hand on my neck.

I can't cry anymore. I don't even want to. I feel as if I have lost all my senses. Is this what I saw the night I held the stone in my mouth? Was this the ending I wrote?

I wore no coat the night I left the house. No use wasting a perfectly good coat. There was a section of beach I could see from my window where a few rowboats were tied together and anchored into the shore. When I reached them, the tide was low and my boots sank into the thick, wet sand. By the light of the moon, I had no trouble unknotting the rope. The water covered my ankles, the waves ebbing and flowing over my feet as the acrid smell of fish stung my nose and seaweed tangled around my legs. A sharp piece of wood cut into my thigh as I climbed over the edge of the boat, and I thought how strange it was that the wound would never have a chance to heal.

I sat on the rough, wooden plank in the middle of the boat, gripping the sides where the oars would have been if I had not tossed them off. I was glad there was a moon, for it was like my dream. I could see it in front of me, and it comforted me as the tide rose and the boat rocked swiftly away from shore with the sound of water lapping against the sides. I reached my hand over and let my fingers trail atop the icy sur-face. I remembered being a child in a rowboat, dipping my small hand over the side, hoping a fish would leap into it, thinking I could catch one. I remembered the feel of the banister under my fingers as I de-scended the stairs at Abbington Hall, hoping I could still make things right with William.

I wanted to go back, to take it all back, to start over, but it was too late. This was my ending, as I had known it all along. It felt good, easy, floating away from shore, the wind so cold it tore straight through my skin. I was glad I had sinned, lived a life of lies, lain with a man who was not my husband, because it made this last sin seem easy and unquestionable. The water was so cold it stunned me into death, swallowed me whole, pulled at my skirts and licked the top of my head. It wasn't hard, or painful. It was the simplest thing I had ever done.

CHAPTER 40

Granville, New Hampshire, 2007

It started snowing on their way to the funeral home, fat flakes parting wildly as they barreled down Route 93. Bradford Funeral Home was in Easton, at the far end of town near the train tracks, in a white house with wall-to-wall carpeting. There were folding chairs lined up in the funeral parlor, bouquets of dyed carnations jammed into green Styrofoam, lit votives arranged along a table and stacks of memorial cards with a smiling picture of Bill above a quote, *"God, I offer myself to thee..."*

This was Reverend Kazmecki's second funeral of the day. He stood near the coffin in a black suit and paisley tie with a Bible and a turned-down smile. His hair was greased as if he were leading a swing dance instead of a funeral. It was a closed casket. People filed past, knelt, said a prayer and moved to a vacant seat.

Dorine was there in a black dress, '50s style with a tight waist and full skirt. She had brought her three kids and a guy with tattoos that curled out from under his cuffs and circled the tops of his hands. Carol Ann was dragging Lillian around as she grasped people's arms and kissed their cheeks, branding the mourners in red lipstick while Abby stood in the back feeling completely out of place. She'd borrowed a black skirt and blouse from Lillian and nothing fit right. People nodded and smiled at her, but no one knew who she was.

Beethoven came from a speaker at the back of the room and

Abby took a seat next to a man in a baggy suit with a thick beard and curly hair. Reverend Kazmecki stood at the podium nodding solemnly. When the violins faded, he cleared his throat and announced that he would be reading Romans 8, after which he led the room in a silent prayer, his head down, the top of his hair shining like obsidian.

When it was over, people filed quietly out. The snow was still falling, shifting like dust beneath their feet, reminding Abby of the shavings on the floor of Bill's woodshop. Zipping up her jacket, she climbed into Lillian's car and they pulled in line behind Carol Ann's red convertible. The top was up, but Abby could see her hunkered behind the wheel with a tortured expression on her face. They wove through Easton, along Main Street, past Chip's Barbershop and Antique Ideas, the line of cars held together like magnets, their headlights disappearing into the muted daylight.

The graveyard was at the top of a steep hill and Abby joined the line of people carefully trying not to slip. The coffin sat on metal rods next to an open grave. The reverend said a short prayer and red roses were plucked from a bucket and placed on top of the coffin, which was already covered in a layer of snow. No one wanted to linger by a graveside in a snowstorm.

Abby was making her way over the wet grass when someone caught her arm. Looking up, she found herself face-to-face with Josiah. He wore a black coat, scarf and a wool cap pulled over his ears.

"Hi," he said.

"You're here," she said, not quite believing it.

"I would have come sooner, but the snow slowed me down."

"I can't believe you're here. How are you here?" Abby wrapped her arms around him, pressing her face into his wet coat. "I feel like a lifetime has passed since I last saw you."

"It has for you," he said as he pulled away, smiling. "Mine has hardly moved." Snow fell around them, dotting Josiah's shoulders and sleeves in sparkling spheres of white. Abby could see Lillian standing by her car watching them, her hands tucked into her jacket pockets, snow falling over her hair and shoulders.

"Come on," she said. "Meet my sister."

They drove in separate cars back to Bill's house. There was a gathering at Carol Ann's that Lillian had no desire to attend. She said a proper meal at her dad's felt like a better way to end the day. Josiah insisted Abby ride with Lillian. The snow was falling harder and they crawled slowly past glistening fields and snowy trees, Josiah following in his rented Jeep. Abby thought back to the first day she arrived, and how she'd followed her dad around the grocery store. She was grateful one of her last memories with him was watching the film of Abbington Hall together.

She glanced at Lillian, her thin face holding so much anguish. "You're going to be okay," she said, and Lillian nodded, keeping her eyes on the road.

It had been three days since Bill's death, and three days since Abby had found the journal. She'd managed to make her way out of the dark attic with it and drive back to Bill's, forgetting all about the cookbook she'd gone to find. She had planned on telling Lillian, but when she'd returned and found Lillian anxiously whipping up egg whites, it hadn't seemed like the right time.

Abby still hadn't told her, or read the journal. Not even a peek, as tempted as she was. There had been so much going on, and the moment needed to be perfect: sacred and undistracted.

At Bill's house, the three of them gathered in the kitchen. Lillian stirred the pasta water, and Josiah sliced tomatoes while Abby chopped an onion that stung her eyes. Josiah explained that he'd been at a conference in New York City when Abby called to tell him about Bill's death. It seemed impossible not to rent a car and drive up. He would have been here for the service, but the weather slowed him down. "I was worried you might not want me to come," he said, brushing his hair out of his eyes with his forearm, "but I took the risk."

"I'm glad you're here." Abby touched his shoulder, and Josiah leaned down and kissed her lightly.

It was after dinner, their plates pushed aside, the crusty bread and wine all gone, that Josiah said he had something to show them. Getting up, he went to the door where he'd hung his coat and came back with a piece of paper he handed to Abby. It was a printed document, the letters faint, but readable. At the top it said,

Name of ship: SS Minneapolis
Date of departure: May 10, 1907
Where bound: New York
Port of departure: London
Steamship line: Atlantic Transport

Underneath was a list of signatures.

"What is it?" Lillian looked over Abby's shoulder.

Josiah sat back down. "It's a passenger list. Turns out Lesley Wheelock from Burford, England, wasn't too hard to find."

He tapped his finger on a name in the middle of the page: *"Lesley Jacob Wheelock."*

"He immigrated to America seven months after Evelyn Aubrey disappeared. I don't know if it's significant, but it says his town of residence was Burford, England, so it's definitely him."

Abby read the name closely, then jumped up from the table. "I'll be right back," she said, hurrying upstairs and returning with Evelyn Aubrey's book of sonnets. Opening it to the photograph of Evelyn, she set it next to the passenger list. "Do you see this name?" She pointed to a signature on the list, *"Emily Winthrop,"* and then at Evelyn Aubrey's signature underneath her author photo.

"Yeah," Lillian said.

"Does the handwriting look the same?"

Josiah and Lillian looked closely.

"I guess?" Lillian said. "Honestly, it's hard to tell."

"It does look similar," Josiah said, "but I'm no expert. Someone could authenticate it."

"I know it's her." Abby dropped into her chair, triumphant. "Emily Winthrop is a character in Aubrey's novel *Mr. Winthrop*. There's no way it's a coincidence. Evelyn and Lesley were friends. These names, side by side on a passenger list? It's definitely her."

Abby and Lillian looked at each other.

"She wasn't killed," Lillian said.

Abby smiled. "She came to America."

This seemingly small discovery, these two signatures on a passenger list, changed everything.

Leaning over, Abby kissed Josiah. "Thank you," she said. Then she looked at Lillian. "I have something extraordinary to show you."

"Oh yeah." Lillian grinned. "That sounds dramatic."

"It is," Abby said, and went upstairs for the journal.

In the living room, no questions were asked and no explanations given. Lillian put a log on the fire and sat on the couch next to Josiah. Abby sat on the other side of him and he put his arm around her.

"Ready?" Abby said.

"Ready," Lillian said.

Abby untied the leather band around the journal, and opened it to the beginning.

CHAPTER 41

Burford, England, 1907

May 7

I have spent the last month alone in my room in Seaton Carew refusing to succumb to a tragic ending. It is my story and I will write what I please.

Miss Granby leaves food on a tray outside my door, but I have little appetite. My laudanum is all gone, and I hardly sleep. I pass the days and nights in my chair, by the window, thinking of Peter and Henry, of Mother and Father. I have none of them anymore. I ask myself if I can live the rest of my life in this house by the sea, so distant from the original vision I had summoned of my future, the thin walls shaking from the wind that howls through the night, the damp chill seeping into my bones. *No one knows I am here*, I keep thinking, but it doesn't matter. The world already thinks I am dead, which is precisely what I wanted.

It is this knowledge that steadies me. If I made my own death come true, anything is possible.

May 9

It took me a day by train to make it back to Abbington Hall, veiled and dressed in black. I spoke to no one but the ticket master, and walked the five miles from Shipton to Burford, where I waited in the woods until dark, sitting on the forest floor with my back against a tree, watching a sliver of a moon rise between the branches, thin as a knife blade. I did not move for hours. I missed Lesley and wondered what the chances were that we'd find each other in America. I do not know what awaits me, or if I will survive any of this, but I have decided I am not going to rot in a house by the sea with an old woman. I do not need Peter, or William, or my father. I have my ticket to New York. The boat leaves tomorrow, and I will be on it.

I never thought I'd be walking up the hill to Abbington Hall again, sneaking in through the kitchen, up the stairs and into the library, where I am grateful the coals still glow in the hearth. They are enough to see by as I write this final entry to you, Henry, my dear boy.

When I started this journal all those years ago at the inn, I had no idea I was writing it for you. When you read it, you must not think your father is all bad. In a twisted way, he gave me a voice, but at a steep price. I would not have written as I did, if not for William. I would not have been as enraged, or driven, or persistent. Not every writer, or poet, is fed by the darkness, but it fed me. Voraciously.

Your father understood this. The problem is, eventually, the darkness can devour you.

It is from this black, sightless, furious place that I have sought my revenge. Framing your father was my final act of rage, and I am not sure who I will become after. But the possibility of opening my eyes to something light and beautiful drives me forward through my shame.

Following Lesley's good sense, I have taken a knife from the kitchen and spent half an hour meticulously cutting out the pages of *The Tides*. Replacing my fictional story with the real one means I get to rewrite my ending. My only sadness, Henry, is that you will not be in it. Maybe, when you are grown, we will meet again, because this time I will survive. I will go to America. I will take on a new name. I will become a writer.

Look to the light, and beauty, my dear boy. This poem is the last thing I have to give you.

ARRIVAL

There was a moment I remember on a day in winter,
When the snow hung from the trees like feathers,
When the ice shimmered like glass and the sky held
no clouds,
Just a pale blue, so clear I could have dived into it.
It was a day when I turned from the sky,
Curled back into my misery
I should never have looked away.
Those are the moments that make up a life
You choose what you look at and there is always
something beautiful.
That is your beginning
Notice the moments and you will find,
That you are no longer waiting for your life to begin,
You will find that you were there all along,
That you had already arrived.

EPILOGUE

Berkeley, California, 2007

The door fell shut behind Abby. The house still held the familiar, painful silence of her teenage years. Her instinct was to flee, to find anything to distract herself, but she didn't. She stood on the mat, suitcase handle in hand, and allowed the silence in.

Upstairs, a door opened and footsteps padded along the hall. Someone went into the bathroom and started running water into the sink. Abby left her suitcase and mounted the stairs, each disquieting step pulling her back in time. Her breath caught at the base of her throat. Why couldn't these stairs hold the memory of her new bicycle waiting for her on the landing, or all the times she sat reading with her feet on the banister, or the times she'd hurried down them for school dances? She looked over her shoulder at the front door. Because those memories were meaningless cast against the fourteen-year-old who sat watching her mother leave for the last time.

A line of smoke curled from a stick of incense stuck in the jade pot on the windowsill in the bathroom. Her grandma stood in front of the mirror in a shimmering, black evening gown. Abby watched her dab perfume under her chin, trace lipstick along the wrinkled lines of her mouth and press powder over sucked-in cheeks.

"Gram?" She stepped into the light, into the smell of burnt citrus, bracing her arms against the door frame.

Maggie's powder case froze in the air. They looked at each other in the mirror. Maggie snapped shut the case and dropped it on the counter, an exclamation point at the end of each gesture. Abby put a hand on her shoulder. "I'm sorry." She'd sworn she wasn't going to apologize. She had talked about this with Josiah, how she was not going to feel guilty anymore.

Maggie shook her head, her eyes welling up with tears. "I'm not upset." Turning, Maggie pulled her into a hug, and Abby felt how strong her grandmother's arms were. They had always been strong, Abby just hadn't been willing to let them hold her up.

"I love you, Gram," she said.

Maggie pulled away, patting her shoulders. "I know you do." Yanking a tissue from the box, she leaned into the mirror and began wiping the streaked mascara from under her eyes. "I should tell you right away, so it's not a shock, that we cleaned out your mother's room." She clicked open her powder case and began reapplying.

"Everything?"

"Everything." Her mother's bed was gone? Her bureau and nightstand? Isn't this what Abby wanted, to stop returning to the scene of her tragic childhood?

"It was time. It was long past time." Maggie set the case down and clasped a bracelet around her wrist, the silver thin as tinsel. "It was your grandpa. After you left. He just went in like he did years ago, only this time he emptied everything out. He even repainted the walls." She gave a weak smile. "I couldn't have done it myself, obviously."

Abby sat on the edge of the bathtub, the porcelain cool against the palms of her hands. It surprised her how devastated she felt.

"Are you alright?" The blush on Maggie's cheeks sparkled under the vanity lights.

"I'm fine." She smiled. "Or, I will be. It'll just take a minute."

They heard Carl before he reached them, his voice sailing

down the hall. "Maggie, what the blazes are you doing? We're supposed to be there already." He halted at the sight of Abby.

"Hi, Carl," Abby said. She'd never called him grandpa.

He leaned into the bathroom without stepping through the door. "You're home?"

"I'm home."

He pulled a gold watch from his pocket. It was the kind you had to wind, and Abby realized how fond she was of this old-fashioned gesture. "It's 6:05. Maggie, we should have left twenty minutes ago." He snapped shut the watch and tucked it back into his coat. When he looked up, his eyes were watery around the edges. Was he crying? Abby hadn't thought her leaving would affect him in any way. "We missed you, kid," he said, running his hand up and down the edge of the door frame. He couldn't look at her. "I know we've never really been here for you in the way we should have. Kind of moved through the years just getting by."

"You've been here for me." Abby wanted to put him at ease, like she had always done. "I never—"

"No, no," Carl said, and put up a hand. "You let me finish." He kept his eyes on the doorframe, moving his hand as if cleaning it. "We didn't give you what you needed after losing your mother."

Abby got up and put her arms around Carl. "You did the best you could." He couldn't manage a full hug, but he wrapped a single arm around her and patted her back, which was the most affection she'd ever had from him.

Carl pulled away, slapping his palms together. "It's been a bumpy road, but here we are. I can't believe you've picked this moment to come home! We have this damn party tonight that we can't get out of."

"It's okay," Abby said. "Honestly, I'm exhausted."

"Maggie, let's get going before we're *un*fashionably late." He pointed a finger at Abby. "Oh, and you're paying back every cent of those credit card bills I paid while you were away."

"No wonder they kept working." She smiled. "I promise, even if I have to grovel for my coffee shop job back."

He nodded, planted a quick, surprising kiss on Abby's cheek and ducked into the hallway.

Maggie frowned. "It's Charles Campbell's eightieth birthday. He's the meanest bastard I've ever met. I suppose money obligates people to attend your party. That, and really good champagne." She lifted the incense from the pot and stuck it upside down in the dirt. "There's stir-fry in the fridge, if you're hungry. I used seitan instead of tofu, which I know you don't like, but I didn't know you were coming, did I?"

"It's fine, Gram. You'd be surprised what I ate in England."

"I want to hear all about it. You hardly told me anything over the phone." Her voice was shaky. "Sorry I have to leave you for this party."

Abby took Maggie's hand, her skin soft as milkweed, the veins raised like braille. "We have plenty of time."

Maggie squeezed her hand. "Turn the lights off when you go downstairs."

Standing in the empty bathroom, Abby listened to her grandparents pull their coats from the downstairs closet, fumble with their shoes, look for keys. Did Maggie have her purse? Of course, since she would be the one driving home when *someone* had too much to drink. *"Just get your purse. Hurry up."* The door opened. A car drove past. *"People drive way too fast down this road now."* The door clicked shut. Silence.

Abby walked past her mom's bedroom without looking in. She didn't get any food from the fridge. She took her suitcase and went out the back door to the guesthouse. It was unlocked, and she pushed open the door and clicked on the light. The note she had left for her grandparents was still on the desk next to her cell phone and computer. From her bag, she took the photograph of her mom and dad and propped it up on her desk. Next to it, she set Evelyn Aubrey's *Poems of Solitude*.

The day after her father's funeral, she'd called Sally and

Thomas and told them a certified package would be arriving. They were each on the line, talking over each other, begging her to tell them what it was, but Abby said they'd find out soon enough. It felt good to return the journal to England. It belonged with the letter, with Abbington Hall. It would need to be authenticated and archived if Sally and Thomas chose to make Evelyn's story public.

Abby hesitated, looking down at the trunk she used as a coffee table. Opening it, she took out her mother's purse. Holding it at arm's length, she went out the door to the row of garbage cans by the side of the house and dropped it in. She did not want to hold on to loss anymore. Being with her father at the end of a life she'd missed had made her see her time with her mother differently. She'd always felt cheated out of a life with her mom, when in reality, their fourteen years together had been a lifetime all its own. Wrapping her arms around her chest, Abby looked out into the night. The sky was dark and clear. In the distance, the city lights shimmered, expectant and hopeful.

The air was dry and weightless against Abby's skin as she rounded the corner up the path leading to the top of Mount Tamalpais. Reaching back, she took Lillian's hand and they scrambled up the rocks together. It was February, a year since Bill died. A week earlier Lillian had flown to the Oakland airport. That night, over dinner with Maggie and Carl, Lillian told them that Nicholas's house had burned to the ground. "Went up like a tinderbox. Burned so fast, by the time I got there the roof had already collapsed in. They told me it started in the attic. Faulty wiring." She'd leaned over, pointing her fork in the air. "But I think it was Evelyn. Her journal was found, so she was done with that wretched house."

Lillian told Abby she'd made Bill's house her own. As beautiful as his furniture was, she hadn't wanted any of it. She gave it all away. The only thing she kept was the carving her dad made the night he died. She still missed him every day, but living in his house made her feel less alone.

Abby had made her own leaps. A month ago, she'd moved in with Josiah. When he found out Lillian was coming, he bought them tickets to the symphony and told Abby she had to stop studying and spend the week being a tourist with her sister. Abby had put aside the film project she was working on for her class at SFSU, and spent the week taking Lillian around the city. They'd gone to the San Francisco Museum of Modern Art, shopped at vintage clothing stores on Haight Street, rode a trolley to Lombard Street, and spent an afternoon at Fisherman's Wharf eating French onion soup from sourdough bread bowls.

Sunset on Mt. Tam was the last thing on her list.

Reaching the top, laughing and breathless, they found a spot on the rocks and sat down to wait for the sunset. There was no fog, just a cloudless blue stretching above, and a deep-sea blue expanding to the horizon below. They sat holding their knees and watching the sun sink, the view of the bay magnificent, the city painted in pastel, the Golden Gate Bridge darkening into a silhouette. When the sun finally dipped beneath the water, Abby reached into her pocket for the moonstone. "Your turn," she said, holding it out to Lillian.

Lillian looked at it, a tender expectancy to the turn of her mouth. "It's bad luck to give it away."

"It finds its way back." Abby took Lillian's hand and placed the stone in her palm, closing her fingers around it. "This way, you won't need to jump off cliffs in the middle of the night."

"I like jumping off cliffs." Lillian grinned. "The curse was just an excuse." She held up the stone. "I keep thinking how sad it is that Henry never found Evelyn's journal. It was right there in a book no one ever opened, and I still can't wrap my head around how this necklace got into my house. The journal makes sense, Nicholas bringing his grandfather's books from England, but how did he end up with this?"

"Maybe Marion Gray found a shred of decency at the end of her life and gave it to Henry, who passed it on to his son."

"It didn't do him much good." Lillian flicked the stone with her finger, setting it swinging on its chain. "Maybe it's the stone that's cursed."

They looked at each other, each thinking the same thing.

When they got back down the mountain, Abby drove out to Stinson Beach, pulling into the empty parking lot and walking with Lillian over the slippery sand. They stood at the edge of the dark water feeling the thunder of the surf in their feet, the power radiating up their legs. Behind them, to the east, a half-moon rose above the hills. It was sliced straight down the middle, the light and dark equal and balanced.

Lillian handed Abby the stone. "You do it."

It was heavy, cool, its opaque whiteness turning an iridescent blue. "It's hard to get rid of," she said.

"It washes up with the tide every twenty years, remember?" Lillian nudged her with her shoulder. "We'll come back for it. In the meantime, this is your leap, Abigail Aubrey."

Reaching high overhead, Abby hurled the stone into the air. It shot up like a single, white spark, and then fell, sinking hard and fast, the water rising over it.

★ ★ ★ ★ ★

ACKNOWLEDGMENTS

I am incredibly grateful to Brooklyn College, and my outstanding professor Roni Natov, for guiding me through a thesis that led to the creation of Evelyn Aubrey. This novel has taken many shapes over the years, but Evelyn's story carved the path that led me here, and I am indebted to everyone who made its final arrival possible.

Thank you to Sanford J. Greenburger Associates for first recognizing this book, and to Trellis Literary Management for an exciting future ahead.

Many, many thanks to my agent, Stephanie Delman. This book was our beginning. I will always have that. Your continued faith in it, your confidence, patience, and impeccable timing, has made it a perfect journey.

Enormous thanks to my editor, Laura Brown. Your ability to see a story from all angles, and guide it where it needs to go, has transformed this book. I couldn't have gotten here without you.

Thanks to everyone at Park Row Books and HarperCollins for your dedication, enthusiasm and hard work: Erika Imranyi, Rachel Reiss, Margaret Marbury, Loriana Sacilotto, Heather Connor, Randy Chan, Rachel Haller, Katie-Lynn Golakovich and Nicole Luongo. To Kathleen Oudit for her stunning cover design, and to my assiduous publicist, Justine Sha, for keeping me organized.

For their friendship and guidance: Melissa Dickey, Heather Liska, Juliana Camacho, and especially to Christina Kopp for your invaluable feedback on this manuscript.

I owe so much to my family who read and supported this book long before publication: Isaiah Weiss, Michelle King, my amazing sister, Lilia Teal, and encouraging dad, Robert Burdick. To my mom, Ariane Goodwin, whose first critical eye on these pages—back when edits were actual red slashes through words—pushed me to improve, and improve and improve. I would not be the writer I am today without her.

To my children, Silas and Rowan, who played with blocks and toddled around while I wrote, unaware of how much their presence in my writing life would mean one day.

And to Stephen, for listening, for believing in this book from those early college days, and patiently letting me run plot points by you for fifteen years.

We did it.